NO
HEARTS
OF
GOLD

NO

HEARTS

OF

GOLD

JACKIE FRENCH

NO
HEARTS
OF
GOLD

Angus&Robertson
An imprint of HarperCollins*Publishers*

I write my books on Dhurga land of the Yuin nation. I give my love and gratitude to elders past, who created the living larder and the beauty of my home Country; my love, respect and endless admiration to the elders of today, who give their knowledge so generously and profoundly to us all; and my love and confidence in the all the elders of the future. — JF

Angus&Robertson
An imprint of HarperCollins*Publishers*, Australia

HarperCollins*Publishers*
Australia • Brazil • Canada • France • Germany • Holland • India
Italy • Japan • Mexico • New Zealand • Poland • Spain • Sweden
Switzerland • United Kingdom • United States of America

First published in Australia in 2021
This edition published in Australia in 2022
by HarperCollins*Publishers* Australia Pty Limited
Gadigal Country
Level 13, 201 Elizabeth Street,
Sydney NSW 2000

Text copyright © Jackie French and E French 2021

The right of Jackie French to be identified as the author of this work has been asserted by her in accordance with the *Copyright Amendment (Moral Rights) Act 2000*.

This work is copyright. Apart from any use as permitted under the *Copyright Act 1968*, no part may be reproduced, copied, scanned, stored in a retrieval system, recorded, or transmitted, in any form or by any means, without the prior written permission of the publisher.

A catalogue record for this book is available from the National Library of Australia.

ISBN 978 1 4607 6132 8 (paperback)
ISBN 978 1 4607 1162 0 (ebook)

Cover design by Mark Campbell, HarperCollins Design Studio
Cover image © Mary Jane Ansell
Author photograph by Kelly Sturgiss
Typeset in Sabon LT Std by Kirby Jones
Printed and bound in Australia by McPherson's Printing Group

For Lisa Berryman, with love and endless gratitude to my most magnificent editor and friend.

Prologue

SYDNEY, DECEMBER 1853

The bride wore blood, a ruby necklace vivid against her white dress, with the widest crinoline Sydney had ever seen. The satin silk gleamed in the sunlight, its lace caught up by seed pearls, as the tiny young woman stepped from the carriage onto the freshly swept road below the church.

The dress was magnificent. But it also emphasised a skin too dark for complete respectability, despite Lady Viola's wealth and title. Perhaps Lady Viola thought her dress so splendid, and her own small shape so insignificant, that her brown skin would not be noticed under her veil and damask gloves.

Her Majesty Queen Victoria had been married in white, but white was still far from the norm even at society weddings. Only the most wealthy could afford a colour that must be washed after every wearing. The drably dressed women in the watching crowd muttered that blue or green would surely have looked better with that brown complexion.

The crowd moved closer, as the Matron of Honour adjusted the bride's veil, under a tiara of more rubies, entwined with fresh white roses. 'Saw her meself!' the women could say. 'Lady Viola Montefiore — a genuine Lady. Of course, you knows about the scandal.'

The men and boys were more eager to earn pennies holding the bridles of the guests' horses for the grooms. And this was Sydney, a colony built on thievery. There were pickpockets and cutpurses cunning enough to slip the cravat from your neck without detection. Besides, some new husbands ordered coins to be distributed to the watching crowd, either in joy at marital bliss to come, or in thanks for allowing his bride to enter the church without having her necklace stolen.

The early morning sky stretched like a blue handkerchief above the church. Seagulls wheeled white above the harbour, and tall-masted ships sailed like swans.

The bride stood quite still for a moment, small, almost childlike, as the governor, Sir Charles Augustus Fitzroy himself, descended the stairs to take her hand. Police in blue uniforms held back the crowd as the Matron of Honour walked towards the church on the arm of one of His Excellency's aides. The bride and His Excellency followed.

The new church smelled of heat and freshly hewn sandstone. A sensitive wedding guest might have imagined the sweat stench of the convicts who had shaped its stones. But this was unlikely, among the scents of gardenia and roses, the starch that had stiffened the ladies' silks, the bay rum that had anointed the chins of the men as their valets shaved them that morning. Few guests knew either bride or groom well. But even though the heart of Sydney society was built on gold these days, or at least from the wealth from selling mutton to miners, English aristocracy still mattered. Besides, Lady Viola's own fortune rivalled any in the colony.

The music swelled. The congregation stood as the Matron of Honour began her slow walk down the aisle, followed by the bride and His Excellency. Lady Viola's face had been solemn as she walked from the carriage to the church, and yet, despite convention that said a bride should look neither right nor left, Lady Viola flashed a smile at the friends in the front pew.

In the days and months to come the guests remembered that smile, as the bride took her place beside the groom, almost twice her height in his frockcoat of mulberry broadcloth, his white waistcoat and lavender doeskin trousers.

The bride handed her bouquet to her Matron of Honour. She turned, and joined their friends.

The ceremony began, and then continued, droning like the flies that buzzed at the stained-glass windows, the words muffled by the rustle of silks, the creak of corsets and crinolines, fans waving, brows being mopped. Bonnets obscured the view of all except those in the front pews or by the aisle. Not that it mattered. The placement of each person according to their social rank was more important to them than the nuptials.

Vows, kneeling for the blessing, signing the registry. The choir sang. The guests grew restless in the December heat, perspiration dripping under waistcoats and jackets, or the corsets that made breathing difficult even when their wearers were not confined in a crowded church.

Then the ceremony was over. The bride smiled again above her vast acreage of white (were the roses in her headdress drooping?). The groom gathered her arm into his. The guests remembered, too, his look of love as he gazed down at her, though only the most sentimental witnesses used that term. 'Dashed fond,' as one gentleman remarked, was a more manly summation.

Bride and groom walked together down the aisle, then paused for the taking of the daguerreotype photographic portrait, arranged as a wedding gift by the bride's dearest friend. Wedding bells pealed above them.

At last, released, the guests clustered round the couple, throwing rice, with laughter and more sideways glances at each other's toilettes. Carriage wheels rolled on the cobbles. Footmen waited to usher their employers down the steps, to be conveyed to the reception. Chair carriers clustered at the far end of the street, hoping to transport those who did not maintain their own carriages and had not been offered a place in the vehicles of the more fortunate.

The first guests had turned to depart when a growing hubbub followed by a shout halted them.

It was impossible, all agreed later. Newspapers in the colony, and then in England, across India and the Empire, even on the Continent and in America, echoed with the story.

No one had left the crowd; nor was there even a bush to obscure the view on what had such a short time earlier been a building site. And yet, as the groom cried out, and gentlemen strode around, busily pretending to search for what all already knew could not be there, the conclusion was inescapable.

The bride had vanished.

Chapter 1

KAT

BRIARGLEN, ENGLAND, OCTOBER 1847

Kat leaned against the stable wall and inspected the object Long William was pointing at the stable wall, ejecting a long stream of yellow that flowed down into the straw. 'That's not as big as a horse's,' she informed him.

Long William started. 'What you doin' here?'

'Looking at you, of course.'

Kat had heard the parlourmaids giggling that the new stable boy boasted that his appendage was as big as a stallion's ever since she'd returned from school a week ago. Kat had been curious, but little Amy, the dairymaid, had been scared when Long William had cornered her in the dairy and tried to kiss her.

Amy had been too terrified to check the cheeses alone ever since. Kat liked little Amy.

Kat wrinkled her nose at the object. It seemed more comical than frightening or admirable. 'It's no more than a wiggle waggle. You know, the big worms the fishermen use.'

Long William closed his trousers. 'You're no proper young lady!'

Kat grinned. 'I don't have to be a proper one, not with a rich papa.' She looked at him thoughtfully. 'Do you know what I learned at school, William?'

'No, Miss Kat. I beg your pardon, Miss Kat,' he added, reluctantly polite. Everyone knew that the master had a heart of gold where Miss Kat and her ma were concerned. This was a good place, and he didn't want to lose it.

'I learned that terrible things happen to young men who try to kiss girls who don't want them to.'

'What kind o' things?'

Kat quickly tried to think of a suitable punishment. 'Oh, it depends how often they've tried it. Nothing can happen for years. But then they try it one more time,' she lowered her voice, 'and their tongue gets covered in boils.'

'I don't believe you! Beggin' your pardon, Miss,' he added carefully.

'Oh, it's quite true. You go to bed one night and then in the morning your tongue's all horrible and oozing. It happened to the butcher's apprentice down in the village, just last year. He was so ashamed he ran off to be a sailor. Ask the other grooms if I'm not right,' she added, guessing that the men had little time for a boaster, especially a newcomer who'd frighten a dairymaid. Besides, Miss Kat was the pet of every servant here. The men would tell the boy that Miss Kat always knew what she was talking about.

'How ... how do I stop it happening?'

Kat looked thoughtful. 'You could try brushing your tongue with horse piddle each night. It has to be steaming fresh, mind. And William,' she looked steadily at him, 'stay away from the dairy. Your advances are not welcome. But I'm sure you've no need to worry,' she added airily. 'Just as long as you don't go near a dairymaid ever again.'

She picked up the skirts of her sprigged muslin morning dress — slightly puckered near the hem from grass seeds — and strolled down the path, leaving William staring and a good deal paler than he'd been before she'd seen him in the stables.

The path led to the stream, its water dappled with beech leaves, trout flickering among the shadows. The stream led to the Irishman's hut: two rooms of stone, a thatched roof, and a chimney with a spiral of smoke as grey as the sky.

The Irishman had come from Wicklow with Mama when she married Papa. Ostensibly the Irishman was a groom, but Kat had never known him even to curry down a horse; nor was he ever known by his name. He was 'the Irishman' to everyone on the estate and in the village too. He spent his winters tending the braziers in the hothouses with their pots of peach and orange trees. Summer saw him checking the ripening fruit and making his selection.

Now in autumn he fed the vats of fruit with yeast he kept bubbling all year in glass jars on the mantel above his fireplace, far from the windows so no wild strain might contaminate the culture. He swore it had been handed down for seven generations.

If the smoke from his chimney was any guide, today he'd be distilling the first batch of the poteen. It was a ritual Kat loved — almost as much as Papa loved the illegal brew — ever since she'd escaped from nurse at five years old and seen the drips emerge from the vast snakes of copper tubing that led from still to flasks.

The wooden door was shut, but she had no hesitation in giving three knocks, then opening it. Any other unexpected visitor might find their head banged by a skillet: the Irishman was ever at the ready in case the revenue men arrived to enforce the law against unlicensed distilling. Miss Kat, though, had entry to any place she wanted.

'I've brought you a seedy cake,' she informed him, as the gust of mutton and cabbage and unwashed man met her face. There was no hint of fruit or fermentation, of course, for the Irishman's genius lay in keeping every skerrick of fragrance for his brew.

'Put it on the table, girl. I've no hands free to take it.' After twenty-six years there, the Irishman spoke almost like an Englishman now, but the name still stuck, just as the gypsies who camped each winter in the river field were just 'the gypsies' and the Frenchman down in the village who'd come to England as a boy after the revolution had become 'Mr French' instead of 'Monsieur du Foret'.

Kat seated herself on the stool by the still, glanced at the coals glowing red under its copper, then at the tubing, and the flask below it, still with no hint of moisture.

'When?' she demanded.

'When the good Lord decides, that's when. You don't hurry a good brew, Miss Kat. Each batch makes its own time. Ah, here's the first now.' They both stared at the drip that grew larger and larger on the end of the tube before finally deciding to fall.

'Now don't you go sniffing it, Miss Kat,' he warned, as a second and third drip followed the first, and then the thinnest trickle began to flow. 'Even the smell of the first flow is enough to kill a man sometimes — or send him blind.'

Kat laughed. 'Wait,' she chanted. 'Wait.'

'That's it. It's what follows has the sun in it, the fire in the fruit ...'

'And finally, the juice that you throw out.'

He winked at her. 'Or distil again, for the dregs are good enough for anyone stupid enough to pay for it. But this,' he pushed a small flagon under the new flow, which had subtly changed colour and texture, 'this now will be good enough for your pa an' his guests.'

Kat stared at the clear liquid, the firelight fracturing the contents so they glowed a soft gold. Just fruit and yeast and nothing else, certainly not sugar or honey. But it had to be exactly the right fruit at the right time, the correct yeast. It was magic, like the way yeast turned silky flour into cracking bread crust, and liquid egg yolks thickened a sauce. Her stomach growled.

The Irishman grinned at the sound. 'Thought that school was goin' t' make a lady of yer, Miss Kat.'

'Miss Thackeray tried,' Kat said complacently. The year at the Young Ladies' Academy had been the first imposition ever placed on her by her father. She hoped it would be the last. 'I must dress for dinner.'

The Squire and his wife and son were dining today. This was unusual, though the early hour of the meal was not. The

Fitzhuberts, like their neighbours, kept country hours, so that in summer visitors might dine and return home without the need of lanterns on their carriages.

But although the Fitzhuberts' social rank and Papa's wealth meant they were on visiting terms with twenty-six families in the county, Mama cared little for socialising. Mama spent her days on the cliffs, hunting for fossils, her hat hanging by ribbons from her head and her skirts tucked up into the new-style pantaloons, made almost respectable by Her Majesty having adopted them.

Mama was eccentric. The girls at Miss Thackeray's used the term as an insult, but Kat always said it with pride, as did Papa. Papa believed he was the most blessed of men, who owned an emerald-eyed wife whose hair rivalled the firelight, and whose laugh the seagulls answered.

Mama was also, Papa declared, the only woman in England whose conversation did not bore him — apart, of course, from Kat's. Papa had even encouraged Mama to become a student of poor Miss Anning, who had died earlier this year. Miss Anning was certain that the bezoar stones she'd discovered were the dung of the giant creatures that had roamed the ancient Earth. Miss Anning had not been able to publish her discoveries, but Papa had had a limited edition of Mama's paper, *The Bezoar Stones and Their Implications for the Diet of Prehistoric Creatures*, printed for her as a gift last Christmas.

Fossilised dung was not a subject that interested many at the dinner table. Nor was the Squire likely to have developed a fascination for Papa's beloved scale models of steam pump engines, nor even his working models of the steam trains on which Papa's wealth from railway shares — and much of his conversation — was based.

The rare guests were almost certainly due to her return from school, Kat thought smugly. She knew that she was beautiful. Papa said her hair was like a flame at sunset, and she had her mama's eyes. She also had a bosom that was twice the size of any other girl's at the Academy, and firm enough out of their corset to balance a raspberry on each nipple without dropping it, and what a fuss that had caused when Miss Thackeray marched in and caught her demonstrating the skill. Only Papa's fortune had meant she was not expelled, which was a pity, as Kat had more than had her fill of school.

Papa's fortune and Kat's return were also the reasons for her invitation to a private dance at the Bellairs' next week, as well as the dinner with the Lambert family. Kat could finally wear her hair up and her new evening necklines low and let Derringer arrange Grandmama's pearls at her throat and ears and thread them through her curls, though the arranging took so long Kat could only be bothered with a formal hairstyle for company. She did, however, enjoy the fresh gowns: low-necked pastel silk evening dresses, sprigged muslin walking dresses, even a new riding outfit, with trousers under a daring divided skirt that Mama declared the only possible garment for any woman who did not want to risk a fall at the next fence.

Her boots clicked on the cobbles of the courtyard as she ran to the back door, through the scullery and into the second kitchen.

'Miss Kat!' Mrs Button looked up from the table where she was carefully unmoulding the jellies for tonight. Peach, Kat noticed, pleased, made with the carrageen moss Mama had sent twice a year from Ireland.

'May I have the taster?' Kat made her eyes wistful. 'We never had anything half so good at school.'

'Get away with you! Well, here it is then.' As if Mrs Button hadn't filled Kat's special teacup for just such a request. She passed it to the girl with a spoon. 'We'll be making blood pudding when the pigs are killed next week, if you'd like to join the stirabout, and I'm making your mama's special receipt for damson preserves tomorrow morning, if you'd care to see how to do it.'

'Yes, please.' Kat closed her eyes at the smoothness of the jelly. Too much carrageen and jelly turned so tough you had to slice it. Too little and it didn't set at all. And that was skill too, not recipe, for all fruit had its own amount of liquid and its own specific sweetness too.

'There was a seedy cake missing after this morning's baking. You haven't been down to the Irishman's hut, have you?' asked Mrs Button suspiciously.

Kat grinned at her over the jelly and didn't answer. Mrs Button shook her head.

People always shook their heads at Kat. Even Mama would tut-tut at the state of her cheeks and hands, for she'd worn neither hat nor gloves today as she visited the pigpens and inspected the new Dorking hens in their coops before meeting Long William and the Irishman.

But Kat had been confined too long in the lavender respectability of the Academy. Mama might sigh at first, but she would laugh too, for hadn't she sent Kat to school for some of the discipline that Mama knew she would not get at home?

Home. It was a lovely word. There'd be green goose at dinner this afternoon, her favourite, and the Rhenish creams Mama loved as well as jellies, and Samuel, the Squire's eldest son and heir, who last Christmas had shown his appreciation for red hair and green eyes, even if the nose was slightly freckled.

Kat wondered what Samuel's appendage might look like, and if there might be any chance of a discreet walk unaccompanied in the shrubbery so she might compare it to William's. The bodice of tonight's pale blue dress trimmed with seed pearls was low enough to permit the intrusion of caressing hands, and its wide horsehair petticoat was easy to lift up, and so might give Samuel access to a little more than kisses.

But not much more. Kat was curious about some of the activities whispered about at night at the Academy, and she had enjoyed Samuel's kisses, but she had no wish for The Act itself. That was irrevocably the right of a husband, unless one chose to be a Scarlet Woman. None of the girls at school had been able to tell her the details of how one achieved Scarlet Womanhood. Kat thought it sounded interesting, especially as it involved no husbands who might have decided ideas about their wives' behaviour.

She grinned again as she scraped up the last of the jelly, making a sound that was not ladylike at all. It was just as Miss Thackeray had said as she shook her head at Kat back at the Academy.

Some girls were not born to be good.

'Kat, would you give me a few minutes after breakfast, please? In my study?'

Kat glanced up from her second rumbledethump, skilfully made of both mashed and grated raw potato, a Scottish dish most definitely not served at the school. Darling Mrs Button knew she loved rumbledethumps, and the strawberry jam in its silver dish, the warm rolls of potato bread instead of toast.

'Of course, Papa,' she said, curious.

What could not be mentioned here, with Mama, sipping her chocolate, and Grimsby filling the coffee pot? It must not be too serious. Mama didn't even glance up from her latest copy of *The Magazine of Natural History* — Papa ensured that Mama had all the latest journals that might conceivably mention coprolites — so she must know what Papa wanted to talk about.

Nor did Grimsby change expression, but then a good butler never did. The Fitzhuberts might be eccentric, but even they would not conceive of a butler who might show that he listened to his employers' conversation.

This, then, was something, that Must Not Be Said in Front of Servants, a subject Miss Thackeray had often focused on.

Kat stiffened. Possibly, now she was seventeen, it was no longer acceptable to visit the Irishman's hut. Perhaps she and Long William had been seen. That was, of course, far more reprehensible, but Kat could sincerely assure Papa it would not happen again now her natural curiosity had been assuaged, and William had been warned against displaying himself to the unwilling.

The library was the warmest room in the large house apart from the main kitchen. Kat, Mama and Papa often sat by the fire after dinner, Papa demonstrating his latest steam device while Kat and Mama embroidered camisoles and other items too private for Grimsby to glimpse.

This morning, however, only a vase of flowers dyed crimson sat in the fireplace. Papa motioned Kat to sit next to him on the velvet sofa, his face sombre, his hands holding a letter. Perhaps his agent had failed to acquire a manuscript he wanted at some auction house in London or abroad.

'Is it bad news, Papa?' A young lady did not Ask Direct Questions, except, thought Kat thankfully, at home.

'Yes, but not unexpected. Your Aunt Bertha has refused to give you a London Season. With your cousin Gabriella's entry into society last year, and Mary-Anne's the next, Bertha says her constitution is not equal to the strain.' Papa raised an eyebrow. 'My sister has the constitution of an ox, but I can easily understand that she does not want a niece outshining her own daughters.'

Kat flushed with pleasure at the compliment. 'Thank you, Papa. But I never wanted a Season, you know.' The discipline of a London Season, not to mention the formality of a Presentation at Court, would be ten times worse than Miss Thackeray's. 'Besides, it makes me sound like a horse. "Miss Kat is now in season,"' she added, trying to make her accent sound like one of the grooms'.

Her father unsuccessfully smothered a grin. 'Kat, my darling, a mare has to accept the stallion her owner has chosen. The purpose of a ... a London "Season" is to give young women of your class — and men too — a wider choice of prospective spouses.'

'I don't want to be married yet.' Kat was not sure she ever wanted to be married, even if the life of a Scarlet Woman proved an unattainable or unenviable ambition.

Most women — except Mama — did not seem particularly happy in their marriages. They filled their days with gossip and fashion magazines and whatever else the Squire's wife had talked about before Kat lost interest yesterday and began to dream about the possible adventures of a Scarlet Woman instead. Look at the poor queen, with five children in seven years, and looking twenty years older than when she was wed.

Women did not have babies as easily as sheep had lambs, and even then a ewe might die. You would need to be absolutely sure you wanted a baby to waddle around for half the pregnancy and then have pain and danger at the end of it. A husband controlled not just his wife's person, but her property, too. Kat would inherit Papa's fortune and it would be *hers*, though not of course for such a long time that she need not think of it.

A husband was needed only for social position, to which Kat did not aspire, or to keep one in a proper style, or if one fell in love, as Papa had when he saw Mama. Kat thought there was little chance of that happening. Young men were all talk of horses and how many partridges they had shot. Despite the flavour of his Christmas kisses Samuel had not even known what a plesiosaur was, nor shown any interest in the miniature steam cart Kat and Papa had contrived with John the Smith's help.

'You will never need a husband to support you in any style you wish, of course,' Papa continued. 'But your mother and I would ... shall we say there is no young man in this neighbourhood I would wish to see you allied with.'

So that was why Papa and the Squire and Samuel had spent so long over the port the previous night, leaving the women to tea and desultory gossip in the drawing room. Had Samuel enquired about paying his addresses to her? A few kisses in the chimney nook, thought Kat indignantly, should not mean that he so presumed.

Papa seemed to read her thoughts. 'The Squire seemed to think you would have no objection to his son making his addresses.'

'I enjoy Samuel's company now and then,' said Kat evenly. 'I don't want to marry him. Or any of the neighbours.'

'You relieve my mind. I admit I would as soon not have you leave home quite yet. We missed you while you were away at school, Kat,' he added.

Kat chuckled. 'Your ideal husband for me would move to Briarglen, have a deep interest in prehistorical dung and be a gentleman metal worker who could weld a seam strong enough to withstand the highest steam pressure.'

Papa laughed, his face relaxing. 'It's so good to have you back where you belong, Kat. That does indeed seem a perfect son-in-law.'

'Failing that paragon, Papa, I shall be a dutiful daughter and care for my aged parents in their dotage.'

'You might marry and do that too,' said her father dryly.

'I might, but I won't. Papa, what is a Scarlet Woman?'

'Where did you hear of those?!'

'At school,' said Kat calmly. 'I thought, perhaps, I might become a Scarlet Woman and never have to leave home at all.'

'Ahem. A Scarlet Woman usually accepts the attentions of many men, not just her husband, and is paid for receiving them.'

'She keeps her own fortune? That sounds superior to marriage, Papa. And Mama says that marital relations are indeed most pleasurable.'

Mr Fitzhubert seemed to be trying not to laugh. 'Pray ask your mother about the disadvantages of becoming a Scarlet Woman. To begin with, it is not generally practised from one's parents' home.'

Kat wrinkled her nose. That last condition seemed to be a clincher.

'If railway shares keep rising as they have the last few years, I believe you could aim as high as you would like for a husband,' said Mr Fitzhubert complacently. 'I would not like to see you condemned to spinsterhood. But after all you are so very young. We might hire a house in London in a year or two. Or travel,' he added with more enthusiasm. 'Would you care to see America? I gather it is possible to hire a steamboat to cross the Great Lakes. Your mother mentioned that there are fascinating prehistoric discoveries in the cliffs of Utah. It's a father's right to furnish his family with every gift he wishes. I would give you the moon and stars if you asked, Kat.'

'That's a safe promise, as you can't obtain them,' said Kat practically.

'Nor can I buy your mother one of what I gather are now called "dinosaur" skeletons,' said Mr Fitzhubert regretfully. 'All my agent can obtain are fossilised leaves. I believe she would love a palaeotherium for the hallway. Perhaps one can be obtained in time for her birthday. But do you think travel would suit you?'

'One day,' said Kat, with the blitheness of a girl who did not believe that one day would ever happen. Papa did not even enjoy carriage rides. He would sketch and experiment in his workshop with the aid of John, and Mama would hunt her fossils or join him riding to hounds, a predilection the more malicious girls at the Academy had whispered was the reason Kat was an only child. If so, Kat believed the sport was further recommended.

Briarglen would stand as a self-sufficient island on its hillside, Kat's life untrammelled by the conventions of the world beyond. There would be rumbledethumps or pigeon pie for breakfast, the scent of pot pourri in the hall, possibly next to a palaeotherium. If she wished for kisses too, or even something more, she was sure they could be obtained.

Perhaps she should acquire an Interest — not fossils or steam engines or, it seemed, being a Scarlet Woman, but something that would build a deeper layer into her life than last evening's gossip about clothes, neighbours, or the impudence of the squire's daughters' latest governess.

She would breed chickens, like Queen Victoria, Kat decided as she made her way down to the kitchen and the scent of stewing damsons. Papa could easily be persuaded to buy some of the ruinously expensive but most productive newly arrived Chinese hens, to mate with Briarglen's Dorkings. The newspapers declared that Her Majesty was even planning to be Patron of an Exhibition for Hens.

Kat would become The Famous Miss Fitzhubert, breeder of a hen that laid three eggs a day, and life at Briarglen would continue forever.

Eighteen months later Briarglen had been sold at a price that did not even begin to cover her father's debts. The boom in railway shares had broken, leaving many more than her father bankrupt, his vision of a steam-driven Britain gone with his riches. Her parents lay in their graves, but not side by side, for Papa's lay outside the churchyard fence, where suicides were buried. And Kat stood on the deck of the *Salamanca*, orphaned, her sole possessions in the valise she carried, the trunk the carters were carrying to her cabin, and the two trunks down in the hold, bound for a husband she had never met.

Chapter 2

KAT

LONDON, DECEMBER 1848

Aunt Bertha found the husband for her while Kat recovered from the emptiness she felt had left her cold forever — a far worse recovery than from the wound in her shoulder, sustained when Papa in his anguish had tried to shoot her too that morning.

The coroner's inquest had determined that Papa's aim had wavered after the flagon of poteen he had consumed. Kat would forever hope that it had not been the poteen, and that at the last moment his love for her had overcome his desire to take his wife and daughter with him from the world he could no longer face, and he had twitched his hand aside.

'There is no hope of a satisfactory marriage for you in England,' Aunt Bertha pointed out, not unkindly, as Kat lay listlessly on the chaise longue in the upstairs sitting room. After the scandal of her mother's murder by her husband, and his own suicide, Kat could not appear where Aunt Bertha's acquaintances might meet her, even if she was not in mourning.

Kat's presence in the house had been kept as discreet as possible, so as not to blight the chances of her cousins in their own potential marriages. It was fortunate that they bore their father's name and thus could be kept separate from the scandal of the Fitzhuberts.

Kat nodded. No fortune. A name that would stay notorious, for she was the daughter not just of a bankrupt, a murderer and a suicide, but a fool who had allowed his passion for steam to lose him his family wealth. The scar on her shoulder meant she could not even wear an evening dress without a lace fichu to cover it.

What now, if not marriage? She had no skills to be a governess, nor even the respectability to be a companion to an invalid who would like her to read aloud and fetch her shawl.

'I might be a cook. Or even a housekeeper.'

'At your age? And with no employment history? One does not change one's estate so easily, Kathleen. What mistress would want a gentleman's daughter in her kitchen? Besides,' her aunt added practically, 'if you must be cook and housekeeper, why not in a home of your own, where you give the orders instead of take them? No, it must be marriage, and not in England. I had thought of India. You might go there quite respectably to help care for a family's children — not a paid position of course —'

'I have no experience of children.'

Aunt Bertha ignored her. '— but then my dear friend Lettice showed me the letter from her brother in New South Wales, Mr Zebediah Markham. A quite acceptable family, my dear. Zebediah is the youngest son. He must be in his thirties now. How time flies! He was in the army briefly in the Low Countries, but decided he could find more adventure and fortune in the colony.'

'Why has Mr Markham not married before?'

'Because it is a convict colony, my dear. Most convicts sent out there are men, and, as for the women, well, one would scarcely expect a man of good family to ally himself with the criminal classes or the orphan dregs sent out for charity. Mr Markham has nearly two thousand acres, a house that is comfortable if not grand, and is prepared to pay the expenses to travel out there, as well as settle five hundred guineas on his wife.'

'Five hundred guineas? Surely Mr Markham must be inundated with possibilities.'

'There are ... drawbacks ...' said Aunt Bertha carefully. 'His house is somewhat isolated — a two-day journey by boat down the coast from Sydney, another boat upriver, and then a three-hour cart ride up the mountain.'

'A cart! Can Mr Markham not afford a carriage?'

'I'm sure he can, but I gather the roads in a new colony can't accommodate one, not where he dwells.' Aunt Bertha hesitated. 'I have taken the liberty of sending Mr Markham the likeness your cousin Sarah painted of you two years ago when you first went to the Academy. I have assured him that you are used to living in somewhat isolated surroundings and have all the skills and more that might be expected of the mistress of an estate that, to a great extent, must support itself. Of course, there will be other ... applicants ...'

'When did you do this, Aunt?'

Aunt Bertha met her eyes. 'A week after the tragedy, my dear, six months ago. Mr Markham should have my letter now. He may well have replied already. Lettice informed me it takes four or five months if the voyage is good for mail to reach the colony.'

'Perhaps Mr Markham will not like the look of me. Nor want my father's daughter.'

'I doubt anyone in New South Wales knows the tale, much less cares what happened to a gentleman's family in the English countryside. The colonists will have scandals of their own. And the likeness of you was charming. I informed Mr Markham that you can supervise a piggery, are familiar with poultry and can instruct a cook in everything from apple pie to a soufflé. Lettice kindly added her recommendation to mine.'

'So he is to marry me for my soufflés? You might have asked me!'

'You were in no condition to think of your future, my dear. But someone must.'

'What if he writes his acceptance and I travel all that way and we cannot stand each other?'

'It is up to you to make sure that does not happen. Mr Markham will want to like and respect his wife. Lettice assures me her brother has no vices. The chief joys he speaks of in his letters home are his estate and the building of his home. Now his affairs are somewhat settled he wishes for a family. It is over two thousand acres, Kathleen,' Aunt repeated, voice growing somewhat exasperated. 'You need not live in each other's pockets. What do you look for in a husband?'

'Absence.'

Aunt Bertha stood, her eyes assessing. 'Perhaps, if you are feeling a little better, you could be of assistance in this household? Mrs McDougal might like help sorting the linen cupboard.'

It was a threat. If Kat stayed on the chaise longue for the rest of her days, meals would still be brought to her, her bed made. There might even be 'new' dresses once her year of full mourning was over — Aunt Bertha's or one of her cousin's made to fit her when they had worn them as often as fashion dictated. Perfectly good dresses. But she would work for her keep.

If she told her aunt she was tired of town — which indeed she was, the rattle of carriages, the street cries, the smells of coal smoke and river stench — she might inhabit an upstairs room at their family's country estate. Perhaps, in twenty years, or thirty, her cousins' children might even ask her to their tea parties, as 'dear old Cousin Kathleen'.

A husband. She could not stand the thought. Her father had been the kindest husband. And, yet, in his ruin, he had still killed, or tried to kill, his wife and daughter, once he could no longer shower them with whatever they desired.

Why had he done it? Kat had asked herself this from the moment she entered the library, glimpsed Mama upon the floor and saw the pistol raised.

Because they belonged to him, legally and in every way that counted. Because he assumed that with his life no longer worth living, theirs must be worthless too.

And if he'd had the courage to live with his failure? There'd have been a little money — Mama's marriage portion — enough for a cottage, a garden. No more steam engines, but it cost nothing for Mama to roam the cliffs. Kat could cook ...

Mama's small marriage portion had been left to Kat, after bequests to Mrs Button and a few of the servants she was closest to '*if no provision has otherwise been left to them*'. But after those bequests there had been nothing left. The Irishman had been left nothing, either.

Kat almost smiled. The Irishman had lost his hut and his hothouse peaches, but she was sure he'd make his way with his yeast, his skill, and whatever other fruit he found. Possibly, even probably, Briarglen's new owners had kept him on, as they had retained the other servants. Kat had not asked.

Aunt Bertha sat and took Kat's hand in her beringed ones. She was not a hard woman, Kat realised, merely a practical one who knew what was important in her own world: the marriages of her daughters and the social position of her family. 'It's a chance for a new life, Kathleen. The best chance you'll have.'

'You think no one else will ever offer for me,' said Kat bitterly.

Aunt Bertha hesitated. 'I think you will probably get many offers,' she said at last. 'You're as much a beauty as your mother, and you have her charm too when you can be bothered. Some marriage proposals will come from sympathy, and such a husband will expect gratitude from you all your life. Some will come from a widower wanting a young wife.'

'None from love?'

'Those would be the worst,' said Aunt Bertha bluntly. 'Love rarely thinks of suitability. Do you really want a husband at outs with his family because he married a penniless subject of scandal broth? A gentleman in New South Wales has even less chance of getting a suitable wife than he might in India, which after all is closer. If there must be gratitude in a marriage, let it be from him to you.'

Kat blinked at her. 'You didn't expect frankness,' said Aunt Bertha dryly. 'I am your father's sister, after all. But society expects a game of coyness.'

'It's a game I don't want to play.'

'Then go to New South Wales. It's a land with its own grim past to live down. Lettice says they are going to abolish transportation now that so many in England believe the use of convicts is little better than slavery. They even have a new word for the country. What is it now? Ah yes, Australia. The colony is coming out of hardship too — I remember Lettice crying over her brother's letter just three years ago, as he wondered if it would ever rain again. Mr Markham began with one thousand acres. He was able to buy the rest for almost nothing because every other farmer walked off their land. He got the last five hundred acres for sixpence and a horse to get its ex owner to Sydney.'

Kat looked at her with the flicker of a smile. 'You make Australia sound so very tempting.'

'In truth, I don't know what you'll find there,' said Aunt Bertha honestly.

'But you think I will be a better fit in a land of thieves, rogues, disaster and strange hopping animals.'

'Strange hopping animals?'

'We had a copy of Mr Tench's book. They are called kangaruhs.'

Aunt Bertha raised an eyebrow. 'If you wish to find a husband with whom you can discuss kangaruhs, I suggest you seriously consider Mr Markham's letter.'

Kat dreamed again that night, the nightmare that had followed her since she had heard the final shot ring out in Papa's study.

Papa's face dissolving, because he had not been what she had thought he was and she did not understand, still could not understand, the man he was. Saw her life melting and her future too. Their lives had been built on gold, and when the gold melted, there had been nothing left.

She woke, chilled with sweat, then crossed to the coal scuttle to add more to the bedroom fire. The flames hiccupped, belching fumes. She was so tired of the smell of coal. I want wood fires again, she thought. I want chickens and fresh air. I want the past to vanish, to have a second chance ...

At least there'd be wood fires in New South Wales.

She could vaguely remember its outline on the globe at the Academy. The continent was — large. It had a healthful climate and strange animals, though she could not bring any one of them to mind. It also had few people.

Kat gazed out through the green velvet curtains, held back by fringed gold cords that matched the green and gold of the room's wallpaper, its pattern matching the wheat-sheaf carving on the chaise longue, the chairs and the mantelpiece. All she could see was yellow sky, slightly tinged with grey, which only changed when the grey grew deeper and it rained.

She was suffocating in this room and under that small sky. Surely, in a land as large as Australia, one might rid oneself of any husband who was too repressive, or even one who loved as immoderately as Papa had loved.

A farm meant horses. One could steal a horse and ride away, with the five hundred guineas settled on her and anything that might fit in her saddlebags. She could disguise herself as a boy and make her fortune, or open a bawdy house, though she would need to find out precisely what a bawdy house needed, apart from Scarlet Women and, probably, good cooking. Well, she could do that, anyway.

And, of course, there might be no fare to Australia, no settlement of five hundred guineas.

This Mr Markham might not even want her.

Chapter 3

TITANIA

THE *SALAMANCA*, MARCH 1849

Mrs Hartley Boot (nee Titania Higginbotham), widow of the late Mr Hartley Boot of the Inns of Court, London, gazed at the girl hesitating in front of her at the hatchway that led down to the *Salamanca*'s under-deck second-class cabins, and then the hold.

'But I was assured of a first-class cabin, opening onto the deck,' the young woman insisted. She was red-headed and delicate under her black mourning clothes and bonnet, as fine boned, perhaps, as the daughter Mrs Boot's parents had hoped for when they named Titania for a fairy queen thirty-three years earlier. Instead, they had received a daughter who was more like a female Hercules, politely described as five feet fourteen inches and once, by her late husband, as being 'tall as an outhouse'. He'd had the kindness to add, 'At least she don't smell like one.'

Mrs Boot glanced at her charge, but the tiny Lady Viola Montefiore still stood on shore in a neat woollen travelling cloak. Several soberly dressed women — her old nurse, a governess, and the ducal housekeeper no less — had come to make their final farewell before Lady Viola crossed the world. Her maid waited behind her, and her brother's footman stood attentive in case some marauder might make his way through the crowd of well-wishers. Lady Viola had been in London for less than a month and yet, despite being in mourning, and with the ... irregularities ... of her position, she already had people who would miss her.

Some girls were born to be loved.

Titania sighed. She had been bade a good journey only by her landlady, and that only in the hope of five shillings slipped into her hand. Titania had given her sixpence, for the roof had leaked and Sunday's roast was served as ragout on Monday, shepherd's pie on Tuesday, and mutton and turnip soup on Wednesday; after that last she had needed at least six pickled onions to remove its memory. Titania also had a most excellent use for every penny this voyage would bring her.

No one seemed to be shepherding the young woman on deck, though like Lady Viola she looked far too young and delicately bred to be alone. Titania's shoes had been made to be worn on slippery decks and were sturdy enough to carry her frame.

'If you will pardon me ...' she began.

The young woman turned, then bobbed a rudimentary curtsey to one who was obviously somewhat lower in station than herself. Titania curtseyed in return. 'My name is Mrs Hartley Boot, employed as companion to Lady Viola Montefiore. I am afraid that the entire deck cabin area has been reserved for Lady Viola.'

The girl glanced again down the hatchway. It smelled of turpentine, carbolic soap and unwashed humanity. 'You cannot expect me to stay down there for the entire five months or more of the journey. Why, they say there are days when one cannot even walk on deck!'

Many such days, thought Titania, who had studied the conditions to be expected on this voyage in detail. But then, that was her job. 'I am so sorry. But perhaps with your companions you will find it not so very bad. This is a most clean ship, and excellently run.'

'I have no companions,' said the young woman shortly.

Titania blinked. 'No maid?' She herself had never had the attentions of a maid — her dresses had discreet fastenings at the side and she wore her hair in a neat roll swept off her plain square face. She gave the young woman's fine wool travelling dress a discreet evaluation. As she had thought, it fastened up the back. She would need help even to get into her nightdress tonight.

'I do not have a lady's maid. The stewardess will give me all the help I need.'

Captain Olsen had informed Titania that the *Salamanca* would not carry a stewardess on this voyage, as Lady Viola had her own attendants. Obviously no one had told this young woman, or her family.

'I am sure you and your chaperone will manage splendidly,' Titania said hopefully.

'I have no chaperone,' said the girl shortly.

'No chaperone either?' asked Titania, faintly scandalised.

'I was meant to join a Mrs Henry Adams and her children. Her maid was to attend me too. Mrs Adams changed the date on which she was to sail two weeks ago. I decided I would keep my booking, rather than wait months for another suitable ship.'

Mrs Henry Adams had undoubtedly been told about the rearranged accommodation on the *Salamanca* and had shuddered at the vision of her family in the cramped, damp and foetid second class, without even a first-class saloon for dining and socialising. Admittedly it might take months to find passage on a ship that did not carry convicts or steerage passengers, with the high risk of disease, but what could be so urgent that the young woman could not wait?

'Your family agreed to this?' Titania asked tentatively.

The girl smiled faintly. 'My aunt does not know I kept my booking. I have no one else to answer to.'

Which explained why there was no one to say farewell to her. 'If you will excuse me, Miss, but Mrs Adams had good reason to cancel. There is no stewardess on board. Even the dining saloon has been reserved for Lady Viola's use.'

'I see,' said the girl slowly. She lifted her chin. 'I will manage.'

'But why?' demanded Titania. This matter was too serious for good manners.

'Because I could not stand another week in London. Because every minute in England wastes the new life I need to have ...' The girl looked embarrassed, as though she had been startled into saying too much. And the truth.

It was, however, the one answer that could convince Titania that the girl had made the right choice. Titania, too, was seeking a new life. The last months had been agony, knowing that a future was within her grasp, and longing for it to begin.

Titania's first duty was to Lady Viola, of course. This was not a hardship. In her plain, hardworking life Titania had never met anyone as endearing, nor an aristocrat so free of a sense of self-importance. Though, to be sure, Lady Viola's ... circumstances ... had been difficult.

But there must be help for this young woman too, who probably did not even know that without a maid she would have to empty her own chamber pot over the rails. She possibly had not even brought provisions to add to the monotonous shipboard meals.

Titania gave a quick glance at her own cabin, next to Lady Viola's, hoping that the spirit lamp and kettle had already been unpacked, with the tea caddy, the teapot, and the cups and saucers, not to mention the sugar basin, the sugar tongs, tea and lemons, and that the trunk with their other provisions, including the all-important jars of pickles, were safely there too, and not in the damp of the hold. The extra trunk would make her cabin sadly cramped, but that was no matter.

Some women were born to be useful.

Titania sighed. In her thirty-one years, not only had she been unloved, but everyone had also always assumed she was capable of looking after herself and others, too. Which of course she was.

'Perhaps, as you have a first-class passage, you might sometimes join us,' she began, resolving to help the girl dress and undress each day, at the very least. 'I must ask Lady Viola's permission for you to use the upper deck, of course, but ...' She stopped, for her charge was finally making her way up the gangplank on Captain Olsen's arm, smiling up at him charmingly, while he looked down with fatherly concern at her.

Indeed, Lady Viola was a girl to be loved.

Chapter 4

VIOLA

Lady Viola Montefiore smiled dutifully as Captain Olsen welcomed her onto his ship with a deep bow. Viola had learned to smile early. As an aristocrat's daughter she had the choice of two responses when an unwary newcomer, whether guest or servant, first saw the changeling of the Montefiore family. Viola could hide or she could smile. She could be outcast, or she could be loved.

It was far better to be loved. Viola had learned that early, too, after a nurse had tied her hands to her crib to stop her sucking her thumb. That nurse had been dismissed, and the next — who, despite Viola's mother's outrage when she was discovered trying to bleach the child's face with buttermilk, tried again with a diluted acid that raised the skin in blisters.

By the time her next nurse arrived, Viola had learned to smile.

Smiling made people comfortable. It eventually even enchanted nurses and nannies, and later governesses and dancing masters who had been employed to tend the daughter of a duke and found their charge — her. They couldn't openly complain of being tricked into teaching a girl with dark skin. Viola might not have her mother's milky skin, but she had inherited her title and her fortune, settled on the female line since Queen Anne's time. Lady Viola the elder would not only hear no criticism of her daughter, she refused to allow acknowledgement of her difference either.

Had Mama thought hiding her dark skin behind the Abbey walls and courtyards with only a library from which to view the outside world would make her life easier? It hadn't. Viola had learned to depend on her own companionship, and the friendship of writers like Plato, dead more than two thousand years, the Bible as she read it, not as it was interpreted by the rector, or foreign philosophers like Soren Kierkegaard, especially since her mother's death from a fast consumption, two years earlier. Her older brother Edgar had gone to school and made his home out of term time at their London house with his father, with brief visits to their hunting lodge for the shooting, until a stumbling horse had meant Edgar assumed the title twenty months ago, only four months after their mother's death.

Edgar's first act as the new duke had been to begin the legal process to make him no longer Viola's guardian or trustee, and to petition her only other relative, a Major Nash in far off New South Wales, to take on the duty until she came of age in four years' time. New South Wales, presumably, was distant enough for society to forget the dark-skinned girl who was legally — and scandalously — the new duke's sister. Major Nash had sold his commission, and so would not have promotion jeopardised by a dark-skinned ward. The income from Viola's trusteeship should also be welcome.

Viola had become even more expert at smiling in the last twenty months.

Yet Viola had discovered that smiling at the world also came at a cost. When you smiled at people and met their eyes you noticed the most fleeting of their expressions — the shadowed eyes despite cheerful faces, envy, fear or loneliness. Smiling was one of the coins you paid for love, but it meant you paid in other ways, for when you smiled you learned to care.

Just now Viola smiled not just to please the captain, but because as she crossed this gangplank she was finally free, or at least more free than ever before. She was no longer hidden in the west wing of the Abbey. She had travelled the entire road to

London, though had admittedly only been allowed to peer around the curtains lest she be seen. She had met some of the servants of her brother's London household. Now she stood, entirely open to everyone's gaze there on the wharf and ship. And no one had screamed or done more than glance at her twice. Some had even treated her kindly.

She had before her an entire four- or five-month voyage, where she could walk in the open whenever she wanted to, unseen except for the sea and sky, and the crew, who in the eyes of society did not count, and Mrs Boot and other employees, who were paid not to mind. She also had seven trunks of books among the many other trunks of dresses, linen and other necessities for a girl of her class.

She turned her smile to the young woman in black unexpectedly standing alone on deck. The girl was possibly two years her senior and twice her height. The girl did not smile back, but nor did she look at Viola with curiosity or distaste. She seemed, indeed, to be locked in her own small world of misery. Viola turned to her new companion.

'Mrs Boot, what seems to be the matter?'

'This young lady had booked a first-class cabin. She was not informed that the deck area has now been reserved, nor that there is no stewardess on board,' said Mrs Boot.

As Mrs Boot had failed in making introductions, Viola ignored convention. She gave the young woman a slight curtsey. 'Please allow me to introduce myself. I am Lady Viola Montefiore.'

The other girl gave her a quick, startled glance. Either she recognised Viola's name and the ancient scandal, or she was surprised that a girl of such dark complexion bore the title 'Lady'. She quickly dropped a lower curtsey. 'I am Miss Kathleen Fitzhubert of ... of nowhere now, except this ship, and bound for a second-class cabin below deck.'

Viola had been under the impression that the whole passenger area of the ship had been reserved for herself and her attendants, with the former passengers offered passage on a ship sailing in three months' time. But Miss Fitzhubert looked as if far more than a first-class cabin had been wrenched from her.

Her accent and her dress also proclaimed her well born and well bred. The young woman might, just possibly, provide companionship on a voyage that, as well as being uncomfortable and dangerous, was also long. Lady Viola's maid, Smiggins, had for decades been her mother's and was still inclined to treat Viola as a child.

Viola's mother had given her everything possible, but never the companionship of someone who had not been paid to be with her.

Viola turned impulsively to her companion. 'Mrs Boot, could Miss Fitzhubert have the cabin next to mine, and my dresses stored in hers?'

Viola watched as a smile of relief spread across her companion's face.

'That would be an excellent idea,' said Mrs Boot. 'Your ladyship is most gracious.' She nodded to the waiting Smiggins. 'Please accompany Miss Fitzhubert to her cabin. The one to the right of Lady Viola's, I think. I will inform Captain Olsen, Miss Fitzhubert.'

Miss Fitzhubert hesitated. 'That is exceedingly kind of you ...'

'It is not kind at all! You will be far better company than a cabin full of dresses,' said Viola hopefully, fully prepared for her offer to be snubbed, despite the extra comfort of a cabin on deck.

The girl looked embarrassed, and slightly angry at being embarrassed. 'I may not be quite the company you wish for on the voyage, Lady Viola.'

Viola's smile was not manufactured this time. Miss Fitzhubert seemed gloriously unbothered about having a dark-skinned companion, and one socially above her, too. 'Nonsense. Come with me now while the luggage is stowed! Smiggins, please unpack for Miss Fitzhubert, too.'

Smiggins gave Miss Fitzhubert a look the girl didn't notice, and then another to Mrs Boot, which that woman ignored.

'Yes, Lady Viola,' Smiggins said expressionlessly.

Viola dispensed an appropriate smile. 'Smiggins, you are wonderful. Remind me to tell you how wonderful you are again tonight.'

Viola would also give Smiggins a guinea this evening, with an implied promise of more to come if she tended Miss Fitzhubert, too, for how could a young woman even do her hair with no lady's maid? Nor would there be much other work for Smiggins on this voyage, for Viola's only changes of dress would be to start the day, for dinner, and for bed.

Viola took the young woman's hand. 'I believe my friend Mrs Boot ordered cakes delivered for our tea.' She smiled again, as reassuringly as she could. 'They will be our last chance at proper pastry till we reach Madeira. I am sure you are longing for a dish of tea.'

She glanced at Mrs Boot, who was obviously hoping that the captain did not forbid the lighting of a flame while in port. Viola hoped so too. She, also, longed for tea, and was extremely glad she would have it on this voyage. Major Nash had been very clear about what his new ward might expect on the voyage in his letters welcoming her to his home. Tea — especially with cakes — was a luxury afforded only to passengers who made their own provision for it.

Viola had no special love for the land of her birth. It had been made clear that it was, in fact, not hers to love. Australia might be more generous. But there was still a strange desolation in leaving all she had known behind. It had been uncomfortable, but at least familiar and protected by the family's position. Her new protector was unknown, except for his letters, and at the other end of the world.

'I would indeed be grateful for a dish of tea.' The stiffness in Miss Fitzhubert's voice was already fading.

Mrs Boot gave a small nod of approval. She looked around for a sailor who might take a message to Captain Olsen, who had vanished for more urgent matters so close to sailing. But Viola had no doubt that her companion and chaperone for the voyage would ensure that the exchange went smoothly.

Nothing, it seemed, fazed Mrs Boot, from the charge of an extra and unexpected young lady to the best provisions for a long sea voyage. She had comfortably assured Viola that she had packed sufficient portable lemonade and jellied soup stitched into oil cloth, tea, plum puddings, fruit cakes, jams, chutneys, jars of preserved fruit and what she described as most excellent pickled onions, with clarified salt butter and bottled boiled cream to see them comfortably through the voyage, as well as a most adequate medicine chest and jars of pickled plums with ginger, sovereign against seasickness.

Some women, thought Viola, envying her, were born to be useful.

Chapter 5

VIOLA

Viola glanced around her cabin. It was far smaller than any room she had ever occupied and the bed was narrow, but the planked flooring had been covered with small Oriental rugs. They were Mrs Boot's doing, she imagined, and most practical, for the rugs could be taken out and shaken or dried on deck. A large bunch of out-of-season roses sat on the hinged table, their hothouse fragrance almost overcoming the scent of salt and the slight, omnipresent tinge of rat. Two small portholes looked out at the oily waters and the ship moored opposite. But the four chairs, while not upholstered except with the loops to fasten them to the wall in rough weather, looked comfortable.

Viola untied her bonnet — an automatic act, for she had never in her life stepped out of doors without one in case her skin darkened further, and even then she had rarely gone beyond her mother's private courtyard, lest some visitor see her. She had spent even Sunday church services in the family box, hidden from the gaze of the congregation. Today had been exhilarating enough, with people actually looking at her, or at least glimpsed under the poke bonnet, the rest covered by dress and gloves.

And now she was 'entertaining'! A young woman, like herself, not a toy giraffe.

'Please, take a seat, Miss Fitzhubert,' Viola said slightly breathlessly.

Miss Fitzhubert flushed. 'Possibly you have heard my name before.'

Viola hesitated, suddenly remembering the item in the newspaper. Fitzhubert was not such an uncommon name, though she would not have associated the murder–suicide with this young woman if she hadn't mentioned it.

Viola looked at her with sympathy. 'It must be disconcerting to have been certain about your life, only to find that you had been wrong about everything.'

Miss Fitzhubert had the startled look Viola always saw when others heard plainspoken insight from an aristocrat with her childlike form and pretty brown face. 'I beg your pardon, Lady Viola?'

'Please call me Viola, if we are to be facing sea monsters together.'

'I'm Kathleen. Kat. Your comment ... about being wrong about everything ...'

'I don't imagine you expected the tragedy of your parents,' said Viola gently. 'You must have assumed your life would keep its predicted pattern, just as your father based his whole life on the false security of his railway shares. You must surely wonder,' she added, 'whether he acted from love or hate, or accident, or something which we can't even guess.'

'Love, I think,' said Kat slowly. 'Papa created a Garden of Eden for us, and then it was broken, so Mama and I must vanish too, because he could not bear it.'

'But you can,' said Viola matter-of-factly. 'Though you must have suddenly felt a stranger in a strange land.'

The young woman stared at her wonderingly. 'No one else has understood that before.'

'Perhaps I do because I have always been a stranger.' Viola began to smile, then suddenly realised that perhaps she had no need to, not with a girl as burdened as herself. 'Surely you've heard of my own scandal? It has been the talk of the town on and off since my birth.'

'I didn't talk much in town,' Kat admitted. 'Or listen.'

'But you must have noticed something ... odd ... about me. I believe I am quite original in ducal circles.'

'You mean your dark skin?' Viola was glad Kat could mention it so easily. 'I thought perhaps your father had married an African princess, or something like that. I know little about the aristocracy,' she admitted. 'Though my papa was cousin to an earl.'

'No, my mother's colouring was as fair as yours. The scandal of my birth died down after a while, as few saw me, but unfortunately the gossip began again on my father's death.'

'I'm so sorry for your loss.'

'Please don't be. His death has meant I am freed from the seclusion of our country estate. I only met him perhaps a dozen times, and then briefly. You see, he was almost certainly not my true father.' Viola shrugged. 'Mrs Boot knows the story, as I am sure Captain Olsen does, and some of the sailors perhaps. Even if they have never heard my name before they will ask questions when they see the colour of my skin.'

Viola waited for the inevitable polite denial that anyone would want to gossip about her appearance. Instead, Miss Fitzhubert — Kat — merely looked at her questioningly.

'My parents journeyed to India two years before I was born. My father had business interests there. He never expected to inherit the dukedom, as he was a mere cousin, third in succession. I'm sorry — I still call him my father, as that is how he was referred to by everyone, even though they knew he couldn't be. My brother was ten years old and kept at school in England. My parents stayed in India for eighteen months, then returned to England when the duke's two sons died when their yacht capsized. Their father had a stroke that proved fatal. He died while my parents were still on the voyage home. My father arrived to find he was Duke of Longmarsh and that my mother was expecting.'

'Was he fond of his cousins?'

'I never asked. I never knew if he was fond of my mother, either. She was an heiress in her own right and he was quite penurious when they married. But certainly, after I was born, tiny, with a complexion that is … not English … he showed her no affection and demanded she stay at Shallowford Abbey, on his estate. I had to stay there too, of course.'

Kat Fitzhubert blinked. 'You mean your father disowned you?'

'No,' said Viola. 'He did not disown me. That would have caused an even greater scandal. My mother remained his wife, who kept to the country because of her delicate constitution, while his sister played hostess for him in town. I remained his daughter, though I imagine few were incautious enough to mention me to him.'

'That is monstrous. I have often seen in breeding pigs where one of the litter may be dark, and all the others fair. If there is one dark ancestor, on either side of your family …'

'There hasn't been,' said Viola. 'Or not at least for the last seven generations of portraits.'

'But were portraits painted of every ancestor? Ha! I expect his own grandmother was dark complexioned.' Kat Fitzhubert showed not the least embarrassment.

Viola felt her serenity melt into laughter. 'No one has put it as bluntly before.'

'Colour can easily skip a generation or two. I've seen a white rooster born after five generations of pure Dorking hens! What did your mother say?'

Viola wallowed in the frankness. 'I only asked her once. She had to pretend there was nothing to explain, you see.'

'Why? You said she had her own money. She could have taken you to the south of France, or Venice …'

'You forget, she had another child, my brother. An open scandal would have affected him, possibly even questioned his legitimacy to the succession.' Viola wondered if that was the reason Edgar had so quickly instructed his lawyers to assign away her guardianship and trusteeship.

'And your real father?'

It was as if the air had suddenly cleared of fog and London smoke. No one had ever said those words aloud to her. 'I only asked my mother when she was dying. She said, "Your father loved me." Then she stroked my hair and said, "You are so lovable, my darling." And that was all she said.'

Kat snorted. 'Beautifully sentimental, but facts would be better. I beg your pardon — I should not have been rude about your mother, especially not when she was dying. But what takes you to New South Wales?'

'My brother decided it would be best if he relinquished my guardianship, and sent me to my mother's cousin in Sydney Town on the grounds that the climate would suit my delicate health.'

Kat snorted again. 'He didn't really say that, did he? A voyage like this to suit your health! The man's an idiot! Oh, I'm sorry. I am being dreadfully rude again.'

'Don't apologise. I like it. But I think perhaps New South Wales will suit me,' said Viola. 'I hear it is a place where even in the best society people are very good at forgetting the past scandals in their lives, and others'.'

Kat hesitated. 'That is also why I am going there,' she admitted at last. 'A Mr Markham has purchased my hand in marriage for five hundred guineas.'

Viola blinked. 'That isn't very much.'

Kat laughed. 'I wish I had asked for more too, especially as I am most experienced at pig breeding, which my aunt says shall be a valuable skill in the colonies, as well as my respectable birth.'

'Fresh lives for both of you,' said Mrs Boot quietly, from where her frame had been filling up the doorway. She entered, somehow balancing a tray in one hand with the cups, cake plates, milk jug, sugar bowl, sugar tongs, teaspoons, tea strainer, cake forks, as well as the teapot, slops pot and hot water pot. The other hand held a cake tier, with jam tarts, cream puffs and other delicacies on the lower levels, and a sponge cake oozing jam and cream reposing on the top. 'Will you take tea, Lady Viola? I apologise for the china teapot, but silver sadly tarnishes at sea.'

'I will accept a china teapot if you call me Viola.'

Mrs Boot flushed. 'It isn't fitting, your ladyship.'

Kat grinned. 'It seems you are sharing a voyage with two scandalous young women. You might call us by our first names.' She examined her. 'I think you have perhaps only ten more years than either of us, though you seem older.'

The flush deepened. 'I have been married and widowed.'

'I'm sorry —' began Kat.

'I was not,' said Mrs Boot flatly, gazing at the silver teapot. 'I married young, and he was older.'

'You don't recommend marriage?' asked Kat.

Mrs Boot placed the tray on the table and sat heavily on the third chair. 'I have only two experiences of it — my parents' and my own. My parents seemed happy enough.' She looked sharply at the two younger women. 'I'm thinking it will be different for both of you. I had nothing to give my husband but my housekeeping and, as he grew feebler, managing his business.'

'Why should it be different for us?' demanded Kat.

'Men treasure beauty.'

'Sometimes it is a burden to be a treasure,' said Kat flatly, staring out the porthole, but not, thought Viola, at the feet and wheels going past on the dock.

'Mrs Boot, what is your Christian name?' put in Viola quickly.

'Titania,' said Mrs Boot bluntly. 'And no use telling me you've never seen anyone less fairy like, because I know it. I'm a troll, more like.'

'Indeed you are not,' said Kat vehemently. 'How are we to know how tall the fairies were before they left England, anyway? Leprechauns now — everyone knows that they are small. But if giants built the great stone circles, perhaps those giants were fairies.' She frowned. 'Though their wings must have been extremely large to carry heavy rocks. Perhaps they were flightless, like hens. I am very fond of hens,' she added.

'May we call you Titania? You don't look like a boot,' said Viola coaxingly.

'I don't look like a Titania either,' said Titania bluntly. 'And I am supposed to be chaperoning and companioning you.'

'I promise to obey Queen Titania quite as much as Mrs Boot.'

Mrs Boot — Titania — sat wordlessly for a moment, then nodded.

'Then Titania, darling, will you make us tea, please?'

Titania let down the table, then began to set out the contents of the tray. Kat stood to help her.

'We are the best provisoned cabin on any ocean,' said Viola with satisfaction. 'Titania has brought tea enough for the voyage, oat biscuits, portable soup, portable lemonade, pickled eggs, plum puddings, crystallised fruit, chutneys, waxed cheeses and trunks of fruit in bran or sand down in the hold, and I forget what else. And now we have companionship, as well.'

'My husband was an agent,' explained Titania. 'One of his clients was a chandler. I ... I shared that side of the work, too, for some time before my husband's death. I enjoy provisioning.'

'And we benefit from it.' Viola held out a tiny hand for her china cup and saucer.

'The three of us will have wider, freer lives out in the colony,' said Kat firmly.

'I am not sure what life I would like, once I am of an age to choose,' admitted Viola. 'But if there is a chance of friendship ... I have never had the chance of friends. Plato called friendship Philia, as great a love as any other kind. The only other love I have ever known is a mother's.' Viola smiled. 'I don't think Plato knew much about that.'

'Who's Plato?' asked Kat.

'An ancient Greek philosopher,' said Viola. 'I'm sorry — my life has perhaps been too much in books.'

'Never known any Greeks, except Mrs Aristides who trades in olive oil, and good quality too,' said Titania. 'But friendship — that's something I've not known either, but I'm thinking that Mr Plato might be right. I'd have friendship over marriage any day,' she added wistfully.

Kat held out her hand. 'We will be friends forever, sisters in scandal. Titania, will you join your hands too?'

Titania offered the cake tier to Viola. 'I'm a paid employee.' She gave a wry smile. 'And sadly, my life has never been touched by scandal.'

Or much else, thought Viola shrewdly. Titania showed no sense of loss for her late husband, nor her parents, nor any part of the life and land they were leaving.

Kat winked. 'We'll have to find you a lovely scandal of your very own. Maybe there is even an Oberon on board.'

'None of that,' warned Titania. 'Oh, very well.' She looked deeply touched, and put her square hand over the girls' smaller ones.

'Tea,' she said firmly. 'And we'd best eat up the sponge cake as it won't keep. And the tarts, too. They'll be the last we'll get till Sydney.'

'See? She is a treasure,' said Viola.

'Viola ...' For once Kat hesitated. 'Do you think you will ever know ...?'

'Who my father was? Perhaps. My mother left me this.' Viola slipped out a thin silver filigree locket, highly ornate. 'She wore it always, but under her collar, or a lace fichu, never too visible. Now I wear it for her sake and ... and for whoever gave it to her.'

'You think it was from your ... the man who was ...?'

'My father,' said Viola firmly. 'Now we are casting off I can say the words. Perhaps he gave it to her. Perhaps someone else, someone my mother was close to out there. Who knows what happened?'

She touched the necklace. 'My mother had the income of her inherited trust, as you pointed out, though her husband controlled most of it under the terms of her marriage settlement. She could afford to journey back to India. Legally, my father could have prevented her, but she could surely have embarked without his knowing. If he sued her for restitution of marital rights, forcing her back to England, he would have created an even greater scandal. If he divorced her for desertion, he would have lost her income. So why did she never return? That,' said Viola quietly, 'is what I would most like to know. Perhaps my father is dead. Perhaps, somehow, she genuinely did not know how she came to bear a half-Indian child. Maybe the elves slipped me into the cradle when the midwife wasn't looking, for I have no features of my mother, beyond my hands. But she always treated me as her child. She always loved me.'

The men's yells outside changed to a more urgent tone. Sails creaked. The ship's cow gave a bewildered moan.

'Seems as if we're leaving,' said Titania.

None of them made a move to farewell the land on which they'd been born. The wind gave a sudden gust through the door as the ship turned, a sharp tang of salt and freedom.

Chapter 6

TITANIA

Titania's pen scratched on the paper. After six weeks at sea she had adapted to the sway of the ship, her hand hardly veering from its neat roundhand. There was barely enough lamplight to make out her letters as she dipped the pen in the ink bottle again and wiped the sludge off the nib. But that did not matter. She did not need to see the book clearly to write. It was indeed a luxury to have a lamp at night again, for in the high winds or storms earlier in the voyage no spark of any kind could be lit. Even the kitchen fire was extinguished.

Day 41

The wind continues light, the Captain informs me, sailed at between 5 and 7 Knots, the Weather so Warm. Today we consumed the last Portion of the 12th Pudding. The Rainwater now consumed, we once again Boil the water from the Barrels to Good Effect on our Digestions. Two Bottles Apricots, preserved, discoloured, and thus thrown Overboard. Mould also on the dried apricotts. Note: Try Spirits of Sulphur for the next Preserving. They may keep better Pickled.

It had been an easy voyage so far. Oh, Kat had not thought so with the first few days of seasickness, when she could keep nothing down but ginger water and bouillon from the jellied stock Titania had so prudently prepared, as well as regular doses of pickled plums in ginger.

Titania believed in open bowels, an open mind, and plentiful pickles. In her experience pickles made most of life's hardships easier, from the sweetness of pickled damsons after a tongue lashing from the late Mr Boot, to the pungency of a pickled onion to help relieve a cold.

Kat could not know how fortunate she was that the *Salamanca* was an unusually clean ship, with few passengers and none in steerage nor, worse, on the 'mid deck', into which, on so many other ships, convicts and migrants were so deleteriously crammed that often a third or more would die of fever on the voyage. Even the *Salamanca*'s rats were almost under control, thanks to Captain Olsen's terrier and the ship's cat.

Now Kat consumed whatever provender Titania placed on the table, whether it was the ship's potatoes and boiled mutton — a sheep was butchered every week, its flavour much improved by one of Titania's chutneys — or the milk from the still uneasy ship's cow, or their own slightly wrinkled apples, the prunes she had dried herself, or the walnuts that opened with a satisfying crack. Luckily, she had brought such a store that there was plenty to share. Viola's brother had at least given her a free hand to buy whatever she thought might be needed. Titania made another note:

Cracking Nuts in the Shell most Satisfactory, as a Way of passing Time.

They also played spillikins, cards, bibblecatch, made paper flowers which wilted in the damp, read aloud to each other, and walked on deck when the weather was calm. Kat even seemed happy, placing whatever had happened to her in the past and what might occur in the future into a realm of 'then', herself existing only in what Viola had informed them that a Danish philosopher had called 'the world of now'.

Viola, perhaps, never left that state. Titania presumed it had been her mother who had had the wisdom to give so vulnerable a young woman whatever book had taught her to be present for each momentary joy. Often Titania found Viola had left her cabin in the evening, to be found leaning on the rail, watching the stars with serene joy.

Viola had brought her translation of Kierkegaard with her, as well as other books of philosophy, some in ancient Greek or even Roman, and so inaccessible to Kat or Titania unless Viola translated, something she only attempted once, when Kat protested in boredom after the first page.

It was Titania who had thought to bring the most interesting reading matter: Sydney newspapers purchased in London from a newsagent who specialised in publications from the colonies for those who had family, friends or investments there. The newspapers were now more than six months old, but gave a portrait of the society they were sailing to. The three of them pored over the columns of Arrivals, Departures and Clearances — none of them were quite sure exactly what 'Clearances' were.

Aborigines, it seemed, had attacked the flocks of a Mr Mundey, causing grievous damage; the governor was disputing something with someone, though the newspaper circumspectly did not say exactly what, or why; six loads of poultry had arrived, but from where and for whom? And what breed had they been? But the hens had sold for from two shillings to two shillings and threepence each, and fat pigs at four pence per pound; and a ship's captain had been impounded for fraudulent behaviour, his ship's crew and chandlers unpaid but no other details given. The newspapers presented even more questions than they answered.

Titania watched their faces as they took turns to read out items, vital, happy, *young*, as they chattered in the soft pool of the lamplight.

Had she ever been that young? Only if you measured it by the clock and sunrise. Youth must be shared, and so these past weeks accompanying Viola and Kat had been Titania's first true acquaintance with youth. She envied both girls. They would not know what a gift youth was until it had vanished.

Her mother had been forty-eight at her arrival, six stillbirths behind her, her father sixty-four. The baby daughter had seemed a miracle, until she grew and kept on growing. She was not ungainly, nor out of proportion. Indeed, from a distance she might seem comely. She had never forgotten two young men watching her cross the moor, their obvious appreciation turning to hilarity as she came close and they comprehended her true size. 'I say, they'll never believe us back at Oxford. That such a thing of beauty could turn to this!'

She was simply large and useful: doing the household accounts, nursing her mother through her last illness, and then cossetting her father's frailty, until he claimed her galumphing got on his nerves and forbade her from his presence. In those final months he had arranged her marriage to Mr Boot, his lawyer and man of business. She had accepted joyfully, despite his age ...

The wedding night was etched into her body. She suspected it would never leave. She lay, as her new husband directed, her nightdress fastened at the neck and raised to her hips. He did not look at her by the faint gas light through the curtain chinks. She saw him take a belt to his own flesh, ordering it to rise; he used it then on her, though she cried out. He covered her mouth with his hands in case the servants heard, and she quietened, lest she choked.

At last he forced himself in, waited for three seconds and withdrew, then stated calmly as he lay beside her, his panting easing, 'No one can claim non-consummation now.'

It seemed that even the consolation of children would be lost to her.

The ship chopped and swayed about her, jolting her pen. She bent to her figures again, as she had kept Mr Boot's figures for three years. He had married her as a housekeeper and confidential clerk. She had thought that as she grew even more able, taking on more of the agency business too, as he grew frail, that her husband might grow to like her — even, in partnership, that she might lose her distaste for him.

But as she gradually began to run the entire office, taking daily orders from his bedside while making more of the decisions — and better ones — his contempt grew greater. Unwomanly in body, she was even more so in her mind and ability to organise. Even then it was only after he had died and the will was read that she understood the depth of his hatred, grown perhaps from his dependence on her, though the seed had already been there.

He had made the agency business over to a nephew, months before his death, a young man who knew nothing of shipping or a merchant's trade, and had even given him the house as well, with a life-tenancy for himself, but not for his wife. The latter had been such a petty malice that she had cried, as she had not since the last hours of her wedding night. Her life had been accounts, and accounts have no emotions, only orderliness. But she had quailed at all the hatred dug deep into the shrivelled man upon the bed, small in life and even smaller now in death.

She had only her marriage settlement. Her father's long slow dying had nibbled his competency away till he agreed to only a hundred and six pounds and fourteen shillings, with twenty-five pounds as a paltry widow's jointure. She also had this position, which brought in sixty-five pounds a year — an excellent wage for a woman, especially as Viola had insisted that her own dressmakers, mantua makers, milliners and even suppliers of fine luggage equip Titania lavishly at Viola's expense. 'For I may need chaperoning to balls, and how can you do that without a gown?'

Her most valuable possession, however, was this book. It never left her person. Every contact she had ever made at Boot, Boot and Boot — all three generations of Boots now returned to leather, bones and bones — had been recorded in this book, just as those generations of Boots had made their entries too. The tonnage of ships and the amount of cordage each had needed; the supercargos and quartermasters who had ordered prime salt pork, and those who settled for the cheapest, rank fat floating in sludge; the recipes for sauerkraut and pickled carrots; for salted limes in rum; for the boiled fruit puddings on which the health of captains and officers depended, for they could not be lost to scurvy like the men: this book had them all.

And the nephew had not even recognised its worth. She had found it in the waste basket, when she took it out to empty it on her last day in what had been her marital home. She had slipped it into the pocket of her apron, not knowing whether to rejoice or grieve that Boot, Boot and Boot would decline into bankruptcy without it. Mostly, guiltily, she rejoiced.

She now recorded their passage each day in the book, judging for herself the efficacy of the diet on the sailors, and any other matter that had escaped her understanding in a life spent ashore.

Viola would never ask her to leave her employ. She would not have done so to any employee, and certainly not abandon a friend. Nor — probably — would Viola's guardian or her eventual husband terminate her position, though Major Nash would undoubtedly restrain the unstinted generosity with which Titania was treated.

But in New South Wales — a land of failed banks and businesses, from the long drought so recently past — Titania was determined to find her own life. To do that she would need luck.

She would also need a man.

Chapter 7

KAT

Kat noticed the change in the ship's motion as soon as she woke: a steep smooth rising, as if climbing a hill, slide, creak, flap, grind, glide, and an equally smooth descent, the creaking subtly different, and the flapping, clapping, slapping of the sails too. Each glide and fall took minutes and were far easier than fast bumps and swaying on the stomach (a portion of the body Miss Thackeray stated no young lady should mention). But how could you ignore an organ that could make you feel as if even leprosy might be preferable to nausea?

She lay under the soft linen sheet, recommended (and provided) by Titania as the only covering needed in this equatorial heat, trying to anticipate each rise and fall, till Smiggins entered.

The maid was still coldly polite, possibly because she had expected some recompense from Kat for her newly acquired extra services, which Kat did not have the money to provide. Aunt Bertha had equipped her with made-over dresses from her cousins to wear, once she put off mourning on the ship, with a plenitude of strips of old sheets for her monthly flows and sundry bonnets only slightly out of fashion. She had not given her money — possibly, Kat accepted, in case her niece used it to escape to some ill-advised employment or other enterprise that might bring more shame to her already burdened family. While Aunt Bertha would almost certainly have given her enough for shipboard gratuities, or small purchases at ports along the way, Kat's escape while her aunt was chaperoning her daughters through an exhausting season had meant that Kat had no more than the five shillings she had obtained by pawning an extremely ugly brooch, left to her by a long-dead great aunt. Those shillings needed to be kept for an emergency, and besides, Kat knew that Viola tipped Smiggins lavishly for the extra work. Smiggins had also been left an annuity by Viola's mother, and might, Kat thought, be worth even more than the unknown Mr Markham with his two thousand isolated acres of mostly untamed continent.

'Your hot water, Miss Fitzhubert,' said Smiggins, without a twitch of a smile.

'Thank you, Smiggins.' It would be salt water that never made one feel entirely clean.

'Will I lay out your yellow dress, miss?'

This was not helpful, as her cousins had an inordinate fondness for yellow, which clashed with Kat's eyes.

'Yes, please,' said Kat, not particularly caring, but glad to be out of black. Back at ho ... *Briarglen* she had drunk tea or chocolate in bed each morning, and nibbled an oatcake made to Mama's recipe. Here on the ship the three chose to drink their early morning tea together.

Kat washed, while Smiggins fetched Titania's and Viola's hot water from the galley — Smiggins' careful propriety showing in that Viola received her water last, and so had another half-hour of sleep. Smiggins returned to drape Kat's petticoat over her shoulders — only one, so close to the Equator — and the light cotton dress, the lace fichu that covered her scar, then dressed her hair. Kat had been firm that her hair must be *up*, for though she had not had a Season, she did have a fiancé, and so was as *out* as any girl might be who was not entirely married.

All the while she felt the ship slow, the waves drop, till they almost seemed to be floating in a millpond — decidedly preferable to waves, thought Kat, anticipating tea and the beaten biscuits from Titania's trunk that were almost as good as oatcakes, and their breakfast mutton, differing only from their luncheon ship's mutton in that the latter was served cold with chutney, while breakfast was the previous night's boiled meat hashed and topped with the sauce Kat herself made of ship's milk, flour and Titania's pickled capers, glad to have at least one useful activity now that she had charmed the one-armed cook into letting her use the charcoal brazier in the small brick galley.

This morning there would also be the marmalade of quinces Titania had made back in England to eat with the small flat breads Titania had shown the ship's cook how to make, using the excellent yeast plant Titania had brought from London; and one of the apples or hard winter pears brought up from the leather and oilcloth chest in the hold where they sat, hopefully still dry, in bran.

Best of all, Kat thought, no waves.

Chapter 8

TITANIA

No waves, thought Titania grimly ten days later, glancing at the flat sea to the horizon as she crossed the deck to Captain Olsen's cabin in response to his invitation, carrying a jar of the pickled walnuts he was so fond of. The ocean looked like glass, with a strange lifeless oiliness.

The ship sat no further on its voyage than it had three weeks before. It floated, every sail set to catch the slightest breeze, smelling of sweat and desperation, as if the Equator had sucked away all movement from the world.

Even the crew sat idle or lay in the small shade offered by the sails for, with the sails limp and the sky an unyielding blue, and it seemed, no fish to catch, there was little to do there in the doldrums except scrub the deck. Even that was no longer the chore it had been, for the sheep were all eaten, or turned to salt mutton.

Sheep drank water. Water was far more precious now than meat. Even the crew had been given all the mutton they could eat. The sad-eyed cow was eaten too. The ship was quieter and less fragrant than it had ever been. Titania longed to smell something more than salt and sea. Only the rats were active, keeping her awake half the night scratching at the ship's hull, as if they could sense the water beyond it.

She had left Viola and Kat in Viola's cabin, the best place to catch the breeze that wasn't there, playing the pitch half-penny that Kat had taught them. Even the brief walks the deck allowed were uncomfortable now, not just because of the heat, but due to the surly glances of the men. Water was restricted to a pint per person each day, but the females did not have to work on that allowance.

Titania felt a stickiness under her shoe. She lifted one and saw blackness oozing from the deck. The pitch that held the planks together was melting. Was the ship about to fall to pieces around them?

Of course not, she told herself. Ships were nailed too, and pieces fitted together so neither nailing nor pitch were needed to keep them seaworthy. But the melting deck was unnerving. She knocked quickly on the cabin door.

'Ah, Mrs Boot, come in.' Captain Olsen himself opened the door, then shut it quickly behind her, despite the heat and stuffiness of the cabin. 'Pickled walnuts! You have a heart of gold indeed, Mrs Boot.'

'Nothing so bright or so malleable,' said Titania dryly. Or not any more, she thought grimly, and never again. Somewhere beyond the thin line of the horizon was a life of her own

Captain Olsen looked at her with appreciation. 'Perhaps I should have said a heart of steel, which is why I've asked you here now. Won't you sit down?'

'Thank you, Captain.' Titania sat. She had met Captain Olsen through Boot, Boot and Boot, and had been the one to recommend him as worthy of the not inconsiderable payment for conveying Lady Viola and her party.

'Mrs Boot, may I speak frankly?'

'I don't know why else you'd have asked me to your cabin,' she said bluntly. 'We're running out of water fast, aren't we?'

He nodded. 'I intend to cut the ration to half a pint tomorrow. That will give us enough for perhaps three more weeks.'

'Enough to see us to Cape Town, assuming the wind decides to ever blow again?'

'Only if it rains as well.'

She had known the situation was serious, but not nearly so dire. 'Thank you for the warning,' She tried to keep her voice calm. 'You think we should be preparing our souls for Heaven?'

'Possibly,' he said shortly. 'I'm afraid of mutiny.'

'What?' Of all things she had not expected this. Captain Olsen not only treated his crew well, but also offered bonuses at the end of each voyage. Titania shook her head, 'The sun must have crazed them. What good is taking over a ship that won't move?'

'It's not the ship they'll be after, but the ship's boat. Fourteen men, perhaps, might row it to shore, if they take all the fresh water on board.'

Fourteen men, out of more than forty crew members. How would the mutineers choose the fourteen? Draw straws perhaps? Or by violence, leaving those left alive to take the boat and whatever else they wished.

'I see,' Titania said slowly. She met his eyes. 'What about twelve men you trust and three women? Might they survive rowing to the African coast?'

'They might. They might even survive the landing ... and the natives, the mosquitoes and whatever else they find there.'

'They?' she looked at him sharply. 'Not you?'

'Mr Johnson can command and navigate as well as I. I'll stay on this ship, and search for you if the wind rises. Nor is that a decision I will make for a week yet, and not even then if there's any movement in the sea or sky. Mrs Boot, every sailor knows stories of ships of skeletons, found years after they were becalmed in these waters. I will not see that happen to any woman under my care.'

'Thank you,' she said. 'A week? Is that what you asked me here for? To be wary and prepare?'

'It is. I've men I trust guarding the ship's boat, and they have weapons too; they are men I have sailed with many a time and who know I'd not leave them behind. But no captain can sail with the same crew on every voyage.'

Of course not, thought Titania. The loss of a third of the crew to disease or scurvy on each expedition was common. The

Salamanca would lose few of her men, a couple washed from the deck in storms perhaps, or an accident up on the mast, but most sailors would take any chance of a job ashore, if one were offered, or be tempted by the higher profits despite the greater danger on a whaler.

'What do you suggest?'

'Keep your cabin doors shut and bolted, despite the heat.' Captain Olsen hesitated. 'There might be some who'd think to take at least one woman with them, or ... mistreat ... you all before they left. Choose clothes to protect you from the sun and a bag of whatever supplies you think most suitable.'

'Captain Olsen, I asked about three women. That was thoughtless of me. I forgot Miss Smiggins.'

It was all too easy to forget Miss Smiggins. Titania did not know why Smiggins had agreed to accompany Viola to Australia — Viola's mother had left her an easy competence. It was certainly not from pleasure in her new mistress's company nor any more than grim politeness to her friends. 'There are also the three men employed to see to Lady Viola's trunks and other welfare,' she added.

'Can any of them row? Even if they can, you must choose one, at most — the boat must have as many experienced sailors as possible. Miss Smiggins — yes. I will not leave a woman alone on this ship. I can't deny though, Mrs Boot, that Mr Johnson will be lucky if he can get the boat away, and luckier still if you make landfall. With luck still to come if you are all to remain alive till rescue.'

Titania thought of her companions. She knew Kat well enough now to suspect she would throw herself at the adventure. But Viola? There was more than kindness in the girl. How much more Titania didn't know — and nor perhaps did Lady Viola herself. Viola would undoubtedly do her duty. But would that duty be to stay, or go?

Her own duty, at least, was clear. As companion to Lady Viola, as well as friend, the choice was not hers to make.

She got to her feet, feeling the deck sway minutely below them, not sure if she wished more for surging waves or just to feel solid ground again, and never leave it. 'Thank you for being so open about our position, Captain Olsen.'

He stood politely. 'Aye, well, I thought you'd likely not have the vapours on me.'

'I wouldn't know how to begin.'

Nor did she quite know how to explain the predicament to her companions.

Chapter 9

KAT

Kat gazed at the mirror ocean through the porthole as Titania outlined Captain Olsen's proposal, still absentmindedly fanning herself with a water-stained copy of *The Sydney Morning Herald*. Rowing for a possibly crocodile-infested shore would at least be *doing* something, instead of sitting there, as helpless as she had been since that moment in the library ...

'But of course we cannot go,' said Viola calmly. Smiggins had caught Viola's hair up in a bun to keep her neck cool, but despite the adult hairstyle she still looked like a child — a small, and most determined child.

Kat turned and stared at her. 'But we will die if we don't.'

'If we go, how are we better than the men who might mutiny, abandoning the others to their deaths?'

'No better,' said Kat, slamming down the newspaper. 'But we'd be alive. Besides, we wouldn't be condemning the men left behind. The wind might rise, then they could sail to Cape Town while we face lions and tigers or whatever else there is over on the coast.'

'We'd have the water,' said Titania bluntly, her face red with heat. 'That's the heart of this. Whoever gets the fresh drinking water has a chance to live.' She glanced out the porthole. 'Most of the world is made of water, but we can't drink the stuff. If only the salt could be filtered out.'

'The only way to do that is by catching steam,' said Kat absently, then started. 'We *can* make fresh water from salt water!' Why the deuce hadn't she thought of it before? If juice could be separated from peaches, then fresh water could be made from salt. I've just been sitting, letting the world be arranged around me, she thought. No more!

She surged to her feet, her skirts almost creating a breeze. 'We need kettles and copper tubing. We'll boil the seawater then condense the steam ...' She began to pace about the cabin.

'Hold your horses,' said Titania. 'We can ask Captain Olsen about copper tubing, though I don't see any reason why he'd have any on board, unless it's cargo. But how long does it take to turn a kettle full of seawater into steam?'

'I don't know! It depends on the size of the kettle and the amount of heat.'

'Smiggins says it takes half an hour for the big kettle in the galley to heat the washing water for each one of us, and that's just warm, not boiling.'

'Maybe it would take an hour to boil a kettle then ...' The Irishman heated his poteen as slowly as possible, but Papa's machines had needed steam fast. 'If it's a hot fire, then maybe another hour after that to turn the water into steam. We'd need to keep tasting till we found out how much fresh we could boil off before it turned salty again.'

Had anyone ever tried boiling salt water instead of fresh? If only she had read more of Papa's correspondence with other steam enthusiasts.

She found Titania looking at her dubiously. 'Kat, that would mean boiling the kettle all day and all night too, for what? Six to twelve kettles' worth? Minus whatever salt is left. Twelve kettles of fresh water at most for about fifty people on board. That's maybe a cup for each person!'

'A cupful a day might be enough to keep us all alive,' said Viola quietly.

'Well yes, it might — assuming the fire stays lit. How much charcoal do you think this ship carries? I doubt it's enough to keep the kettle boiling for more than three or four days.'

And you still don't think it would work, thought Kat. But it would! Salt was heavier than water, so it would be left behind, just like the fruit pulp. 'We could burn the furniture! And maybe bits of the deck too. A cup is better than no water. The wind has to blow some time!'

'Make a big fire and you'll burn the ship down. And how do you think Captain Olsen will feel about chopping up his ship?'

'Better than he'd feel about abandoning her,' Kat pointed out. 'Far better than dying on her.'

'It's worth trying, Titania,' said Viola softly. 'Anything is worth trying now.'

'Titania, darling, you must ask Captain Olsen!' Kat cried. 'He'll listen to you!'

Titania gazed at them. 'Very well,' she said at last. 'I'll ask Captain Olsen if there is any copper tubing to attach to the kettles. But it's likely there's none, just as there's not enough wood to keep a kettle boiling either ...'

Kat stopped her pacing and stood quite still. A memory flashed before her: she had been five years old perhaps, and Papa had held her hand as they walked down to the pond. He had taken out a lens to show her how focused light could make the water steam on a sunny day at midday. But the hottest day at Briarglen was tepid compared to mid-ocean on the Equator.

Puddles evaporated, even at Briarglen. Oh yes, some water soaked into the ground, but moisture also floated into the air, because that was how rain was made. She and Mama had sat on the cliffs with a picnic lunch and Mama's tools about them, and Mama had pointed to the rain shower drifting across the sea. Mama had told her how the sun had lifted all that rain up ...

I should have saved one of Mama's coprolites, she thought. I should have hidden one of Papa's steam engines, too, as tokens for the memories. Yes, there had been currents in her parents' lives she had never guessed, but she had not just imagined all the good. She had to keep those memories, too.

She looked at the others. 'We have sunlight. All the sunlight anyone could want!' She grinned triumphantly. 'And we have oilcloth lining every chest down in the hold, and more oilcloth besides. We have the coppers in the galley ...' She leaped to her feet. 'Come on!'

'Where to?' asked Titania cautiously.

'To save the ship!' said Kat grandly.

Chapter 10

VIOLA

Queen Boadicea probably looked like Kat did on the deck of the *Salamanca*, thought Viola, all fire and flashing eyes and crying out orders. Boadicea had given courage to a defeated people, had led them into battle. But in the end, Boadicea had lost. How many had died for Boadicea?

Viola loved Kat for her courage, her laughter, her loyalty too. Yet Kat was loyal only to those Kat saw. And Kat only truly saw those she laughed with, those she loved. Kat wasn't thinking of these desperate men scurrying to fill containers of seawater and rig up oilcloth, but of the challenge and victory. If this didn't work Kat would let herself be rowed from a stranded ship and give no thought to these men left behind, though she'd give her life for her companions.

Viola saw everyone. But if she refused to take a place in the ship's boat Titania would not go either and nor would Kat. Perhaps, just perhaps, this scheme of Kat's would work, or at least would give them time enough for the wind to come miraculously back.

Viola moved into the meagre shade of the sail and prayed. She wasn't sure to whom she prayed — almost certainly not the God of Mr Bentley, the vicar, who did not seem like the God Jesus had spoken of in the Bible. Perhaps each person glimpsed another face of God. She almost smiled: possibly if death came soon, she would find out.

She didn't want to die, she realised. She was not afraid of death. She just felt ... unfinished, as if her life had only just begun, and her soul was not yet complete. Mr Bentley would say her sins would be forgiven and she would feel whole but, in fact, she had done very little sinning. She had neither coveted nor stolen; she had honoured her mother and the man who'd allowed himself to be registered as her father. She had kept the Sabbath, though more by convention than intent. Even lust had not marked her, though maybe she would grow into sexual desire as she grew older ...

If she grew older.

Viola opened her eyes, but some of the calm of prayer stayed with her as she watched Kat ordering and organising. Every container the ship had was on the main deck, it seemed, each one filled with seawater, with an oilcloth umbrella suspended by ropes above it and more oilcloth propped up on chairs and stools and sleeping pallets below to catch the drips of fresh water, if there were any drips, and if it was, indeed, fresh. The deck looked like it was crowded with assorted, round-backed turtles, with men half amazed, half hopeful, and wholly under Kat's spell.

'No, pull that bit out more!' instructed Kat. 'Chamber pots! I forgot chamber pots. They're shallow so will evaporate faster.'

'You really think this is goin' to work, missus?' The man who spoke had two long teeth top and bottom and only half the usual allocation of ears.

'Of course it will work! I've been playing with steam all my life. My father ...' Kat's voice broke then resumed more strongly. 'My father experimented with every aspect of steam, the best fuels to use to build up a good head of it ...'

'I'll warrant old man sun up there warn't one of they.' This man was young, watchful, with eyes that kept glancing at the ship's boat.

'No, but my father tried focusing lenses — big rounds of glass — on the water to make it steam faster. He even got enough steam to turn a small propeller ...'

'It'd take a mighty big propeller to move a ship like we got.'

'I'm not trying to power the ship with steam,' said Kat exasperated. 'Though there are steamships on these waters already. I warrant one day soon all ships on this route will be run on steam whenever the winds fail to blow.'

'Happen that day will be too late for us ...' But the young man had begun to look at the containers hopefully.

Viola let her eyes move from Kat, from the watching crowd of men and the watchful eyes of Captain Olsen, to look at the oilcloth umbrellas too.

And suddenly she saw it. As the shortest person on the ship, possibly she was the only person who could see it. The ghost of water condensing under the peak of the oilcloth, then suddenly a drip, sliding to the edge ...

... and down.

'Water,' she said softly.

The young man immediately touched it with his finger, barely wetting it. Yet his eyes were filled with triumph when he announced, 'Fresh!' then gave a cheer.

One drop, thought Viola, catching Titania's eye, and nor could he really have told if it was fresh from that thin smear. But other drops were falling now, a steady rain of them.

The cheers increased. A barefoot boy ran to Kat and kissed her cheek, then ran off to shouts and jeers and scattered applause.

The drops kept falling, plop, pause, plop. Men crowded round now, everyone eager to taste the miracle of water. The ship rolled a little with their movement, back and forth, but never forwards.

Viola moved back to her cabin doorway, next to Titania. 'It won't be enough, will it?'

Titania kept her face carefully expressionless. 'No, not for every person, not even a cupful a day by my reckoning. Maybe, if it could keep going, there'd be enough for a few, but this evaporation stuff will stop when it gets dark.' She glanced over at the sun, already red hazed and sinking towards the ocean. 'But

Kat's bought us a few days, till the men realise they're a crop short of a harvest.'

'Do you think she knows that?' Viola gazed at Kat again.

Kat met her eyes.

Kat knew. Kat also understood that, just like she did, these men felt safer doing something, anything, rather than just waiting for death.

Yes, Kat knew.

Chapter 11

TITANIA

Kat's umbrellas had caught eight cupfuls by sundown, enough for every man and each woman, even Miss Smiggins, to have a sip, and announce it 'sweet as spring water', which it wasn't, for it tasted of oilcloth and something more but not, at least, of salt.

That was triumph enough for every man to plan to spend the morrow hunting for more containers, more oilcloth, and every old sail to catch more drops too — and for Captain Olsen to announce the galley would begin to distil seawater from its kettle as well, capturing the steam not in copper tubing, but with upturned bowls and plates. There would be a close study that night of the manifest, to see what items of cargo might be utilised as well.

Captain Olsen also knew the value of occupying his crew.

Titania fastened her nightcap — even in this heat she would not dream of sleeping with an unclad head. She had just settled into bed when she felt it.

A change.

No breeze. No movement. But something different ...

She pulled her dress back on over her nightdress, hoped the skirts would disguise her bare feet, opened the door and slipped out into the darkness.

'Mrs Boot?' said someone softly.

'Captain Olsen?' She heard his boots on the deck — the sailors to a man went barefoot.

'What are you doing out on deck? I told you to keep your doors locked.'

'I'm not sure why I came out,' Titania admitted. 'Something about the ship, the sea, maybe the air — I don't know. It just felt different.'

She could feel Captain Olsen's gaze in the darkness, even if she couldn't see it. 'There's not many that can do that,' he said. 'Seems like you're one. Look up there.'

She looked. Stars, like a vast canopy, as if Kat's oilcloths were spread across the sky and sewn with a million jewels.

Except, just possibly, a single dark smudge, close to where the sun had sunk.

'Clouds?' she whispered.

'Maybe. But I can smell it.'

'Smell what?' She knew but did not dare to say the word.

'Rain.'

It arrived with the dawn, a thickening of the air too vague to even be mist, but making Kat's contraptions useless without the sun to power them. The ship shivered, for the first time in three weeks. A drooping sail moved.

Men moved, too, spreading the sails and oilcloth to catch water falling from the sky now, not rising from the basins of seawater. A little and then some more. A sail flapped.

A sailor with a seamed face under a bald and speckled head turned his face away, so his shipmates would not see his tears. Kat stood, as triumphant as if her sprinkle of fresh water had called the clouds, holding her face up to the moisture.

The ship moved, an inch maybe, unwilling to leave its resting place. But by dinnertime the sails were filled and emptied by tiny gusts, growing stronger and more frequent by the hour.

By next breakfast they were sailing.

'She'll keep blowing now,' said Captain Olsen. He'd invited Titania up onto the quarterdeck, his face turned into the wind, as if to drink in the entire force of it. 'We'll be water-strapped till we get to Cape Town, unless we get a proper downpour, but we'll get there, every one of us. We can fill the water barrels, buy more stock — they have good sheep at the Cape, and a million scrawny hens. A goat, if there's no cow in milk for sale.'

Kat's 'umbrellas' had been abandoned, interfering with the due running of the ship. The crew, it seemed, shared the captain's confidence.

'And after the Cape? Might we be becalmed again?'

Captain Olsen grinned. 'No, we'll have weather enough from then. We'll catch the trade winds soon enough. You'll feel speed you never knew possible. And maybe ice and storms and even icebergs. But those winds will take us round the globe faster than a man can spit.'

I must check the stock of pickled plums with ginger, thought Titania, and try to rent a kitchen in port to boil down broth to jellied stock. Winds and waves would make Kat seasick, and maybe Viola and herself as well, or even Smiggins, though she had shown no sign of it before.

But they had wind, and every day would take them towards Sydney.

Chapter 12

TITANIA

CAPE TOWN 1849

Kat rode an elephant in Cape Town, and Titania purchased hunks of goat to simmer for bouillon, for Captain Olsen had given her the use of the galley while the ship was in port and the crew were easing past terrors with two weeks of drunkenness, and three days to recover from it. Titania also managed to purchase more dried fruit, some of it strange, but undoubtedly healthful, including limes to pickle, mango for a most excellent chutney, and fresh tea and spices.

Every day she made new notes: who she had purchased from, at what price. At each place, she asked if they dealt only with customers in person or might they ship orders to Australia.

Viola provided the funds to buy fresh fruit for the men. The sailors would undoubtedly have preferred casks of rum, but instead their quarters were filled with cases of oranges and weird knobbly fruit that weren't quite grapefruit. Viola also obtained enough coins from a draft on a Cape Town bank to bestow each man with five guineas on their arrival at Sydney. She purchased a sturdy Persian rug for Captain Olsen's cabin, or his home in Sydney if he preferred, as their gift to him.

Meanwhile the water barrels were drained, the algae and dead rats that had fallen in on the voyage had been scraped out, and the barrels filled with fresh water again, which stayed fresh tasting for perhaps five minutes. Ropes and sails were replaced; the deck recaulked; barrels of salt meat and pulses stored; a fresh supply of vinegar put aside; and the chloride of lime to scrub the decks clean while at sea replenished, all of which Titania noted. Sheep once again complained from a pen on the deck. A tribe of skinny hens occupied the ship's boat, and a yellow-eyed goat gazed balefully at anyone who came near, except for the boy who bribed the animal with a bucket of oats so he could milk her.

The ship now sped south and, as promised, caught the trade winds, speeding them through air thick with tiny spears of sleet, riding waves as tall as mansions, then rushing down to climb another. They also met the dark, the days so short they had an hour perhaps of grudging daylight, and two of dawn and dusk. The rest was simply black, embroidered only by the ice stars that bit any part of their exposed skin.

Kat suffered seasickness again for the first week. The pickled plums seemed to restore her, but she stayed subdued and needed to be coaxed to eat or drink the bouillon. The goat died, from cold or overmilking, or possibly simply from general resentment of the life forced upon her.

The cry, 'Batten down the hatches', was heard daily now, scarcely an hour after they had been opened again. Miss Smiggins did not even attempt to bring hot water, nor warm bricks for their feet or beds. All fires were doused, even lamps forbidden, so the ship sped unlit through the darkness, and rain threw itself against their cabin doors, so that a pot left out at dusk would be full of frost-fresh water an hour later

Mostly they sat in Viola's cabin, clad in every layer of garments possible, with rugs around their legs and another round their feet, stitching to keep occupied while Kat told ghost stories her mother had passed down to her, all too believable with the howl of sea and sky. It was too dark for drawn thread work, but embroidery could be felt with the fingers, a task like spinning wool on a spindle or carving wood or bone, evolved to keep hands busy and minds sane in long dark winters. Titania's sampler read 'A stitch in time saves nine'; Viola stitched 'Friends are the fairest winds'; while Kat's first tea cloth for a home she had never bothered preparing for again showed varied bloodstains from pricked fingers in the brief light of midday and the words, 'I do not like to see the sea.' Water rose and fell over the porthole, bringing the strange green dapples of phosphorescent sea creatures.

It was impossible to venture on deck alone. They went together, arm in arm, if moments of comparative calm coincided with the daylight, but mostly ate in the cabin, not with the captain and Mr Johnson in the saloon. Titania had raised the delicate matter of emptying chamber pots with Captain Olsen and received a brief reply: 'Use the decks, Mrs Boot. They will be washed clean by the sea within a minute.' Even the twice-weekly scrubbing of their cabins was abandoned.

Two icebergs floated past in pale mist, but a safe distance away, and Captain Olsen assured Titania that their gleam could be seen even by starlight. One morning a frozen rat, its whiskers white, slowly slithered across the sloping deck and stayed lodged against the rail till Kat used her boot to edge it overboard. An albatross soared high overhead, peering down, then let the wind carry it away.

At last the ship turned north. Australia, it seemed, had been above them for some time, but Captain Olsen wished to make up the time he'd lost in the doldrums and had kept as far south as he dared to benefit from the strongest winds.

The days grew longer. Wind blew steadily at their backs now, as they stood on deck to watch the coast slip by, or rather trees and hills, and still more trees and hills and high blue mountains, rocky cliffs and just occasionally a spire of smoke.

'Villages?' asked Kat.

'Natives,' said Captain Olsen, passing by. He seemed relaxed now, port so close at hand and several protected bays along the coast where a ship might take shelter if a storm blew up.

It didn't.

Dolphins swam in blue waves around the ship, then vanished. A bird Kat declared an eagle hovered briefly above them, to be replaced by gulls that followed in their wake, hoping for rubbish. Sailors lowered lines into the water and even caught fish, one of which was always presented to the ladies, with appropriate congratulations and a florin given in return.

Captain Olsen ordered a farewell supper in the saloon on their last night: a suckling pig, bought at the Cape and fed on boiled pulses down in the hold, and now served in all its nakedness, parboiled then briefly spit roasted; buttered sweet potatoes; a pickled African green leaf; small currant cakes cooked in a skillet; the last of the plum puddings, and claret and lemonade, with a toast to the queen and royal family, the captain and officers of the ship, to the crew, to steam engines to power ships across the doldrums and to the winds.

Kat sang a ballad her mother had taught her, 'The Lark in the Clear Air'. Viola contributed several tunes in her high, clear voice, including one in French that Titania didn't understand, but at which Kat and the captain giggled.

Titania herself — after an unaccustomed glass of claret — demonstrated her only parlour skill, playing 'God Save the Queen' on glasses of water; during this the entire company loyally and solemnly stood. Captain Olsen volunteered a comic song, 'The Calais Packet', and, as an encore, 'The Post Office'.

The next day they reached Sydney.

Chapter 13

KAT

SYDNEY, SEPTEMBER 1849

Kat had expected beauty, as the pilot finally arrived to guide the ship between the narrow cliffs and out into the spreading glory of the harbour. Bright birds broke from the trees in clouds of green and yellow. Seagulls swooped in the ship's wake. Scattered cottages, huts, farms and mansions, each with a small portion of England fenced around it, dotted the narrow inlet. They finally thickened to become a city, clambering over the hills, shadowed by a smudge of woodsmoke above it all.

She had not expected terror. Mr Markham had not seemed real till now. The five hundred guineas, yes, the new beginning: but the heavily treed landscape she had watched all along the coast and even in the harbour did not seem the kind of country it would be easy to ride away in and escape.

And where should she go? There were other settlements along the coast, but Kat hadn't realised till she and Viola perused the newspapers how closely connected all were by trade and by the circumstance of being small islands of occupation in such a vast land. Even the names of each passenger on every ship had been listed in the paper. A husband could easily find an errant wife if he did not choose to let her go ...

'Kat?' Viola's hand slipped into hers. Kat gripped it, peering as the wharf grew closer, wondering which face might belong to the man to whom she now belonged.

'Mr Markham almost certainly won't be there,' said Titania, coming up behind them. She leaned on the rail. 'How could he know when the *Salamanca* might dock? He couldn't stay in the city for weeks or even months, not with a farm to care for. Viola, can you see a man who resembles the likeness of Major Nash yet?'

'Not yet. He may have changed — the likeness my mother had was painted before he joined the army, almost twenty years ago. Kat, Titania,' she added quickly, 'you must know that you both have homes with me, forever if you wish.'

'Your home will be your guardian's house,' said Kat briefly. 'Titania has a claim on you, but Major Nash may decide that I have none.'

'I'll be of age in four years' time. My guardian will have no say in my affairs. Till then I have my allowance. It is ample to allow you to rent a home of your own with whatever servants you need until I can join you.'

Kat turned to stare at her. 'Your *allowance* is enough to run a household?'

Viola shrugged. 'My brother let me name the figure. I don't think he even bothered to check the amount I asked for. I wished to have enough for any purchase on the voyage, especially if we had to put into another port.' She gave a rueful grin. 'I had no idea how much even an orange would cost. I'm glad I so badly overestimated.'

'Major Nash may well reduce the amount, now you are safe in his care.' Kat resumed her searching of the pier.

'That did occur to me in England.' Viola smiled. 'I have no more knowledge of Major Nash than you have of Mr Markham, beyond my mother's trust in him, and she hadn't seen him since he was eighteen years old, although they corresponded.'

'Not to mention that he would want to keep on the right side of a wealthy woman, with him dependent on his army pay and the interest on five thousand pounds left to him by his father. I made enquiries about your major,' added Titania.

'So half the weight of what seems to be a heavy chest of books is gold sovereigns,' said Viola calmly. 'I may be bound to Major Nash for four years, but you need not be.'

Kat gazed at her with admiration. 'I wouldn't have thought you'd be so cunning.'

'Prudent is the better word,' said Titania.

'You helped her? Of course you did. Viola couldn't even carry half a trunk of sovereigns.'

'Well, nor can I, Kat Fitzhubert. I employed three men to do it.'

'I will simply say I do not need the books yet, and they can be stowed in the attic. Kat, whatever security money can provide, we have.'

'Thank you.' Kat hoped Viola would take the dampness on her face for sea spray. 'You could always employ me as your maid, if Major Nash will not allow a guest.'

Miss Smiggins had announced that she would stay a month to train a colonial replacement, but then would leave to marry. One of the male attendants, though a decade younger than herself, had decided on the voyage that a woman with such an excellent annuity should not be wasted on the hoi polloi of Sydney. Viola's brother's agent had provided for the return of the men.

'You certainly can't be Viola's maid. You can't even dress your own hair, much less hers.'

'I can,' said Kat, stung. 'I've been arranging my hair by myself for the last fortnight, in case Mr Markham has not seen fit to provide me with a maid.'

'I would not call your hair "arranged".'

'You are my friend,' said Viola, tactfully not elaborating on Kat's hairdressing skills.

Kat bent to hug her. 'And you are the best friend in all the world.'

'You two are the only friends I've had,' said Viola simply.

'You're both certainly the only ones I've ever known,' added Titania. 'My ma and pa and Mr Boot weren't ones to let me waste my time with tea parties.'

Kat found herself stammering. 'I ... I have had chances to make friends, but never cared to. Briarglen was enough. Besides,' she managed to recover herself, 'all the girls at school were dreadfully boring, and the Squire's daughters worse, and the two neighbouring girls hated me because boys they fancied preferred me, or possibly my fortune.'

'A man said long ago — yes, another of my ancient Greeks, Kat! He said that souls choose their soul to make them complete, each adding what the other has not. Perhaps that's what we have done, three women so unalike and yet, whatever happens,' said Viola steadily, 'we have each other.'

'Scandal sisters, always,' agreed Kat.

'I shall have our samplers framed,' said Viola. 'To keep the memory of our voyage with me.'

'Kat's will be a memorial to poor sewing,' said Titania.

'Nonsense,' declared Kat. 'The bloodstains are arranged most artistically.'

The small hand in Kat's tightened. 'I think that is Major Nash. You see the tall top hat towards the right?'

'Whiskers and a gold-topped cane? At least he doesn't look like he will bite,' said Titania.

'If he bites we can tie sheets together and lower you from your bedroom window and then lower the trunk with the sovereigns too.'

'Or hire a man to carry them and walk out the door and not come back.' Titania sounded as if she had once dreamed of doing this herself.

'He looks ... amiable,' said Kat, thinking he also looked quite handsome, if a trifle old, forty perhaps. They moved back towards Viola's cabin as sailors swarmed, trimming sails, hauling ropes, shouting as they followed the mysteries of their craft.

Chapter 14

VIOLA

The man who must be her guardian caught her eye as the sailors tethered the ship to a vast iron stanchion. Other sailors hauled the gangplanks. Major Nash lifted his hat and bowed to her, smiling. He was as tall as Titania. His hair was brown, and fashionably short, parted on the side and combed back from his face. His white neckcloth and grey frockcoat seemed perfectly tailored.

Viola smiled in return. This was perhaps the first person who had ever smiled at her on first sight. Of course Major Nash already knew what to expect. Nonetheless, the smile warmed her.

'Lady Viola?' Captain Olsen offered her his arm. Strange, she thought, for he had talked far more to Titania then her on the voyage. Now they were on land again, she once again had precedence.

Land. She wondered if she was the only person on board who hadn't longed for this moment. The last months had been the most free she had ever known, the small community of the ship so familiar with her that they no longer saw the brown skin, and only herself.

'Can you see your wife here, Captain?' she asked politely.

Captain Olsen laughed. 'No. Bertha has a widow's walk up above our house and a telescope set up there too. She'll have seen the ship come through the Heads and be putting on the roast beef and Yorkshire pudding, and apple tart.' He looked apologetic. 'It's what I always crave, first night ashore.'

'I hope that she and your children are all well.' Viola also hoped this conversation covered the beating of her heart.

'I happen to have a telescope of my own. Bertha flew the "all is well" flag for me to see as we came in.'

'A good wife for a captain.'

'She is indeed.' They had crossed the gangplank onto the wharf now. It felt odd, as if the world still swayed beneath her feet. Viola was vaguely conscious of Titania and Kat behind her, and Smiggins and the men, who had already gathered the most urgent of her luggage, up on deck.

'Cousin Viola!' Major Nash bowed, then laughed. 'I refuse to stand on ceremony after you have come such a long way to my care.' He bent almost double to kiss her cheek. 'Why did no one tell me how pretty you are?' The compliment even seemed genuine.

Viola felt tears sting in relief. He hadn't quickly shuffled her away from the crowded wharf. He seemed truly glad to meet her — herself, not just her income for the next four years. She would always be grateful for this moment.

'Major Nash, may I present Captain Olsen, who has cared for us so well?' Now on shore the major should have precedence, she realised, but her guardian didn't seem to mind. The men bowed to each other. 'And Major ... I mean Cousin Lionel ...' He bent another smile to her, clearly pleased. 'Mrs Boot's name will be known to you as my companion, but she is now my dear friend too. And this is Miss Kathleen Fitzhubert, who has become most dear to me as well.'

The major bowed politely, first to Kat, then to Titania. Of course, thought Viola, as an employee, Titania should have been presented last. She must get used to society manners now.

The ladies curtseyed.

'Are you any relation to Lieutenant James Fitzhubert of the 14th Foot?' Major Nash enquired civilly.

Kat curtseyed again. 'Not to my knowledge, sir, I'm afraid.'

Major Nash laughed. 'Excellent. The man was a bounder.'

'Cousin Lionel, I hope I have not offended you by offering Miss Fitzhubert hospitality?'

'Your wish is my wish, in this as in all else,' said Major Nash, slightly too evenly, for naturally he should have been asked first, so the invitation to Kat could be his. She would be more careful from now on, Viola vowed.

Major Nash offered his other arm to Kat, leaving Titania to follow, and smiled down at Viola. 'Come, let's leave all this bustle, so you may see your home.'

Chapter 15

TITANIA

Sydney had excellent wharves, Titania decided, solid, and a goodly number of ships, exactly as she had expected. Titania gazed out of the carriage — a most sumptuous one, silk lined with calfskin seats: new, if she was any judge — and peered at the shanties as they passed. Rotting, crumbling, mired in filth, but no more so than in the streets by the docks in London.

The carriage soon left them behind, rolling up cobblestones that were almost clean, turning several times, past shops growing steadily more elegant, and then houses or, rather, mansions, each of dressed stone and looking strangely even more newly built than they must be, in so young a colony, till she realised the dwellings' apparent youth might be caused by the absence of coal smoke, for the scent in the streets was surely of wood fires.

The carriage stopped by a house much like the others, with steps possibly more recently whitewashed, and certainly more populated outside.

The grandeur of a house can be judged by the number of unnecessary individuals waiting to greet you, Titania thought. A young man in green livery opened wrought iron gates that guarded the steps. Two rigid-spined footmen framed the front door until the exact moment the carriage stopped, when they ran down the stairs to open the carriage doors.

Titania found herself helped down the three steps of the carriage onto a small immaculately gravelled courtyard, where another individual in the formal cutaway coat of a butler bowed to his master's ward.

Another row of serried servants seemed to appear within a blink, beginning with a woman who must be the housekeeper, with a barefoot urchin who might be a gardener's boy or in charge of the firewood peering out from the middle, the only one not trying to hide his curiosity, and then a string of white-capped maids.

Bows, curtseys, the clop of hooves on cobbles behind them. The sun was overbright, despite their time at sea. Titania followed Viola and Major Nash up the stairs, and into a capacious hall. A Persian runner on polished wood; a multitude of gilt-trimmed carved tables, large and small, each with a vase of flowers or feathers, and each one new, Titania was sure.

This house must have been purchased or possibly leased with Viola's money. Titania frowned. She would investigate. Yet as guardian and trustee Major Nash had the right to use Viola's income as he pleased, even to purchase property in his own name. And of course it would be expected that a 'Lady Viola' would live in luxury.

Titania mentally shook her head at herself. She was being ridiculously middle class, expecting a trustee to be as niggardly as possible to give his ward the accumulation of income at her majority. It was hard to adjust to thinking of Viola as a wealthy aristocrat, after the simple life on the *Salamanca*. Yet something about this household niggled ...

'I am sure you are all longing for quiet and a dish of tea. This is Mrs Higgins, the housekeeper. Mrs Higgins, my ward, Lady Viola Montefiore, her companion, Mrs Boot, and her friend, Miss Fitzhubert, who will be staying with us.'

A curtsey. A respectable woman, in a plain dark dress, with an air of quiet confidence that must cost her employer a good deal in wages in a colony like this.

'Mrs Higgins, will you show the ladies to their rooms?'

'Certainly, sir. I hope all is to your liking, your ladyship.' Mrs Higgins uttered the title with extreme satisfaction. Few housekeepers in the colony could ever use it for their employers. Mrs Higgins raised her voice slightly, so the servants behind could hear, and could quickly make the changes necessary for an extra guest. 'Miss Fitzhubert will have the Blue Room opposite yours, your ladyship. I have placed Mrs Boot in the room next to your private sitting room.'

'That sounds splendid, Mrs Higgins.'

Mrs Higgins lowered her voice. 'The hot water is on the boil, your ladyship. I can imagine,' she added, with a spark of humanity beyond her role, 'how much you will all be longing for fresh water.'

'Enormously, Mrs Higgins.' For the first time Viola was the same height as Titania as she preceded her up the stairs.

'Tea before you have bathed or after, your ladyship?'

Viola caught Titania's eye, then Kat's. 'I think we would all prefer to bathe and change,' she said. 'Perhaps there is someone to attend to Miss Fitzhubert and Mrs Boot?'

'Alice is nearly trained already and can attend Mrs Boot, if you approve, your ladyship. If Miss Fitzhubert has no objection, I will attend to her myself this afternoon, with Millie, one of the chambermaids, to assist. I have some experience in dressing hair, at least in a simple mode suitable for tonight.'

Excellent, thought Titania. Kat's hair was still hidden by her bonnet, but now she would not shame Viola by appearing at dinner with hair like a bird's nest at the back.

The carpet was thick on the stairs, the rooms furnished with a mix of London fashion, frills and more gilt and carving, and what must be Chinese-made furniture. Of course, Shanghai was a most convenient port ...

Comfort, thought Titania. Luxury for the first time in her life, for all her life perhaps, if that was what she wanted.

It wasn't.

Chapter 16

KAT

Mr Markham arrived on the fifth morning, just as they had changed into walking dresses for a sail across the harbour to a sandy cove where tea might be brewed and a picnic laid out by the footmen. They were to be escorted by Major Nash, who had himself gone down to the harbour to ensure the hired vessel was comfortable enough for his ward.

Viola peered down at the visitor on the doorstep from her sitting room. 'It must be he!'

Kat crowded next to her. The gentleman wore a top hat, so it was impossible to see his face or build from above, and a cloak of modish design. Only his long, highly polished boots showed that he might be a country man, though a friend of their host might wear such boots if he had been riding. 'He doesn't look like a farmer.'

Viola stood back so Titania could glimpse the visitor too. She shook her head as the door below opened. 'Any other gentleman caller at this hour would have brought his wife. Or sister.'

'I thought I would have had longer ...' Kat whispered.

'Mr Markham must have arranged for a message to be sent to his farm as soon as the *Salamanca* came through the Heads,' said Titania.

'I am a most valuable property and he has come to claim it.'

Viola took her hand. 'Remember, if you do not care for him, you may stay here.'

'Thank you,' Kat managed. But how did you tell a man who had waited for four ships to cross the world and had paid for a wife to come on a fifth that, after all that arranging, she had changed her mind?

Should she change? But she particularly liked the blue dress she had chosen for the picnic, and besides, why change if you might dismiss a fiancé, rather than attempt to entrance him? At least her hair was in an elegant French pleat.

The sitting room door opened. Mrs Higgins' eyes showed a flicker of disapproval. 'Your ladyship, a gentleman has called — a Mr Markham to see Miss Fitzhubert — but the master has just gone out. I have put the gentleman in the drawing room.'

'We will all go down immediately,' said Viola. 'Mr Markham must be greeted properly. Please, could you serve tea?'

The housekeeper bobbed a curtsey, slightly relieved she would not be party to a stranger making off with the silverware, nor to a breach of etiquette. The man's name was obviously known and having three young women to see a male visitor was acceptable, where a single man and woman was not.

The newcomer had been relieved of cape and hat. He stood, gazing out the window, but turned as they came in, Viola first, in some degree the mistress of the house as well as senior in rank, then Kat, with Titania behind.

Zebediah Markham had brown eyes, was perhaps fifteen years her senior ... And he's enormous, thought Kat, trying to subdue her terror. Why had Aunt Bertha's friend failed to mention her brother was so large? He stood at least a head taller than the major and was twice as broad across the shoulders. A vast ox of a man, she thought, whose size the fashionable, close-fitting and obviously new coat and tight hessian trousers only accentuated.

Mr Markham bowed to Viola, then less deeply to the others, his gaze lingering on Kat as he rose. The three curtseyed in unison. Indeed, they were now practised at curtseying together.

At second glance none of Mr Markham seemed out of proportion. It was only that every portion was so very large.

'Mr Markham, you are most welcome. I am afraid my guardian, Major Nash, has not yet returned, but I am his ward, Lady Viola Montefiore. These are my dear friends, Mrs Titania Boot and Miss Kathleen Fitzhubert. I'm glad you found where we are lodged.'

'Captain Olsen informed me of your address, Lady Viola, and that Miss Fitzhubert was with you. It is a pleasure to meet you in person, Miss Fitzhubert.' Zebediah Markham bowed again to Kat. His movements were graceful, despite legs that bulged muscle above the long shining boots. 'I am sorry I wasn't here to meet the *Salamanca*. We are shearing, you see.'

Kat curtseyed once more. 'It is good to meet you, Mr Markham.' She suddenly took in his words. 'Shearing?'

'We take the wool from the sheep,' he said patiently, still eyeing her. Almost as if I were a ewe he had purchased unseen, Kat thought indignantly. 'My sheep are Romneys, bred mostly for their meat, but must still be shorn.'

'I know what shearing is, Mr Markham, but not why it requires your presence.' Kat had not meant to be so rude. She blinked in sudden fright. Would he send her back on the next ship, as a shrew? But thank goodness, she reminded herself, he was not a husband, only a fiancé. He had no power over her, now that she had refuge with Viola if she wanted it.

Did she want it? This was a refuge only, not a home. Viola had no need of two companions, nor even one, now she had reached her guardian. Kat's original plan would have given her five hundred guineas to find a life ...

'I shear with the men,' said Mr Markham evenly. 'Indeed, I can only stay until tomorrow.'

Tomorrow! Kat felt like she'd been pulled back from the hangman's noose. She could delay any decision at least till he had time to return to Sydney after the shearing was completed.

'I hoped, perhaps, you might come back to Rainbow's End with me.' His gaze remained on Kat. Suddenly he smiled. 'I hope you don't think the name hopelessly romantic. But there really was a rainbow, you see, and it ended right where I built the house. We often have rainbows across the valley.'

'It's a delightful name for a home,' said Viola, smiling politely.

'Very pretty,' said Titania gruffly, her eyes narrowed, so Kat knew she was evaluating everything from Mr Markham's boot leather to the make of his hat.

'My mother told me once that leprechauns bury their pots of gold at the end of the rainbow,' said Kat, then mentally kicked herself for inanity. Leprechauns! What must he think of her?

But he smiled again. 'We didn't find any pots of gold when we dug the foundations. Just good soil, dark as a cup of hot chocolate and smelling almost as sweet. I'd rather build my future on rich soil. The fruit trees thrive in it. Besides, doesn't fairy gold fade away the next day?'

'Fruit trees? How interesting.' Viola obviously had little experience of making drawing room conversation, but was doing her best. 'Will you take tea, Mr Markham? Or a glass of claret perhaps? Please, do sit down.'

He stayed standing, ignoring convention. 'I thank you, but might Miss Fitzhubert and I speak privately for a while instead?'

No, thought Kat desperately. Surely he couldn't expect her to leave with him so soon, a stranger, despite the letters between their families. And, unless there was no chance of a match between them, she suddenly didn't want to blight the hope and, yes, joy in this man's face, who had waited nearly two years for a bride and must now wait perhaps another two if he wanted one from England.

She turned to the others, hoping they would object to leaving her unchaperoned. But Titania merely gave a brief nod, as if to say that Zebediah Markham had passed inspection as a potential husband.

Viola held Kat's gaze for longer, perhaps saying silently, 'You need to have a chance to get to know each other before you can make a decision. Superficial social chitchat with others in the room will be a waste of time.'

Or did Viola mean something quite different? But Kat did, indeed, need to find out more about this man occupying such a large portion of Major Nash's carefully chosen Chinese silk carpet. She gave a tiny nod in return.

'Of course. You will have much to say to each other,' said Viola, as calmly as if she had been managing her own household for twenty years. 'Ah, Mrs Higgins has brought tea anyway. You are very good, Mrs Higgins. Kat, perhaps you would be so kind as to pour for Mr Markham? Come, Titania.'

Kat watched them curtsey politely, then leave. Zebediah bowed, his expression changing to a combination of eagerness and apprehension. He glanced down at the tea tray. 'I would indeed like tea. I haven't breakfasted yet but came straight up from the harbour. My ship is there — a small one. We use it to get to and from Rainbow's End.'

Kat felt manners flow back into her. 'Of course, Mr Markham. Please sit. I gather your property must sit at the end of a valley?' She sat herself on one of the chairs — not the sofa, where he might join her — and lifted the pot. 'Do you take milk and sugar, or a slice of lemon?'

'Just the tea, thank you, strong as it comes. No, the house sits above the valley, but I own a good part of the land below as well. Fertile, as I said. Not much grassland cleared yet, but good tall timber, and so many lagoons that you can fire a musket into the air and three ducks will fall on top of you.'

His eyes were on the tray. Kat held up the plate of asparagus rolls, and chicken and cress sandwiches, probably meant for their picnic. 'Please, sir, help yourself.'

'Thank you.' He sat on the chair opposite her and inhaled a chicken sandwich and then an asparagus roll. 'Miss Fitzhubert, I know this haste is awkward for you. It is for me, too. But lambing starts a month after the shearing and, if I'm not there to supervise, the dingoes get the lambs — aye, and sometimes two-legged dingoes take them too. After lambing there's the first corn harvest and then the potatoes to be dug, and truth be told I don't have a foreman I'd trust for more than two days, if that. What I'm saying is, I don't have time to stay in Sydney to be courting you.'

'It would be most improper for me to accompany you to your home with no chaperone, sir. Mrs Boot is Lady Viola's companion, not mine.'

'I'm asking that you wed me tomorrow by special licence, and then we sail back,' he said bluntly.

'Tomorrow!' Kat took a deep breath. 'Mr Markham, I apologise, but you see —'

He cut across her words. 'I'm sorry, I'm making a poor fist of this, and not giving you any reason to flout convention. Miss Fitzhubert, you have sailed across the world to wed me, and I have waited nearly two years for a wife; nor do I think we would get to know each other in a few weeks or even months of tea parties and picnics and a dance or two. We'd be on our best behaviour, both of us, and learn no more than we already know from the letters of our families.'

Except I mightn't want to wed you, she thought, so I mightn't be on my best behaviour at all. I might be doing my best to make you change your mind and pay me the money as a token of your breach of promise.

'Have you taken me in aversion? Is it my size? There is perhaps too much of me.'

'No, not at all, sir.' To her surprise his size had become almost endearing. He looked more like a bear than a husband.

'I was afraid you'd think me more like a bear than a husband,' he said, startling her so she almost dropped the plate of quince tarts she was about to pass him. 'I even shaved my beard off, too.'

'A ... beard!' She had never known a gentleman to have a beard, beyond the most elderly who had grown past caring.

'I won't grow it again if you don't want it. Miss Fitzhubert, we do need to know each other. But either you can trust me not to ... to make myself unwelcome to you, or you do not. I do not think that will change in a few months of polite Sydney courtship.'

Either he was the best liar in the colony or those brown eyes shone with truth.

'What if I never ... welcome you, Mr Markham?'

'Then perhaps we could live in companionship.'

'You only want a housekeeper?' she demanded, startled.

He grinned. 'No. I want someone to talk to at the dinner table. Lettice told me your mother had a passion for fossils, and your father for steam engines. I don't know if you share either of those interests, but I doubted that the offspring of two such parents would be dull.'

'You know what ... what my father did, Mr Markham? You know I still bear the scar on my shoulder?'

'I know, and I'm sorry for it. Or rather, if truth be told, I am almost glad of it, for without that tragedy I would have had no chance of meeting Miss Kat Fitzhubert, much less asking her to be my wife. But I do not see that your father's mistaken faith in railway shares, nor his actions on a single day of despair, need concern our life together.'

He met her eyes. 'I want exactly what the marriage service promises, Miss Fitzhubert — comfort in sickness and in health, and with my body I'll thee worship when you're comfortable with the idea, but if you think I want to marry to get myself a quick heir then you're mistaken. I will have near on five hundred lambs this spring. Five hundred lambs to rear will do me for a while.'

She stared at him, wordless.

'Miss Fitzhubert, will you excuse me if I speak plainly?'

'I rather thought you already had, sir.'

'Then, in more plain speaking: I think most people of our rank marry knowing not much more about each other than we do now. I think by the end of today we may even know more than most. You can't know if I'm a wife-beater till after we're wed, nor will I know if you'll put arsenic in my tea when I tread mud into the carpet. But I give you my word — if you wish to be free of me any time in the next six months, we can have the marriage quietly annulled. That's one advantage of a courthouse wedding with only two witnesses and no notice in the newspaper, you see — few will know we've tied the knot, and no more than that need know if we've untied it. You can say you've been staying with friends, which will be true enough, for I hope we might still be friends. Surely your other friends will support that claim. But if we wait more than six months to separate — well, that would be harder, as you'd be expected to prove the marriage wasn't consummated, but still possible, and I'd be willing to do my best to make it happen.'

Kat flushed, not knowing how to ask what would happen to the five hundred guineas if the arrangement did so end. But she didn't think this man would leave her penniless.

He misunderstood her silence. 'Have you dreamed of a big society wedding? We can have one later, if you want. But except in the towns the colony's a place of catch-as-you-can marriages or, more often, no formal ceremony at all. There are many who marry for law in a courthouse, then have a proper wedding party years later when they come to town.'

Kat had never dreamed of a wedding. She had not, in fact, had any ambition beyond seeing if the new Oriental hens lived up to their reputation for laying, or flirting at the next ball, for Papa would give her whatever she wanted; and when Papa had gone there had seemed nothing good to hope for beyond freedom from the corset of society.

'What life do you want, Miss Fitzhubert?' Zebediah Markham flushed and lost his grin. 'I am aware it was not your hand that wrote the letter to me. That letter asked only for a comfortable home and the companionship of a man of gentlemanly manners.'

What did she want? She knew what she didn't want ...

'I don't want to live in the city.'

The grin returned. 'Well, you won't be doing that.'

'I want beauty around me, the freedom to move without censure of my stride or riding habit. I want a kitchen with an enclosed stove where I can have fresh rolls baked each morning. I want hens and, yes, good conversation too ...' She raised her chin. 'I want an orchard of apples and a hothouse of peaches to brew poteen.'

She did not expect the shout of laughter. 'They've sent me a lush for a wife! Miss Fitzhubert, you do not look like a drunkard.'

'I'm not. A sip after dinner with tea perhaps, now and then. But I enjoy seeing it brewed.'

'Then you can have it. I'll not deny poteen sounds ... interesting. But you won't need a hothouse. The peaches grow themselves with no need of glass to protect them. I've plums, too, and cherries, apples, quinces, oranges, lemons, pears — all I could order from the Cape and a few fruits I'd never seen before from China too. I planted the orchard before I began my house, so that when this day came I would have all that a wife might require. Except,' he added thoughtfully, 'a still. I was thinking more of plum jam and apple pies than poteen. But I am sure we can order what you need in Sydney. If your poteen needs the same equipment as rot-gut brewed from wheat or potatoes, this colony has an oversupply.'

'I ... I have never seen rum distilled, sir, only poteen, though I can brew an ale from hop flowers, and one from beetroot or ginger.'

'I've no ginger growing, nor hops either. Would mangelwurzels do instead of beetroot? I'm sure the men would welcome the ale. I'll ask my agent to procure a sack of hop flowers to send to us when the boat next comes to Sydney then, and perhaps some hop vines? There are hens already at Rainbow's End — or there are if the native cats haven't got at them while I've been away. And the enclosed stove in the kitchen, at least, is too heavy for thieves to bother with. Is there more you want to add to the list now?'

He was not just asking about hop vines.

She should say no. Tell him clearly, tell him now. But what else did she want that he had not offered her?

And besides, flushing, she found herself wondering just what he looked like under those clothes. With my body I thee worship ...

But only with his body, she reminded herself. This was not the deep passion Papa had had for Mama. He had promised her freedom, if she wished it.

'Very well, Mr Markham. I will marry you tomorrow.'

The eyes lit till they had a tinge of the leprechaun's gold. 'Excellent. I have the special licence in my pocket. Now that is settled,' he smiled at her with relief, 'do you think I might eat all of those small sandwiches before the ladies return and finish off the tarts as well?'

Chapter 17

KAT

Her best Sunday frock must do as a wedding dress — or rather her cousin's dress, altered to fit her, and made in the fashion of four years ago, but Kat hoped Mr Markham would not know enough of fashion to judge. There'd be no wedding breakfast as the tide turned at ten am that day.

'Kat, are you sure?' Viola asked as she did up the buttons at Kat's back, Kat being unable to face Smiggins, nor having any wish to have her hair formally dressed. Mrs Higgins had shown Kat how to achieve a French pleat, with two plaits twisted into a bun for every day, which was all she would need at Rainbow's End. Mr Markham had said he had a housekeeper but had explained there was little chance of finding a lady's maid before they left, at least not one who they could be reasonably sure would not open the door for a bushranger lover to steal the place empty.

'Bushrangers?' asked Kat.

'We'd call them highwaymen if we were in England,' he'd explained. 'Except we have no highways, just muddy tracks once past the cities. They're men who range the bush — what back home we'd call forest — but this ...' His eyes had lit with that spark again. 'This forest seems to go on forever. You can see a hundred mountaintops from Rainbow's End, Miss Fitzhubert, green and blue and purple and every shade between.'

'Excuse me, your ladyship.' Mrs Higgins stood at the door. Kat thought she might disapprove of Viola doing up buttons, but she seemed slightly amused at her enterprise. 'Mr Markham has brought this for Miss Fitzhubert.' 'This' was a small jeweller's box.

'Did you ask him in?' asked Viola.

'And offer him breakfast?' added Kat, thinking of his appetite.

'He took a quick beefsteak with Major Nash, your ladyship, but would not stay longer.'

'Thank you, Mrs Higgins,' said Viola, taking the box.

Mrs Higgins gave the box a look of only mild curiosity — Kat suspected she had already shaken it to see what might be inside — and closed the door. She took the box from Viola and untied the ribbon. A pair of emerald earrings glinted from their tissue paper, exactly the shade of green she loved.

'They match your eyes,' said Viola. 'Titania, look what Mr Markham has brought.'

Titania closed the door again behind her and put down the yellow blossoms she must have just bought from the market. She peered down at the stones, then lifted them up to the light. 'Good. Excellent colour and no major blemishes. He's not one to cheat his bride with aquamarines or paste.' Titania glanced at Kat doubtfully. 'But no enterprise should be decided in haste. And this is perhaps the biggest venture of your life.'

'I will ride back to Sydney if we do not suit.'

'Over rivers and those great mountains? And what about when you get here? Once you're married he can claim you back, no matter what he's done to you.'

'He promised I could return,' Kat reminded her.

'Promises are easy before a wedding,' said Titania heavily. 'A wedding's not like any other contract, where you can each set out the clauses straight and go to law if you break them. Once that piece of gold is on your finger the law is on his side, no matter what he does.'

'I know,' said Kat, trying for lightness. 'But I don't believe he'll beat me. It might interfere with the cooking of his dinner.'

Indeed, Mr Markham had shown a prodigious appetite at the meal Major Nash had politely invited him to share. 'And I don't have a fortune for him to waste.'

More importantly, she thought, *he did not adore her*, and nor did he plan to lay whatever life she wanted at her feet. Instead he clearly wanted someone who would share the life he was creating, the kind of life she wanted too. He valued her skills, her company. He had promised freedom if she wanted it. He would not believe he had the right to shoot her out of love ...

There had been no time for wedding gifts, beyond the earrings and Titania's bunch of yellow flowers, lightly scented and already dropping small gold balls of blossom as they slowly shed from their stems.

Kat and Zebediah Markham said the vows with only Viola, Titania and Major Nash in attendance, and the portly shape of a Mr Graham, Mr Markham's solicitor.

'For richer, for poorer, in sickness and in health, till death you do part,' declared the registrar, who had barely glanced at the licence and was obviously annoyed at fitting a wedding in to an already full schedule. Kat had not even caught his name.

But she had vowed for richer or poorer, and so had Zebediah. If he lost his farm and fortune he had no cause to shoot her. Though she imagined Papa had vowed the exact same things.

Mr Graham presented papers for Kat to sign for her settlement, which came not as the large bag of golden guineas that she had imagined, but instead as a slim book inscribed *The Bank of New South Wales*.

A bank book would be easier to escape with than a bag of guineas, but a bank account would probably require her presence in Sydney. Kat had no experience of bank accounts. But she had (almost) lost any fear that escape would be needed.

The signatures and witnessing took so long that Major Nash's groom had to spring the carriage horses down to the harbour, afraid that the pilot might grow tired of waiting to guide his ship through the Heads.

'That's the *Rainbow* on the left-hand side,' said Zebediah Markham, pointing to a ship that was larger than Kat had expected, with a broad open deck and probably a good large hold too, suitable for carrying sheep, but which seemed to have only one small cabin.

Her husband, who she had yet to address by name, strode across the gangplank to assure himself that all her chests had been brought aboard as well as the other purchases he had arranged to collect, from flour sacks to a tea chest, barrels of tar and nails, and tools wrapped in sacking. This journey to Sydney, Kat thought wryly, should not be wasted just on bringing home a bride.

She watched uneasily as the broad shallow *Rainbow* bobbed in the wake of a departing whaler. More waves, she thought. Just as the ground had finally stopped going up and down ...

Viola clasped Kat's hands in her small ones. 'Write every time the *Rainbow* comes to Sydney,' she urged. 'Or more often, so we can read a pile of your letters.'

'I promise,' said Kat vaguely, her attention still on the ship. Somehow at school she had forgotten to write letters home, and rarely got around to thanking Aunt Bertha for birthday gifts.

'Let me know if there is anything you need procuring in town,' offered Titania. She gave Mr Markham a dubious look. 'Men do not always know the best places to procure life's necessities.'

Kat looked round at that. 'Nor do you,' she pointed out.

'I will soon enough,' said Titania calmly, bending to kiss Kat's cheek.

Viola lifted her face for a kiss too, then stood back. 'We will visit as soon as you invite us.'

Kat glanced at Major Nash, deep in conversation with another gentleman along the pier. Possibly Viola's guardian might allow her to venture into the wilderness, but Kat suspected he would prefer his ward not to further her friendship with Kat.

Major Nash had frowned when Kat ignored etiquette and spoke to Titania across the table at dinner, instead of merely to him on one side, and Zebediah Markham on the other. He had merely wished her a polite, 'Congratulations and happiness to you both,' at the ceremony, with what was most politely *not* a look of relief at his ward losing a possible pensioner for life.

Titania abruptly hugged her again. 'About the wedding night,' she muttered. 'My ma told me to wriggle my toes till it was over. You can't concentrate on the pain if you wriggle your toes.'

'Pain?' Kat blinked. Mama had never mentioned pain, nor had the ewes or mares seemed to feel discomfort, just a vague impatience to have it done. And long ago — how very long ago it seemed — she had rather enjoyed the preliminaries. 'That bit is over fast,' Kat assured her. She hesitated. 'Isn't it?'

Titania glanced at the large figure of Zebediah emerging from the cabin. 'I hope so,' she whispered. 'I've heard onions pickled with garlic are good if you don't want a man to kiss you. Take care, Kat love,' she added more loudly. 'Don't be bitten by kangaruhs or swallowed up by bears.'

'Major Nash says the native bears are small, no bigger than a spaniel.'

'The major also said native bears bite. And you wouldn't want a spaniel dropping onto you from a tree either, would you? There's poisonous snakes and spiders and native wild dogs, too, and remember the Aborigines we read about in the newspaper. Has Mr Markham said if there are any wild Aborigines about?'

'He didn't mention any,' said Kat.

'Just look where you're going and take it slow.'

'Yes,' said Kat, who had never taken longer than an hour to decide where fate would take her next.

Zebediah held out his hand to her. She took it, smiling up at him, caught his grin.

'Will you come aboard, Mrs Markham?'

'Willingly, sir.'

This might work.

The feeling lasted as she stood with her new husband's solid arm around her while she waved to the receding figures on the quay. The *Rainbow* turned the corner into the main harbour and the docks were lost to sight.

It was only as they neared the Heads that she realised ...

'Excuse me, Mr Markham?'

He smiled down at her. 'Don't you think you might call me Zebediah? Did you see the bird on the rock over there? I think it's a sea eagle. We have eagles over the valley, but darker feathered than that —'

'Sir, I think I am going to be ...' She made it to the rail before her breakfast cutlets and gravy were lost to the following seagulls.

He was kind to her the whole evil, wallowing day, heading south into a wind that pushed waves like small hills in front of them.

Despite the familiar wish to die or at least to be carried off to a ledge by a sea eagle to be meat for its chicks, she appreciated the buckets he offered, then emptied, the mugs of water he held to her lips, the damp cloth on her forehead. He even wiped her face when she missed the bucket almost entirely, splashing his boots.

Kindness to the seasick should possibly be added to any clauses in a contract for a husband. Possibly as a wife she should also have brought a dowry of pickled plums with ginger.

They anchored for the night in a bay too buffeted for the boat to be still. Kat glimpsed a small rough-built tavern on the shore, almost swallowed by barely cleared bush, a carefully lettered sign proclaiming it *The Harbour Inn*, but the sound of drunken song floated across the water, possibly from the sailors who crewed the two whaling ships anchored nearby, and Zebediah did not suggest they disembark and stay there.

Kat endured the billowing darkness, hardly noticing when the craft began to move again, with oars as well as sail now, up a wide and shallow river, greenery like a wall glimpsed through the cabin door, and strange bird calls among the yells of the crew.

At last the boat stopped. She heard the thud of rope as it was tethered to a wharf, the snicker of horses, and found herself carried by her husband, limp as month-old celery, she thought, vaguely indignant at herself, and laid in a cart. The sky above was blue. The hills on either side were green, with an occasional smudge of cliffs.

'The fresh air will revive you,' Zebediah stood next to her, peering down from his vast height, resolutely cheerful.

She scowled at him. 'If the wind had been any fresher on the way here it would have mooed at us.'

She felt the cart sag under Zebediah's weight. It began to move. But the jolting in the back of the cart was almost as bad as the ship, and the swaying as they turned corner after corner even worse. She closed her eyes ...

... and kept them closed, as the cart wound and bumped around a mountain track forever and forever, then finally, blessedly, stopped.

Kat opened her eyes. A million stars winked at her. The air smelled of woodsmoke and sheep. 'If you move,' she muttered at the stars, 'I will ...' She couldn't think of a punishment for stars.

'Here.' Zebediah's large hand helped her out. At least he had the sense not to enquire proudly, 'How do you like your new home?'

The house was a dark blur beneath the starlight. Someone, bent of back and long of nose, held a lantern in the doorway. Kat climbed two stone steps, seemingly undressed blocks of rock fitted together, then stepped onto a wooden verandah floor, through a doorway onto another wooden floor, unadorned by carpet or indeed any decoration beyond its polish, then up wooden stairs she was too tired to inspect or count, then into a room with a bed, a blessed bed.

A narrow bed, surely not big enough to share with a giant. She only wished to sleep undisturbed, and definitely not rocked by ship or cart or husband. She glanced back at the door, but instead of Zebediah there stood a woman in a grey and white apron, with grey-white hair, and an irregular scatter of long yellow teeth.

'I'm Mrs O'Connell, missus.' Her Irish accent was thick enough to spread on toast. 'Can I be helping you wid the buttons?'

'Please,' said Kat. She pulled the dress off as soon as it was unbuttoned, and then her petticoats and chemise.

'That's a fair pretty nightgown in your valise. Will you be wanting to put it on?'

Kat nodded, but even this made the room sway.

The nightdress was cotton, not the silk intended for a wedding night. It smelled of salt and slightly of last night's vomit, even though it had been in her valise, and not on her person. Probably her whole valise smelled disgusting. She probably did as well …

'Give me a yell in the mornin' when you'll be wanting sum hot water, an' I'll bring it up.'

'Thank you,' said Kat, too limp to even think of washing now. The woman left, taking the lamp, but leaving a candle on the side table. Which Kat blew out, and found the sheets unironed but clean and soft, then shut her eyes waiting for blessed unconsciousness.

Chapter 18

KAT

RAINBOW'S END

She woke before the sun had brightened the bare windows. Her curiosity won out over the remnant weakness of motion sickness. She sat up, and looked around in the pre-dawn light. Her room was small, the walls and floor were of highly polished wood, and held only this narrow bed and a plain but well-made chest of drawers. She ran to the window. The stillness stopped her.

An ocean of trees lay before her, without bird call or rustle. It was as if she had become the centre of a portrait, the valley below the foreground already completed by the artist.

Even as she watched, gold light spilled from the eastern ridge, suddenly reflecting in a thousand small lagoons up and down the course of the river below. All at once birds laughed, carolled or yelled in harsh coarse voices, as if amused at being woken. Ducks rose in great sweeping curtains, for some duckly reason exchanging the lagoon where they must have spent the night for another a few moments' flight away, while another flock of ducks glided down to take their place.

The beauty kept her locked in place for minutes before she thought to inspect the foreground. The house seemed to be perched on a wide ledge halfway up the valley. Vegetables — prosaically familiar cabbages, carrots, turnips — lay in neat beds below the house. Paling fences surrounded fields of potatoes, mangelwurzels and Indian corn, then a tide of grey-backed sheep compacted tightly into a single field, waiting, sheep-like, for whatever the day might bring. Beyond them stark white sheep had obviously been recently shorn.

She needed to see more. She flung off the nightdress, grabbed a petticoat and the first day dress to hand, managing to do up the first two buttons at the back before grabbing a shawl to cover the gap. She thrust on her boots without bothering with stockings or even buttoning them, then slipped out the bedroom door, casting a quick glance at the three doors along this landing, all shut, and narrow steps at the far end that must lead to an attic.

The main stairs did not creak as she walked softly down them. The house was silent, without even a clock's tick to break the peace. The bannister was smooth with polish and the floor below was also polished to mirror smoothness, smelling of beeswax and turpentine. A wifely wife would have inspected the kitchen, larder and scullery, the possibility of a root cellar or at least the drawing room.

Instead, Kat unbolted the front door and stepped out.

The valley widened to her gaze, uneven steps of mountains, the nearest green and the furthest away a purple-blue below a cloudless sky. More birds rose now: a wave of pink that turned grey then pink again. Others, red and green or red and blue, whistled at her from a taller, more prosperous version of the trees she'd seen near Sydney, as well as shorter leafier trees, clad in the same gold flowers Titania had given her.

Large white birds topped with yellow feathers yelled at her from the familiar branches of an oak tree, protesting perhaps at the nets placed over the young orchard on the other side of the house, and so hidden from her bedroom.

The orchard looked as extensive as the vegetables: two hundred trees at least, apples, pears and quinces that she could recognise by their leaves, peaches miraculously growing out in the open, taller than she had ever seen them and many others, unknowable at this distance.

She would investigate that later. Now she walked downwards. The air smelled vaguely of the yellow blossom and carpets of strange leaves, and tangles of vines with cream-coloured flowers that flowed from almost every wild tree. No sea breath here, no tang of humankind, the scent of spring so thick she could almost float on it, the trees, the sky, the birds and cliffs so bright an artist seemed to have laid out the colours.

She walked into the painting, becoming part of it: a path, made simply by feet going back and forth, not gravelled or cobbled, led into the potato field, then through it to the maize, taller than it had seemed from her window — shoulder high.

A gate beyond that opened onto another path, thinner but still clearly worn among tussocks and quartz-sharp rocks that glinted back the sun, leading to a creek carved into solid rock, bending and tumbling over bands of red and grey and pink, a few narrow-leaved trees above it. An animal like a lumpen badger was slowly drinking. It started at Kat's tread, then dashed into a vast hole between tree roots in a flash of fur and claws, leaving a strong whiff of unfamiliar animal.

The trees on the hill on the other side of the creek were entirely leafless for some reason. The grass below them was tall, with yet to be shorn sheep below them, a host, a crowd, a multitude of sheep, surprisingly dull against the stark white tree trunks. The sheep peered at her as one animal, then dismissed her and bent to eating once again.

She turned and, for the first time, properly saw the house where she was to live, with its outbuildings forming a series of levelled courtyards up the mountain behind. The house was mostly timber, as she had expected, but certainly no log hut. In England its eight stone chimneys would have declared it a 'gentleman's residence' if not a 'commodious' one.

The structure was simple: one long verandahed building, the first storey of stone, the same grey pink and the rocks of the creek, and the second floor and the attic made of wood, all with windows arched in an almost grand procession that must take in the sweep of the whole valley.

The roof was shingled. A roofed walkway at one end of the house led to a stone cottage from which a thread of smoke was finally appearing. Presumably this was the kitchen, separate from the house in case of fire, and a common design in the colony, as she had seen during her brief time in Sydney. Behind the main house rose stone barns, what was certainly a stable, workshops, and what might be a men's barracks slightly uphill from the shearing shed and field of unshorn sheep.

As she watched three men in trousers and braces ambled out of the barracks and began to wash in the trough out front, unaware a woman might be watching, followed by maybe a dozen more. Zebediah's farm hands, or the shearers he had mentioned who would move on?

This was not a gentleman's residence. Gentlemen had gravelled courtyards, grassed areas not munched by sheep, and rose gardens and herbaceous borders instead of potatoes. But in a decade this might easily become one.

Something moved, too large to be a dog. It was a pig — massive, dirty pink and black. It settled, dog-like, by the front door. No, not a gentleman's residence at all.

The front door opened and the gentleman in question appeared, in trousers and braces much like the men's, but wearing a shirt and waistcoat and the boots she had admired in town. He bent to scratch the pig behind the ear. The animal peered upwards appreciatively. Then Zebediah looked out and down. He seemed to know where she had gone instinctively, not in flight on the track back to the coast and Sydney, but to this stream.

She waited, smiling, in the dappled light, and, the moment that his eyes found her, knew that she could love him.

Chapter 19

KAT

They breakfasted in a dining room containing only a long table, sized for six, but with an almost invisible seam that showed it might be extended, and a sideboard carved in a pattern of gum leaves and sheaves of wheat, made from a rich almost-red wood, grained like oak, without a hint of fashionable gilt.

'She-oak,' Zebediah said, when she remarked on the wood, drawing her finger down its smoothness. 'Do you like it?'

'It's beautiful. All the furniture here is, and the carving above the doors and on the bannisters. Who is your cabinetmaker?'

He grinned. 'I am. I began because I had to, back in Sydney — it was a case of make my own table and chairs or use half barrels for furniture. I didn't like what I had made, so I asked an old man I'd met at church, Thomas Moore, if he would teach me. I had no idea that I was asking one of the colony's grandees. Mr Moore had started as a ship builder, and still loved the feel of wood. His wife was in poor health, and I think that he was lonely and passing his business interests to others. He taught me carpentry every Saturday afternoon for a year, showed me that the beauty of a chair is in its shape and balance, not decoration. It was his influence that bought me the land here, and he lent me the money for my first stock, too.'

'I'd like to meet him.'

'He died nine years ago. He left his entire estate to the church, but stipulated that the loans he had outstanding to myself and others like me should not be repaid. A most good man.' Zebediah stroked the bevelled edge of the table, remembering his mentor.

'Here's yer eggs.' Mrs O'Connell placed two plates before them.

Kat stared. 'Are you sure those are eggs?'

'Fresh outer the hens and cooked in mutton fat. What can ye see that is wrong wid 'em?'

'Nothing, if used as cannon fodder in a siege. Is there nothing else?'

Mrs O'Connell looked at her as if she had asked for the moon, thinly sliced, for breakfast. 'Sure, and himself has niver found fault wiv me cookin' afore, have yer master? You and Her Pigship has et eggs just like those on yer plate there for the past two year except the times we have a bit o' liver.'

Kat raised her eyebrows and grinned. 'Her Pigship?'

'I sometimes eat my meals out on the verandah with her,' Zebediah admitted. 'Her Pigship's very fond of Mrs O'Connell's eggs,' he added tactfully.

'Then she may have them,' said Kat sweetly. 'Are there more eggs in the kitchen, Mrs O'Connell?'

'What if there are?'

'Then I will cook them. Do you cook for the men too?'

'I do not, thanks be to all the saints. It's Bill One-arm who cooks for dem.'

'Sensible men. Mrs O'Connell, the floor gleams, the sheets are soft, I haven't seen a speck of dust and I suspect you are a treasure. But perhaps I should do the cooking,' Kat added as the old woman seemed to be deciding between being pleased and affronted. 'Just for this morning, would you care to join us for breakfast? You and Mr Markham sit here and I will ... will see what I can find.'

Mrs O'Connell sat, slightly stunned but not unwilling. Zebediah grinned, and pushed his chair back, as if to enjoy whatever might happen next. Kat followed the hall to the back door, through an immaculate scullery and then down the open passageway leading to the kitchen, stone walls and stone flagged floor, a vast fireplace with a spit and hanging kettle, and yes, the promised enclosed stove, though only the fireplace was lit, and the stove would take a good half hour to heat.

She looked around. The room was scrubbed fresh even in the corners where woodsmoke mixed with fat could have lingered or combined with spiders' webs. Mrs O'Connell clearly seemed to have a hatred of dirt, unexpected in a colony of rogues, though she had none of the graces that showed she had been trained in a good household. She was certainly not the housekeeper Kat had expected, nor was this kitchen provisioned as she'd assumed it would be, either.

Eggs in a blue dish, at least three dozen, mostly white and a few speckled. No butter, but a tin of mutton fat that didn't smell rancid. A lump of what might have been intended to be soda bread but might also crack the paved floor if dropped on it. Another feast for Her Pigship. A sack of well-washed potatoes; strings of onions hanging from a rafter; a sack of flour, another of sugar, and yes, a door that opened to a wide larder, with a box of salt, cans of treacle, a hunk of cheese as hard as one of the boulders, a pot with honey comb draining its sweetness into it, and a few other necessities.

But not yeast, or even commercial saleratus. She'd have to capture and grow her own yeast, then test to see if it brewed sweet. You never knew what you'd get with wild yeast, so she placed three tumblers on the windowsill with water, flour and sugar to see what might arrive, then found — ah ha! — a bag of raisins that likely had a yeast attached, and made a brew to coax theirs from them, too.

For this morning they'd have to make do with soda bread, made to rise with home-made saleratus — water run through some of yesterday's ash from the fireplace. And by the smell of it this milk was sour, which would not do for tea — where was the tea? Ah, in that chest there — but sour milk and saleratus would do excellently to make a good, fast, light loaf.

Within twenty minutes she had fried a platter of potato cakes, mixed with sprouted onion tops to give them flavour; a dish of pancakes, rolled with honey to cover the faint odour of mutton fat; the soda bread, nicely risen, to eat with more honey and three folded omelettes containing the hard hunk of cheese grated fine so it melted in the heat. She carried the lot out on a tray to find Mrs O'Connell had set another place; Kat grinned at her and fetched the teapot and hot water jug.

Her husband had begun eating, and Mrs O'Connell too, with surprisingly neat manners with knife and fork. Kat found that she was starving.

'We need to discuss supplies,' she told him.

'I know it. Black John — you met him on the boat — will take your order back to Sydney to my agent there as soon as you've made your list. You'll want carpets, tablecloths, folderols and furnishings. I thought it best if you saw the house before you chose.' He looked at her almost shyly. 'Do you like it?'

'I love it. I'll make that list.' And Titania would see it was filled, and filled properly, not an agent. Titania might interview more servants, too, though Kat found herself suddenly unwilling to share the peace of the house with others.

She must also tell her friends she was happy.

Chapter 20

KAT

She had spent eight months on the ship and never felt that the cabin was hers. But within three weeks Rainbow's End was home.

Kat spent part of the next week of shearing cooking vast breakfasts and dinners for Zebediah, which he ate with great appreciation and even greater speed.

After that first meal Mrs O'Connell preferred to eat her portion in the kitchen. The rest of the time she scrubbed, or washed, or preferably polished for hours on end, not even looking up as Kat passed. Despite her initial protest, she seemed relieved to have relinquished the cooking duties. While she obligingly did up Kat's buttons and undid them morning and night, and brought up hot water, she made no offer of other lady's maid's work. Her conversation seemed limited to 'Y'm. I must get on wid the polishin'.'

Kat made the acquaintance of the house — four bedrooms, not counting the two servants' rooms next to the kitchen, dining room, and a drawing room where even the chairs had obviously been made by Zebediah, and needed cushions to make up for their lack of upholstery. She wandered through the straggle of buildings above the house, taking care to avoid the shearing shed, as Zebediah had informed her the men would down clippers if a woman approached.

Storerooms, four quite substantial cottages and a long, low barracks. Zebediah had explained that he had fourteen regular workmen, five of whom were convicts still serving out their sentences — transportation may have ended but their servitude did not. The others were 'ticket of leavers', which meant they were free to leave his employment, but not the colony. More than half the men worked as shepherds, spending most of their time in huts around the property. There were no other women.

She inspected the dairy, fruit trees, the vegetables, two cows milked by one of the workmen, and the hens, who seemed to be a cross between English Dorkings and the wilder breed she had seen at the Cape. She also managed to lure Her Pigship into the pig sty, where she glared at Kat every morning when she brought her scraps and mash. With no boar, it seemed Her Pigship's role was simply to eat, or possibly to keep Zebediah company, though there was a sheep dog too, Ben, rarely seen except at Zebediah's heels outside, but often heard barking at o'possums, and the badger-like animal she had seen the first day, which Zebediah informed her was a wombat called Digger, though it would not answer to that name or any other, but accepted carrots or parsnips left on the verandah at night.

Kat made butter, proud of her first solo attempt. She also achieved clotted cream; a green cheese; raspberry jam; a marmalade from the oranges and lemons — such luxury — growing behind the house; four fruitcakes; and twenty-eight fruit pies. She cooked vast amounts of sheep: from crumbed brains or fried liver or kidneys for breakfast, to sheep's-head cheese, spiced tongue, roast leg, stuffed shoulder, pickled neck or crown roast and shepherd's pie.

She continued to sleep in the small single room, nor did Zebediah make any hint he wished her to share the larger bedroom two doors down. But every meal, as she watched his open enjoyment of the food she'd made, she wondered if he would extend the same happy enthusiasm to matters of the bedroom.

He did not even kiss her hand, but one morning, as he happened to pass as she was about to call Mrs O'Connell to button her frock, he quietly offered to do the task for her. His hands were warm, even through her petticoat, and gentle. He made his way downstairs as soon as the last button was fastened, but every evening she found him somehow on the landing when she opened her door to call Mrs O'Connell, and lingering there each morning, too.

She grew to love the smell of him; soap, for he washed both morning and evening at the tub with the men; the faint tang of sheep, and a musky scent that was his alone. She learned each wrinkle around his eyes as he bent to his buttoning; how the hairs grew upon his wrists; the freckles on his ears, otherwise too high above her for examination.

Breakfast must be hurried, after that first day, to join the shearing. Instead they talked at dinner: of coprolites and steam engines, which somehow didn't hurt when discussed with him; of Zebediah's early years at Rainbow's End, at first with only two convicts, one of whom tried to stab him in the night to steal whatever he might carry off, slowly building up his holdings and his labour force, and finally his house.

'I had it planned ten years before a single stone was laid. The stone masons were Canadians, convict rebels, with their tickets of leave. The timber was all cut on the property, two years before I began to build. The long-leafed trees give a good hard red wood for outside walls, but it must be properly dried before you use it, or it twists and the nails pop out, and you have a ruin, not a house. The she-oaks give the best wood for inside, a golden grain if the trees get sun, and a deep red in the shady gullies.'

'Do you plan to buy more land?'

He shook his head. 'I have enough for the moment, or will have when more slopes are cleared of trees and I can increase the flock. I want an estate I can run myself, though if we have children ...' he stopped, and gazed at his roast potatoes.

'If we have children,' said Kat calmly 'We may need a property for each of them too. Is there still land to buy?'

His face cleared. He swallowed a mouthful of potato, peas and gravy. 'Plenty of land, and no one else likely to want it.'

'What about the natives?'

He looked thoughtful. 'They move about a lot. I'm not even sure how much of the land they use — all of it, perhaps, but not each year, or even every five years.'

'Are they savage?' she asked, with a little concern. 'I read about them in the newspapers.'

Zebediah laughed. 'The colony is mostly rogues, Kat. If the scum of Britain attack the natives they can only expect them to fight back. I've found the natives to be good people — they laugh a lot, and are generous too. They helped me build my first hut out of stringybark, then showed me where to build the house to keep it out of flood reach — you'd be surprised at how much water can flow down the stream after one of the deluges we can get here.'

'How many natives are there? Do they come up here much?' she asked cautiously.

'Not up to the house, except for the corn harvest. They come to help pick the crop each year, and feast on the cobs while they're tender enough. There's only about twenty-five of them, if you count the children, though every few years there's a big gathering in early summer.'

'The dark lad who does the milking — is he one of the local natives?'

'Little Summat Sam? No, he's a half-breed, I think, a Sydney orphan. Had another master before me. Left great whip scars on the lad's back. He's glad enough to be out here.'

'You don't want natives working here?'

He gave another shout of laughter. 'Swap a band of drunken rogues from England, brought up on gin and thievery, for strong fit men who know the land? There's nothing I'd like better. But the natives live far better than most in England, or even workmen here, for all they have no cottages. They've no wish to grub up tree roots or stop the sheep from straying.'

Which meant the women wouldn't want to be house servants either, Kat thought. How sensible of them. Nor would they know how to scrub a scullery.

'If you find a fish outside the kitchen one morning, it'll be from them. There are some monsters down in the lagoons. The natives and I seem to have come to an accommodation. They don't spear my sheep, though if I've slaughtered and they ask for a share I give it, and I don't run the land so hard there are no more kangaruhs, or wallaby or o'possums — we must get you a cloak of o'possum skin for next winter, Kat. There's nothing like it for softness and warmth.'

'Will the natives trade for o'possum furs?'

'It's not trading, exactly. If I ask, they'll give the skins to us, if there've been plenty of o'possum born. If there's a good crop of potatoes or carrots they'll take without asking — but only if the crop is good.'

'But that's stealing!'

He smiled at her. 'There's not many of them, Kat, and they won't take more than they want to eat, not to sell or store, and only if they judge there's more than we can use. They give far more than they take. They're only here from spring to midsummer, anyway.'

'Where do they go then?'

'I've no idea.' He looked down at his plate, now empty of shoulder of mutton stuffed with breadcrumbs, lemon and herbs, and vegetables. 'I don't suppose you made pies today?'

'I did not.' She chuckled at his disappointment. 'I made a ginger pudding, with clotted cream and a caramel sauce, and a savoury of crayfish, if you'd fancy that too.'

'Of course,' he said, grinning at her, exactly as she'd known he would. For Zebediah Markham had spent his life working towards all he loved in life, and he would not neglect a single mouthful of something good.

The day the shearers left Zebediah looked up from the establishment's first successful toast — it had taken longer than Kat expected to capture a truly good yeast — and rather shyly suggested Kat might like to walk the boundaries of the farm with him.

The air smelled of lanolin and sheep dung, of gum trees, of rock and lingering spring blossom, the thorn bushes now clothed in white and a shivering hum of insects feeding on it. Ben ambled at their heels or pushed his nose into wombat holes. It seemed the valley was rich in Digger's kin. Kat had already learned to watch where she put her feet, for while the wombats were excellent diggers, they were not good engineers, and the small hollows of collapsed burrows were a trap for the unwary.

They walked up to the ridge behind the house first, so Kat could see the land crumple into a series of gullies where the stream began, reeds and rushes and tiny swamps till the water finally cleared to a proper stream, then tumbled over pink grey granite. Large grey and white pigeons trotted, fat as hens, and only waddled faster when Ben rushed at them then stopped, startled, as they declined to show fear.

Along the ridge, then halfway down into the valley, till they came to the property's far boundary, marked so far only with axe marks, not a fence.

At last they sat on a scatter of boulders, grey with lichen. Ben leaned his head against Kat's leg as she scratched his ears. She gazed out at trees, boulders, the fields carved from the green, the skeleton forest she now knew had been ringbarked, so the trees could be burned and their roots grubbed out next winter.

This was not the young country those in England and Sydney had spoken of. It was the oldest she'd ever seen, every rock carved by rain, each tree sculpted by the wind. You could almost feel its ages in the sun. A young colony perhaps, still finding its way but, oh, the land ...

'How did you find this place?' she asked at last.

'Old Mr Moore had heard of it from a surveying party. I wasn't the first here — the Johnsons have a place down where the valley curves and the Richardsons live over that far ridge. You can't see their properties from here. They're a good day's ride away. There's a tributary down river too, that leads up to

Sibber's Beach. There are a couple of prospectors up that way, but they're a two day sail from here.'

She shuddered at the thought of another boat ride.

'I saw smoke down the valley yesterday.'

'Just the natives.'

'But your sister's letter said you visited with five families.' She'd assumed she'd meet the neighbours after shearing.

'Well ...' Zebediah grinned ruefully. 'That's strictly true. There's the Johnson brothers, but no Mrs Johnson, just the two men, each with their own house and farm. There's three generations of Richardsons, but there isn't a Mrs Richardson among them — just two assigned convict women, too rough even to be given tickets of leave.'

'Slaves?' asked Kat sharply.

He looked at her, surprised. 'No, quite willing. They'd have met plenty of men who'd take them back to Sydney if they wanted it, to get reassigned to them. The women each have their own cottage, and the ordering of it, though they prefer rum to carpets and folderols. They've been drunk each time I've met them,' he admitted.

'That's your five families?'

'It's not as bad as it sounds,' he said, looking at her with concern. 'You can take the boat to Sydney as often as you like. Stay as long as you like, too — months, if that's what you wish.'

'I don't think I will ever want to stay as long as that.' Or get on a boat again forever, she thought. Viola and Titania must visit her here. To her surprise she was almost glad they had no close neighbours. She needed to learn this place, and Zebediah too. Neighbours meant tea parties, and tea parties meant dressing her hair and putting on a corset and enduring inane conversation. One day, perhaps, she'd like more company. Now a new life opened, allowing her to shut the door more formally on her memories.

Zebediah looked at her for a while, then just nodded. 'Good.'

'What about Mrs O'Connell?'

'Ticket of leave. I had her assigned from the Parramatta Female Factory, where she'd gone straight from the transport that brought her to the colony. Fourteen years for theft. I'm not sure how many years she has left to serve. It doesn't matter — she can go where she likes in the colony with a ticket of leave, and I can't see her returning to starve in Ireland. Not many older women are sent out to the colony, but she even came with a letter of recommendation as "clean and industrious" from a convent.'

'Why would a convent give a thief a letter of recommendation?'

'The convent had been closed. She'd lived there nearly all her life, as an orphan first then as a servant. I assumed the theft was instead of starving. You tend not to ask about people's past lives in the colony. They either want them forgotten, or it's too painful to remember what they'll never see again. But she's certainly clean and industrious.'

'She undoubtedly is that.'

'She goes through beeswax and linseed oil like bran through a pig. I assumed she could cook when I hired her,' he added wryly.

'How have you survived?'

'I ate with the men a lot of the time, mostly meat on a spit or stew and damper. Truth be told, I've no idea how to find a cook. I thought you would.'

Servants at home were usually recommended by other families, or by other servants, or occasionally by the vicar's wife. She smiled. 'I expect Titania — Mrs Boot — will know where to find the best servants within a month of living in the colony. You've been here fourteen years?'

'Coming up to that. A friend of my father's was coming out and I joined him rather than go to Oxford. Nor have I regretted it.'

'No women in your life?' she asked quietly.

At last he said, 'One. Her name was Myrtle. Had her passage paid by one of the immigrant societies who sent orphan girls out here to make the colony civilised with wives and servants.'

'Which was she?'

'She'd been a housemaid. Knew nothing about the kitchen, or farming, couldn't write her own name, and the bush terrified her. But she stuck it out here for five years — said she'd like as not get a worse master than me back in town.'

'What happened to her?'

'She died losing a half-term baby six years ago. Yes, the child was mine. I would have married her,' he added.

She believed him. She also believed that his family would not have accepted such a connection, nor possibly would society in Sydney, though even a few days there had been enough to realise that women of low birth could marry into a higher estate far more easily than back in England. An ex-housemaid might even be invited to Government House, as a courtesy to her husband — but only once. She'd heard that the wealthy Wentworth family home did not even have a proper front entrance, for why bother when no formal calls would come?

Zebediah stayed silent beside her and, suddenly, she heard what he didn't say. He would speak no word against the girl he 'would have married'. But after her death he had obviously decided to actively seek a socially acceptable wife.

A wife who would walk up here with him, daughter of a mother who'd roamed the chalk cliffs by herself and shared most unsuitable conversations with her daughter.

A wife he could talk to.

Chapter 21

TITANIA

SYDNEY

It was easy enough to find a man in the colony. Finding a trustworthy one was harder.

Titania had observed him for three days now, having noted first the orderliness of his workshop. A rope-maker, who kept his product coiled neatly in piles of different ages, sizes and strengths. She had seen no sign he mixed new cord with old, except in the product he advertised as such and sold cheaply.

She had walked back and forth under her parasol, as if waiting for a ferry, hearing the creaks of the wharf under her feet, the splash of waves, the cries so similar to home, the small hands reaching for her reticule as sly, but just as possible for a woman of resolution to avoid.

She had pretended to wait as a passenger ship unloaded; she had attended two auctions of goods on deck, though she had bid for nothing. And all the while he worked, solidly, his mind on his trade.

On the third dusk she had followed him back to a cottage in The Rocks and the wife she had deduced he had from the luncheon tin he carried, and the flask of what smelled like fresh weak ale — a spouse's brewing, not a shanty's. The next day she watched the cottage and the wife.

The area was not salubrious, but the walls were freshly whitewashed and the doorstep scrubbed before the bells chimed nine. Cleanliness did not necessarily mean honesty, but it did denote pride and hard work. One child, a boy of perhaps five, played hopscotch with the others in the road in the morning, but his clothes were darned, as theirs were not, and he had boots upon his feet. In the afternoon, she could glimpse him through the front window at a table making pot hooks on a slate and reciting his alphabet.

Both man and wife, then, knew how to read, and were giving that skill to their son, as well as a childhood, instead of taking him to sweep the workshop every day. The boy's head, bent over the table, gave her the final certainty.

She knocked on the cottage door the next afternoon, while the husband worked on his ropes by the docks and Lady Viola napped in preparation for the dinner her guardian would give that night, now Viola's unpredictable guest had departed so soon. Thankfully Titania had convinced Viola that employed companions were not required to dine with company.

The cottage door was answered by a woman wearing a clean white cap, a well-darned apron, and an enquiring smile: tradespeople mostly came to the back door down the alley.

Titania held out her card.

The woman looked at it closely. 'Boot, Boot and Boot? I'm afraid I don't understand.' She looked at Titania suspiciously. 'My husband can't be assigned to no one. He's a free man. Born free, too.'

'I know. May I come in, Mrs Anderson? I have a business proposition for your husband.'

'Can you not ask him directly? His workshop is not far away. Just head down the lane, then —'

'I know where his workshop is, Mrs Anderson, but I'd rather speak with you. I think a woman will better understand my proposition.' And if Mrs Anderson approved, her husband was more likely to agree.

The front room was rarely used but dusted. It smelled of years of home-made stews, the lingering scents of baking bread, of brewing. The boy, 'our son, our Peterkin', proudly bore in two mugs of what was indeed a light home-brewed ale, made fresh every few days with no chance to grow to strong drink and, as Titania knew, most sovereign in making impure waters safe to drink.

Mrs Anderson sipped and listened, frowned and asked intelligent questions. 'So my husband would give his name to your new business? Why?'

'Not just his name. Some captains already know me, from the days when I worked as an agent in London, but the majority of ships here seem to be whalers and sealers, and American at that. I doubt their quartermasters will easily trade with a business run solely by a woman.'

'Henry has no knowledge of the chandler trade. I must be honest, Mrs Boot — I'd say he has no ambition to, neither.'

'He would not have to. His own work would be interrupted only in so far as to spend perhaps an hour a day approaching prospective quartermasters for our products — he deals directly with them already, not through Mr Campbell nor any other merchant, doesn't he?'

'Nay, they all know James and trust his cordage. They'd rather buy direct from him than have a rope fray in the Southern Ocean,' Mrs Anderson added proudly.

'I will warrant all the goods we sell will be the same fine quality. Your husband will be free to leave the firm at any time he doubts this. He will keep what he makes at his own business and also receive one-tenth of Boot and Anderson's profit, to be renegotiated after the first year if he finds he has more wish to be involved in the business. We will have this drawn up by a lawyer, so there can be no mistake. I will hire the premises and purchase or make all we plan to sell, and pay all costs.'

'So what's to stop him waiting till the fourth or fifth sale and walking off with cash in hand?'

Ah, an intelligent woman, as she suspected. 'Nothing, except I judge that he is an honest man, as I am an honest and plain-dealing woman, and that you'd both like an easier life for your son than one where his back is bent by the time he is forty, and the feeling gone from hands by his old age.'

Mrs Anderson nodded.

'With a family business — Boot and Anderson — your son might work in an office, or go to school as a gentleman, or even join his father's workshop if he wishes. But the craft of roper may not survive his generation, Mrs Anderson.'

The woman looked alert and alarmed.

Titania looked at her with patient sympathy. 'Ask your husband if it's not the truth. Machines in England do much of the work already. The rope-makers' trade is only profitable in the colony because old hokum is easy to obtain here, with so many ships using the harbour as their supply base for the oil trade, exchanging worn rope for new. This will give your son a chance, Mrs Anderson, that he might never glimpse otherwise.'

As if he knew they talked about him the boy peered in, his face proudly washed and hair combed for the well-dressed visitor. 'The water man is at the door, Ma. He says one barrel today, or two?'

'Two, and to take the two empties as well.' Mrs Anderson waited till the boy left then said, 'I will speak to my husband.'

Chapter 22

TITANIA

A week later she had a warehouse hired and scrubbed, a full-time rat catcher with two industrious labourers hired, a night watchman, two porters and a boy to sweep the street, two enclosed stoves installed and a gross of empty barrels and two cauldrons delivered and stowed. With Mr Anderson's help her notebooks had six pages of reliable sources for not just rope, sails (old and well repaired), coke, firewood, pitch and soap, but for all the other goods a voyage required.

It was time to find some buyers — ones who would pay a deposit on their orders, for her capital would not stretch to buying all the stock she needed immediately. Viola had offered her a gift of money, then, when Titania refused, to lend it to her. She would accept if necessary — but only if necessary.

She dressed in the new fine wool skirt and matching dark blue jacket Viola had insisted the dressmaker back in London provide for her, then asked a footman to fetch her a chair. Viola had offered Major Nash's coach, left entirely for his ward's use while her guardian drove a sporting phaeton, but Titania preferred to grasp as much independence as she could.

The chair carriers left her on the wharf. She finally found Captain Olsen in a hostelry just up from the docks, about to address himself to a mutton pie.

He looked astonished to see a lady in the tap room, but stood politely. 'Mrs Boot? Will you join me? Though this fare is nothing like your London firm supplied. I should have taken a chair back home for luncheon. The sheep that gave its life for this pie had already seen twenty summers at least, I reckon, and the pastry would serve as an anchor.'

She reached into her reticule and brought forth a jar of tomato chutney, made under her supervision with Mrs Higgins' permission. 'Perhaps this will improve it, Captain.'

He brightened. 'I remember your chutneys, Mrs Boot. They indeed improved our whole voyage.' He pulled off the wax covering and helped himself liberally.

She smiled, spread her handkerchief quickly over the seat he offered, and sat. 'That is what I wished to speak to you about, Captain. I hope that cleaning the hull is proceeding satisfactorily?'

'It is, Mrs Boot. The shipyards of this port are efficient, though whether I will have a crew after three months on the rum or offers of whale oil wealth from the Yankees is another matter.'

'A well-provisioned ship might attract sailors — the kind who'd prefer a captain of known ability to the perils of harpooning. Please, do continue with your pie, Captain.'

'Thank you.' He took another bite and chewed resignedly.

'Captain, I am here to claim a favour.' She took a breath. 'I would be grateful if you would allow my new chandlery to supply the *Salamanca*. I would be even more grateful if you would recommend Boot and Anderson to any quartermasters of your acquaintance. I will give you my word that everything supplied by Boot and Anderson will be of the same quality as, or superior to, any goods you received from Boot, Boot and Boot in London.'

She handed him her new card.

Captain Olsen fingered it thoughtfully. 'Anderson?'

'He is the roper down from the main wharf.'

'I know his work and use it. But he's no chandler.'

'No. His is an acceptable male face for a business run by a woman.' Titania met the captain's eyes. 'Just as Boot, Boot and

Boot was in effect entirely run by a woman for three years back in England.'

Captain Olsen carefully removed a small piece of bone from his pie, then grinned. 'Mutton pies included?'

'Mutton pies sewn into oilcloth to last a fortnight and puddings that will last three years or more.' Titania could guarantee that, as she would supervise their cooking herself. 'I can provide you with sauerkraut for the men at half the cost and better quality than any for sale from Mr Campbell. Ship's biscuit will be baked no more than a fortnight before sailing, and from this year's harvest. Cheese in quantity and quality I can't always promise, but I can provide well-salted fresh butter in brine instead. The corned mutton will be new brined, fresh tasting for at least two months as it takes the pickle, a third fat, two thirds lean meat. I have found a source of potatoes and have it on good authority they will last at least three months at sea.'

'All at the same cost or lower than Campbell's for everything?'

'No, sir, for my food will be better quality, and last better, and your crew will be healthier for it. But I will warrant the total cost to you will be no more, for I can make economies I believe Mr Campbell doesn't dream of.'

'What kind would they be, Mrs Boot?'

'The meat will be brined under my supervision, so there will be no waste in gristle or bone. I will supervise the puddings, biscuits and a most extensive range of pickles and chutneys too, far better than any others available in the colony, using local ingredients, not stale ones from the Cape, so there will be no waste and the ingredients cheaper.'

'Go on.'

She smiled. 'You will also have gratis a supply of the herbal sachets I used upon the *Salamanca* to add to the men's stew. It is best I provide you with a list of the common supplies that your quartermaster can choose from. But for your own use — at extra cost, of course, but economical — there may be a marmalade of oranges and grapefruit, extra rich puddings of the finest raisins and prunes, fruits preserved in brandy, and the pickled eggs and onions you so much enjoyed on the voyage out here.'

'And port?' he queried.

'That, too.' Purchased from the merchant who supplied Major Nash's household, whose name and address she had from Mrs Higgins, who did not order it, but who had seen the accounts of Tilson the butler, who did.

'Mrs Boot, I have never shook hands with a woman, but today I offer you mine. If you assure me these can all be procured by the time the *Salamanca* is ready, you have a deal.'

She accepted the hand, a callused one for all the title of Captain, and smiled in relief and happiness. 'No, sir. If all goes as expected, you will have yourself a bargain.'

And, she thought, I will finally begin my life.

Chapter 23

VIOLA

Viola looked at Titania's tiny cottage dubiously. It was made of stone, at least — so many of the cottages near the docks were of round sagging logs that smelled of rot and damp. But this cottage was still in an alley, and even if the cottages on either side looked well cared for, the building on the corner was undoubtedly a shanty. Already drunk men lay, tankards in hand, sprawled on the footpath against its walls. A woman who might be fourteen or forty served them in a dress that did not quite cover her bosom.

Titania grinned at her dismay. 'My front and back doors are sturdy and have bolts and shutters. I had a ship's carpenter guarantee the place mouse proof.'

'But is it man proof?'

Titania shrugged. 'There's naught here for them to break in to steal, beyond my sheets and cooking pots, and there's women enough for tuppence for ten minutes around here without they go bothering me. Besides, I'm twice the size of most of the wretches round here. I know how to wield a skillet, too.'

Viola was silent. It had never occurred to her that one could live entirely by oneself. This was the first time she had even been in a dwelling that boasted only three rooms, and one of them a storeroom. Her mother had visited tenants on the estate, but Viola had not accompanied her.

To dress oneself, to cook one's meals — there must be far more needed, too. Cleaning and ... and such like. Viola had no doubt that Titania was proficient at them all.

I should feel dismay, she thought, at my friend leaving the comfort of George Street. But instead she felt only a prickle of envy. To be alone, without the need to smile, to summon tact and empty speech.

'Well, what do you think of it?'

She would not insult her friend by saying, 'You could have stayed in comfort with me all your life.' This, perhaps, was the beginning of true friendship, with no salary to mar the bond.

'May I help you buy linen and furniture?'

Titania flushed. 'I can buy what I need. I don't need much to start with.'

'I've never had the chance to buy plates or pillows or even a soup tureen. It would be enjoyable.'

Titania gave a gurgle of laughter. 'A soup tureen? Don't think I'll be wanting one of them for a while. The soup will go straight from the pot to the table.'

How could Viola explain that equipping a home would give her purpose, while walks along the gardens and tea parties did not?

She didn't have to. 'I'd like your help, and welcome,' said Titania gruffly.

Yes, thought Viola, this is friendship.

Chapter 24

KAT

RAINBOW'S END, 1850

Kat had thought her first months at Rainbow's End had been happy. Now she began to glimpse Zebediah's fulfilment in the long years he'd spent dreaming of his farm, his house, and then achieving it; it was what Titania, perhaps, was enjoying now she had twenty-three ships fully supplied and orders for fifteen more.

Rainbow's End was hers to plan now, from decorating her home and adding comforts, to planning extended chicken runs, for she'd found her wish to breed hens had not diminished.

The house wore blue curtains at its windows and Chinese silk rugs by its beds and sturdy Indian woollen carpets for the drawing room. A stone storeroom had been constructed next to the kitchen, for the larder was devoted to a breakfast, dinner and tea service, chosen by Boot and Anderson to Kat's instructions, all rimmed with a green design and a pattern of roses in the centre. Chop plates, fish dishes, poultry servers with drainage holes for the juices, sauce tureens, gravy boats, vegetable bowls with well-fitting lids to keep the contents warm, china butter rests encircled with water to stop the butter melting, relish and celery dishes, cake stands, cream pitchers and sugar bowls, as well as silver place settings with the required seven forks for every plate, each one for a different food, and pea spoons, iced tea spoons, cream soup spoons, bouillon spoons, hot teaspoons, demitasse spoons, dessert spoons, sugar spoons and all the rest in heavy silver and a design that matched the plates, commissioned from a Sydney silversmith.

Mrs O'Connell took to polishing silver with a joy, the heavy scrubbing now done by a new arrival, recommended by Titania, who soon called herself 'Mrs' Torrens, though Kat suspected the relationship with the stockman was not so formal. A dairymaid had also quickly become a 'wife', taking the best of the cottages, churning the butter and even making a slightly salty but quite acceptable fresh cheese. Kat enjoyed talking to both women about matters of the house, dairy and weather, but they had too little in common for friendship, and both seemed wary of 'the missus'.

Two more ticket-of-leave men had been hired to plant and tend a garden of roses, rhododendrons and herbaceous borders from a Sydney nursery. The only things missing were the Chinese hens that had been impossible even for Boot and Anderson to procure, and the still for the poteen, which also needed a new, discrete addition to the dairy to house it. But life had joy enough without poteen.

Kat also now had a husband in every sense. As Mama had suggested, the marital experience was quite delightful. It was also fun, which Kat had not expected, especially when performed in the deep pool below the house, sheltered from view only by the she-oak trees and boulders, or in rooms other than the bedroom.

It was still a private home, for Titania had been unable to find a lady's maid willing to face the isolation of Rainbow's End, and Zebediah seemed content with Kat's hair simply plaited and wound in a coronet on her head. He took delight in doing up her buttons and even more in the undoing, and made no comment when she failed to wear first her corset, then later as the weather warmed, even petticoats.

Nor had a competent cook or trusty housekeeper prepared to face an isolated bush farm been found — it seemed they were as rare as lady's maids. But Kat discovered she enjoyed the charge of the kitchen, especially given Zebediah's lusty appreciation even for gingerbread too crusty on one side and meringue boats that turned into strands of toffee when he took a bite.

Today they dined on turtle soup — an unwary beast had retreated into its shell when it was heading up the path and Zebediah coming down; dressed eels; saddle of mutton with redcurrant sauce; and a ham on the sideboard — not Her Pigship, nor piglets from her, for Zebediah said she had attacked both boars he had tried to mate her with, but a ham sent down from Sydney; baked potatoes, potted carrots and buttered spinach; and a remove of curried eggs on toasted and most excellent bread — Kat fed her yeast each morning on the windowsill — and lastly an apricot tart, and walnuts from the previous autumn's picking.

Dinners were never boring, with the days doings to be dissected, a wayward ram bucking his fence to get to the ewes too early, the new wombat hole through the rose garden fence. Zebediah had a fine loose baritone to serenade her with after dinner, while Kat embroidered tapestry chair covers, for distracting idle hands.

Tonight though, they lingered over the nuts, for today's boat up the river had brought the mail, as well as sacks of flour and rice, more turpentine, linseed oil and wax for polishing, barrels of coarse sugar and fine; a vast amount of the golden syrup the men required; and chests of tea, as well as the preserved ginger, spices and pineapple in syrup and other luxuries that Titania added at her discretion as supplies arrived.

Two months' worth of newspapers: year-old copies of *The Lady's Newspaper and Pictorial Times*, so useful for new receipts and household decoration, even if the fashions were a year out of date by the time they reached the colony; two copies of *The Zoologist* to which Mama had subscribed and which Kat ordered in her memory; *Punch*, which they both enjoyed, even if the political references were also long out of date; as well as the colonial *Sydney Morning Herald*. The pile of copies would be slowly read over the next week, not that either Kat or Zebediah would recognise the names in the social pages, apart from the governor's and Viola's. Zebediah had never made an attempt to join Sydney society, and seemed relieved that Kat was content for now with letters.

The mail was the chief attraction that evening, so much so that etiquette was abandoned as Zebediah cracked the walnuts and handed Kat their meat, and each read the most important. Through the open windows Kat could faintly hear the clap of not quite drums and native singing, far down the valley, as well as laughter from up at the men's quarters, and the thin music of a penny whistle.

'Lettice has been to a Venusian Breakfast,' announced Zebediah, squinting at his sister's tiny, crosshatched handwriting. 'Have they all dressed up as ancient Romans and partied at a Temple of Venus?'

'Venetian Breakfast, I expect,' said Kat distractedly, still reading Titania's neat copperplate. 'They were all the rage, though I never attended one. Titania regrets that business keeps her in Sydney this year, but promises to take at least a fortnight to visit us next year ...'

'Would you like to spend some time in Sydney, love?'

'No,' said Kat, grinning up at him. 'And no more would you.' She glanced down again. 'Titania has a new neighbour who she fears is a Woman of Loose Behaviour. Did you know I once wanted to be a Scarlet Woman, darling?'

'You are definitely a Scarlet Woman, totally shameless, but thankfully you prefer one man,' said Zebediah smugly.

'Well, the man I have is large enough for four and eats enough for ten. I warn you, if you throw walnuts at me you'll have no toast for your breakfast! Ah, Titania says her neighbour's clientele are well behaved and only comprises one customer each night, so the house is quieter than with the seven children who lived there before. And she has dined twice with Mrs Olsen. I'm glad. I was afraid she would be lonely.'

'With a hundred carters and wheelwrights and sail-makers around her every day?'

'You know perfectly well that isn't what I meant. Oh, wonderful — Viola says she will come and stay! I most carefully did not invite Major Nash — he was most kind, but he did not quite approve of me — so, it will just be her and her maid and probably a groom — he can share Thompson's cottage. Viola will love the lyrebirds. I told her all about the one that copied your song ...'

'"Oh Nancy Mine"?'

'What else do you ever sing? I want to show Viola Flat Rock and we can ride down to the lagoons. I wonder, can she ride? Her mother and then her brother kept her so confined ... but surely she rode about the estate, even if not beyond it. It was so sad on the ship, Zebediah. Titania and I would talk of places we had seen, but Viola spoke only of scenes in books, or what people in books had said. I'm glad that she is free at last.'

Zebediah put down the nutcracker. 'Shall we retire to the drawing room? Or possibly,' he added casually, as Mrs O'Connell gathered up the remnants of the dinner table, 'you feel like practising for that former ambition of yours?'

'My what?' Kat blushed. 'Oh, that. Yes, I think possibly a little practice would be a most excellent idea.'

His hand was warm in hers as she rose from the table.

Chapter 25

VIOLA

SYDNEY

Viola stood as Alice lowered the dress over her corset and petticoats and began to lace it. Alice had taken Smiggins' place as lady's maid but continued to use her first name '... because takin' me pa's name after all the years as Alice would be nothin' but botheration, begging your ladyship's pardon'. So Alice she remained, despite Mrs Higgins' disapproval.

Today's was a morning dress, not a walking dress, for Viola had no wish to tread again down the familiar streets of shops or public gardens. To be sure, the views of the harbour were invariably delightful and always slightly different, the water grey or blue or turquoise, the flocks of birds colourful, the trees free from the clouds of anonymous little sparrows so common back in England. But even a simple walk meant being followed by a pair of footmen to guard her against the criminals of Sydney.

In her year in Sydney Viola had dined, partied and soireed more than she had believed possible. The chance to entertain a genuine 'Lady' and sister of a duke meant more to colonial Sydney than the colour of her skin. It seemed Sydney society had decided to pretend her brownness didn't exist. Sometimes Viola felt that she existed to them only as her title.

She had also paid her membership of the public library and

attended fourteen plays and several operas and entertainments at the Victoria Theatre. She had arranged for a local dressmaker, recommended at a dinner, to liaise with Madame Fleurette in London. Madame would continue to design, create and consign Viola's more important dresses, shoes, slippers, hats and all else necessary, using the 'shape' that all good dressmakers kept so their clients need only have final fittings for their gowns — and that could be done here in Sydney.

Madame would be notified of any alteration to her figure; and Viola need not worry about changes in fashion. Dresses, pelisses, fichus, mantles and basques would arrive, and she would wear them. It had never occurred to her, who had been so well attended, to have her own taste in clothing. But with her clothes provided for, and Major Nash's house so impeccably furnished, there was little pleasure in shopping except for gifts for Titania or Kat, no matter how exquisite the shops in parts of George Street might be to one of good taste and means.

And this morning? Mr Hastings and his mother had offered to escort her to a vantage point where they might see the ships coming through the Heads. The last of the convict ships was due to arrive, surely a most historic event, though one Viola had no wish to see, and had refused the invitation. The sight of the poor chained wretches laying cobbles hacked from the quarries was only bearable knowing their slavery would end with their sentence or, as Cousin Lionel had explained, an even earlier 'ticket of leave'.

Even worse had been the 'famine ship' from Ireland she had watched unload last month — its frail remaining living cargo at last released from steerage where some had managed to survive while the more affluent passengers tried to ignore the smell of death and the bodies tipped overboard at dawn, to inconvenience their enjoyment of the decks as little as possible.

A maid — Millie — curtseyed at the doorway. 'Master asked if you would take a luncheon with him today, my lady.'

Viola smiled at her. 'Of course.'

This was how women of her class — women, at least, with the correct skin tones — occupied their days. They dressed for one meal, and then for another, or for walking, sleeping, for entertaining others or being entertained.

Titania glowed with the growing success of her business. Kat's letters proudly described their shipments of fat lambs to market, the excellence of the fleeces, the strange velvet-nosed creature like an enormous hedgehog that had taken up residence in her new herbaceous borders and was consuming the ants there, as well as the measures she had taken, so far unsuccessfully, against the wallabies that consumed every single rose bush, except the ramblers that had been protected by stout fences until they grew too tall for the wallabies to reach.

But Viola had no wish to design a garden, much less be a farmer or a proprietor of any business. She had rarely even handled money — the only time she had kept coins on her person had been on the journey here. The gold guineas in her trunk in the attic had remained there, as unused as she herself had no true purpose. If a beggar appealed to her she smiled at the footman to give him a coin, which her guardian would repay, as he paid the dressmaker, the milliner, the subscription library, the box at the theatre and all other bills, for even in the colony no shop of worth or even stallholder would expect an aristocrat to pay on the spot. Any goods she selected were delivered to the house, and the account settled there.

Nor did she envy Kat her country life. Viola had lived most of her life on an estate with a home farm attached. She knew how milk arrived in the pail but had no interest in getting it there herself. She enjoyed white lambs bounding onto rocks in spring but didn't want a closer acquaintance. Life lacked ...

She did not know what it lacked.

She sat still so Alice could arrange her hair.

Luncheon was set out informally in the morning room: it was a meal men rarely indulged in and so did not need the formality of a dining room. Cold chicken, sliced and jointed, sat on its platter on the sideboard, along with a cold beef sirloin, a ham, and always bowls of the abundant fresh fruit of this country, even at this season, oranges and tangerines, the last of the winter apples, the first of the strawberries, even a pineapple sent down from the Queensland colony perhaps, or from Cape Town, grapes kept over winter in tubs of bran down in the cellar, which as quasi-mistress of this house she had, of course, inspected, giving smiling approval to all the housekeeper's deeds and plans.

Cousin Lionel stood as she came into the room. 'Good afternoon, my dear. You look beautiful.'

Words that had been said to her most days of her life, polite but meaningless, at least applied to her small self, to which she replied as always, 'Thank you,' as the footman held her chair out for her. She sat and accepted a slice of chicken as the footman offered the platter.

'I have received an offer for your hand,' Cousin Lionel said casually, helping himself to mustard for his ham.

Her eyes widened. 'Really?'

'Are your affections engaged?'

'Of course not, sir.' She laughed. 'I fear I don't even know which gentleman it might be.'

So her brother had been correct. Here, where civilisation perched on the edge of a vast continent, across the world from every family who mattered, a respectable marriage and married life were possible — assuming the petitioner was eligible. But if not, she was sure Cousin Lionel would neither have wasted time with him nor mentioned the offer to her at all.

He raised an eyebrow. 'You're not going to ask who it was?'

'I would prefer not to know, sir. Any man who made an offer after such small acquaintance that I can't even guess his name must be solely attracted by my fortune, or even title. It would embarrass me when I met him again to know you have refused him permission to make his addresses.'

'How do you know I refused?'

She looked at him, surprised. 'Because you are a man of sense, and experience, and extremely kind to me, Cousin Lionel.' Nor had he ever shown more than the slightest embarrassment introducing his dark-skinned ward to newcomers. 'You make me feel most welcome, not an imposition!'

If the other end of the table had been closer, he might have taken her hand. 'Never that, my dear. You light the house.'

'I'm glad, for I have no wish to leave it, nor to think of marriage yet, till I know the colony and its society and ... and myself, sir. I know too well how little I have seen of the world, beyond the walls of Shallowford Abbey. I may never marry, and certainly not until I reach my majority, if that is not too long to trespass on your care.'

'It could never be that. I hope you are still finding the colony interesting.'

She smiled. 'Of course, Cousin Lionel. You have been so assiduous in entertaining me.'

She ate a little of the chicken, and crumbled a bread roll, then glanced up at him again 'You will soon have a break from care of me though. Mrs Markham has invited me to visit her and her husband. It will be fascinating to see more of the country. Her descriptions of the valley are most vivid.'

Cousin Lionel carefully speared ham onto his fork. 'Ah, Mrs Markham.'

Cousin Lionel did not approve of Kat. Had he resented a guest thrust upon him, despite his welcome? Kat's free manners? If he had heard of the tragedy of Kat's family he had never mentioned it. Or was it Kat's hasty wedding?

'I would like to give Kat a proper wedding breakfast when they next come to Sydney,' she said carefully, waiting to see his reaction.

He nodded politely. 'That would certainly introduce them to society. Markham is of excellent family, it seems. It's a pity he has not thought to establish himself properly here.'

As Cousin Lionel had not either, despite his many years in the colony. Viola had slowly noticed that the invitations they received came from those attracted to her title, all of them from hostesses who were not previously acquainted with her guardian. She knew the major had lost money in the colony's long drought, but that should not have barred him from the acquaintanceships he'd made before. She thought, perhaps, they might mostly be male, given his army career, even if he had sold his commission when the regiment returned to England. Single men rarely gave the kind of entertainments a lady would attend.

'I think this is probably not the best time to take even a short voyage down the coast ...' His pleasant face grew sombre. 'You have heard of the latest ship from Ireland?'

'I saw some of the poor souls disembark last week. I wondered if I might join one of the charities that waited to assist them. I gather the colony has many such.'

His face gentled. 'You have a heart of gold, dear child.' No, she thought. I have a fortune and a gilded family crest, far more significant to all except Kat and Titania, and — perhaps — to you. 'I am more concerned that the ship may have brought typhoid, despite all quarantine precautions.'

Titania lived so near the waterfront. She would be most vulnerable to contagion ...

'I think it best if we remove to my property on the Hawkesbury for a few months, till the worst of summer's heat and the disease risk are over. I know you will miss your social life, but you will like the river, I think, and there are several families to dine with.'

'It sounds delightful,' she murmured and accepted a tangerine. She must write to Kat to say there would be no visit in the next few months. But Cousin Lionel hadn't forbidden it. So far he had refused her nothing that she had asked for, not even querying the dressmaker's bill that he must guess covered garments made for Titania as well, and the crystal glassware that had been her wedding gift to Kat.

And this afternoon she would call Mrs Higgins to her sitting room. Mrs Higgins would know how best to keep watch on Titania, so that if she sickened a doctor and nurses would immediately be sent for, and a message to the Hawkesbury too so Viola could nurse her. Her mother's long illness had prepared her for that.

But with so much work just now to establish Titania's business Viola would otherwise only be a nuisance, at best a distraction from the necessary mixing of puddings or chopping of vegetables for sauerkraut.

The Hawkesbury would no doubt be delightful, just as Cousin Lionel had said, and the journey there interesting. She did not even consider whether her carriage would be well sprung too; her journey would inevitably be accompanied by suitable picnic baskets, tea brewed on spirit lamps, and lemonade packed in ice, for she'd had such comforts all her life, except for during the inevitable rigours of the voyage on the *Salamanca*.

Those months, with its tide of stars above and friendships in a small stale cabin, had been the richest she had known.

Chapter 26

TITANIA

SYDNEY, 1851

Years later Titania remembered the exact moment the news stampeded through the docklands: ten minutes to twelve, far enough from breakfast to have her thinking hopefully about the mutton pie she'd kept aside from the last batch, and for Quartermaster Jenkins to have gratefully accepted two of the oat biscuits she had offered him with the traditional tot of rum to seal a deal.

It was as if a wave of chatter passed — men ran, and all work stopped behind them. Wheelwrights stopped hammering; blacksmiths stopped beating; and even the cries of 'Oysters! Fresh oysters!' vanished as the babble spread down the wharf. She watched it all through what was possibly the only clean window in the district.

'Excuse me, Mr Jenkins.' Titania pulled the bell for Porter. He loped into her office, as tall and broad shouldered as the ancestor who had won the family name.

'Yes, mum?'

'What's the commotion outside?'

'You ain't heard?' Porter said it as though the world must know the news already, even though it had been ten minutes at most since it reached the docks. 'There's a fortune in gold over the mountains, mum! A Mr Hargraves found so much in one morning he filled his saddlebags with it. They say Mr Hargraves made a fortune on the Californian fields and came back 'cause he saw we had the same kind o' rock out here. He galloped straight from Sydney to Bathurst without stopping once and there wuz the gold, just waiting to be found.'

'Hargraves!' Mr Jenkins laughed. 'Big hefty chap, got an arse like a pair of puddings? Begging your pardon, Mrs Boot.'

'They say he's a mighty big man, sir,' agreed Porter. 'Has to be to carry all that gold.'

'I know him,' said Mr Jenkins dismissively. 'He shipped back to the colony with us — and in steerage too. Made a fortune my sweet ... I mean, stuff and nonsense. The man had led a group to California promising to find them gold and instead he lost every penny. The man's a trickster. It'll be naught but stones covered in gold paint.'

'But Mr Hargraves took the gold to the Treasury! They took it, too. The men there should know if it's gold or not. He's asking the gov'ment for a reward.'

'Ah, that's the con job then: the reward. Happen Hargraves got himself a few grains and hopes to trick the government into paying him for his so-called discovery. Mark my words, there's nothing in it.'

Titania gazed out the window again. The hammers were still silent. Even the men repairing a high mast had monkeyed down. Men stood in small huddles, arguing, gesturing, excited.

It is like a fever, she thought, spreading faster than typhoid, and like typhoid, would soon burn itself out and the hammers would sound again.

She set herself to the task of persuading Mr Jenkins that a few barrels more of sauerkraut and lime juice for the crew would pay for itself, as a ship needed fewer men when you could be sure they wouldn't sicken with the scurvy. It was an easier task than she expected. Mr Jenkins would probably have agreed to supply the crew with pickled elephant so he could head out to join in the golden gossip.

Titania brewed herself a dish of tea, unwrapped her mutton pie, accompanied it with bread, cheese and pickled onions, and sat back in her chair to allow herself a few moments' to enjoy them. It had been a good morning's work. It had also been a good year, too busy to be eventful beyond the small triumph of adding yet another quartermaster to her customers, another farm, or wheelwright to her suppliers.

She had scarcely seen Viola, for Major Nash had kept her mostly down on the Hawkesbury, for fear of the typhoid, and her visits back to Sydney had been too filled with social engagements to allow more than visits in the short periods between the end of Titania's work day and whatever invitation to a dinner or musical evening Major Nash had accepted for them. Even on Sundays he shepherded Viola to an acquaintance's family pew, to which Titania had not received an invitation.

Viola seemed content, but Titania was concerned that despite the fresh air of the river she didn't have the bloom of the months on the *Salamanca*, nor even her occasional looks of deep joy that Titania had glimpsed as she gazed at what to Titania seemed to be far too slowly changing sea and sky.

Titania frowned. She had indeed made enquiries about the major. She had found nothing bad about him. But there had been ... hints.

'Left the regiment sudden like,' one of the carters told her. He'd been a private at the same time as the major.

'I thought he left because the regiment returned to England, and he preferred to stay here?'

'Nay, he left afore that. There was talk ...' the carter shrugged.

'Don't tell me he misappropriated funds!'

'Nah, nothing like that.' Was that a blush? 'Don't you worry about it missus. Just talk.'

Titania worried. It sounded suspiciously as if Major Nash had been asked to leave his post, to avoid disgrace to the regiment as well as to himself. There were many other peccadilloes besides making off with the mess funds: cheating at cards, or even having an affair with the colonel's wife. But the former would have made him unacceptable in Sydney society, the latter a joke, to all except perhaps the colonel and his lady. What could have been serious enough for him to be asked to leave — if indeed he had — but without charge or public humiliation?

But there was nothing she could do about it, beyond tactfully questioning, and not too often, least her enquiries be reported to the major, and he became even less amenable to her visits with Viola.

Kat, on the other hand, she did not worry about at all. The shipments of wool and fat lambs from Rainbow's End spoke to her business mind and a prospering estate. There was no stinting in the household orders, either — even the crockery for the workmen's cottages was good quality, and Kat had a permanent order for Titania to look out for Chinese 'ever laying' hens 'no matter what their cost'.

Kat was a poor correspondent. A monthly letter — and scrawled in a poor hand, too — was the best that could be expected, despite Titania's dutiful weekly missives, even if there was not much more than the weather to write about. Viola's letters from the Hawkesbury were more likely to include poems or passages from books that she thought her friends might enjoy, usually of the kind that Titania regarded as 'improving'.

Kat's infrequent letters were far more fun: 'Digger' the wombat had decided to undermine the front step. Every day Zebediah had the hole filled with rocks, and every night Digger removed them, till eventually Zebediah had conceded defeat, and moved the steps slightly to the left, so that everyone had to walk in a diagonal to the front door.

Titania wondered why Zebediah didn't just take his shotgun to the animal. But there was no doubt that Kat's household found the battle hilarious, nor any doubt at all that Kat was happy.

The colony itself was thriving, just as she had expected it would after the long period of drought. Rain delivered itself at the right times and intervals, and despite the ships of skeletal wretches from starving Ireland — and much of England not much better, with almost no sunlight for harvest — most of the outbreaks of typhus and other diseases had been confined to their ships, and only rarely spread to the docks area or beyond.

Transportation was ending, free emigration increasing — including growing numbers of single women sent out by charitable institutions to civilise a colony where men so outnumbered females, and with the withdrawal of convict labour, jobs enough for anyone who could stay off the rum long enough to work, even if only oakum picking for the less able. Titania finished the last of her pie and bit into a pickled onion. The colony had no need to dream of gold. The glitter of Hargraves' claim would surely fade.

Chapter 27

VIOLA

Mrs Higgins stood at the door of the drawing room, where Viola was reading a most interesting work by the ancient philosopher Epicurus. No governess had thought philosophy suitable for a girl, but luckily the Abbey library had been well stocked with classics, even if it appeared the books had been bought in bulk, and never read until Viola opened them. This, however, had been found at the Subscription library.

Mrs Higgins looked at the young woman indulgently, as she raised her head from her curtsey. That was the Quality for you, a pretty girl wasting her day reading. 'Ahem, I don't want to disturb you, your ladyship …'

'Of course you're not, Mrs Higgins.'

'Could you have a word with young Blackhill? The silly fool is packing his bags to go out to Bathurst after gold and not even waiting out his notice. Says he doesn't need his wages as they're walking on gold out there. He thinks the world of you, your ladyship,' added Mrs Higgins, 'ever since you noticed he was in pain with that carbuncle and called the surgeon. He won't pay any attention to us.'

Viola reached for a bookmark and put her volume down on the side table. Blackhill was the youngest of the footmen, one of the men who rode behind her carriage, let down the steps and opened the door for her. His life consisted mostly of waiting — waiting for the carriage to stop, waiting for her to emerge from the lending library or the ball and the carriage to roll again, waiting for her to send a message asking an acquaintance (she did not call them friends) to dine. No wonder the young man wished for adventure.

But the governor himself had assured Viola only two evenings earlier that what he called 'this gold nonsense' would soon end. Gold belonged to the Crown, not to those who dug it up. Indeed, Mr Hargraves' 'discovery' was no such thing, for many had long known of the gold's existence. The government was not going to license gold digging, His Excellency declared, not with insufficient official surveyors or magistrates to police the lands beyond the towns already.

She smiled at Mrs Higgins. 'Of course I will speak to him.' And reassure the young man that his position would be waiting for him when he returned, for she doubted anything she said could dull the lure of gold. She let Mrs Higgins open the green baize door that led to the servants' dining room.

But Blackhill had already gone.

Two more servants had left by the next morning, Mrs Higgins informed her. Their defection was disturbing, a small insanity that seemed to get larger every day. So many of the world's problems seemed to suddenly become vast like that, just as a small swell out at sea had grown into a wave towering over the ship. Indeed, it was just such a problem she wished to discuss with Cousin Lionel that morning.

Viola waited till Tilson had poured the coffee from the silver pot engraved with Mama's family crest, the sight of which always embarrassed her, for one did not engrave one's crest on new silver plate, though it might be inherited. Tilson quietly shut the doors of the breakfast room.

'Cousin Lionel, would it be possible for me to have an increase in my allowance?'

Cousin Lionel looked up from his kidneys and bacon. 'Of course, my dear. How much do you need?'

'As much as can be spared,' she said seriously.

She could see him trying not to smile. 'Oh dear, as bad as that? You haven't taken to penny whist, have you?'

Viola produced a smile. 'Of course not. It's not for myself. The tragic news from Ireland ... so many starving.'

'You wish to contribute to a charity? Very laudable, my dear. Shall we say ten pounds?'

She hesitated, unsure how to phrase her next questions. 'I thought my income might cover far more than that.'

'It does,' he said pleasantly. 'But that is why I am your trustee, to make sure your income isn't wasted.'

Only until I am twenty-one, she thought, and less than three years off now. 'This is a better cause than new dresses, sir.'

'Let me be the judge of that.'

'Cousin Lionel, you have been so generous with everything I might need or want. Surely I can give more than ten pounds?' No one had yet told her the extent of her fortune, though she had heard it described as 'immense' and herself described as 'extremely wealthy'.

He looked at her seriously. 'You know I happily pay whatever bills you incur for clothes or fripperies, even jewellery, but it would be betraying your mother's confidence in me to let you dispose of your funds to strangers.'

'Sir, what is my annual income?'

He laughed. 'Not for you to worry your head about. Let us just say you are wealthy enough never to have to worry about whatever you wish for.'

'I wish to give money to the Irish Appeal. Sir, they say small children lie curled up in the streets, starved to death.'

'Ah, your heart of gold is working overtime again. Your sentiment does you credit, but my dear, the poor are always with us.'

'I believe my heart to be of firmer metal than gold,' she said quietly. 'I do not speak from sentiment, Sir, but from knowledge that the present starvation is worse than any Europe has known.'

'Such a sweet child. Two hundred pounds then.' He said it so carelessly that she knew her estate was, indeed, so large that an amount that would pay the wages of six skilled men for a year mattered no more than a penny given to a boy to sweep the road before she alighted from her carriage.

'Thank you, Cousin Lionel,' she said quietly. 'May I pour you more coffee?'

Chapter 28

KAT

RAINBOW'S END

Kat sat by the lagoon on what was not grass, but which carpeted the ground with green except where tufts of daisies lifted yellow faces to the sun. Around her children brought her mussels they'd plucked up from the silt of the lagoon, quickly cooked in their shells by the fire; a hunk of roast duck; and berries of at least ten kinds. She had no idea what they were but ate them anyway, smiling when they were sweet, wrinkling her nose at bitterness, slightly puzzled when the fruit had little flavour.

The children thought her expressions as she tried the new foods hilarious. They stroked her dress, shrieked with laughter as she took off her boots then put them on again, then pulled at her plaits till she loosened her hair and cried in wonder yet again at its flame. A tiny girl giggled, grabbed her bonnet and raced off with it, chased by two small boys.

Definitely boys. A year or so back, Kat had found the natives' almost nakedness embarrassing. But she was used to her body and Zebediah's now. It was amazing how quickly a string of tools around the waist, or an o'possum skin wrap, seemed the only clothing necessary. They were certainly more sensible than corsets and crinolines.

The other children left too, chattering to each other, too fast for Kat to pick out any of the few words she knew of their language. She glanced around at the other women. They seemed as amused as the children by the ludicrous garments and ignorance of a white woman. One young woman fed an elderly man and woman a paste of grubs and fat — Kat had watched it being made. Two even older women wrapped in o'possum skins dozed in the shelter of sheets of bark that kept off the wind and reflected the heat of the small fire, where three ducks slowly roasted on spits above the coals, their fat sparking now and then.

A small whirlwind of children raced back again, scattering more wood on the fire. Three young women wandered up from lower down the valley, carrying string bags of grass seeds that Kat had seen ground to an oily flour and baked into paper-like bread on hot rocks. Apart from the old ones being fed, the men were elsewhere, as men so often were, presumably hunting or making spears or whatever else men did.

Which reminded her that Zebediah would want his own dinner, and even though she had put it all in train before she wandered down here, there was at least another two hours' work to finish it. She spent a second's envy of life at the camp: no hours tending the stove to exactly the right temperature for bread or roast mutton; no days spent polishing floors and furniture and silverware — all the necessities of life in an hour or two a day, and that more fun than work.

On the other hand, she loved her stove and the scent of polish, the feel of carved wood as she sat at the table, the softness of her bed and the security of walls and roof from the rain that she suspected would fall tonight: the air hung hot and still over the valley in a way she had learned meant moisture would gather into cloud.

She stood and brushed leaves from her skirt, and decided to forget about the bonnet. It might turn up on the doorstep tomorrow, or it might not. She turned to the nearest woman whose name she had still not quite caught, for the natives seemed to use sounds she couldn't even hear though they laughed patiently when she'd tried to use these words, and then promptly forgot the little she had not quite learned. 'Goodbye. Thank you so much for having me. It has been quite delightful.'

The woman laughed, and Kat laughed back. This language, at least, they had in common. The woman said something, or possibly many things, gesturing at the children, then down the valley, with a motion of her hands that suggested walking, which probably meant that in a day or two Kat would no longer find them there: according to Zebediah the natives spent the colder months down at the coast. He had met them there a couple of times on his way to Sydney.

Kat nodded, smiling, hoping it was the right response. She suspected the woman in front of her spoke some English and might even use it at the next corn harvest feast, when farm workers and natives plucked buttered corn cobs from the cauldrons cooked on the fires in the paddocks after the fields had been picked and the cobs husked.

But this camp was the woman's home. It was not unreasonable to expect that a guest in your home learn your language, even if Kat found it difficult, just as she'd been unable to learn the piano. Tone deaf, Mama had called her. Kat could finally remember that with no pain now that home awaited her up the valley.

It seemed the ship from Sydney had returned in her absence, the cart with their supplies winding up the track on the far side of the valley from the camp. Rainbow's End was bustling as men unloaded sacks and barrels and tea chests, tools wrapped in hessian, the bolts of calico Kat had ordered. All was stowed just as the first drops fell.

Kat damped down the stove and opened the oven door a crack. Dinner could wait. Instead, she settled on Zebediah's lap on the cushioned settee on the verandah, watching the pale wave sweep up the green valley: a vast curtain of water.

Down in the gully the ducks had settled back to the reedy edges of the lagoons, the eagles to their ledges and branches, the laughing jackass birds to the hollows, the wallabies to their crevices. Even the giant insects that shrilled so loudly that eventually your ears no longer heard them had gone silent. The workmen and their wives had retreated to the cottages and barracks. Only the sheep did nothing except stand mournfully staring at the ground, waiting for the wet affliction to pass.

The drops landed heavily on the shingled roof. Splat, splat, then drip. She could almost hear the fruit trees sigh and drink, the wilting leaves of lettuces and cabbages perking up to catch the rain. There is no scent as good as the fragrance of earth after rain, thought Kat.

The valley grew white, then slowly green again as the rain passed, leaving only the drops from trees and shingles. Then suddenly there was the rainbow — a perfect one from the far end of the valley to the house, so the colours striped the garden, shimmering red and gold and violet. They watched in silence for the moments before it faded, warming each other against the chill the rain had brought from the south-east. At last Kat said, 'Why is the rainbow always in the same place?'

'Maybe because the rain comes up the valley, and the sun in the afternoons is at exactly the right angle?' He laughed. 'I don't know.'

'Well, at least we know the leprechauns haven't left a pot of gold there,' said Kat practically. 'Or we'd have found it when the men planted the roses. I should take the mutton out of the oven.'

His hand stroked her back. 'Perhaps it's time we have proper servants, so you no longer have to cook the dinner.'

'I like cooking. And a proper servant would look out the window at us and be shocked.'

'A very proper servant would carefully not remark on what they'd seen master and mistress up to.'

'True. But it wouldn't be the same.'

This was peace: a partnership quite different from her father's adoration of and jealously guarded provision for his family. Zebediah worked and so did she, from sun-up to sunset, and then after dinner by lamplight too; she sewing, darning, he carving or sanding a new shelf or, just lately, the ribs for the cradle Kat suspected they would be needing. The hard work was more for the satisfaction of achievement than true need. But not every morning, nor every night.

And yes, they would need more servants, possibly soon, for after one child there'd be more. Plucking and roasting a pair of ducks for dinner for two was one thing, especially when the duck would stretch to a luncheon the next day and a ragout for dinner too. But with babies came napkins and schedules and extra scrubbing and more sheets to wash, and a social life as well if the children were not to grow up wild bush babes.

They would need to visit Sydney, and stay for weeks, not days, and make acquaintances who would come to visit, or 'send on' acquaintances of acquaintances from England in the time-honoured way of the aristocracy, who assumed they would be welcomed anywhere, especially if their hosts might need company, visitors who would probably never associate Mrs Zebediah Markham with the bankrupt suicide Fitzhubert. Visitors would mean beds made up and water carried and tea trays, and all that meant more servants. This, too, was why Zebediah had looked for a socially adept wife. When children came it would be time to join the world of ladies and gentlemen once more.

Zebediah had even accepted the position of magistrate last month, quite an honour, as he'd said, in a district with only four white men who were not convicts, ticket-of-leave men or emancipated, and him the only one of the four sober for more than two days a month. In ten years or twenty, though, the position would gain in importance, and their family and their estate would grow in dignity as well as size.

Kat found she didn't mind the thought at all. But for now ...

She bent her lips to his.

Long afterwards, lying on the bed, the sheet and quilt flung down, the single candle guttering, they talked, as they often did, not wanting the day to end.

'Are the men going to keep ringbarking past the big boulder?'

He glanced at her. 'I suppose so. You seem uncertain.'

'That's getting close to where the natives camp.'

'They have most of the rest of the valley to camp in.'

'I'm not sure they'd think so.' Somehow she had gained the impression that the place, as well as the timing, was important.

'We can ringbark the slope on the other side, down to Honey Gully, if you think it better.'

'Please.' She stroked the muscles of the arm nearest to her. The woop-woop pigeon called from the after-rain mist she could just see through the window, twisting through the gullies in the moonlight. Ben gave a single bark. Digger must have emerged to graze now the rain had stopped.

'What did your aunt's letter say?' he asked. They had both glanced at the mail as the wagon was unpacked, though, as always, such a pile of mail and papers needed several days to consume and discuss; and nor was there a hurry with any of it for by the time they heard news any urgency had long passed.

'Mary-Anne's wedding to Viscount Enderby is apparently still being spoken of as a triumph and Sarah is to have her coming-out next year if her spots have cleared, and Aunt Bertha tried a new hairstyle with ringlets on either side that takes an hour and a half with a curling iron to create.'

He did not even bother to ask if she regretted that life was no longer hers. Nor the ringlets. 'One of the newspapers had an interesting headline. I meant to tell you, but old Judders interrupted us with that snake he'd killed. Turns out that man Hampton, no, Hargraves, that was it, was no fraudster. There is really gold there. A thousand men have descended the mountain trail to Bathurst and thousands are following.'

She laughed. 'Thousands?'

'That's what the newspaper reported.'

'Thousands of men, all after gold. Hard to imagine.' She rolled over and let the sweetness of the breeze play on her body. 'I'm glad they're far away. The gold and Sarah's ball.'

He laughed, and bent to her again. 'They can't touch us here.'

Chapter 29

VIOLA

SYDNEY

'You look beautiful, my dear,' said Cousin Lionel. He said those exact words at least twice each day. Miraculously, he meant it, thought Viola, as he held out his arm to her as she descended the stairs. Cousin Lionel was one of the two people she had ever met who did not glance past her when he spoke to her, or quickly introduce her as 'Lady Viola' to excuse her brown skin. He genuinely did think that she was lovely, dark skin, childish figure and all.

She took his arm as she always did at least twice a day. Only the clothes varied. 'Thank you, Cousin Lionel.'

The second gong had gone for dinner and ... people ... were expected. Viola would remember their names in time to greet them, but how could you truly know people who only spoke in pleasantries, acceptabilities, and respectabilities? Viola suspected this was even more the case in the colony than England, as so many there — herself included — had at least a small cloud hanging over the reputations they left behind in England.

Only clouds of a certain kind, of course. A man like Mr Macarthur, before his sad illness, had been accepted despite his financial irregularities back in England. A man might even be in trade, as long as that trade only involved the acquiring and sale of properties, the produce of his estate, or the goods his agent acquired for him and then resold — and as long as that man had the ton not to mention money when asked to dine, unless perhaps his host had arranged a game of cards afterwards, or wished to exchange a bet on a horse or curricle race.

Having a title — as well as a fortune — might be enough to ensure her social acceptability even if she became apprenticed to a cobbler — if one would take on a female — when she became twenty-one. But that acceptability had not bought friendship, only invitations. Viola was offered coffee, gossip, and the careful display of new possessions, but not confidences. Viola didn't know if that was due to scandal, skin, or her own personality.

Nor did she mind. The values and the interests of those she met in society here were not hers. She had her books, her walks along the cliff or river, even if trailed by footmen. She had Titania and Kat as surety that friendship was possible for her. She had an entire life to create after her majority. Till then, she would play the game of 'ward' and 'hostess' with an ease that had been slowly growing since her arrival, thanks to the well-ordered home her guardian had prepared for her.

Tonight's evening dress was new, and low necked now that she had been officially presented to the governor at a ball. She had only met him at dinner parties previously, as well exchanged pleasantries after church.

The dress was pale yellow satin, heavily embossed, with puffed lace sleeves, and gold lace at the hem, as well as embroidered with pink and gold roses in a deep V from her waist. She had ordered it chiefly as an excuse to have Titania accompany her, so that she might order more of the fashionable outfits Titania needed as proprietor of a prospering business. Titania had assured her it was now a profitable one, more than covering the costs of its establishment, but Viola knew that her friend would use those profits to extend her warehouses rather than for her own adornment.

Major Nash paused on the stair below her. 'You are not wearing your new sapphire earrings?'

Viola flushed. 'No, sir. The pearls seemed more suitable for this dress.'

'I noticed them on the account that came in a few months back,' he added lightly, 'but I haven't seen you wear them. You decided you didn't like them?'

Her flush deepened. 'I gave them away,' she said honestly.

'To the Irish Appeal?'

'Yes, sir.' She had also given two-thirds of the sovereigns in the chest in the attic three months ago, transferring coins every few days in her reticule to give to the Appeal, keeping a third of them for her own security. Guilt had wracked her every night for a month, until she had transferred every single coin. How could one have wealth in an attic when children lay starved along the streets? And even that had not been enough. She waited for her guardian's reaction to her underhandedness.

But he just laughed and dropped a kiss lightly on the curls the hairdresser had created with hot tongs that afternoon. 'You are a sweet child.'

'I am not a child, Cousin Lionel,' she said quietly.

'No, my little girl? That just shows how young you are.'

She preceded him into the drawing room, realising he had not even bothered to insist that she not do the same again.

The dining table was long, and the evening would be longer, thought Viola, as she smiled attentively at the gentleman on her right, who had bought a horse, or bred a horse, or perhaps even sold a horse, and was enthusing about that animal and Arab horses in general. The polished wood shone under the chandeliers. The silver epergne, the filigreed celery holders, the embossed dishes of peaches that decorated the table gleamed even brighter. Cousin Lionel at the other end of the table seemed to be genuinely enjoying the conversation of his neighbour, a matron in puce.

Viola wondered what would happen at one of these occasions if she spoke of something that truly interested her. What do you think of Epicurus's view that the goal of human life is happiness through modest pleasures, Mr Tanqueray? Can one be truly happy knowing that one's comfort is based on slavery, as his was, just as this colony is built on convict labour?

What would the lady in puce say if after dinner Viola offered not just tea or coffee, but a suggestion that it was the starvation across Europe from poor harvests and unequal access to land to grow food that had led to the ever-growing hordes of the desperate heading to dreams of gold in Australia?

Her reverie was broken as the dining room door opened to reveal Tilson bearing the silver soup tureen, footmen like a row of liveried ducks in white gloves behind him. Viola watched as the lady in puce — Mrs Harrington, that was it — was served.

'Soup, your ladyship?' They dined à La Russe, of course, course after course with each guest selecting what they wished to eat as Tilson or the footmen offered it, though the more conservative in the colony still preferred à La Française, with the entire feast set out on the table before them at the same time.

'Thank you, Tilson.' Viola blinked at the soup. She had ordered crayfish soup for the meal tonight and, though this was undoubtedly crayfish, as she could see small shreds floating with the vermicelli, it was not the clear soup she had ordered.

Tilson's face was expressively expressionless. It remained so through the baked fish that should have been a lobster mousse and the jellied eels that followed — they were covered in a delicate curried aspic, to be sure, and decorated with watercress, but nonetheless they were plebeian eels. Then came spring chickens jointed and sautéed with a green sauce, instead of the more impressive roast baron of beef. Cousin Lionel glanced at the dish with brief annoyance. He was fond of beef, and even more of presenting vast portions of various animals on his table.

A fricassee of pheasant, bred on the Hawkesbury estate — they should have been roasted, the portions served on toast spread with pâté from their giblets; lettuce salad with cheese biscuits; a lemon sherbet instead of pineapple ice cream; a croque-en-bouche instead of Gâteau à la Antoinette, and poached peaches under an orange crème Chantilly instead of orange mousse. All dishes that could be prepared quickly, Viola realised. She might not be able to cook beyond leaf tea or blancmange for invalids, but ordering a menu required knowledge of the time that needed to be taken to procure ingredients and prepare them.

Tilson still did not meet her eyes.

She followed his example, continuing to talk of weather and wild fowl, listening to the minute description of her dinner partner's new horse, then giving the polite cough it had taken her months of being hostess to learn when she judged it time for each person to turn to speak to the person on their other side, rising after the grapes and fondants, the almonds and raisins, to leave the men to port and lead the ladies to the drawing room and tea tray.

'Don't you think so, Lady Viola?'

'I am sure Lady Viola agrees ...'

'Lady Viola said only last week that ...'

Did they all come just for the pleasure of using her title?

The evening at last drew to a close. She walked wearily to the staircase as Cousin Lionel farewelled the last guests, longing for the moment she was released from her corset, petticoats, hairpins, garters and heavy satin.

'Your ladyship!' Viola turned. It was Mrs Higgins, not Tilson, who had the courage to break the calamity, but Viola had guessed the news anyway.

'Monsieur Hugh has left our kitchen for the diggings?'

'Yes, your ladyship, and two of the kitchen maids with him. Two! Straight after we had our luncheon and the beef not even on the spit! I sent down to Mrs Boot straight away ...'

'Mrs Boot does not run an employment office!'

'No, your ladyship, but she can cook, and I didn't think an employment office could give us dinner by eight o'clock.'

'Titania cooked our meal! Is she still here? I hope she has stayed the night after all that labour.'

'No, your ladyship. She asked Tilson to have a chair called for her straight after taking the profiteroles out of the oven. I told her I could do the rest,' said Mrs Higgins stoutly. 'I might never have been a kitchen maid, your ladyship, but I've been in kitchens most of my life.'

'You are wonderful, Mrs Higgins!' A chair! How like Titania to not even ask for the carriage.

'My dear, what is the matter?' Cousin Lionel had farewelled the last of his friends, or Viola assumed the jovial men were bound in friendship.

'Monsieur Hugh has left for the diggings.'

'How unfortunate. But that explains the eels and the chickens. Thank you, Mrs Higgins, you may go.'

'I am so sorry the dinner was not as you wished, Cousin Lionel.'

'No matter at all, my dear. It was adequate, and no one noticed any deficiency.'

'That is two grooms, two kitchen maids, the boot boy and a footman lost to us in a month, as well as a French chef.'

'And at least half the men on the estate.' Major Nash seemed amused, not worried.

'Why didn't you tell me?'

'My dear, your happiness is my chief purpose in life. Why should you be harried with such worries? I have it all in hand. Our household should be restored to full strength within the fortnight and by tomorrow, or next week at the latest, the deficiencies in our kitchen will be made good again.'

She looked at him with admiration carefully untinged by her mild annoyance that he continued to see her as a child. 'You are too good to me, sir. How shall this miracle happen?'

'The easiest way for miracles to occur. With money. One of the junior cooks at Government House will undoubtedly accept four times his present salary to work here. Possibly the senior cook might too, but His Excellency would notice we had purloined him. Mrs Higgins' wages have risen accordingly in the past week, as have those of all the staff who remain loyal — but those wages will not be paid until the end of each quarter, and only if the full quarter has been worked.'

'But if the servants must leave to tend to a sick relative, or are ill themselves ...'

'Then of course they shall have their due wages. I also sent a message to your friend Mrs Boot last week, asking her to make a similar offer to the new immigrants flooding through the port. Some, at least, must have knowledge of house or farm work and may prefer the certainty of a generous wage to dreams of gold.' Cousin Lionel shrugged. 'Already would-be miners are trickling back, starving, ill, complaining they could not pan enough to pay for bread, much less dine on the venison and jellies they expected. I believe the labour shortage will be short lived.'

He bent and kissed her forehead. 'Sleep well, my dear. It was a most enjoyable evening.' He waited till she had begun to ascend the stairs before he followed her.

I must visit Titania tomorrow to thank her, Viola thought. She would take roses, from the rose gardens at the estate, grown from the stock imported by Mrs Macarthur. Cousin Lionel had fresh flowers sent up by the night coach weekly. Titania loved flowers and too rarely saw them.

Viola made a vow to make sure that Titania too received flowers every week, enough for her office near the waterfront and her cottage too. She had realised something tonight. The sharpest pang this evening had come from knowing Titania had been here all evening, and yet Viola hadn't seen her.

She needed a larger portion of friendship in her life.

Chapter 30

VIOLA

Cousin Lionel's carriage conveyed her to the warehouse, though Viola recognised one of the gardeners as the driver, and his son Billy in the too-large footman's livery as her guardian groom today.

There was no need to lift her skirts above the muck outside Boot and Anderson. The road there was swept several times a day, and was clean today, despite the labour shortage. Billy opened the carriage door for her, and then the warehouse door, bowing each time, a trifle jerkily.

'Well done, Billy,' she said softly, pressing a shilling into his hand. She had asked her guardian for the coins that morning in case no footman was available to dispense them. Indeed, it was unlikely Billy had been provided with money as well as uniform, for he was not old enough or large enough to defend her property. But such a willing lad ...

'Viola, love! You are looking prettier than ever.' Titania stood and came around her desk. She took the roses with deep pleasure, sniffed their fragrance, then to embrace her.

'And you, too. You seem thriving.' A careful compliment, for Titania had drawn her hair back in a style that did not suit her, and looked as if it might have been weeks since she last laughed, but her business certainly seemed to be going well. 'I came to give you my most profound thanks for rescuing us last night, but thought you might be too busy to see me.'

'"Too busy" would mean "too disorganised". All is well in hand.'

Of course it is, thought Viola. Mr Anderson's name might still be on the letterhead, but his role these days was still no more than roper, the job that suited him well, though as his son was now a schoolboy it seemed unlikely he'd follow his father in the declining trade.

Six clerks now worked in the larger office outside — six before the gold rush and six still. The original warehouse space was five times what it had been before, including a covered courtyard for the bulk of the cooking, leaving Titania's cottage purely as a dwelling space. Viola assumed Titania could afford far better accommodation by now, but she said she liked the neighbours on either side of her, including the Scarlet Woman, and found the alley as quiet at night as Sydney allowed.

To think that four years earlier she had not met Titania, nor Kat, and had no knowledge of what a Scarlet Woman might be, she reflected as Titania led her to the well-cushioned sofa in her office.

The familiar spirit lamp stood on the much-embellished sideboard, as did the water jug, kettle, teapot and all the other appurtenances Viola had grown so attached to on the voyage. Even the jar of oat biscuits seemed the same. She took one with pleasure. 'Thank you. Breakfast was ... slight.' And might be so tomorrow too — even if the chef from Government House arrived, he would not condescend to breakfast dishes.

'You will breakfast well tomorrow. I sent a Mrs Goodwin up to your house a half-hour ago. You must have passed her chair on the way. She calls herself "a good plain cook", but I invited her to stay with me for a couple of days. She didn't touch a drop of gin or rum in all that time, I'll warrant, and her apple pie is the best I've tasted.' Titania arranged the roses in a Chinese vase as she waited for the kettle to boil.

Mrs Goodwin also sounded unlikely then to complain about being undercook to the personage from Government House. 'I cannot thank you enough.'

Titania flushed. 'What else are friends for?' She transferred the water into the pot, turned it three times, then poured it, weak and fresh, just as Viola liked it. 'Viola, I have meant to speak to you about a matter of ... of delicacy. I'm afraid I am not good at delicacy.'

Viola looked at her, puzzled. 'You know you do not have to curb your words with me.'

'It's Major Nash. He's using your gelt to feather his own nest,' said Titania bluntly.

'Is that all? May I have another biscuit?'

Titania passed her the jar. 'You don't mind?'

'Why should I? I have always assumed that he must do so, for I knew he wasn't plump in the pocket when my mother appointed him as default guardian. Keeping an establishment for me must be far more costly than one for a single gentleman.'

'The word I'm hearing is that he was in financial trouble before he became your guardian.'

'I thought that might be the case. Why else should he accept me as his ward, knowing what he did about me? He isn't in debt now?'

'Not that I've heard. Just lavish.'

'He lavishes quite a lot of money on me.'

'Viola, you don't understand. He bought the house and the estate in his own name, but with your income, or at least made the down payment, for both are mortgaged.'

'Titania, darling, I do understand, and I truly do not care. Cousin Lionel can't touch my capital, and has no say in its management. He is my guardian, not my trustee. He only has access to my income, nor am I liable for his debts.'

'I didn't know that,' said Titania, looking relieved. 'Nor that you knew, either.'

'I may look like a child,' said Viola gently. 'But I am not one. My mother made sure I knew about the terms of my inheritance — it is unusual, after all, to have a trust and title passed down the female line. A large part of my income comes from the lands linked to the title, and those can only be sold with my permission, after I am of age, as well as the permission of any female heirs I might have at the time.'

'Someone could forge your signature.'

'Not until I am twenty-one, and not until I have formally taken possession of each property in my estate.' She sighed. 'I suspect it will be a long process. The senior partner of my mother's firm of solicitors will travel to Sydney purely to fulfil that duty.'

'How much are you worth?' asked Titania bluntly.

'In total? I have no idea, nor can I demand an answer till I am twenty-one, though I suspect my income is at least ten thousand pounds a year. I asked Mr Barren for more details — he is the senior partner, and I have known him all my life — but he just laughed, and told me not to worry about my estates till my majority, and he was sure by then I'd have a husband who would take the burden from me. But he did assure me that if I was unhappy with Cousin Lionel, I could ask to have my wardship transferred, either to another suitable person, or even to become a ward of court.' Viola shrugged. 'Cousin Lionel attends to my every wish,' she met Titania's eye, and smiled. 'And my friends are in the colony, so I would rather be here than England.'

'You don't mind that he has put the properties in his name?'

'He's welcome to them. And yes, if he is in difficulty paying his mortgages after he no longer has my income, I will help him with them. It's a just reward for his care and the ... restraints ... that must be placed on his life, having his ward live with him.' Viola didn't mention she was even more grateful to have a guardian who liked her. 'Cousin Lionel does not even look for a wife. I suspect he won't, till I'm out of his care, and that is kind of him too. I own, it would be uncomfortable to take a subordinate position after having the household for my own. Besides, in less than two years I will become independent, though I hope he will allow the current arrangement to stand until I find what I'd like to do with my life. If I ever do,' she added.

She was no closer to that than she had been on the ship. She only knew what she did not want. Viola wept for the starving in Ireland and gave most of her allowance to charity too, but she felt no call to work for the poor. Small, and with no skills — how could she help, except with money? A university course of study in philosophy or theology would be interesting, but closed to a female, no matter how wealthy. But she was also tired of being confined to rooms, and rules ...

'Perhaps the major hopes to marry you.'

'He thinks of me as a child. Perhaps he always will. Besides, I have told him that I will probably never marry. At my age I should have felt some attachment if I were ever going to.'

'I'm glad of that,' said Titania slowly. 'There's gossip about him, you know.'

'Gossip I should know?'

'I'm not sure,' Titania admitted. 'Word on the wharves is he was asked to leave the regiment before he sold out, but I can't find out why.'

'Possibly he couldn't pay his debts because he'd lost his money,' said Viola pragmatically.

'He shouldn't have run up debts then.'

'Titania, I can only judge what I see, not what others say. Sometimes I think the colony's only occupation is gossip. Everyone is touched by it, whether the stories are true or not.' She smiled. 'It was probably the same in England, but I never had to listen to it before.'

'You're maybe right,' said Titania slowly. 'As long as you're sure he can't touch your capital, and that you won't want to marry him. A girl needs to know more than her marriage settlement before she weds, in my opinion. You really never have felt any ... attraction ... to a man?'

'None, not even to a handsome dancing master or the most dashing of the Governor's aides de camp. I have loved people, of course, but that is not the same; nor is any person I love someone I would marry.' Viola looked at Titania consideringly. 'I am not sure who I am, you see. I think — I am almost sure — that until I know that I will not find the kind of love that says, "Live with me all of my life."'

'Then you don't intend to always live with Major Nash?'

'Of course not.' Did she see a flicker of relief on Titania's face 'Though it would be convenient to keep staying in his house while I become familiar with my income, and the responsibilities that come with spending it. Do you know, I have never yet paid a bill!'

'May I ask a favour?' said Titania gruffly.

'Of course!'

'Take me with you when you see this solicitor chap, and if you need help after that, ask me, not the major. Don't let him come within a whisker length of any of your sources of income.' Titania considered a moment, then added 'And make sure he knows that I'll be involved, too, just in case he's making plans that involve your money after you come of age, the kind of plans that might lead him into debt again. I may be a woman, but I know more of investments and contracts than a thousand Major Nashes.'

'I'm happy to promise that. I'm grateful, too, as long as you won't try to persuade me not to make Cousin Lionel an allowance. He is going to need one, and I can well afford it. Don't try to stop me giving to those who need the money far more than I, either.'

'I'll support whatever you want, as long as it's what you truly want,' said Titania slowly. 'But I'll be glad when you leave the major's care, and that's a fact.'

'It would seem ungracious to leave him on the day I turn twenty-one. But in a year or so I think, perhaps, I might travel.' The grin that had not been used for many months peeped out. 'I will need to find another chaperone though, as Mrs Boot is so gainfully employed. But any voyage from here will be long, and not undertaken lightly. I'm content to wait until ...' She laughed. 'Shall we just say ... until.'

'If this were a novel you'd fall in love with a handsome captain at the next ball and marry him on your twenty-first birthday. But it ain't.' Titania regarded her thoughtfully. 'Nor do I think you will, either.'

'Exactly. You are happy in a single life. You are, aren't you?'

The worry left Titania's eyes. 'Extremely happy.'

'There you are then.' Viola watched her friend for a moment. Titania worked hard to make her business profitable, but she did not think she did it because she loved money, but for her joy in industry and organising the world and being independent. Could Titania perhaps understand?

'Sometimes — often — I wish I had no fortune,' Viola said slowly. 'You know the passage in the Bible, where Jesus says it is easier for a camel to slip through a needle than a rich man to get to Heaven? Do you think that might mean being rich condemns one in life, too?'

Titania stared at her, saying nothing, but not objecting either. Viola continued with more confidence. 'I don't just mean that being rich condemns one to a life of changing dresses, and inanity. It means you need to protect your investments, to ... to have to think about money far too much, at the cost of thinking of things that matter more. Money isn't interesting at all.'

'You've never been poor,' said Titania bluntly. 'The poor have to think about where their next scrap of bread comes from, and that ain't interesting either.'

'I know that. But please — understand why I truly don't care if Cousin Lionel or anyone else helps themselves to some of my income. Perhaps money is like water — we need enough to stay alive, but if we have too much, we drown in it. I need enough, that's all.' She smiled. 'But if you ask me what "enough" is, I can't answer, because until I know what life I want I don't know what I need for it. I do know it won't be the kind of riches I have now. I need to see more of the world than the Abbey and Sydney to do that. Does that sound too idiotish?'

'Sounds like uncommon sense to me,' said Titania. 'Enough seems about right for everything, and not just money.' She winked. 'Though I don't know that it's ever possible to have too many pickles.'

'Thank you.' Viola tried to smile back, and unexpectedly found herself near tears. She stood. 'I mustn't take any more of your time, nor will I waste my breath asking you to come to dine with us.' She forced the smile to emerge. 'You would find the conversation extremely boring, and poor Cousin Lionel would be so polite to you that you'd want to flee down to the harbour before the fish course. But when our kitchen is settled, I plan to descend on you with a picnic dinner.'

'I'd like that,' Titania admitted.

'Every week, perhaps?'

'I'd like that too.'

Viola closed her eyes briefly in sudden, deep pleasure. A friend one could say anything to. A friend who took you seriously, and not as a child, or one who must live up to the concept of 'lady'. She knocked lightly on the office window for Billy to escort her back into the carriage.

Chapter 31

KAT

RAINBOW'S END

It began with a single man down in the main valley. Kat did not know how long he had been there before she noticed him.

Men, white and black, often moved through this landscape. This man stayed focused on a small patch of earth at the far end of one of the lagoons.

Zebediah rode down to speak to him the next day, Ben at his heels. He returned two hours later and shrugged. 'Gone. But he has been digging.'

'Gold?' It was hard to say the word. The Ophir rush had spawned more, literal rushes of thousands or tens of thousands of people to wherever gold and its promise of wealth might be next. Ophir hadn't lived up to its promise, but the papers said the fern and lyrebird gullies the miners had left behind were now just mud and muck, worthless and hopeless too.

'I didn't see any gold.' Zebediah shrugged. 'Wouldn't know what to look for. He hasn't dug deep, just shifted the gravel in a dozen places.'

Two weeks later one man had become six, then three groups, then perhaps a dozen. It seemed there was gold to be found among the sand and gravel beds of the valley's streams, ignored as glittering uselessness by the natives, now enough — just —

to breed dreams of wealth based on gold. Eight weeks almost to the day a tide began to pour down from the tableland, men on horseback first, forging a road where there had been none from who knows where, then using the farm track down into the valley.

Men on foot humped swags, men with wheelbarrows, men dragged carts or sledges, the latter moving easily now that the track was mostly mud. A hundred that first day perhaps, swelling to uncounted plodding feet and eager hungry faces, sure that the few specks they'd found in their gold pans meant that a fortune lay below.

More men than trees, campfires outnumbering stars, then tents. Boats sailed upriver and then a track formed along its banks and cliffs: men and more men ...

'Can't we stop them somehow?' Kat pleaded, knowing the answer. Who could prevent a gold rush, a contagion, a vast dream? The government had tried to enforce the law that all gold belonged to the Crown, not to the person who found it, but had given in to public pressure. The law did not have the resources to prevail, and nor did the law try. This was hunt and take; winner take all and loser starve.

And the miners weren't even on Zebediah's land. Rainbow's End was soil over bedrock, not the sand and gravel washed down from some long-eroded reef. The land being panned and sieved and dug and washed was probably the Richardson's, but old man Richardson didn't own the minerals it held; nor were he, his sons or men at the huts that had been their homestead when Zebediah rode over to see if they needed help. The Richardsons too, it seemed had been swallowed by the rush, had abandoned their corn, presumably sold their cattle and begun to dig and pan.

Within a week every farm hand at Rainbow's End vanished, even the two with wives and cottages, those who'd not yet got their ticket of leave, all but young Summat Sam, who disappeared too, but returned battered and terrified two days later and would not speak of what had happened.

Mrs O'Connell stayed as well. She did not even seem to notice times had changed, but scrubbed and polished just as she had done for so many decades in the convent. She did avoid the verandah now, Kat noticed, and the old woman refused to look down the valley as she carried in pails of water up from the stream.

Their lower paddocks now ended in hillocks of dirt. A water race, dug into the ground with a rough bark viaduct to channel it across the gullies, carried off the water only two hundred yards down from the house. Zebediah could have removed it, but that would only have achieved enmity, and it would certainly have been replaced. Half the sheep were stolen in a week.

Zebediah and Kat rounded the remnant up and put them in the still fallow corn paddock. It was impossible to cut feed for that number, so they sold most of them for meat, for a hundred times what they'd have fetched a year before. There was no shortage of buyers, nor of thieves who would take what they couldn't buy.

The stench and the noise grew as thousands of ants toiled below them, and still the tide of men flowed over the ridges and even some women, too.

The morning they found the hens had vanished, Zebediah put it into words. 'Do you want to leave?'

'No,' said Kat.

'Are you sure?'

'If we leave they'll claim it all — everything you worked for: the house, the orchards, even the paddocks.'

'Are they worth staying for?'

'Yes.' Because she loved them. Because Zebediah loved them, had put his life towards them. Because she knew the answer her husband desperately wanted her to give. 'Maybe a new goldfield will open and they'll all move on again.'

'It depends how much gold is here,' said Zebediah steadily. 'I think it's a good field, love. There may be no nuggets, or seams of gold to be dug, but there must be specks enough in the sand. Men keep coming, but far more than are giving up.'

'Do you want to go?'

'No. But the two of us can't take on ten thousand miners, if they decide to take Rainbow's End.'

'We can try,' said Kat.

Chapter 32

KAT

They managed.

They even did well, if money — or specks of gold — hidden under the floor or in jars buried in the garden were the criterion. The household's silver, Kat's jewellery and all other valuables were buried too.

Miners needed food, and the wheelbarrows of groceries and barrels of flour rolled down the muddy slope to land against a newly erected wall of dirt weren't enough to feed the horde below, though few could afford even enough flour for damper. The valley that had fed so many families since the hills were young now gave nothing except tiny grains that might add up to a week's food — if you were lucky. Those who weren't lucky starved, and died of starvation or the diseases that filth and starvation breed, their bodies flung down abandoned mine shafts, according to the gossip of those who'd managed to scrape enough glitter to buy Kat's potatoes, or even the luxury of carrots or parsnips.

How many had died already? Kat wondered. She supposed no one would ever know, just as there was no way of guessing how many men scrabbled down there in the dirt. Even if this field never yielded a seam big enough for real riches, enough diggers made enough to keep the dream alive — and to buy food from anyone who had it to sell.

Zebediah sold most of their potato crop within a day, from a stand he erected at their front gate. Now there were only four to feed on the farm he sold most of last harvest's corn and pumpkins, too. But the vegetable gardens, the fruit crop, the supplies in their storeroom were a treasure now — a treasure that could keep you alive, when specks of gold could not, and envied by men who had forgotten laws and rules, even if they had once obeyed them. There was no one they could ask for help — the colony's police force couldn't even properly control Sydney. The single local representative of the law was Zebediah. They could not even buy guards, even if there had been any way to get a letter to Sydney to ask Titania to hire them. Any men willing to trek out here would be most likely to stay a night, to help themselves to what they could steal, then join the diggings in the morning.

Zebediah had a bed made up in the drawing room with the door to the verandah left open. Kat took the first watch, sitting with pistols and firing at anything that moved, and if it was a kangaruh then that would be gutted and its meat sold too. Zebediah relieved her at two am and caught a couple of hours sleep at six o'clock.

Her courses came again. She didn't know whether she had indeed been pregnant or they had been merely delayed. Had her body decided this was not the time to bring life into a world that was ravaged more each day?

Time seemed to have vanished, as if the confusion below had affected the universe about them too. Kat was not even sure of the week or month when she woke to a gunshot and ran out, pulling a shawl around her, feeling frost crisp on the grass under her bare feet. Zebediah bent over a twitching shape among the new crop of potato plants. 'Just a roo!' he called to her.

Roos did not eat potatoes. She walked towards him, pistol in hand.

'Kat, love, go back inside.'

'No.' She glanced at the shadows around them. 'I'll keep watch while you dig a grave. Best do it here.'

He was too tired to show incredulity. 'Why?'

'New digging won't be noticed among the potatoes. We can plant over him tomorrow.' She nudged the body with her toe. 'I'll just go and put my boots on. Was he alone?'

'I think so,' he said grimly.

She shrugged. That could be good or bad. Bad, if they were accused. But who would anyone complain to? The only magistrate in the district had fired the shot, and no court would convict a gentleman who had fired at an intruder. Better, perhaps, if their determination to keep what was theirs was known and understood by the hordes of newcomers.

She looked down at the dead man. No one she had seen before, but he had the shrunken shape of most convicts, reared on gin and crusts and smog instead of daylight. Impossible to tell more from just a face of whiskers and the usual drab and shapeless clothes he likely wore sewn onto him to stop anyone stealing his trousers when he was drunk.

A lost life, she thought, long before he lost it here.

She should feel pity, guilt. Instead, she just felt fury, and protectiveness of Zebediah, who had built so much and dreamed so far and had now seen it dug away from him within the swell and shrinking of a moon. Even the child she had thought she was carrying had proved to be an illusion.

One had to hope. Keep faith, that one day ...

What? She did not have the energy even to imagine what that miracle day might be.

'Go get the spade.' She began to watch the shadows, looking for those that did not fit their fields or garden.

He retreated to the shed. Before dawn they had buried the body deeper than a plough would pull.

Kat didn't know if the death was suspected. Possibly not, for men came and went both to and from the diggings and to other spots along the vast wombat diggings of men, and he didn't look like a fellow with friends. But within a fortnight it seemed the word went round the valley: don't approach the farm up on the mountain except by the proper track and only in daylight hours.

Was it a week later she heard sobbing in the night? It was her watch; Zebediah snored exhausted on his pallet. It was a woman's cry. Kat nonetheless took the musket as well as the candle when she went to the verandah to investigate.

Two women sat there in a slump that meant they could go no further tonight, the younger one's arms around the older, their wails soft as they gazed out at the gleams below that were not starlight reflected in the lagoons and never would be again.

She did not recognise them; nor did they greet her. Kat said nothing, just slipped to the kitchen and came out with bread and stew still warm, for she had reheated it for Zebediah before he slept. Meal times, too, had lost solidity. Food was now sustenance and not a celebration of the richness life could bring.

She put the food down a little way from the women and waited, afraid she might scare them further and cause them to run into the bush. But they knew bread, plates, spoons and stew. The wailing stopped. They knew chairs too, for they each sat on one and put the plates up on the table.

'My name is Mrs Kat Markham,' said Kat.

They didn't answer.

'Kat,' said Kat, pointing to herself. They kept on eating stew, but she thought they understood. At last, the stew finished as well as the loaf of bread, the younger woman looked at Kat.

'Why?' she asked.

At first Kat took it for a native word, even a name, then realised it was a question.

'Why do they look for gold?'

The girl nodded. The old woman kept her head bent.

'Because they hope to be rich.'

The girl made an impatient gesture, as if she understood that. 'Why gold? You cannot eat gold. You make no tools of gold, no guns. Why pay money just for gold?'

'I don't know,' said Kat honestly. The earrings Zebediah had given her were bound in gold. Some of her mother's jewellery had been gold, which had made it valuable enough to sell to pay the debts and help the servants. But she had felt no attachment to the metal in any of them. Their value came from the skill that went into their crafting, from the love with which they had been made, given and worn. Gold had a value simply because some people — many people — decided it had value.

And gold made some men rich quickly. But that still didn't explain the frantic squalor below. Any man in the colony could find land to squat on, make a hut of stringybark, grow vegetables enough to eat and buy some sheep, though admittedly many of the 'new chums' sailing in their thousands to Australian ports might not know that, or anything else about this land besides the fact that it had gold. The desperate and the starving had nothing but a few shreds of hope. Others had left good jobs for a barrel of dreams and a whisker of reality, the grains of gold among the mud and faeces and bodies rotting from days spent in muck and damp nights too.

'I don't know why it happened,' said Kat slowly. 'Gold is like an illness, maybe, that people catch.'

'Or a snake,' said the young woman softly. 'One that wriggles into them and eats their hearts.'

It was as good an explanation as any. 'Will you come inside?' The verandah could be seen from the road. The women should not be there in daylight.

The older woman said something in a long guttural speech. Kat recognised not a word of it and yet understood it all: a lament, a wondering, a deep pity for the madness of the newcomers to this country; a grief so deep she was in tears by the time the old woman sat silent.

The tears were for herself, too.

The women stood up, clearly about to go.

'No, please, stay here — I can hide you inside. Do you need food to take with you? Money?'

The young woman laughed. For the first time in the flickering candlelight Kat noticed that a cut below her eye had been bleeding. She moved as if her side hurt. And yet she laughed.

At the thought there might be safety indoors, or anywhere so near the seething tide of men? At the offer of food? The natives' usual diet was far better than Kat's own, in this rag-time of their lives. Did she laugh at the very concept of money? Or was it simply friendship?

The women left, darkness swallowing them the instant they left the small pool of candlelight that they clearly did not need to show their way.

Kat did not mention the visit to Zebediah or Mrs O'Connell. By daylight she even wondered if she had dreamed it, had eaten the stew herself, the loaf of bread.

She must begin to be careful how much flour she used now, for the river was so silted up it was no longer navigable. Zebediah had sold the *Rainbow*, for like all their possessions it was only theirs as long as it could be guarded, and they had no guards. They had not yet managed to send mail to Sydney to arrange for supplies to be sent overland.

Life became ... not normal. She could never accept this frantic scurrying rabbiting for what was mostly an illusion as a part of what humanity should be. But she added potato and pumpkin to the bread to make the flour go further. She grew used to starving faces, men more filth than skin, desperate men trying to find the strength to trudge away even as more slipped and slithered down the track that had appeared overland for those who could not afford the easier way by boat down the coast, and then along the rough track that followed the river.

The diggings stretched across the entire valley now. And still no nuggets had been found, nor any reef. Kat suspected they never would. The specks the early miners had panned up had been washed down when the hills were young, perhaps. The gold had spread where the lagoons seeped, and as men dug and poured and plundered sometimes a corner by a rock yielded enough to live on, or even buy a cottage if the finder had the sense to go while he still had strength instead of sinking his winnings into yet more digging.

The lagoons stank, shrank then became a swamp of mud with labouring muddy monsters who were men. Waterwheels and water races and mullock heaps grew like vast rock worms then disappeared, in case the rock within might carry gold.

The hills and then the lower mountain ridges grew sparse of trees, then bare, not because there was gold beyond where ancient floods had been, but because timber was needed for pit props as men dug into deeper sand and mud. Ringbarked trees were used for firewood — wood, any wood, might turn some cloth into a tent or rough shelter, and if you had no wood the stringybark might do as well. Fires needed wood, of course. At night the smoke rose up, green woodsmoke on fires lit by men who had never cut or ordered firewood in their lives, and did not know green from dry. Kat stared at the bare skull shapes that had been forest, but refused to cry.

It had been one month, two months, or much longer, since Kat had seen a bird, a wallaby, or a sky that wasn't dust or smoke. She fried up the last of what had been Her Pigship — she'd heard the pig shriek as her throat was cut and the lead from her musket had lodged in the leg of the miscreant who did it, but you did not bury a pig. You butchered it with Summat Sam, and had it cut up and the pork frying before your husband returned from a dispute he'd been called to, claim jumping or some such, for word had also gone around that he was a magistrate. There was little Zebediah could do in such cases but give an opinion, but it seemed the opinion was mostly followed.

He would mourn Her Pigship. Strange to grieve over a pig, amid so much desperation, but Kat found she cried for the pig, too, even as she cleaned her tubes and chopped her fat for sausages.

When she heard the steps on the verandah she thought it was Zebediah, returning, but instead there stood a black man, a native, not the black of a New Zealander or the dark-skinned crewmen on so many whalers who had jumped ship to join the rushes. The man was clad in clean trousers and shirt, barefoot, bare headed, beard and hair trimmed. 'Morning, missus.'

'Good morning,' she said hesitantly. His accent was educated, which meant he'd probably worked on a farm and learned his English copying a gentleman, not a convict who only used a hundred words, his brain too rotted by rum to remember more.

'I would like to see the magistrate, missus.'

'He will be back soon.' She didn't know when Zebediah would return, but a woman did not say she was alone except for a lad and an old woman, not to any man, black or white.

'I wait?'

The manner was so polite she found herself saying, 'Please sit. Can I bring you a dish of tea?' It was mint tea now, as the tea chest was empty.

'Yes please, missus.'

She brought him a plate with two slices of potato bread on it and buttered too — the cow lived in the kitchen courtyard each night now to protect her from thieves — not quite knowing why she offered food to a well-fed man while ignoring the desperate who starved below them. He ate quietly, politely.

'What do you want to see the magistrate about?' she asked at last. 'Perhaps I can help you?' It was unlikely either of them could, for if she and Zebediah had been dispossessed with no chance of redress, this man's people were a thousand times less likely to ever regain a campsite in the valley, or to have any other wrong against them righted.

'I would like to buy land up there.' He pointed to the tableland. 'Where there is no gold, but where potatoes will grow and cabbages. I would like to buy land for myself and my brothers and my uncles. Six of us.' He held up six fingers, as if she might not understand numbers. 'Six farms of thirty acres each.'

'But ...' Kat stopped. There was, indeed, no law that said a native could not be sold land. Zebediah had mentioned that the land the man described had been surveyed before he bought this farm. Zebediah even had a copy of the survey map framed in the drawing room, which showed the district carefully marked in to saleable portions.

'Do you know how to grow potatoes?' she asked cautiously.

'Yes. I have grown potatoes. So has my uncle. The land by the gully is good, but the land around it is not good, so others will not want to buy near there. We would like to buy six farms,' he repeated.

'Do you have money to buy the farms?'

'I have six shillings.'

He said it with the dignity that knew a shilling would not buy thirty acres, except a plot with the poorest soil perhaps, a very long way away with no water source nor feed. His tone also said that he should not even have to offer a shilling to buy what had never been bought by those who declared 'we will have a colony'. She suspected the land this man and his relations had chosen might not look promising but would be exactly what they needed, water source and all. Six shillings would not buy it ...

Or would it? she thought suddenly. In what must be the chaos of paperwork in Sydney now, letters from a magistrate recording the sale of land and enclosing the money might simply be transferred to the record, with the true value of the land uninvestigated. Legally, and just possibly irrevocably, Zebediah might be able to sell them the land.

The man in front of her glanced subtly down towards the valley, the merest sideways movement of his eyes. But she understood.

This man and his family should not need surveyors or even a magistrate for this small recompense: thirty acres each instead of boundless paradise. But justice had no part in this exchange. Parcels of thirty acres were possible. Paradise was not.

Her loss, and Zebediah's, was infinitesimal compared to his. She could not even conceive the magnitude of it, for uncounted generations past and to come. She could do only a little, and even that might not succeed. But she must try.

'My husband will write the necessary letters and ask that the records be put in your names,' she said at last. 'It would be best if your names ...' She could not quite say, 'did not sound native'. She substituted. 'Would you object to being John Jones, Mick Murphy and other names my husband will give you?'

He shrugged as if to say, 'Names change.'

'I will ask him to write and sign a letter for each of you, identifying you and your names as being the same ones that are on the titles.' She had no doubt Zebediah would agree, from kindness as well as moral need. He might even know of ways to ensure natives might keep the land once a colonial administration had assigned it to them.

'It may not be easy,' she warned. 'Even if you are given title, people may still claim your farms later on, especially if there are potatoes growing or other things they may want.'

He nodded. 'Hard to find us there.'

She hoped Zebediah could work out where the land they wanted was on the map. She hoped, desperately, they might succeed with their potatoes, with a life. 'It will be difficult,' she said.

'Always is now,' he agreed.

Chapter 33

TITANIA

SYDNEY, 1852

For the first time since her wedding night with Mr Boot, Titania seriously considered the virtues in acquiring a husband. Sydney Harbour's traffic had fast become ten times what it had been, ships lining up outside the Heads waiting for the pilot's boat. The figures they unloaded were corpse-like, except for the light in their eyes, and the shillings that might have bought them food for the voyage had been hoarded to buy spades, pans and sieves for the goldfields.

Boot and Anderson had flourished even more as the port traffic grew. Ships that brought men clutching fantasies of gold out to the colony needed provisioning for their return journey, and cargo had to be loaded too, which she could help arrange. But word of mouth alone did not suffice these days — the ships from California, from Italy, from anywhere men imagined fields of gold, did not know quartermasters or captains who had dealt with Mrs Boot. She did well, but it was the men who made the fortunes.

True, she had made Mr Anderson a partner, partly because he was happily wed, so she would never be tempted to try to make a business arrangement personal, or more personal than Sunday lunch after church sometimes with the Anderson family, and the exchange of gifts at Christmas. Nor had there ever been overtures from any man who wasn't six sheets to the wind, and even those had been accompanied by jeers of, 'Look out, or she'll squash you.'

A useful husband was an idle dream. A man with no head for business would drink her profit; any man, with a business head or not, might decide to control it and her, too. And a second marriage would be like her first — contempt mixed with envy and resentment.

She brought up the subject of marriage again when Viola brought the picnic dinner they now shared once a week, chicken mayonnaise and fresh lettuces from the estate, with meringue nests, an omelette *Imperial* and apricots. Her ladyship's footmen had wandered down to the shanty, confident their mistress wouldn't report them for this brief lapse in guarding.

'You are still set on spinsterhood?' Titania asked idly, applying cream dressing to the lettuce hearts. She had heard no more gossip about Major Nash — the colony had better tales to spin now, of nuggets or the newest digging. Titania was less concerned about Major Nash now that she knew the greater security of Viola's affairs, and she herself could keep an eye on them. And after all, Viola had the protection of her title and Sydney society looking on. The only danger to her fortune would be her husband, if she were to change her mind and acquire one.

Viola laughed. 'Spinster is a terrible word, isn't it? It makes one think of keeping many cats and hiding port behind the sofa. But, no, I haven't been tempted.'

Titania wondered how many offers for Viola's hand there'd been, or men who would have offered, given the slightest encouragement. Enough, surely, for there to be good men among them.

'What about children?' she asked gruffly, taking an apricot, small and freckled red, such a luxury that she had never eaten one back in England, yet here any slightly spoiled produce was fed to the goats or hens, unless their owner could be persuaded to make jam or chutney for Boot and Anderson.

'I like to see children laugh. The few I've met have been interesting. But I have no wish for children of my own.'

Titania gazed at her, shocked. She would have loved a brood of children, to feed on mutton pies and puddings, to teach bookkeeping. Her arms would not feel empty if she'd had a child.

'I am dreadfully unwomanly,' said Viola without concern, choosing her own apricot. 'Perhaps it comes of being so confined. I never learned the correct habits of men and women. Or maybe being small there is no room in me for passion.'

And Viola had her courses. None of them had been able to entirely hide the necessary washing and drying in the close confines on the ship. There was no doubt she had grown to womanly maturity.

'You haven't heard from Kat?' Viola carefully changed the subject.

'Not since the note asking for their stores to be sent overland. I did as she asked, but have no idea if the stock reached them — the men never came back to Sydney. I hope they just made off to the diggings, and didn't come to harm. It's not just bushrangers on the road now — any group of miners can overpower a dray and steal the contents.'

'Cousin Lionel hires outriders when we go down to the estate and guards for all shipments from there. At least there is no shortage of guards now.'

The stream of men trudging back from the diggings was growing, most of them desperate for any work that might advance them enough for a meal and sufficient rum to drown the memory of failure. The brief desperate labour shortage was over.

'I need to send her more provisions even though there's been no order. This time I'll offer decent reward for any man who comes back with news of her, and a letter to prove it true.'

'Cousin Lionel would think a visit out of the question now,' said Viola. 'Though the diggings would be interesting,' she added wistfully.

Titania raised her eyebrows. On this subject at least she suspected she and the major thought alike.

'Let me know when you have found men who'll take the stores so I can send a letter too,' Viola added.

'There's no difficulty finding men to go,' said Titania. 'The hard bit is finding men who will bring the dray back.'

'Offer them each fifty pounds on their return. I will pay it.'

'Fifty pounds! Will the major let you have that much?'

'He pays the bills for my jewellery,' said Viola lightly. 'And sometimes I sell it.'

Titania gazed at her. It was easy to underestimate this childlike figure. 'That was leery of you, lass. The major doesn't suspect?'

'I confessed the first time he asked me about it. He must have guessed I have done it since, but has not mentioned it again.'

'Why not just give you the money? That would be more sensible.'

'It would not be fitting,' said Viola primly. They laughed. 'The world is mad, except for you and me, and possibly Kat too. Will you have another apricot?'

Chapter 34

KAT

RAINBOW'S END

They worked, harder than Kat had thought possible — the labour that had been mostly by choice before was now forced on them to keep the vegetable plots productive and safe and to tend to the remaining sheep.

Summer turned to winter again. The diggings grew muddier and more crowded, shanties growing up as well as tents, even some slab huts where hard-faced men sold rum and women sold their bodies or watery stew or both, and a seamstress or washerwoman could make more in a day than a digger.

Every evening the air was rent as men fired their weapons to check the powder was still dry. Every night campfires glowed below them where once the moon had shone on the lagoons. Every day the line of bush eroded higher on the slopes as trees were turned to pit props, water races, warmth. Even the river was broken into a thousand desperate shallow channels now.

Spring arrived, unfurling leaves across the orchard, loquat fruit from China ripened, the Beauty of Bath and Jonathan apples fattening, but below the paddocks not a hint of green showed across the valley. Orange slashes in the hills were the only colour: after each rainfall more steep land slipped, the dark soil vanishing, leaving the clay below.

Zebediah and Summat Sam managed to shear the reduced flock, dawn to dusk most days, Zebediah's hands trembling with exhaustion as he took the mugs of ale, the plates of stew, the slabs of apple cake Kat carried to the sheds.

The rain held off over shearing and then a new front moved in from the coast and lingered, soft dappled drops that dripped from the shingles and splattered Kat's hair as she dropped potatoes into the furrows and raked dirt over them, following Zebediah and the single-tined plough pulled by Grey Girl, part-Clydesdale and the only horse they had left. Hair dried more quickly than a shawl or bonnet, and the rain did not pull her firmly plaited hair out of shape. Zebediah, too, was hatless, whistling the song she had heard the first day there, and countless times since.

'*Oh Nancy mine, I'll meet you in the flower time,*
Oh Nancy mine, I'll meet you in the glen
Oh Nancy mine, I'll kiss you in the flower time,
I'll hold you close, oh Nancy mine and then ...'

Kat's back ached from bending and straightening. Her skirt felt heavy with mud. But there was happiness too, despite the mud, the weariness, the destruction below. There would be fresh bread with their dinner, and real tea again since Titania had actually had stores delivered to them: they'd come on bullock drays that were the only large transportation possible now, in a trek of many weeks up the Blue Mountains and down the mud and slides to Bathurst, and then the even rougher tracks that eventually led to them.

Other drays passed them daily now, halting on the track just below the house to roll barrels of supplies down the mudslides, for these days even bullocks couldn't make their way down the track. Zebediah rode down the ridges if he needed to visit the valley floor, rather than risk a horse on the ruts left from rain and wheelbarrows.

Kat suspected that Titania made a considerable profit from her shipments to the Rainbow's End goldfield, even though she refused to let Kat and Zebediah pay for their part of the stores. Flour sold at ten pounds a sack these days, or thirty ounces of gold. One fossicker in ten might make enough to keep himself in damper. The others starved. Some left if they were strong enough. Many were not.

Zebediah no longer let Kat venture even to their lower paddocks, much less into the valley. The deeper mines had all been duds, so no more had been dug to throw rubbish into, or to use as latrines. Instead bodies were flung into shallow graves above the gravel pits — those who'd starved or died of typhoid, scurvy or the other diseases rampant among so many close-packed tents and shanties. Fights broke out over claims or blatant theft, and few had the will or energy to intervene.

The strongest ruled. The weakest died. Dingoes carried skulls up to the hills to gnaw. And still a thread of dreamers trailed down the mountain or up from the coast, drawn by the displays of wealth of those who'd made their fortune in a few days at other diggings, sure that if no rich vein of gold had been found, it must still be there to be discovered.

Meanwhile Zebediah sold peas at six shillings a pound and potatoes at three shillings a small bag. Potatoes were a relatively safe crop, for few miners had the energy to fork them up at night after a long day's digging or panning, and then Ben's bark — and teeth — gave warning enough to catch those who tried it.

It took a man ten minutes to find a feed of potatoes and even more to find pea pods in the darkness, but only seconds to slit a lambing ewe's throat. It seemed insane that men laboured below for an illusion, when far more could reliably be made from potatoes. There was no arguing the worth of a potato. But even though Zebediah had offered work to those trudging back up the mountain, none had accepted, either unable to face the scene of their failure, or hoping that a fresh goldfield might provide the life of luxury this one had not.

At last the entire paddock was planted fence to fence with potatoes that now must be watered, hilled as they grew, the ladybirds picked off, then the crop dug up, but at least they were fed by the manure of the sheep who'd occupied the land before.

Those animals were mostly mutton chops now, and long since eaten. They had kept reducing the numbers, keeping only the best breeding stock, till finally they had grown too tired to keep up the night watch. As soon as they had been shorn Zebediah had sent the remaining animals to Major Nash's estate on the Hawkesbury where, at Viola's urging, he had kindly agreed to keep them until …

Until what? The day they had saved enough for another property, and found the will to abandon the house Zebediah had laboured so long to craft, the orchard with its plump fruit, the outbuildings? A time when those below accepted they dug for a dream, and those leaving outnumbered the men who'd stayed?

At least now the sheep and most vulnerable crops were gone they no longer had to take it in turns to keep watch, relying on Ben to bark at intruders, though each night Zebediah kept a musket freshly loaded by the bed, firing it each morning to keep the powder fresh, as well as to let the valley know the inhabitants of the stone house would protect their own.

They trudged up to the house together, the mist hanging above them, wetting the air but too thin to be named drizzle. Small frogs leaped across their boots.

'Soup,' said Kat longingly. The stove's firebox just needed to be stirred up and the pot heated, leek and potato, the leeks cunningly scattered in clumps around the garden so would-be thieves might not recognise them as food, like the ferny carrots that grew under the peach trees, the parsnips under the apples. She had baked the bread last night.

'I'm sorry,' Zebediah said suddenly.

She turned a wet face to his muddy one. She guessed her own was just as filthy. 'Why?'

'I offered you a fair estate. Now you're a wife to a cocky farmer, trudging around the farm in your husband's boots.'

Kat considered. He was undoubtedly correct but … 'I've never thought that. Not for a second. I'm happy. I'll be happier when I'm in dry stockings.' And in bed tonight, she thought, then laughed.

'What's funny? Other than the mud on your nose.' He wiped it off.

'The teachers at school told us all good women have a heart of gold. Well, I'm not a good woman, and my bosom is the colour of mud.'

'I like your bosom,' said Zebediah.

'Then you can help wash it,' she grinned. 'I just remembered another saying from the past. A wiggle waggle.'

'What the deuce is a wiggle waggle?'

'I'll show you tonight, or rather, something far superior.' She glanced up at the sky as the rain began to thicken. 'I'm going to spend the afternoon by the kitchen stove darning your old trousers.' Firewood was too precious for more than one fire in the house now. 'Would you object to a wife in trousers? I'm sick of dragging my skirts through the fields.' She saw the pain in his eyes. 'Truly, I don't mind.'

'I should take you away from here,' he said. 'Say the word, Kat, my love, and we'll go.'

'No! We're not leaving all this behind! And there's less gold every month and not one man has struck it rich. Another big rush somewhere else and half of them will be gone.'

'Gone?' He gestured down the valley. 'There's a city growing down there, love, hotels with stone foundations, and slab huts too. A stinking slum city, thousands of souls, with all their stench and greed. It's like the worst of London descended on us.'

'And we're above it and will outlast it. Let's spend the afternoon in bed.'

'Can't. Summat Sam and I have to take those peas down to Tompkin's shanty. Besides, we'd shock Mrs O'Connell.' He grinned at her suddenly. 'I've never yet told you how much I love you.'

'You tell me every day.'

'But not how much.'

'I love you too. Zebediah?'

'Yes, love?' He paused at the stairs.

'How many letters of application did you get for a wife?'

'Only one. Lettice decided we would suit, and your Aunt Bertha did too.'

'I ... I assumed you had advertised.'

He gave a shout of laughter. 'How would I know which of the applications was genuine? No, I just asked my sister. I did think she might send me a few more choices.' He shook his head sadly. 'I might have found a wife who could play the piano, or even the bagpipes.'

'I can play the piano!'

'Really? You never mentioned it.'

'I can play the piano very badly. But I'll consent to learning the bagpipes as soon as you find me a tutor.'

'Remind me to pin a notice to a tree tomorrow: *Wanted, tutor for bagpipe lessons. Will pay two potatoes for the hour.*'

Kat grinned. 'Just what did Lettice and Aunt Bertha say about me?'

'That unfortunately you'd never learned to play the bagpipes.'

'No, seriously.'

'They said you'd probably enjoy the life here, despite the isolation.' He glanced grimly down the valley, then smiled at her. 'I kept their letters.'

'Really?'

'Of course. I'll get them out for you after dinner if you like.'

'Excellent. We can read them together. Then I'll explain about the wiggle waggle.'

Kat heaved her wet skirts and herself onto the verandah and sat to let Zebediah pull off her boots, and the three pairs of woollen stockings worn under them so they would fit.

She dozed that afternoon, for though the nights began with loving she still woke at every sound, and knew that Zebediah did as well. It was a rare night when he didn't pad out to investigate a bark from Ben, or even a creak that might be a footfall in the house.

The drumming woke her. It were as if an army marched, shaking the ground. She ran out to the verandah and found

Mrs O'Connell already there staring at the white water that had taken the place of air. 'The sky is fallin' on us!'

'The clouds are low, that's all. But listen to that rain!'

'It's the creek, too. Never known it to flood like that. Ah, lucky we are to be well above it.'

But Zebediah is not, thought Kat, trying to see through the almost solid water; nor would theirs be the only creek flooding down into the valley. The sooner he was back, the better.

She sat on one of the verandah chairs and waited. It was growing dark and raining still when Mrs O'Connell brought her out a lamp and shawl. 'The master'll be stayin' down at the shanty till the rain has eased, to be sure. Don't you be frettin' yourself, missus Kat.'

'Or he and Summat Sam might be on the track with no lamp to find their way.' Though hopefully Ben could smell the way home. Kat pulled her boots on again. 'I'll walk a way and call.'

'Not out in that! May Jesus, St Joseph, St Patrick and Our Lady watch over you!'

'I won't melt. Nor will I leave the track.' She held the lantern high as she ran down, round the first bend, past the peas then the potatoes, the second and third bend, and stopped.

The track had vanished in a landslide of orange clay, more dirt still slowly slithering or trickling in a hundred streams down the hill. The single lamp light not enough to even guess at its extent.

She ran uphill, panting, in case the slide took more of the track, but the mud came from downhill where the trees had been cut for the mines below. This part still seemed solid. But the lost track explained why Zebediah had not returned. She hoped he was safe in Tompkin's shanty, though dry was too much to hope for.

She squelched back to the house, where Mrs O'Connell, lovely woman, had warmed her nightdress and another shawl, and even heated a pot of hot water to wash in.

The rain fell.

Chapter 35

KAT

Kat woke, and knew that he was dead.

She could not tell how she knew nor why. Just that there was an emptiness, not just in bed, nor in her heart, but in her very self.

He was gone and some small cord had snapped.

The rain had stopped, though drips from the soaked shingles splattered on the soil outside.

'Missus Kat?' Mrs O'Connell's face was grey as her hair. 'I think ye need to be looking at this.'

Kat followed her down the stairs, and onto the verandah, and stared down.

The valley she had known had vanished. Instead, five hundred yards below her, there roiled a lake, in shades of brown and dappled with what might be trees, or pieces of roof, or what had been a horse or bullock. Across on the opposite slope another great slash of orange clay showed where the land had slipped there, too.

Kat imagined the earth trembling under her feet. But she and the house were anchored by a goodly stand of bush and orchard trees. The land that was lost was land already destroyed.

'May the good Lord protect us. More rain must'a come down during the night,' whispered Mrs O'Connell. Strange, that a whisper could be heard above the roar of the water and her own heartbeat too, but nothing else. The whole world was water and this an island in the misty cloud.

'He'll have found his way uphill, darlin',' Mrs O'Connell assured her. 'I bin prayin' for him all the night.'

And I did not, thought Kat. I slept.

I don't think I'll ever sleep again.

Or live.

She lived. She baked bread from dough that had risen overnight and ate the slice that Mrs O'Connell fussed at her to finish. She made soup for the old woman and drank some herself, too. Then as a trickle of white-faced men finally staggered up around the landslide from the sea below, she ran from one to another asking, 'I'm looking for Zebediah Markham. A big man, very big. Sold potatoes. Have you seen him?'

One by one they shook their heads or dazedly stared straight ahead and simply walked.

On the third day, the sea below developed small brown humps of newly swirled hills. The streams were down to only twice their previous size. Half the lake below, perhaps, had swirled out to sea. Kat had been asking each passer-by on the track again, but there were fewer now, as those survivors who could had already fled. At last a small man, carrying an injured dog across his shoulder, stopped and waited till she came up to him. He had only one eye — an old injury — and walked with the aid of a rough crutch, his leg bound between two branches used as splints.

She could not bear to look at the dog, or even ask about its injury, or its owners'. Ben was gone too, and Summat Sam, but there was only so much that one could grieve and her well was already overflowing.

'Missus Markham? I bought potatoes off you, and you gave me a scrag end for me dog. You lookin' for your man? I saw him. Mr Markham were down at Tompkin's, sheltering with fifty others, the walls near to bursting with men. Aye, and his dog too, up on his shoulder like Red here. I left to find me tent then heard the roar. Came like a wave it did, mud and water and men too. I just had time to grab Red and clamber up a tree. I tied meself to the tree as the water rose then tied Red onto me.'

'Tompkin's?' she asked tightly.

'Washed away. I saw it go. Roof and all, and every man that was in it. Nothin' there now. Nothin' at all.'

'You ... you're sure it was Mr Markham?'

'Can't mistake a cove his size.'

'Thank you.'

I should feel something, she thought. Relief, that was it. She need no longer keep asking. 'Can I offer you some soup? Maybe Red would have some, too.'

'Broke his leg. Don't think mine is broke, but just wrenched a bit. He'll drink the soup. Eat anything, will Red.'

She watched them eat on the verandah, the man and dog, then made them a parcel of bread and mutton. She watched them leave. She sat and watched the sad straggle from the valley, the desert of mud that had once been an almost city, and before that a paradise, and wondered how to go on.

'Kat, me darlin', I made ye some toast, an' wid lovely strawberry jam on it too. Come in now, and eat it.'

She followed the old woman back into the kitchen, sat like a child and ate the toast.

At last, she managed to think. There was food enough for her and Mrs O'Connell. They had the vegetables and fruit. She could trap the birds who came to eat the fruit the way the stable lads back in England had shown her. There were enough gold grains and coins in the jars dug into the garden for her and Mrs O'Connell to live simply, perhaps, even if Titania no longer sent charity supplies.

She shook her head. She had no real idea how much things cost, beyond the extravagance of a ball gown. How much was a barrel of flour, a chest of tea? Zebediah had provided for her, and her father had before.

One day, she thought, I will be able to cope with the magnitude of all I've lost. Not just the man, but the years of partnership together. Children, laughter, Christmases, nights in the big carved bed. One day I will be able to add up the totality and then, maybe, measure out my grief into small portions, just enough to manage it each day.

One day, perhaps, there might be more than mud and potatoes.

Chapter 36

KAT

The water dried over the next two weeks, leaving rock and clay behind it, the remnants of the lagoons, the gravel and sand where they'd been drained, clearing away men, shanties, gold ... all washed away and, it seemed, most of the bodies, too.

The flood had been merciful in that at least. It had taken, but also cleaned, leaving the land a bare skeleton behind.

Or almost, for down below a few men still worked a dozen claims where seams of rock had kept the dirt. Those men dug, and stayed, putting up rough huts from the scant debris and the few remaining trees. Weeds grew on the lower slopes of clay, shaggy as sheep. The top slopes gleamed hot and orange as summer passed and eroded further with each storm.

Kat expected letters from Viola and Titania, and eventually from Aunt Bertha and Lettice in England, asking how Rainbow's End fared. But it seemed the rain had been widespread, and the floods and mudslides, so theirs must have been lost among the many other tales and had not reached the newspapers. And who was there to write of it? No one had ever counted the valley's inhabitants. The figure 'thousands of people' was only Zebediah's estimate, for how could individuals in such chaos be numbered? Had there been ten thousand, or one thousand? She didn't know. If any journalist or writer or even diarist had been down there, they too were gone.

Ironically, the flood that had washed away the valley's gold had uncovered a bigger reef at Tumble Mountain, not fifty miles south — a far more major news story than the loss of a goldfield that hadn't even produced a notable nugget. Kat heard from the men who still arrived to buy potatoes that there was even a road from that outpost up to Bathurst that passed not far from the valley, or at least a track that could be followed by a bullock cart.

One day she'd need to journey to that road, and then along it. The river was still no longer navigable. Perhaps it never would be again. The thin track along the bank had been washed away as well. Those who knew the country could probably ride from the valley to the coast. She could not until a track was cut.

Meanwhile she dispatched letters with men heading to Sydney, hoping the messages would reach Viola and Titania. The letters assured them of her safety, in case the news of the flood had reached them. She did not mention her loss. She could not bear to.

She had not notified anyone of Zebediah's death. Once the first vastness of shock wore off, she did at least consider what she might say and how to say it. At the very least the government must be told they had no magistrate.

But what could she say? I saw a valley wash away an entire town out to sea. A man who tied himself to a tree claimed he saw the shanty where my husband was sheltering tumble away. No, I don't know his name. He had a dog called Red.

Without proof of death — a body at most — her husband would be missing. What of that? Husbands went missing every day, especially with gold to lure them.

Zebediah had lost so much of his farm; perhaps the authorities would think his wife was a shrew or, like many men these days, that he simply dreamed of making his fortune and coming back to her, and then had found another girl to warm his bedroll at the diggings in Bendigo.

The colonies were overrun with too many men and had too few police or officials of any kind. At most, there would be enquiries sent to England to see if Zebediah had written home: two years or more to get a reply. And then, perhaps, a wait of seven years till 'missing' became — maybe — declared dead.

'Seven years' felt proper. She would wait seven years till she uttered the words, 'He's dead.' No one else was likely to. Wifelike, she had taken to writing the family letters to his sister. Mrs O'Connell did not speak to anyone, except perhaps in silent communion with the ghosts who peered over her shoulder to check she polished well.

Over the next four months, Kat fielded two matters brought for a magistrate to deal with: a dispute about the borders of a claim and, for the first time, a trooper bringing in a thief and who wanted his arrest recorded. Each time Kat claimed her husband was away from home, expected late that night. She forged his writing and his signature and had it ready for the claimants and the trooper the next day. Most likely even the forgery was not necessary, for who would have noticed the change?

Winter. The tree shadows darkened to purple and the dull yellow peach leaves had long since dropped. The valley stayed mud-colour, it's heart ripped out by gold, and now that glittering heart was gone too.

Kat woke one morning and saw the mist clinging to the window, a sea of pure white hiding the devastation, and admitted she was lonely.

Chapter 37

TITANIA

SYDNEY, 1853

The dinner basket Viola had brought this week held game terrine. Major Nash bred partridges and pheasant now and the overseer had sent up a basket of wood duck. It also contained a duck roasted with oranges with an almond sauce, an endive salad, dressed, a cherry cream and rose water jelly: nothing that resembled the heavy puddings, hams, corned meats and cheese Titania dealt with every day.

She laughed as she spread the contents on the tablecloth that covered her kitchen table: the starched and embroidered linen cloth that happily proclaimed this to be a cottage, not a gentlewoman's house with a polished table that never needed scrubbing. 'You always bring me enough to last the whole week.' She considered the meal, then added a jar of pickled pumpkin to the repast, a new receipt, and excellent if you added enough allspice to the vinegar. No meal was truly complete without the bite of pickle.

'You need someone to cook for you sometimes.' Viola stroked the ginger cat who purred complacently on her lap, appreciating the scent of game terrine. Mr Tom had offered his services as rodent controller a few months earlier. Viola sliced a piece of terrine and offered it to him with her fingers. Mr Tom accepted it and looked expectantly at the duck.

'You spoil him,' said Titania. 'He'll expect duck every night.'

'I expect he gets the best that's in your larder.'

Titania chuckled. 'He's a restful companion after the bustle of the day. I like to watch him wash his face.'

'You sound happy.'

'Oh, I am. Two quartermasters on my doorstep this morning, both never dealt with us before, and another farm wife from Liverpool way offered me more than a hundred-year-old cheeses and the promise of a regular supply. I've got twenty-two women making salt butter now and sixteen cheesemakers, and all of them bring cabbages and eggs, too. I owe your major my thanks, as well. His doubling the supply of mutton made a world of difference and it's good quality. But I shouldn't be boring you with facts and figures.'

'It's not boring. It's good to see you happy.'

Titania stopped carving the duck and examined her. 'And you're not, quite.'

'No. Not quite.'

'The major not behaving himself?' asked Titania sharply.

'Cousin Lionel always behaves impeccably. It's a trifle boring. No, I think ... in fact I have decided ... that I will travel as soon as I turn twenty-one. I'd like you to look for a passage for me, a comfortable ship and, if possible, a captain who travels with his wife, who might act as a companion of sorts on the voyage and for my first weeks in India.'

'India? Why?'

'To find my father,' said Viola simply. She touched the silver pendant at her throat. 'I always knew I'd have to. Why else would Mama have left her fortune so? She wanted me to be free to use the money once I am twenty-one, and not be dependent on approval for an allowance.'

'You're too young to travel by yourself. If I could find the time ...'

'You can't. A year from your business? You'd have none left. I wish to travel alone, too, or rather, I want to be free from supervision — I don't mean I will attempt to manage by myself. I don't know what I will find and that ... that is why I need to find it.'

'He may not be a rajah, you know.'

Viola smiled. 'I am fairly sure that he is not, or he'd have sent an emissary to find me.'

'He might not be alive, either. Might not even have known of your birth.'

Viola shook her head. 'Mama said, "He will love you." She'd not have said that if he were dead.'

'And it may be impossible for you to find him.'

'I'm sure it will be,' said Viola calmly. 'But it will be very easy for *him* to find *me*, if that is his wish. The gossip that the dark-skinned Lady Viola, daughter of *that* Lady Viola, will spread across Calcutta and beyond. I imagine I'll find hospitality once I get there.'

On reflection, Titania was sure the girl was right. Her title, her fortune, her beauty, would be welcomed in a land to which eligible single Englishwomen travelled on the 'fishing fleet' each year to find a husband desperate for an English wife. Even the scandal would make her an interesting guest, although perhaps only for a memsahib who did not have a son who might decide himself in love with a half-breed.

'What does Major Nash say?'

'I have not told Cousin Lionel.'

Ah, thought Titania. 'When will you tell him?'

'When you have found the ship and the companion and booked my passage. I do wish him to hear the news from me and not from gossip.'

Titania placed a slice of duck on her plate and a lettuce heart. 'Eat.' She took a hearty slice of the terrine for herself and chewed. 'Losing your income so suddenly may be a shock to him. He probably thinks you'll let him keep it till you marry.'

'I have already asked him if he'll continue to "manage my income". He can send me bank drafts as I need them. There's enough for us both. As long as he sends the bank drafts when I request them, that need not change.'

Unless you marry in India, thought Titania, or decide to buy a palace there to move this Indian Pa of yours into, or a ruby mine. A good businessman — or woman — liked to be able to predict the years ahead. Nash had proved himself a businessman, profiting well from his guardianship, though it would be an insult to call a gentleman by that name.

Viola fed Mr Tom a shred of duck breast. 'I'm going to send Kat a letter by messenger, asking if she'll come to Sydney for a good long visit before I go, though I won't tell her I'm leaving till I see her. You know it's been over six months since we heard from her?'

'They'll have been busy harvesting, and letters get lost these days.' Titania frowned. 'I'm sure Mr Markham would have found a way to let us know if anything was wrong. It will be good to see her again.'

'Very good.' But Viola didn't smile as she fed Mr Tom another piece of duck.

Those who knew her little thought the Lady Viola the most open girl in all the world. She wasn't. Titania had not been surprised at the plans for the Indian visit or that it had been of such long and steady standing. The girl about whom everyone must pretend had learned to pretend extremely well herself. But Titania had been startled by the suddenness of the request, almost an urgency.

Something was wrong.

Chapter 38

KAT

RAINBOW'S END

Kat found the letters where she should have known they'd be, behind the portrait of herself that Aunt Bertha had sent with the 'letter of application'. Zebediah had made a frame for the sketch several months after their wedding. She appreciated his tact in not claiming even her image until their marriage was a true one, even as she wept at the memory.

He had inserted both letters behind the cardboard. She only noticed the thickness when she took it up to wonder at the innocence of the girl portrayed there. She had been sixteen and on her way to a year of school, her hair curling on her shoulders, her face laughing at the cousin who took her sketching so seriously, though the subject looked a little impatient too, at having to sit still so long. There had been a proper portrait, painted by an eminent artist the year after, that had hung in Papa's study. Kat wondered vaguely what had happened to it as she carefully pulled aside the pegs that held the frame to its contents.

Aunt Bertha's letter to Zebediah was matter-of-fact. She outlined Kat's circumstances, openly describing her parents' deaths and her sudden lack of fortune; she asserted that her niece had a lively mind; was considered beautiful; was used to country life and some degree of isolation, that she had shown herself proficient at all aspects of household management and especially talented at cookery, able to both supervise kitchen staff as well as prepare meals herself, from household basics like bread, marmalades and butter to soufflés and pastry, and that she possessed a deep interest in the management of poultry, pigs and other rural matters.

She almost smiled at the image of Zebediah reading that, sitting with a leaden slice of Mrs O'Connell's soda bread. The cookery might have snared him.

She picked up the second letter.

My dear Zebediah,
I trust You are as well as this leaves Me.

Well, I have met her, though briefly, at a visit to her Aunt. I do not think Miss Fitzhubert even realised I was there. She is a Beauty, no doubt, and as sulky as a Mare who has been sold to new Owners and longs for her old Stable. She was clearly bored by the Drawing Room Conversation. I mentioned that the Weather seemed warm for the time of Year. She merely answered, 'Is it? I haven't noticed.'

I am painting a winsome Portrait of her, aren't I? She kept gazing out the Window too, but not, I think, at the fog outside, and despite sitting in a most Ladylike manner seemed somehow restless, as if she longed to be outdoors and active. I believe her Mind is as nimble as her Mother's was in the years when we met more frequently. She is likely to be as Stubborn and as Unpredictable as well.

If Miss Fitzhubert does not like you, I expect she will tell you so frankly and possibly ride off the next Morning, confident she can find her Way across a mostly unknown Continent and face Anything, as long as she is not confined to a Drawing Room again.

She likes Animals — I brought Pug with me, and she reached down to scratch his Ears. He liked her smell and would have joined her on the Sofa if I had not reclaimed him. She conversed with Hugo for nearly twenty minutes on the advantages of Her Majesty's

Oriental roosters over Dorkings, and they even exchanged opinions on how many Hens one Rooster might cover in a day.

Hugo, at six, can be forgiven for the want of Delicacy, but I was amused at Miss Fitzhubert's readiness to discuss the subject. I would suppose her most interested in Country Matters of all kinds, and She is too lovely to have been ignorant of the effect of her Charms upon the Males of her Acquaintance before her tragedy, but I also think her too Intelligent to have gone beyond the bounds of Propriety. Certainly, She accepts the Restrictions of Mourning at the moment, though possibly that is Shock and Grief rather than respect for Convention.

Bertha, no doubt, wrote to you by the first Post and sent you Miss Fitzhubert's likeness, which I have seen and which captures her quite well. Bertha no doubt is eager to have her from the house, as once she is out of Mourning she will quite eclipse her daughters, even if their spots diminish. There is also the worry for a Hostess that a Charge who converses freely about the Husbandly qualities of Roosters in the Drawing Room might say something even more Outrageous at a Ball.

Zebediah, my dear, I am convinced that you will like her, be charmed by her, and even Love her, as I was very close to doing even in that brief Meeting. She has Courage and Character and it is impossible not to Admire her as much as Pity her. I also believe she will love the Eccentric way of Life you have chosen, though possibly you may need to purchase some Oriental Hens with as much Speed as is Possible in your Remote Situation.

I am also a fond enough Sister to believe Miss Fitzhubert will love my Brother, too.

Your affectionate Sister,
Lettice

Kat placed the letters back behind the frame and fastened it again.

So that had been the beginning. This was the end.

She was not sure what to feel. Anger at Lettice, for it was this letter that had sent her across the world. She might be wed to a vicar's son by now, a curate with the promise of a small but comfortable living when the present elderly incumbent died. She might even have been happy, or believe herself happy, though cribbed and confined.

No, she owed Lettice gratitude. She had known nearly three years of freedom and fulfilment and knowledge of what a marriage might be, experiencing passion without possession.

She also owed Zebediah's sister the story of his death. But why grieve Lettice just yet, when, after all, she would never have seen her brother again, except in the unlikely circumstance that either brother or sister chose to endure a couple of four- or even six-month journeys?

Instead, she would send a letter talking about the rainbow that had dutifully appeared across the valley after the last storm; how a goanna as long as a pony had wandered through her rose garden, its tongue flickering; how Zebediah would send his love too if it were possible to get him to put pen and ink to paper. She would enclose some pressed wattle blossom, which might even retain a ghost of scent by the time it reached England.

She would send Zebediah's sister an illusion, and for a while she might share it too.

Chapter 39

VIOLA

HAWKESBURY ESTATE

'Viola, my dear, would you care to walk with me by the river?'

Viola laid her embroidery aside. 'Certainly, Cousin Lionel. That would be delightful.' She kept her sudden unease from her smile.

Her guardian had never suggested a walk together before, nor to her knowledge did he enjoy the activity, though he rode each morning both in Sydney and on the estate, and often joined friends in the colony's version of a fox hunt, the hounds following a trail of aniseed rather than the foxes Australia lacked.

She waited while Alice arranged a shawl of Norwich silk around her shoulders, tied the ribbons of her bonnet at one side of her chin in a modish manner, and exchanged her silk indoor slippers for more substantial ones suitable for a gravelled walk. Major Nash offered her his arm.

They did not, in fact, walk far: merely beyond the house to the first view of the river, where a rustic seat had been placed in an arbour of climbing roses, planted by the wife of the previous owner who had sold the estate cheaply towards the end of the long 40s drought. Across the placid water sheep grazed, heads down, uninterested in humans who brought neither food nor dogs to harry them.

'My dear, you must know that I am most fond of you.'

'I know you have shown me the most affectionate care possible, Cousin Lionel, and I am more grateful than I can say.'

'Would it surprise you to know that I have grown to love you, most deeply and sincerely?'

She had become concerned that he might propose to her six months ago, when he presented her with a brooch that had belonged to his mother, and his great-grandmother before that. A man of honour did not marry his ward. She had made the arrangements to leave the colony to forestall any possibility he might propose once she had turned twenty-one. She had not thought he would have raised the matter so soon. Surely he regarded her as a child, and as such, one who'd remain in his care.

And yet the offer had come. She did not sigh, even internally, and wish that for once he had at least proposed with some originality. He was an almost blank canvas, with polite manners vaguely doubled on top. The peccadillo she presumed had meant he stayed in Australia rather than return with his regiment remained the most interesting thing about him, though she had told herself it would not be right to try to find out exactly what gossip Titania hadn't passed on.

For a brief while she had wondered if the major's blandness concealed as much thought and wonder as her own careful lack of expression. She now believed there was little to hide, beyond convention, a fear of flouting it, and a reasonable concern now that the last affluent and fashionable years might be erased once her income was lost to him.

'Cousin Lionel, I feel great affection and the deepest gratitude to you, but as you know, I do not wish to marry.'

'Childish nonsense, my dear. All women wish to marry.' He lifted her hand, and kissed it. 'Once you are no longer my ward it may not be seemly for you to continue to live in my house with no chaperone.'

'Surely Mrs Higgins is a sufficient chaperone? But I could engage a companion, if you think it best.'

'My dear, I think it best that you have the protection of my name, as well as my house and affection.' His expression now was earnest. 'Truly, this is not cream-pot love, even if it may seem so to you. I'd wish to marry you even if you didn't have a farthing.' He gave a mock grimace. 'Though, of course, in that case I could not afford to. But truly, I care for you most deeply.'

She moved slightly away from him, still keeping her calm smile. 'Cousin Lionel, please do not be concerned about money. For some time, I have been determined to make over half my income to you on the day I come of age.'

He looked as if a sparrow had changed into one of the careless big white birds that feasted on their walnut trees. 'My dear little girl, that would be ... an act of ... such generosity ...' He sought more words. 'It is not to be thought of. The gossips would be bandying about the news for years.'

'The gossips need know nothing of it. It would be between you and me and the man who I hope is your most discreet lawyer.'

He smiled indulgently. 'You are so sweetly innocent, my dear. I cannot allow you to do any such thing.' He took her hand and kissed it. 'I can, however, most earnestly beg you to be my wife.'

She sat quite still. Major Nash had made no overtures to any woman in the colony during her time there nor did he seem to have women friends, especially disliking those of vigour and determination like Kat and Titania. And myself, if he only knew it, she thought. At first she'd supposed his financial circumstances had prevented him from marrying before, then assumed he simply had little interest in women or marriage, and was delaying any courtship so that she might remain mistress of the house till her majority.

She glanced at his face. To her shock he looked at her with the expression she had observed on men looking at women they ...

She lacked the experience to finish the thought. That they loved? Wish to possess? Something else, that she could not understand? But there was no doubt that she was looking at a man who sincerely wanted her to be his wife.

'I ... I planned to go to India ...' she blurted.

'India!' He laughed. 'What a notion. It's a long voyage, and I fail to see the attraction at the end of it. But if that is what you want, my dear, we will travel there one day.'

She shook her head at her own inanity. 'I'm sorry, that was a silly answer. The unchanging truth is I do not wish to marry anyone, as I told you before.' How had she mistaken his feelings for so long? Titania saw them, she thought. Titania tried to warn me.

It was as if he hadn't heard her. 'We have been happy together, have we not? I will make it my life's aim to keep you as happy as you have been the last four years.'

She had not been happy, except for brief periods with Titania, or engrossed in a book, or watching the gulls soar over the cliffs. She had simply been not unhappy. She had been waiting.

She looked at him steadily, trying to work out how to convince him. 'I am sure you would make a delightful husband, Cousin Lionel. But I am not the wife for you. I am quite sincere — I do not intend to marry.'

He frowned. 'All girls must marry.'

'I am lucky in that there is no "must" in my case,' she said lightly.

That, finally, seemed to penetrate his conviction that she would be as malleable in this as in all other matters since her arrival here. 'Viola, you cannot be so cruel as to intend to leave me. Please, tell me at least you do not plan to set up an establishment of your own next year.'

'I can certainly assure you of that.' She was glad that she hadn't told him that she had already planned the journey to India. No, she would not set up her own establishment, but nor would she stay in his house once she was twenty-one.

She must see Titania again, and ask her to make the arrangements more urgently. Perhaps she could stay with Titania till the voyage, though her house was tiny, or Kat. Kat would be better, she thought — she had never seen Rainbow's End, and it would be two day's sail from Sydney and Cousin Lionel. She longed all the more to feel the sea wind again, the deck roll under her feet. Those months at sea had been as close as she had ever come to freedom. Her money had been her prison, forcing her to comply with the social conventions of her estate.

But that money would soon free her, too. She stood before he could say more. 'Thank you for the honour of your offer, Cousin Lionel, and thank you too for all your care. I am still determined that you should not lose when I gain my majority later this year.'

He looked at her strangely. 'You have been unhappy in my house? The estate does not please you?'

'Everything about it is most pleasant, sir.' She handed him another smile. 'I am sure you would have changed the colour of the trees if I had wished it.'

He didn't answer. She offered him a smile again, feeling uncomfortable that while she had not lied to him, she had certainly misled him. 'Shall we go back to the house? I find the breeze is chilly.'

He stood and proffered her his arm again. 'Of course, my dear.' He smiled down at her. 'I shall keep trying to persuade you.'

'Truly, sir, I have long been aware I am destined to be a spinster. But I am grateful for the comfort of your house and all your care.'

She waited till they had walked up to the formal garden again, before saying casually, 'Would you mind if I returned to Sydney tomorrow, Cousin Lionel?'

'What is so urgent?'

She tried to find a suitable reason. 'It's Titania's birthday. I had quite forgotten.'

'I'm afraid I need the carriage tomorrow,' he said pleasantly. 'But I can send a footman on horseback to convey your birthday wishes, with flowers too, perhaps, if you like.'

'That is kind of you, sir, but I'd rather give them in person. When do you think I might return?'

'In a few days, perhaps. I need to get Jenkins to look at the rear axle. I would never forgive myself if you had an accident.'

'You are most thoughtful, Cousin Lionel.'

'I am indeed,' he answered lightly.

She carefully did not meet his eyes as they walked up the neatly tended paths, past the rose bushes, the hedge of lavender and back towards the house, where Tilson would be waiting to open the door for them and Alice to remove her bonnet, and everything from the timing of the dinner gong to the direction in which she spooned her soup — mulligatawny today — was assured.

Chapter 40

KAT

RAINBOW'S END

'Kat? Kat me darlin', I think ye'd better be coming down.' The old woman's voice wavered from the foot of the stairs.

Kat flung herself out of bed. Had Mrs O'Connell slipped and broken her leg? Or was it her heart, perhaps?

'I'm coming.' She didn't bother with slippers or a shawl, half tumbling down the stairs, then stopped.

A young man stood in the stairway, her age perhaps, thin as a whippet, with rusty red whiskers and a pistol pointed at Mrs O'Connell's heart. He also wore a coat red with blood on one side. Blood that had dripped upon his trousers too, and even onto his boots.

'Who are you?'

'He's a bushranger, Kat!'

'I can see that. Well, Mr Bushranger, we have some sacks of potatoes, as many as you can lug away.' Kat made sure her voice didn't shake. Had he come for the syrup tins of grains of gold or coins, as well as the household silver buried under the rose bushes?

By the look of him he might faint from blood loss before Kat had time to dig them up. But by then he might have shot Mrs O'Connell too. 'We might even find you a loaf of bread and some honey,' she added. 'But I'm afraid you'll find nothing else we have valuable.'

'I think you have exactly what I need, ma'am.' He sounded like, but was not, a gentleman. 'I need your hospitality for a few days. Some bandages would be good too. And one thing more.'

'What's that?' Kat took another step down. If she could get close enough she could grab the pistol. If only Mrs O'Connell had warned her, she'd have grabbed the musket still kept at her bedside, shot him from her doorway before he had a chance to blink. But if the old woman had shouted a warning, likely he'd have shot her before Kat had even heard.

'Your husband's name.' The bushranger smiled with what in other circumstances would have been considerable charm. 'It's like this, you see. There are troopers after me. They're not sure what I look like, but they are damned sure I have a bullet in my shoulder and must go to ground. My usual companion is ... indisposed.'

'You want us to hide you here?'

'On the contrary, I wish to be seated in your drawing room as Magistrate Zebediah Markham, with my foot resting on a stool — the gout you know — to excuse my not getting up. And I will stay as magistrate and your guest till I am healed enough to leave.'

Kat kept her voice steady. 'What do you think my husband will say to that?'

'Nothing. I know that he is dead.'

Kat stood silent.

'Come, Mrs Markham, we have been watching your place for two years, Jimmy and I. Not to rob you. I liked the look of you, the pair of you.'

'Thank you.'

'It's true. The gold transports had to come past here. I saw you and your husband work together day after day. Then since the flood, I've seen only you. But I listen to the gossip too, and there's been no word of Magistrate Markham's death. The world seems to think he's still alive.' He grinned. 'And for a few weeks he will be.'

'How dare you!'

'I'm sorry.' He suddenly looked it too. 'I should have realised your grief is raw. But I have no choice but to take his name for a while. I promise you I'll do no more than that. I ...' He staggered, then clutched the bannister, though the pistol hardly wavered in his hand.

'Oh, put that away, you fool,' said Kat. 'If you shoot me, you'll have no one to pretend that you are my ... and the magistrate too. And if you hurt Mrs O'Connell, I will wait till you are asleep and cut your balls off and leave you bleeding to death faster than you are now.'

'No need for that language, Kat darlin',' said Mrs O'Connell surprisingly. She turned to the young man. 'We'd never give a man up to them troopers, would we, missus?'

'Wouldn't we?'

'I wouldn't,' said Mrs O'Connell simply. 'Bad cess to the lot o' them, and English soldiers too. Your ma was Irish, Kat. You understand these tings.'

'Perhaps,' said Kat slowly. Mrs O'Connell, a rebel? Or maybe a rebel's daughter, orphaned and ending up at a convent orphanage? That seemed more likely.

'Very well,' she said crisply. 'How long do we have before the troopers appear?'

'An hour perhaps. They've got a good tracker with them, Gully John, who'll follow the bloodstains.'

'It's the front steps then that will need cleaning, and the garden too, God love you,' said Mrs O'Connell, queen of scrubbers. 'I'll see to it at once.' She vanished towards the scullery for brush and bucket.

Kat inspected the bushranger again, pale but still on his feet. 'Into the kitchen,' she ordered. 'What is your name, by the way?'

'Captain Quicksilver.'

Kat snorted, half a laugh. 'I won't be calling you that.'

'You'll call me "my dear".'

The phrase would do. At least the man had the tact not to expect her to use Zebediah's name.

'Then give me the pistol and put your hand over that wound till I can get a towel under you. Mrs O'Connell has enough blood to mop up without you donating more.'

It was two hours at least before Kat heard horses on the track as she stirred the pot upon the stove: one of their precious chickens sacrificed, for a magistrate would be expected to have meat on his table. The hen's bloody head and neck was hanging from the apple tree with a dose of strychnine in it to kill any prowling wild dog. A freshly killed hen would also handily explain any stains Mrs O'Connell might have missed.

Kat removed her apron and checked her newly neat hair. How long had it been since she'd arranged it properly? It felt strangely good to be in a fresh cotton dress and to see Mrs O'Connell in an apron she too hadn't worn for over a year. Why wear out an apron when it was easier to wear the same dull dress day in day out? Such dull days, the heart of her life vanished ...

She hesitated at the kitchen door. Was she sure about this? The man could be far more of a rogue than he appeared, even a murderer. What if the ruse failed? She could say truthfully that she had been forced at gunpoint now, but what if Zebediah's body had been found, and it was discovered that his wife had claimed another man was him? She would need to say ...

But there was no time to think of that now, not with the troopers almost at the door. She grinned, suddenly excited by the challenge.

Mrs O'Connell appeared at the back door. 'They're here, Kat darlin'.'

'I heard the horses. You know what to do?'

'I'll be answering the door and bringing them to the drawing room, and when ye ask for tea, I'll bring them the apple tarts cooling on the sill. I've missed your pastry, Kat darlin'.'

'I've missed it too. We've flour and fruit enough. I'll do more baking. But just for now ...' She stepped quickly into the drawing room — luckily impeccably dusted, polished and scented with lavender as always, even though it had been more than a year since it had been used — sat on the sofa and picked up the darning she had not touched since the flood: one of Zebediah's stockings, too well washed to have the scent of him.

The bushranger sat in the armchair opposite, his face pale, one foot bandaged and resting on a stool. Luckily, his wound was shallow — obviously he'd been shot from a distance — and Kat had been able to dig the ball out. He now wore one of Zebediah's shirts and waistcoats over the thick wad of bandages. To Kat's surprise it didn't hurt to see another wearing Zebediah's clothes, for the shirt looked completely different on this small, wiry man. Mrs O'Connell had tacked up the back of the shirt and waistcoat in a thick seam to make them appear to fit and tucked the excess hessian into Zebediah's boots.

The rough attempt would not withstand scrutiny, especially not if the bushranger had to get up, but Kat doubted he'd be able to for long, anyway. She had also dosed him with laudanum, shaved off the red whiskers, and placed a tasselled smoking cap on his head to hide his hair colour, then made him drink a strong cup of the last of her precious coffee — stale, but it would still have its stimulant effect. He had nearly brought the whole thing up, but seemed alert now, relaxed, even amused.

She suspected he did indeed think the situation amusing.

Kat heard the front door open, voices, footsteps coming down the hall. She put the sock down. Mrs O'Connell curtseyed. 'Master, missus, it's the troopers.'

'Sergeant Dwyer and Constable Morrison, Mr Markham, Mrs Markham.' Sergeant Dwyer had the look of an old lag made good; his uniform was neat but faded and he had faded tattoos of the kind the convicts scratched on the voyage out on the backs of both his hands. Kat gave him a minute curtsey and sat again.

'That's Tracker Gully John out on the steps,' added Sergeant Dwyer. 'I'm sorry to disturb you and your good wife, Mr Markham, but we're following a thief.'

The man in the armchair laughed. 'Well, you'll find as many of those down in the valley as you care to choose. Excuse me not standing up to greet you. Touch of gout, you know.'

'It's a cove calls himself Captain Quicksilver. He tried to hold up the gold coach from Tumble Mountain again, but we winged him this time.'

'What a ridiculous name,' said Kat. 'Mrs O'Connell, would you please bring tea? And some for the man outside too. Sergeant, Constable, please sit. How can we assist you?'

The bushranger tapped the leg propped onto the tasselled stool. 'Afraid I can't help you hunt, old boy. I've been laid up for weeks now. Dashed rum, the gout.'

And you are doing it slightly too brown, thought Kat. But the sergeant was no gentleman either and with little experience of their conversation, she suspected.

'No, sir. Wouldn't expect you to help in the hunt, sir. I wondered though if you had heard a horse pass?'

'No horse has passed all day,' said Kat truthfully. 'Nor all week, either.'

'He might be on foot. Managed to get a shot at his horse, too. It kept going, but wouldn't have lasted long.'

Kat repressed a shudder. She forced herself not to glance at the dead horse's owner. 'You are certainly welcome to search here. The local miners know my husband would see them off if they tried to rob us, but I hate to think a stranger might be hiding nearby.'

'We no longer farm.' The bushranger twitched his good shoulder in the ghost of a shrug. 'Stopped bothering with the gold rush and haven't bothered since.' He grinned. 'Got used to an idle life, eh? But it means we don't have workmen any more — even the convicts assigned here took off for the goldfields, and you know better than I there'd be no hope of finding the miscreants among the diggings. I'd be grateful if you'd give the outbuildings a thorough going over, and the fields around too.'

Kat shivered theatrically. 'What if the wretch has come through a window? You have a tracker? He might be here then! Under the bed, or behind a door! Constable, please, for my peace of mind ...'

The sergeant laughed indulgently. 'I'm sure he's not under a bed, ma'am. But Constable, if you'd be so good as to look upstairs ...'

Kat was glad she had left Zebediah's razor, comb and even nightshirts exactly where they'd always been, but hoped the constable didn't compare the size of the clothes hanging in the wardrobe to the proportions of the man in the drawing room. She put her hand on her heart. 'It would relieve my mind, sir. Thank you. Ah, tea. Will you have a tart, Sergeant?'

The bushranger smiled indulgently. 'My wife makes the best apple tarts in the colony. No, not for me thank you, my dear. I ate too many when they came out of the oven. Tell me, Sergeant, where are you based? Over at the Tumble Mountain diggings?'

They left two hours later. By then Kat could see the effort the bushranger was making to keep his voice steady. She managed to farewell the troopers as they came around the house from inspecting the long-empty granary and equally empty hen yard and dairy, and Mrs O'Connell's small cottage, between the house and the privy.

'Have they gone?' He looked at the point of collapse.

'Yes. Let's get you upstairs to bed.'

'You'll let me stay?' It was almost a whisper now.

'A right idiot I'd look if they found you half dead tomorrow and I'd claimed you as a husband today.'

'At pistol point.'

'Be quiet and put your arm around my shoulders. It's lucky there's just a handful of you.'

He made no reply, focusing on the steps. Nor did he protest when she undressed him of boots, hessians, waistcoat, leaving him in a shirt for nightclothes. Only after he'd been lying for some minutes while she brought a jug of water and a glass, then checked the wound was not bleeding, did he say, 'A good thing you know how to dig out musket balls.'

'I don't. I watched my mother dig out shot from a stable boy shot by accident. Well, he and the other lad both said it was an accident. I've bound up some bad gashes, just like any mistress of a house, but no more than that.'

'Kat ...' He took her hand. He had been holding it for some minutes before she realised he was asleep.

He developed a fever the next day; his eyes were bright and impatient when Kat found him struggling to pull his trousers on one-handed.

'How far do you think you're going to get like that? Besides, the troopers may return.'

'I'll make sure they don't find me. You can say your husband is "away from home on business".' He grinned. 'Which I will be, as soon as I'm on a horse again.'

She didn't tell him his wound would almost certainly break open if he had to ride far. 'Your partner will be worried about you?'

'Jimmy? Jimmy's at home, safe and respectable, and will be relieved there's been no word of Captain Quicksilver's capture. I was a fool to try the hold-up on my own.'

'Where's home? Come on, at least lie down till you've had some breakfast. It's good soup. I made it myself, and fresh bread too.' If she could get him talking he might find the sense to eat and sleep.

'On my family's farm.' He laughed at her expression, but let the trousers fall and swung his legs back into bed. 'Maybe I had better not say exactly where it is.'

'Jimmy is your brother?' She handed him the bowl of soup.

'No. Works with the cattle.' He looked up at her, amused. 'I'm not the son of some poor but honest parents who robs the rich to keep food on his old ma's table. My ma is dead, anyhow. The farm does well enough — a hundred acres, but it's all good soil and, as you undoubtedly know, even a potato brings a decent price these days if you can get it to a mining camp. But why break your back when a year or two on the road will have you living like a gentleman?'

'Jimmy agrees?'

'Jimmy's folk know every inch of this land, routes across country the troopers can't guess at.'

'Jimmy's a native?'

'Aye. Jimmy gets us there and back, and I do the ... persuading.'

'Successfully?'

'Until this,' he said shortly. 'The constable was hidden under the tarpaulin. I won't be tricked a second time.'

'What do your family think?'

'My stepfather, stepbrother and two stepsisters believe I make my living from a neat clerking job on and off in Parramatta and take Jimmy with me as my servant. But that's why I couldn't go home. Anyone with a hole in his shoulder will be suspect.'

'Then you'd better stay here till there's no hole.'

'Maybe.'

She took the empty bowl from him. He was asleep before she reached the door.

The troopers did not return.

He stayed in bed that day, and most of the next, getting up to eat with her and Mrs O'Connell in the kitchen.

Mrs O'Connell seemed most disappointed that 'Captain Quicksilver' was no rebel, holding up gold coaches to avenge the wrongs that England had inflicted on Ireland, but she still chattered with him more freely than she ever had with Kat while Zebediah was alive.

Zebediah had been an English gentleman, Kat realised. It had been that which kept the old woman silent, what she saw as an unbridgeable stream that could not be crossed till Kat was alone and grieving and, after all, half Irish too.

The bushranger healed quickly after that, though his wound broke open if he tried to use his arm. He chafed without occupation. The women talked to him instead, Mrs O'Connell with stories of the leprechauns who offered three wishes that inevitably brought disaster, and ancient heroes like Ó Súilleabháin, who'd one day drive the English from Irish shores.

Kat found herself talking about her mother, her fossil collection, and even of her father's crime.

The bushranger leaned back in the armchair and watched her face. 'You must hate him.'

'I wish I could. But I had seventeen years with the best father in the world and only one day with ... with the other. Not even that. He did it as soon as the letter brought the news. I still wonder if by evening he'd have found a way to live, seen that we all could have been happy ...'

'So what now?'

'What do you mean?'

'Will you stay here, living on potatoes? How much did your husband leave you?'

'In the bank? Or other property? I don't know.' She realised she had never even thought that Zebediah would have at least some money in the bank. But she probably couldn't access his funds until he was declared dead.

How much was there? She was fairly sure there had not been enough to build up another farm like this, with a sturdy house and enough land for sheep, and without a mining camp encroaching on its boundaries. Or was there?

She had never asked Zebediah if they stayed because there was no other choice, or because he did not want to choose. Just like her mother, she had left that to her husband. There might, indeed, be enough in a bank account to keep her and Mrs O'Connell in new dresses and silver teapots all their lives, or even just to restore and restock this farm, if she thought there was no chance of the prospectors returning to ruin the valley all over again. But with the sand that had held the flecks of gold mostly washed away, there seemed little risk of that.

I have five hundred guineas settled on me that I can draw on too, she remembered. But Zebediah had never suggested that she should. I have a silver tea service and cutlery that could be sold, the emerald earrings he gave me when we wed, the jars with grains of gold and coins buried about the garden.

What was the interest on five hundred guineas? Or was it more now? Twenty pounds a year would probably buy all she and Mrs O'Connell would need ...

She found him gazing at her, eyes twinkling. 'Have the little people stolen you away?'

'I'm sorry. I never thought ... I haven't thought about money.'

'You will marry again,' he said with certainty. 'Then your husband can do the worrying.'

He doesn't know about the five hundred guineas, she thought, though he probably has a reasonable idea of how much was buried in tin cans if he and Jimmy have been watching the farm. 'No, I won't marry again.'

'This isn't India, where a widow is supposed to burn herself alive for her husband,' he said impatiently. 'One day you'll want to.'

She shook her head. She had risked her independence once and won. It seemed unlikely she would ever meet a man like Zebediah again.

'Kat ... I didn't tell you. I gave a traveller a letter to take to my stepfather. It says I'm staying at the house of a friend of my employer. Jimmy will guess where I am and be coming for me soon.'

Kat thought: Mrs O'Connell and I will be lonely. And then, perhaps we do not need to be. Not always.

She needed to come to terms with the fact that she was not penniless. She did not need Titania's charity, though she was glad of the friendship that offered it. It was time to look for help on the farm, too, or at least someone to chop firewood. They couldn't keep cooking on fallen branches roughly broken with an axe.

She found the bushranger looking at her intently. 'I'd like to say I'll see you soon. I probably will, but you won't see me. Kat, it's hard to thank a woman for saving your life.'

'Then don't try. I enjoyed it,' she said honestly. She managed a smile. 'I wasn't born to be good. I just was, with Zebediah.'

'Ah, you'd make a fine wife for a bushranger, but bushrangers make their wives widows too.'

'Just don't get shot again.'

He put his hand on his heart. 'I give you my solemn word, I will do my best to not be shot.'

'An' I should hope so too,' said Mrs O'Connell, coming in. 'I took the pies out of the oven afore they was singed. An' there's a basket of oranges if you want to be making that honey marmalade of yours ...'

The sound of horses woke Kat the next morning, but she did not get up to see. Jimmy must have been camped above the house to be here at first light. She waited till she heard Mrs O'Connell clang the stove door shut with its morning wood before she dressed and went on down.

As she had expected, he had gone.

Chapter 41

KAT

A week later ten new hens and a goodly rooster, more resplendent than any she had ever seen before, sat on the perches in the hen house when Kat went to investigate the noises of poultry. She laughed, wondering whose hens they had been.

A gold crucifix, the kind worn by any prosperous Irish shopkeeper's wife, had appeared in Mrs O'Connell's favourite teacup overnight, too, along with a puppy in a basket under the table that Mrs O'Connell cuddled like a baby and called Ó Súilleabháin — definitely NOT Sullivan, Mrs O'Connell declared, even if they sounded much the same to Kat's ear. Not Sullivan attached himself to whoever was most likely to dispense food, and barked dutifully at every man, kangaruh and parrot who passed by, and at Digger, who had returned to the burrow under the steps now the human tumult had vanished, and grazed the garden every night.

Five weeks after those arrivals a vastly pregnant sow glared at Kat from Her Pigship's sty, safe enough, probably, with so few miners in the valley now, and all of them seeming to be hardworking men with good claims that meant they had no need to steal a pig, especially not one who might take your leg off if you displeased her. A cart from Tumble Mountain delivered six bags of flour, two barrels of sugar, a tub of treacle, a chest of tea and an enormous box of peppermints, all paid for, and the delivery too.

The peppermints, Kat thought as she crunched one, were a particularly nice touch.

The next day a dark-skinned man — not a native, Kat thought, but one with features like the freed slaves she'd seen working on the docks back in England — appeared at her back door. She brushed the flour from her hands onto her apron and wondered if she should run upstairs for the musket. But his expression was polite, not threatening.

'Yes?' she asked.

'I'm Black Harry. Cove told me you might want a bit o' work done in the garden, mebbe some wood chopped. The wife thought I should come up an' see.'

'Where is your wife, Mr Harry?'

He jerked a thumb down at the valley. 'Down on our claim. She's got a better eye for the grains among the sand than I have. We've built ourselves a hut down there since the floods, but there ain't no soil left that's fit fer growin' vegetables.'

'How much do you want to be paid?' She realised she had absolutely no idea of a proper wage for a farm labourer, either now or before the gold rush.

'Not money. Thought I make take me wages in fruit from your orchards — the wife has a fancy for fruit, and the cove I spoke to says you got plenty. Mebbe eggs too? As for vegetables, what say I grows 'em in your paddocks, with the muck from your hens and your horse, and you gets a third? Well, mebbe half,' he amended, at Kat's look.

Which meant she'd be lucky to get a third, but he'd still make sure she got enough not to complain.

'I'm willing to give it a trial, Mr Harry.'

He spat on his hand, then held it out to shake on the deal, just as if she were a man. She watched him stride down the track, obviously glad to tell 'the missus' that their standard of living would rise considerably. As would hers and Mrs O'Connell's, if this worked out. And if one man was prepared to return to work, there would be more.

She might even turn the property into a farm again one day. But did she want to?

She went back to her kneading, still pondering. She wanted Zebediah, and the life they'd had, the hopes they'd had, the valley of lagoons and waterlilies. What did she want that she *could* have?

Not to live in Sydney, even if Zebediah had ten thousand pounds that she could access. Nor did she want another property. If she'd wanted to leave she'd have remembered the five hundred guineas some time during the last months of grief. Her place was here, in the house she loved, that had been built of love. Here, Zebediah was with her still.

But she had to fill her life, too. She had enjoyed tricking the troopers. She'd also enjoyed seeing the bales of Rainbow's End wool carted down to the boat, but she was not fond enough of sheep to ask for Zebediah's flock back from Major Nash, or at least not yet. Sheep needed shearers as well as plentiful shepherds, more reliable labour than she was likely to have for some time.

There were no fossils there to hunt, and nor had she ever shared her father's passion for steam trains. The one activity she had truly found fun ...

... she stopped kneading, and looked out the window at the ripening apples, at the peaches too, far more than they could eat, or even Black Harry and his missus.

Zebediah had once said ruefully that nine-tenths of the potato crop they sold was probably turned into rum in some illegal still, terrible stuff that often sent men blind, but they still paid sixpence for a dram.

What would the colony pay for liquid gold?

Chapter 42

TITANIA

SYDNEY

Titania looked at the list in her hand. What was Kat thinking of? Please procure her twenty yards of copper tubing, ten copper kettles, the largest size, a dozen wooden barrels, twelve dozen bottles ...

She sighed. She knew exactly what Kat was thinking, and so would anyone who saw this order. She'd need to break it up, buy it from half a dozen different places and disguise it with sheets and carpets and chamber pots.

Kat! No word for months, and then this! Some girls were not born to be good.

She glanced through the pile of letters but there was none from Viola. She had only received one since Viola's quick note informing her that Major Nash was moving the household to the Hawkesbury for the spring after typhus broke out briefly once again.

Titania had written a discreet note informing her that *the purchase she'd required was available* — a good ship and a captain's wife who travelled with her husband, and who seemed well liked and sensible. Her husband ran a fleet of three ships on the Calcutta route. The captain and his wife even had their house there, where 'her ladyship' was most welcome to stay after their arrival.

But Viola's answering letter had spoken only of the weather, and the extremely large fish one of the men had caught and presented to the kitchen. An almost cold note and not like Viola at all — no reference to the 'purchase', nor even when she planned to return to the city for the arrangements with the solicitor coming from England for her birthday and majority. Surely Major Nash would celebrate the event. Was he keeping her there to surprise her with a party or a ball?

The arrival of a supercargo from an American ship from the Netherlands — an old acquaintance now — interrupted her thoughts. It took a civil two hours to take his order, to suggest a mix of fermented carrot and radish as an excellent addition to the sauerkraut; quinces preserved in honey as an essential for the officers; and that a long bunch of still-green bananas was an experiment well worth trying, for they ripened slowly, fruit by fruit, and could thus be eaten every day by those who had acquired the taste. Could she also recommend dried potato? Not suitable for the table, but an excellent and far lighter substitute in chowder than ship's biscuit, and sovereign for the scurvy ...

It was late when she finally left her office, but even by the yellow gas light she had no fear passing the shadows of the wharves, the drunken sprawls outside the shanties.

News of Mrs Boot had got around. One shove of her elbow could have a man singing soprano for a year, and when she'd told Dick Three Toes she'd pull his boots out through his throat if she saw him near her premises again he'd up and moved to Parramatta.

On the other hand a cove down on his luck could always get a shilling and bread with mutton and chutney carting barrels of sauerkraut for her, and there might even be soup left on your table if your old lady or the little'uns was poorly, and a jar of pickled onions or basket of apples.

Titania made her way up the hill, then around the corner to her alley. The boys playing marbles were long asleep, unless they'd been sent to empty a drunk customer's pockets in a shanty. Miss Marigold La Belle next door had extinguished her red lamp, which meant that as usual she already had her single client for the night and would not welcome another hopeful knocking on her door.

Titania inserted the key in the lock, then blinked at the lamplight from the kitchen. Mrs Halligan who came to clean each day must have left it on ...

'Viola!'

The young woman looked tiny, huddled by the stove, though the early-spring evening was warm. A small valise sat at her feet. 'I ... I'm sorry. I didn't know where else to go. I pretended I was taking clothes to the Poor Relief meeting this afternoon, then slipped out through the courtyard and walked up here. Mrs Halligan let me in. I must leave soon. This is the first place he will look for me.'

'Who? Nash?' Why else would Viola seek shelter?

Viola nodded.

She's right, thought Titania. First here, then at the warehouse. A ship ... No — though she knew the captains, so did Nash. But there was one place ...

'I'll get you a shawl. One of mine, to cover your head and most of the rest of you.' She held out her hand. Viola's was cold, but Nash might come at any moment.

She led her quickly down the alley, then knocked on the door. The woman who answered wore a red silk dressing gown and a frown. Her blonde hair hung loose on her shoulders. 'When the lamp is not lit, I'm not takin' callers ... Mrs Boot!'

'May we come in, Miss La Belle? Please? We need a refuge.' And of all the places in Sydney Major Nash would not look for them here.

Marigold La Belle held the door further open. 'Didn't you bring me mutton broth and barley water for a week when I had the influenza? Not to mention the jar of pickled cucumbers at Christmas. Now I'll have had two respectable women across my threshold. You know where the kitchen is? You won't be disturbed there.' Which Titania took to mean that they would not hear her relations with her client. 'There's a maid's room next to it if you need it — only a lean-to, but the bed is made up if you need it too, and the sheets are fresh — I keep it in case I feel like slipping out for a few hours by myself some nights.'

'Thank you. Please, don't say that we are here.'

'Who's here indeed? Just the night and a man who'll need another half-hour of work if I don't get back to him soon, and I want some sleep tonight. Put the cloth over the kitchen lamp if you hear knocking at the door, and help yourself to anything in the larder, Mrs Boot. Don't worry. I offer my gentlemen bed, but never breakfast.' She vanished up the narrow stairway.

The kitchen had once been the main part of the house, the front rooms added on. Its stone was crumbling a little, but it was clean, and the settee comfortable. Titania got Viola seated, a small pile of face and skirt, her arms hugging herself, and found the bread bin. 'Toast,' she said. 'You'll eat it, too.'

'I couldn't.'

'You will. And this ale smells fresh to sop it in, with some sugar. Come now. I won't talk until you've eaten some.' She turned and made the toast without waiting for a reply, stuck the hot poker in a mug of ale, then brought both over.

Viola sopped and ate, and a small amount of colour came into her cheeks.

'Now, what is it? It's been so long since I've heard from you! I nearly hired a carriage to see how you were.'

'I ... I wish you had. Cousin Lionel has brought me back to Sydney for our wedding preparations.'

'What?! You said you didn't want him.'

'I don't. But I have to marry him,' Viola whispered.

'What malarky has he been feeding you? When you're twenty-one you're free.'

'You don't understand. I didn't understand — I have been so stupid!'

'Viola darling, what is it?'

'I ... I'm breeding. He came into my room, night after night ...'

Titania gasped, and wished she could roar. The rage, and astonishment. And, immediately, the guilt, at not warning her, not protecting her. 'What?! How *dare* he?'

'He said I would understand one day,' Viola said wearily. 'He said I was too young to know what was best for me, to trust him, to be quiet and it would soon be over ...'

Titania shut her eyes at her own memories. She hoped Nash had been quicker at it than Boot.

'I tried to stop him. I truly did! After the first time I asked Alice to sleep on my trundle bed, as I wasn't feeling well. Mrs Higgins offered instead — I think she guessed that something was wrong. But Cousin Lionel sent her back to Sydney, and Billy and the other servants I know best too, except for Alice. She said that he'd told her there was no need to stay with me, as he'd give me a sleeping draught. And he did after that, every night, and watched till I took it. It made me feel sick every morning, and sicker too to ... to feel between my legs and ... realise what had happened while I slept.'

'Viola ...' Titania had no more words. She simply hugged her, and felt the small body tremble.

'I would have run, and tried to escape, but he was always with me. Always! He only stopped forcing me to take the draught when I told him my courses were late, that ... that if we were breeding the sleeping draught might be bad for the child. He ... he said we had to marry the day after I turned twenty-one and stopped being his ward.'

'You don't have to marry him! Marry the man who abused you! A cad who only wants your money.'

'I have to marry for the child,' whispered Viola. 'Titania, it isn't just the money. He truly wants me as his wife. I could stand a marriage in name only for my money, but ... but this ...' Her voice broke.

Titania hugged her again, guilt consuming her. It was her fault. She should have guessed Nash would not let Viola's fortune slip away. But it had never occurred to her Nash might turn rapist.

She found her voice again. 'You will not marry him. You'll sail away to India and call yourself a widow.'

'No,' said Viola, suddenly steel. 'You think I haven't thought of that? I will not make my child a bastard. My own birth was not ... regular. I will not do that to my child too.'

'You can't tie yourself to a man who forces himself upon you!'

'I have no choice. The wedding date is set for six weeks' time. The day after my birthday.' Her lips twisted. 'No man of honour can marry his ward.'

'He loses control of you and your fortune one day and gains both the next?' I should call the police, thought Titania, and accuse him of rape. But that would mean even more scandal for Viola, and scandal all her child's life, too.

'He says we have been happy. He assures me that we can be again. He says he promises he will not ... force me ... again. He only wishes for a son.'

'In the name of all that's holy, what if she's a girl?'

'I imagine he has considered that,' whispered Viola. 'I am well aware that husbands have rights, no matter what they say before the wedding.'

'Marry him, then leave him at the altar. Go to India as you planned.'

'And have him fetch me back? There may be many ships that leave the port now, but not so many that I could vanish on one. He'd find me.'

'Are you sure he'd try? He'd have your money.'

'He'd want his child.' She closed her eyes. 'He wants me too. The law entitles him to take us both.' She opened her eyes again. 'Titania, I think there are times when there is no escape. I must give my child a name, and a home too. How can I hide my child away, as I was hidden, year after year? I ... I have to make the best of this. If I can be a wife, conventional, obedient, affectionate, I'll have the life of any woman in society. I'd not have the life I want, but it's the life that I must have. Then somehow,' her voice grew cold. 'I will make sure that my child will be free.'

'There must be some escape!' cried Titania.

Viola looked at her hands, such small hands in their pale gloves. 'For me? None, or not for long. The ancient Greek Stoics taught that the path to true happiness lay in living each moment, not anticipating either pleasure or pain. They believed that true virtue is enough for happiness, and will shield you from pain. I ... I think I must be a long way from true virtue. I just want a few days of peace. A ... few days when I need not see him, not have to smile at him, and not pretend. I might find the strength for stoicism then.' She looked up. 'Do you think I might rent the room here?'

'Here?' It was at least safe, and indeed, more comfortable than the ship's cabin. Nash would never think to look for his ward in a whore's house, and Titania would make sure Viola had proper comfort, too, good soups and fresh cheese and pickles, and hugs as well, which none of those ancient Greeks were able to give her. 'Yes, most likely.'

'Could you lend me the rent?'

Titania felt her heart would crack. 'Yes.'

The kitchen door opened. Marigold La Belle entered, still in her red dressing gown, her blonde hair loose down her back. 'Well, that's him done and dusted for the week.' She pushed the kettle back onto the stove. 'Now, what's the trouble here?'

Titania glanced at Viola. Viola put her face into her hands, and nodded. Titania explained, as briefly as she could.

Marigold did not exclaim in shock. Titania expected she had heard far worse. She merely reached over and patted Viola's hand. But when Titania mentioned the major's name, her eyes narrowed.

'You don't mean "Nanny" Nash, do you?'

'His name is Lionel,' said Viola.

Marigold gave Titania a quick glance, then turned back to Viola. 'Let's get you into bed, with a tot of rum and honey to help you sleep. You can borrow one of my nightgowns — the ones I sleep in, not the flash I wear for customers.' She put her arm around Viola and helped her up. 'Mrs Boot, would you warm the brick for the bed? It's over by the stove. Come on, love. I warrant it will all look better in the morning.'

Titania busied herself heating the brick. She found the jar of dried chamomile flowers she'd given Marigold when she'd been ill, and made a tea, adding rum and honey, then took it in to Viola, and sat with her while she drank it, and stayed sitting there till finally Viola dozed.

Marigold sat at the table, a mug of rum and hot water in front of her. 'A bad business,' she said quietly.

'It's ... it's a nightmare. Miss La Belle ...'

'Marigold.'

'What did you mean by "Nanny" Nash?'

'The major likes them young. Got a name for himself, has Nanny Nash. He'll only take a child, and she must be virgin too. He pays well for it,' Marigold added briefly.

'I'd heard he'd been asked to leave the regiment,' whispered Titania. 'I thought it must have been for debts, or maybe stealing.'

'He was found with the daughter of one of his fellow officers. The girl was only twelve years old. Luckily, he hadn't had time to hurt her.'

Sweet Heaven, thought Titania. No wonder no one had told her, a respectable woman, the story.

Marigold nodded towards the bedroom. 'Reckon she's just what Nanny would like, for all she's a bit old. Got a real look of innocence about her, that one.' She hesitated. 'You wouldn't see me weeping over some rich bit o' jam who has to take a man she don't fancy. But Nanny Nash? He's a skilamalink. One o' the quiet ones,' she added, when she saw Titania didn't understand. 'Polite as all-out, except when he isn't. One o' the girls he had went and killed herself, and two others said he made it so's they couldn't be taken by no man again, no use on the game again, even if they'd had the heart for it.'

'Why didn't they go to the police?' whispered Titania.

Marigold laughed shortly. 'When would the peelers listen to the likes of us, against a man like him? But there's been girls who've come out of it well enough, and with gold to show for it, especially the last few years when he's had barrels of dosh to throw around the fancy. But a girl like your friend can't be bound for life to a man like that.' She hesitated. 'There's ways a woman can make a man turn away from her, but a husband can punish a wife if she tries 'em. Ah, well, at least a man like Nanny Nash won't give her the pox.'

It was worse, far worse, than Titania had ever thought. And the trap seemed inescapable. Titania felt her finger nails bite into her flesh, as she tried not to scream, or sob.

She had to write to Kat.

Chapter 43

KAT

She met him as she made her way from the ship, leaving her two valises to be taken to Titania's cottage for her. Two valises were too little luggage for a visit to Sydney, but all that was practical to take as fast as possible on horseback, for from Rainbow's End she had chosen to send a message down to The Harbour Inn at the river's mouth, to hire a guide who could bring a horse for her to ride to a ship that would sail her up the coast.

The inn was a fine stone building now, and the harbour hamlet there was bustling — it had become a regular stop for whalers and the like. Men were even working on a proper cart track along the river, too, for the small farms that now supplied the whalers. Even as her friend's world fell apart, hers was being rebuilt.

Titania's letter had been frank, furious and urgent. Nanny Nash, indeed! There was no time for the arduous trek along rough tracks to Bathurst and then the climb over the mountains to Sydney, with a choice of bullock dray or mail or gold coach from Tumble Mountain. While a coach trip would be faster than a dray, days rather than weeks, the presence of gold and other valuables the passengers might be carrying made a hold-up by bushrangers more likely. And she didn't imagine she'd feel any less ill in a swaying coach than in a rocking ship. And what did seasickness matter, with a dastard like Nash to foil?

She almost smiled, despite her horror and worry, as she picked her way around a dog scratching fleas on the wharf and then paused to allow a man wheeling a load of barrels to pass. She had helped one of the very bushrangers who made coach travel unpredictable, especially if the driver was shot or the horses stolen. Even if, like her, a passenger carried nothing a bushranger might want to rob, except perhaps her wedding ring ...

It was as if her thoughts had conjured him up. She stared at the figure walking along the wharf towards her.

'What ...?' she began, then stopped, for despite the weeks in her house he hadn't given her a name.

'Mrs Markham!' He bowed politely, then grinned. 'You have just met John Smith, come to sell the family's potatoes. You're looking pale.'

'The sea doesn't agree with me, and I don't agree with it, either.' Though she suspected her expression was due more to worry than the nausea she'd hardly felt this time.

'May I offer you my arm?'

She took it automatically. He looked both the same and entirely different, no longer in the faded anonymous clothes of a bushranger — nor Zebediah's borrowed shirts and waistcoats — but the moleskin trousers and bright shirt and neckcloth of a prosperous small farmer. 'I'm not going far, just to Mrs Boot's warehouse. Oh, my Lord, you don't sell your potatoes to her, do you?'

'Mr Smith' laughed. 'No. I know of her as a good businesswoman, but Pa's dealt with Campbell's since his first crop. I've just been overseeing their delivery to a ship at dock here.'

And if Kat went to Campbell's she might possibly find out his true name. But Quicksilver suited him. Just like 'Nanny Nash' suddenly seemed the perfect name for Viola's guardian ...

'How are your new hens, Mrs Markham?'

She wrenched her mind back to the man beside her. 'Extremely well, thank you, Mr Smith. We have an abundance of new chickens, too.'

'Guard them well. I suspect your rooster is an Oriental. You may not know that since Her Majesty's Poultry Exhibition, Oriental fowl may fetch up to ten thousand pounds.'

'Ten thousand ...'

'That is in England. I don't know what one would fetch in the colony. I don't believe any have sold yet, as only a few have been imported by certain large landowners. Nonetheless, I would sell some of your stock quickly, as the Oriental hens lay so productively that the price even of crossbreeds is sure to drop quickly once they are more common.'

She narrowed her eyes at him. 'How did my hen house come to have an Oriental rooster?'

He grinned. 'I can't tell you that. Every trade must have its secrets. How I escape and how I find Oriental roosters are mine.'

Kat stopped suddenly and stared at him.

He laughed at her expression. 'Do I have a smut on my nose? Or have you suddenly decided my company isn't respectable enough for you?'

'I think I have met the one man in New South Wales who might be able to help,' she said slowly.

'You need help?' He immediately looked serious.

'Desperately,' she admitted. 'I have a friend who needs escape. A friend in danger, trapped by convention and her own conscience and the law. Mrs Boot can think of no way to get her free, and nor can I.'

'I will do anything you need,' he said, and she knew he meant each word.

'Even marry my friend?' she asked impulsively. That, at least, would give Viola's child a name and keep her fortune from Nash.

He stared at that. 'Are you serious?'

'Most serious.'

'Yes,' he said slowly. 'I might even do that for you, but only if we can think of no other way to solve this problem — and only if your friend won't be clinging to me all my life. I would like to choose my own wife, thank you.'

'She's wealthy.'

'I stand by what I said, though in that case I might charge for my services.' He glanced at the crowds around them. 'Is there somewhere we can be private?'

'Mrs Boot's office.'

'Devil take it, Kat, you don't expect me to marry Mrs Boot, do you?'

'No. It's another friend — a far more wealthy friend, who will pay you extremely well if you can help us in this. Whatever price you demand.'

'Money is always welcome,' he said lightly. 'But I'd do anything for you, Kat, money or no. Let us go and see your friend.'

She flushed. 'Let me explain the problem first, then we can see my friend.' She would not, however, tell him about the desires of 'Nanny' Nash. Even Viola had not been told about those. Her anguish was deep enough already.

'Kat, me darlin',' began Captain Quicksilver, John Smith and whoever else copied Mrs O'Connell's tone and accent, but she heard something deeper there as well, 'I promise you, I will sort this for you.'

Viola glanced at him curiously, as they sat in Miss La Belle's kitchen. Marigold was not entertaining tonight. Now that she had a generous rent coming in, Marigold enjoyed nights where she could say, 'Not tonight, darling,' and be in bed, asleep, by ten o'clock. 'A whole night's sleep, just to meself. Haven't had one of those since I were twelve years old and ma auctioned a good price for the fun o' takin' me cherry.'

Some time in her professional years Marigold La Belle had also learned to cook — a skill still in short supply in the colony, for most city dwellers ate from street stands or at shanties. Or, rather, she had discovered how to put a large pot on the stove with meat and vegetables and let it turn itself into a stew, portions to be heated over the next few days, for whatever meals fitted into her schedule that day. 'In my business you need to be able to eat as you can,' she said frankly.

Tonight's stew was rooster, a luxury, from the two birds Titania had delivered the day before, along with the vegetables to flavour them. Marigold had already 'lined her pudding house for the shanty's gut rot' later that evening, and Viola and Titania had dined with her. Now Kat and John Smith spooned up the stew too.

'Not as good as Kat's,' he said. 'No offence, Miss La Belle, but Kat is a cook in a thousand.'

'You've stayed with her and Zebediah?' asked Viola, obviously assuming that was how he and Kat had met.

'Zebediah? But he —' The bushranger stopped as Kat kicked his ankle, hard.

'Zebediah couldn't come with me,' said Kat quickly. 'Yes, Mr Smith visited Rainbow's End.' It had never occurred to Kat that of course Mr Smith would assume she had told her friends her husband was dead. She had indeed planned to do so now she was in Sydney. She could not do so just now, however, when Viola's tragedy was so immediate.

Mr Smith gave Kat a sharp glance. 'I was ill,' he put in quickly. 'Mrs Markham was kind enough to nurse me. Indeed, I owe her my life.'

Kat flushed, even though the words were true.

'Mr Smith, I am pleased to meet you,' said Viola quietly, 'but I don't understand why you are here, nor why you seem so ready to help me — or think that you can do so.'

'I'm here because I owe a debt,' he said softly. The grin reappeared. 'And because I like a challenge. And as for why I can find a way to help you — Mrs Markham has most tactfully not said that I turned up on her doorstep with a bullet in my shoulder, and she fished it out.'

'Someone shot you? Appalling.'

He laughed. 'Quite reasonable. He was a constable and I was robbing a coach.'

Marigold laughed. 'Me first bushranger, and he's sitting in me kitchen, not in me bed and offering me a chest of gold!'

Titania stared, then looked from Kat to Mr Smith then back again. Suddenly she began to laugh. 'Kat, you are impossible. Does Zebediah know you have asked a bushranger for help?'

Mr Smith's look sobered. 'Mr Markham knows nothing of this, Mrs Boot, nor did Mrs Markham seek me out. I met her on the wharf this afternoon, coincidentally, just after she landed. She recognised me, greeted me and only then asked for help.' He raised an eyebrow at Kat. 'I think she thought that a man who committed crimes might be a match for another kind of criminal, one guilty of far worse than I have ever done.'

'There can be no way to help me now,' said Viola tightly. 'I have to marry him, for the sake of my child. Just now I ... I can't bear the thought of him touching me, of even being in the same house with him. But I will find the courage to do what must be done.'

'There are other possibilities,' said Mr Smith, surprisingly gently. 'Mrs Markham's first thought was that I might be paid to marry you, to give your child a name, then leave you free. But there's a disadvantage in that.'

Viola blinked, as if suddenly realising her path ahead might not be as straight and inevitable as she believed. 'You might want to marry another,' she said slowly.

'There is that. Lady Viola Montefiore also deserves a more respectable husband than I will ever be. I'd advise you not to trust any man who offers to marry you to save you, including me. An illustrious marriage might also make me the subject of scrutiny I would prefer to avoid. But I am expert in escapes, I have another plan. One that will leave you free of unwanted husbands and your child respectable.'

Viola shook her head. 'There can be no such escape. A child must have a legal father.'

His eyes gleamed. 'You're talking to a man who has spirited himself out of the end of a blind canyon and vanished from what seemed like a long straight road with the troopers not five miles behind, watching my dust.'

But that was Jimmy's work, Kat remembered. Was Jimmy to be involved in this, too? 'What's the plan then?' she demanded.

He chuckled. 'A most ingenious one. It came to me as we were walking up here. I still need to sort some details out, and have a chat to a few coves I know — the kind of coves I wouldn't want to introduce to ladies. I'll make sure they don't know who they're helping, either.'

He looked at the four women, one by one, meeting Kat's eyes last. 'I'm not going to tell the four of you the whole of the plan, either. There are going to be questions, a lot of them, and possibly for a long time. You'll need to appear innocent as morning dew, and not one of you has experience in lying, if I'm any judge. You'll each play your own part in this. If you won't give me your word you won't share it with the others, I can't take this on. I'm asking you all to trust me. Just do what I say, and Lady Viola will be free, entirely and absolutely and forever, and her child too.'

Titania turned to Kat. 'Is this a load of gammon, or do you think he can do it?' she asked bluntly.

Did she trust his word, or his confidence in his own abilities, Kat wondered? But 'John Smith' had tricked the troopers, not just at Rainbow's End, but who knew how many times before that. Nor did she think he would lie to her. She met the bushranger's gaze. 'We can't afford for this to fail,' she warned him. 'It's Viola's life.'

'It won't fail. I'll be in control the entire time. I'll get Lady Viola safe and keep her safe.'

'For gratitude to Kat?' asked Viola, her eyes entirely distrustful.

His eyes were hard. 'No. Because a man who forces a woman has no right to walk upon this Earth.'

'What's that got t' do with you, matey? Men mostly doesn't care what another cove does to a woman.' Marigold's voice was suddenly grim.

He hesitated. 'Doesn't matter.'

'Yes, it does,' insisted Kat.

'Very well. My step-pa married my ma when I was four years old. He's a good enough man, but I've never truly been his son. My ma was fifteen years old when I was born. She died ten years ago. The man who fathered me was ... shall we just say I have my reasons for hating men like Major Nash.'

'You're doing this for your mother?' asked Kat incredulously.

His eyes crinkled. 'No. I'm doing this for you.' He turned to Viola. 'And, your ladyship, Mrs Markham did mention money ...' he added delicately.

Titania's expression cleared a little. 'How much do you want?'

'Five hundred pounds? For that I will not just make sure that Lady Viola is safely beyond the reach of Major Nash, but I'll ensure he never hurts a woman again.'

Kat blinked. 'You don't mean you'll shoot him?'

The laughter returned to his eyes. 'You know, I didn't even think of that. It would sort everything out nicely. But although I threaten to shoot, I haven't killed a man yet. Shame on you, Mrs Markham.' He winked and added. 'My way will be far more interesting, and a far better revenge than a shot to the chest.'

'I don't want revenge,' said Viola tightly. 'I just want safety, for myself and for my child, and freedom, if such a thing is possible.'

He took Viola's hand. His look was kind now and she didn't draw her hand away. 'Marrying you would be trapping you, even if I left the cage door open. I'm a man who doesn't like cages. Will you trust me? Do what I say and believe that, at the end of it, you'll be free?'

'I think ... I think I am beginning to believe it. I can give you five hundred pounds. I have that amount, and more, in the jewellery I've bought in the past three years, as well as pieces I have inherited, if Mrs Boot can sell them for me. What would I need to do?' For the first time that night — after how many nights, how many weeks? thought Kat — Viola's voice had hope.

'You'll do what I say? Exactly what I say?'

'Yes,' said Viola simply.

John Smith glanced at Titania.

'Very well,' she said, unwillingly.

'You can count on me,' said Marigold. She took Viola's other hand. 'Men have got this world all sewn up nice and tight for themselves. They take our bodies, and tell us what we ought to feel with our hearts. We women got to help each other, just like Mrs Boot helped me, or we go under.'

'Kat?' John Smith demanded.

'I'll follow your orders. But if you let her down you'll wish you were in Hades,' Kat added fiercely.

'I won't let her down.' John Smith sat back. He looked as if he was enjoying himself. 'Send Major Nash a letter,' he said to Viola, 'saying you have been staying with a friend, considering your future and that you're now making wedding plans. Tell him you'll return one week before the wedding for the final fittings of the wedding dress, and that Mrs Boot will accompany you to help you with ... with whatever women need help with for their nuptials. You can stay with her, Mrs Boot?'

'Of course,' said Titania, 'he's a hugger-mugger, and no mistake and she can't be left alone with him.'

'Visit your dressmaker tomorrow, your ladyship — Nash may have watchers out for you, but I'll warrant a dressmaker is the last place he'd expect you to be. Order the most spectacular wedding dress the colony has ever seen, one that will stand out in a crowd, and make all who see it gasp.'

'Cloth of gold,' suggested Marigold. 'With red roses embroidered around the hem.'

Kat shook her head. 'Pure white would be more noticeable.'

'I've got some of those new horsehair crinolines in,' suggested Titania. 'Wider than a carriage, some of them, but they don't creak like whalebone. She'd look like a vast ship in full sail all in white in a giant crinoline.'

'Perfect. I can safely leave all that to you. Buy whatever other bride clothes would be customary, as well, and have the bills sent at once, so that Nash thinks all will be as he wishes.'

Viola nodded.

'Ask Major Nash in the letter to have your jewels cleaned. You know where he'd send them? Good. You can pick them up yourself, for Mrs Boot to sell what's needed. Give him instructions for whatever else you think needs to be done before a wedding, food ordered, things like that. Send him a list of guests you would like invited, to be added to his own.'

'And then?' whispered Viola.

'And then you marry him.'

Chapter 44

TITANIA

Her bed was a narrow one, but the advantage of being a ship's chandler was that there were usually spare mattresses in the warehouse — most ships' captains replaced their own at the end of every voyage, even if not those of the passengers — and certainly not those of the crew, no matter how bug infested. Several of these piled on top of each other made up a bed for Kat on the floor.

'Do you trust him?' Titania asked abruptly.

'Strangely, yes.' Kat stared at the ceiling.

'Has he told you more about this plan of his than he told me and Viola?' The bushranger had taken them separately, one by one, into Marigold's bedroom to outline the roles he wished them to perform in his play.

Kat did meet her eyes now. 'He told me some of it outside when I went to say goodbye, just like I know he told you some more of it at Miss La Belle's. I don't know what he told Viola privately, either. But he's right. We each have our parts to play. Best if we know nothing of what the others do. What we don't know, we can't say, and if none of us knows more than part, we'll look surprised exactly as we aught to be.'

'If this doesn't work Viola is shackled to a monster.'

'No. If this plan doesn't work we will find another way to free her, even if it does mean shooting him.'

'My sainted aunt, you mean it!'

'Yes,' said Kat, not quite calmly. 'Down on his estate when there's no one to see. I could play the innocent little woman afterwards, too, because why should I shoot my dear friend's husband? But that's not the plan, for which I'm glad.'

Titania sat back up in bed. 'What else haven't you told me, Kat?'

'What do you mean?'

'You are thin as a twig with the wood shaved off, with hollows under your eyes and calluses on your hands. Zebediah hasn't turned out to be a monster too, has he?'

'No. He died.'

'Kat!'

'A year ago. I ... I couldn't bear to write it. I would have told you sooner if I could have.'

Titania saw Kat's face set like plaster as she gazed up at the ceiling again. 'The gold rush took our farm. Not the land, but we couldn't run sheep because they'd be stolen. It destroyed the valley. All that beauty, the lagoons and all their richness, just became a vast stinking mess. I ... I had no time to write then. No, that's not true. I just didn't have the words to say what I couldn't understand: how a farm, an entire valley could change so drastically so fast. And then the flood came. But it was more than just a flood. The valley washed away as well, and my husband with it.'

'Kat, my darling Kat.' Titania scrambled from her bed and kneeled to hold her in her arms.

For a long time neither said anything at all. 'That's why I have to save her,' Kat sobbed at last. 'I could do nothing, nothing at all, not about the diggings nor the flood nor losing Zebediah. But I can do this. The three of us, well four of us, for Marigold will help too, and Captain Quicksilver too.'

'That's never his name.'

'As much as it is John Smith.'

'He's been in the newspaper then! There's a reward out for his capture, Kat.'

'But not his picture?'

'No. I've not seen that.'

'He keeps his face hidden during his crimes, except from his partner, who helps in the robberies and plans the escapes, I think. And me because he was wounded and had no choice. And now you know who he is too.'

'Viola will probably guess, eventually.'

'He's trusting us. Which is why I trust him.' Kat paused. 'He loves a challenge, and making the high and mighty look like fools. And there's the money too. But I think the main reason he's doing it is because this time he can play the hero, not the villain.'

'Maybe,' said Titania.

'Titania, marriage should be ... good. I never thought I'd want it,' Kat added candidly. She paused to blow her nose. 'When I agreed to marry Zebediah straight away I still thought, I'll give it a few weeks and, if I don't like it, I'll use the five hundred guineas to sail away again, so he can divorce me for desertion. And then one morning I found that now I couldn't live without him, I had to find a way.'

'Have you found a way yet?' asked Titania softly.

'I'm still here, aren't I? Or most of me, anyway. It helps that I will live in the house he built and loved for all the days of my life. But I'll never have another man in his place again, not even in my bed.' The faintest smile crinkled her face. 'I've a plan to keep me occupied, too.'

'The tubing and kettles and kegs?' replied Titania dryly. 'The village idiot could see what you plan to do with it all. Making rum from your potatoes instead of selling them to the miners? Yes, you'll make a lot more money. But it's illegal, Kat. Not a hanging crime, but you'd go to gaol.'

'In England it's a gaol term. In New South Wales distilling is practically respectable. Part of the Macarthur fortune was made importing and selling stills and buying then selling what was made in them as well. It's a fifty-pound fine and a warning for the first offence.'

'And for the second?'

'I'll worry about that if I've been charged the once. Who'd suspect me?'

'Anyone who buys it,' said Titania wryly.

'I'm not setting up as a shanty keeper. I won't be selling to diggers either — the flood swept the gold away too, or most of it. Those who are left couldn't afford what I plan to charge. Nor will I distil rum, either. I'll make poteen, just fruit and yeast and sunlight and a long slow heat. New South Wales has never tasted anything as good. My father ... my father bought the best whisky, and brandy too, but he admitted they were a mere flicker of star light compared to the glow of poteen. I plan to sell it at a vast price to the most discriminating households here in Sydney. You wait till you taste it, Titania darling.'

'You think you know how to make something better than whisky?'

'Well, I watched it being made for seventeen years,' Kat admitted. 'I've yet to do it by myself. I admit I've never had but a sip now and then either, one for each new batch, and my mother gave me a spoonful whenever I was feverish. But I watched a master at the trade, and he told me all its secrets. Oh, he loved to talk, that man, and I was a child, so safe to talk to, for why should a girl like me ever want to make poteen? A draft of sunlight, Titania, that takes all the pain away. Or enough so that you can bear what ... what must be borne. But there'll be none of that till we have Viola safe.'

Safe. Viola must be safe. Titania lay back in her own bed, unable to even shut her eyes. No matter what, Viola must be safe.

Chapter 45

VIOLA

SYDNEY, DECEMBER 1853

Viola had learned to smile, no matter what. She had been taught to smile charmingly.

She needed every skill now, as Major Nash himself opened her carriage door, his own smile a mix of caution and relief. 'Welcome home, my dear.' He reached for her gloved hand, and kissed it.

Viola managed not to flinch. She glanced at the servants lined up to greet her. 'A most wonderful welcome, indeed, Cousin Lionel.' She had carefully practised her lines, keeping the tone almost playful, even admiring.

'Don't you worry none,' Marigold La Belle had informed her. 'Even gentry morts don't listen to what's behind a woman's words. Tell 'em what they wanter hear, an' they'll believe you. Come on now, try it. You'll get the hang of it soon enough. "Ooooh, but aren't you the handsome one?"'

'That is a most handsome coat, sir,' Viola said now, letting her fingers stay in his as he led her into the cool of the house.

'I'm glad you approve. We have missed you, my sweet little bride.' Viola made sure her expression did not change at the new endearment. 'I have missed you.'

'A wedding needs preparation, sir! And not in the home of

the groom.' She kept her tone lightly amused. She turned to the housekeeper. 'Mrs Higgins, you wonderful woman, I am so sorry to have burdened you with a feast at such short notice.'

Mrs Higgins went pink, curtseying deep. 'A pleasure your ladyship. My very best wishes, your ladyship. It ... it is so good to see your ladyship happy.' She obviously struggled to find a discreet way to say that she had been worried, and was deeply relieved to see her master's ward safe and apparently content.

'Please accept the good wishes of the entire household, your ladyship,' said Tilson, bowing.

'I hope you have followed the instructions for the servants' ball too, the day after our wedding? We shall be travelling down to the Hawkesbury the next morning.'

Viola glanced at Major Nash. 'I hope that suits you? You were quite right, sir, to remove us there this spring, as you always are. I've found the city air stifling now summer is here.'

His eyes had lost their watchfulness. Marigold had been right. He heard only what he wanted to hear. 'We shall go wherever you wish, my dear.'

'Then that is settled. Mrs Higgins, you have no problems with the wedding breakfast menu I sent you?'

'None at all, your ladyship.' Mrs Higgins seemed even more reassured to be on such a familiar subject. 'The ducks and pheasants are hanging in the larder as we speak, and Cook has ordered the ice special so the aspics don't melt in this heat, nor the Boeuf en Gelee. The cake has six tiers each with six arches, just as you ordered.'

'A bride has only one wedding day,' said Viola lightly.

'If you don't mind my asking, my lady, when will the dress be delivered?' asked Mrs Higgins eagerly.

Viola managed a laugh. 'When the groom is not in the house. Sometime tomorrow — and I shall send for you to see the fitting. Shall I see you at teatime, sir, or at dinner? I hope you don't mind that Mrs Boot is joining us? It seemed ... convenable that she might chaperone me until the day.'

'I have matters to attend to this afternoon, but dinner, certainly. Of course your friend is welcome.' He lifted her hand once more and kissed it again. She flushed and hoped the smile would make it seem a blush.

She managed to keep the smile as she ascended the stairs, greeted the waiting Alice and answered questions, as she let her pelisse be removed, her dress unbuttoned, the waiting fresh day dress lowered over her head and fastened, clean stockings and the silk slippers of the kind she liked to wear indoors.

Alice must guess she was breeding. The one personal task a lady performed was to remove and replace her own monthly napkins, but even so, a maid would know when her mistress had her courses. But she had only missed two and might have had the second while she was with Miss La Belle. Alice could not be sure, despite the sudden haste of the wedding.

Yes, Viola assured her, the dress would arrive tomorrow, and the veil and petticoats. It was white, so, she would wear the rubies, rather than diamonds which would not show as well against the cloth. Viola prattled carefully on. 'My mother's necklace, and the bracelet too, and the matching tiara over my lace veil. Such good fortune that Mrs Boot knew of a consignment of fine lace.'

'White will be beautiful, your ladyship,' said Alice, awed. 'Just like Her Majesty's wedding dress. And no one in the colony has anything like your rubies.'

'Mrs Markham will be in blue silk. She'll be my matron of honour. Mrs Boot will wear a paler blue satin. She refused to be an attendant, but will be arriving after her work has finished tonight to stay with me till the wedding, just in case anyone thinks I should have a chaperone.'

'Mrs Higgins told us Mrs Boot will be here, your ladyship. She is a most pleasant lady.'

'She is the best of friends,' said Viola quietly.

'She is that, your ladyship. I'm so glad she'll be with you. I'm so glad you're happy, too. All of us downstairs were worried,' Alice flushed. 'I mean, I hope I don't presume ...'

'Not at all. Thank you, Alice. Thank you for everything.'

At last the girl was gone to check on the white rosebuds she had ordered and see to the starching of the widest horsehair crinoline Sydney Town had ever seen. 'Not whalebone. A bride should not creak! Mrs Markham will have horsehair too, though Mrs Boot insists that only whalebone will support her figure.'

Viola sat, her hands in her lap. She could not move, not even to lie upon the bed. She simply sat and let the tears slip down her cheeks.

The dress was indeed magnificent, the work of seven seamstresses for a week, led by a woman to whom the words 'No matter what the cost' was the sweetest music she had heard. Thick satin silk — another of Mrs Boot's contacts — had been embroidered a third of the way up from the hem and all down the bodice with white roses, till they met in a point just below her waist, the whole thickly sewn with seed pearls, which also trimmed the hem and the veil of Brussels lace.

'Sydney has never seen such a dress!' exclaimed Madame Lucie (the surname Bottomly discarded years earlier), and Mrs Higgins and half the female staff, who all just happened to be passing at the door opened to admit her, agreed.

'And I'll warrant that's true,' said Titania grimly, when finally they had the bedroom to themselves again. Titania had slept on the trundle bed in Viola's room the previous night, despite ostensibly occupying the room across the hall again. There had been no interruptions, however, till Millie came in with the morning tea. Millie had not commented on the trundle, though perhaps downstairs they laughed at, 'That Mrs Boot, deciding to have a last week of jam as chaperone again.'

'I never dreamed a dress could be half as fancy.' Titania still seemed shocked by its extravagance.

'Mr Smith directed that my dress should be both expensive and remarkable,' said Viola wearily. 'I don't know if that is part of his plan, or if he thinks it shows my conformability to my guardian's wishes.'

'My word, it's remarkable. You'll blind the seagulls with all that white. Now I'm going to call for some soup and toast, and you're going to eat it. It'll settle your stomach.' They breakfasted in the bedroom too, an excuse to cover Viola's new bouts of morning sickness. Titania had tactfully covered the chamber pot with a napkin and emptied it herself in the lavatory, installed for the ladies' use at the end of the corridor.

'Yes,' said Viola.

'It'll soon be over, love.'

'Yes,' said Viola, her eyes empty. 'Oh yes.'

Chapter 46

KAT

Marigold La Belle helped Kat button the sea-blue silk bought for the wedding, most fashionable, courtesy of Madame Lucie and Major Nash's account, on which Kat had also bought two new bonnets, a lace cap, one silk hoop petticoat in the latest style, three flannel petticoats, a muslin walking dress, two stout Indian cotton dresses, one of the new-style crinolines wide enough to sweep away small children, plus a pair of boots, two pairs of slippers, a green cashmere shawl, a green-blue flannel work dress and an emerald green silk 'Sunday best' to give Mrs O'Connell, which the old woman would adore, even if they had nowhere to wear their best to on a Sunday, and a red flannel petticoat which would scandalise her but that she would wear and enjoy nonetheless.

She only realised as Marigold La Belle fastened the dress for her in Titania's house, where she had stayed the week, that it had never occurred to her to wear mourning dress for Zebediah, although she had black in her wardrobe aplenty, from her mourning year for her parents. Perhaps if there had been a proper place and time to mourn, a funeral, a wake, she would have thought to do it.

And would be out of mourning now.

Marigold looked at her own reflection in Titania's mirror. Her purple silk dress was also courtesy of Major Nash, though he would never know it nor, probably, the identity of the woman who would sit next to Titania on the bride's side of the church this morning. Kat had done Marigold's hair in the sober roll at the back of her neck that was one of the few styles she could manage. Marigold's elegantly trimmed bonnet would cover any wisps that escaped.

'The woman who invented bonnets knew what she was doin',' said Marigold, fingering the hat's lace and satin trim. 'Don't think no gentry cove is going to recognise me at the church in this. There's been gents among me customers too.'

'The other guests will all think you are the beautiful Lady, er, Beatrice de Vere, come out from England for Lady Viola's wedding. Mr Smith says you have a role to play too.'

'I do, and glad I am it's a small one. I ain't sure of that beau of yours, Mrs Markham. 'e's a captain sharp an' no mistake. He's enjoyin' this far too much. I don't know what his game is, but I warrant it ain't just rescuing Lady Viola.'

Kat frowned. 'He's not my beau.'

''e thinks 'e is.'

'Then he's wrong. Besides, he's getting five hundred pounds.'

'Five hundred pounds! I could live like a queen with five hundred pounds.'

Kat thought of her own five hundred guineas, still incredulous she had once forgotten it. Perhaps she had not wanted the choices it would bring. But she knew what she wanted, now. 'Viola's made provision for you, too,' she admitted. 'She opened a bank account for you, though I don't know how much is in it, and she had her lawyer draw up an annuity. That means an income for life,' she added.

'I hoped she might do summat like that,' said Miss La Belle artlessly. 'Guineas being as common as mice to her. Be nice not to have to work nights, except for me pets now and then to keep me hand in. But that ain't why I'm helping her.'

'I know,' said Kat.

There had been a brief visit to the lawyer this afternoon with Major Nash, to confirm Viola's majority and the ownership of her income, as well as to open a bank account in her own name.

Hopefully Major Nash did not know of Viola's second visit to the lawyer with Kat, as well as to the bank just before closing, to withdraw both the maximum amount of coin and notes available, as well as to arrange several bank drafts made out to Mrs Boot, and the new account for Marigold. Viola now had access to far more money than the sale of her jewellery would bring.

Viola had also authorised the transfer of two of her properties in England to Titania and Kat. There was no way to prevent Major Nash from controlling Viola's estate once they were married, but he would find less than half the property he expected. Kat had urged her to try to liquidate it all, but Titania had argued for caution. Major Nash would still be a most wealthy man. Losing more than half might well prompt him to take legal action to try to regain what had been signed away, on the grounds of undue influence on his innocent bride.

Had Mr Smith been paid yet? Apart from a quick conference at Titania's office Kat had not seen him again, though she knew Titania had.

Marigold gazed at her reflection again. 'I do look fine, don't I? I suppose I could be taken for a lady if I keep me trap shut and me knees together. But I'll slip into the church by the side door, just to be safe, not go through the crowds out the front. There's bound to be crowds, for a wedding like this. Half o' Sydney will want to see the bride.'

'You know St John's?' asked Kat, surprised.

Marigold looked away. 'Me gran was half dead on the Second Fleet of cons when the Reverend Johnson went down into the hold an' carried her up. Gran an' Ma an' me always gone to church every week on account o' that, and no customers all Sunday neither, not till Sunday night. Last Sunday when we were all planning was the first church service I missed since I was off for a month last winter with a bout of the whites.'

Kat was not sure what a bout of the whites was, and nor was this the time to ask. She peered out the window. 'Major Nash's carriage is here. I'll see you at the church.'

'She ain't really goin' through with it?'

'She says she has to.'

'You ain't gammoning me? I was sure Mr Smith and Mrs Boot was going to do a bolt with 'er instead of goin' to the church. Come on,' she urged. 'Is that the plan? I won't split on yers.'

'As far as I know Viola is going to marry Major Nash this morning, and I hope he rots in hell for it,' said Kat.

'Oh. Well. At least I gets to choose who I lie down with. An' I get paid for it, an' paid well since I made me reputation. You know that little kitten didn't even have a shillin' of her own when she came? Some blessed footman always carried the readies for her if she wanted to tip the boy who swept the roadway. Mrs Boot had to lend her the gelt to pay me, not that I wouldn't have taken her for nothing.'

'You're a good woman.'

Marigold grinned, showing the gaps in her back teeth. 'So the gentlemen tell me. I'm very good indeed. A heart of gold, that's me — but only the outside bit, an' it's gold 'cause that's what they pay me. The rest of me heart's me own. I learned early that if we tarts don't look after each ovver we're scum under their boots when they've had enough o' us. I just never thought it happened with the gentry too.'

'Oh, yes,' said Kat. 'We need to ... look after each other.' In the past year she had forgotten that. Life seemed real again ... since she had told Titania what had truly happened.

Kat had finally checked her deposit at the Bank of New South Wales and found she had not only the five hundred guineas, but an extra seven pounds two shillings and threepence interest on the account.

Her copper pipes, casks, jugs and kettles were being shipped in three wagon loads to the farm even now, divided and disguised among new bed linen, a long red and blue carpet for the hall, six large baskets and two small, a set of saucepans and sundry other items, none of which she needed, as well as the usual sacks of flour, a tea chest, and — very carefully — no more sugar than would otherwise be used in a household of two women.

Rum distilling needed sugar, though poteen didn't. The respectable Mrs Markham should never be suspected of the crime of distillation, despite the purchase of copper pipes. Without sugar, how *could* she be doing anything wrong?

She checked her reflection in the mirror, adjusted the bunches of cream ribbons on either side of her curls — no bonnet for the bride's attendant — and stepped into the carriage, waving a lace glove at Marigold, who would hire a chair to carry her to the church so as not to appear at a wedding with a dusty ruffle at the hem, a sure sign of someone too poor to afford either a carriage or a street sweeper.

I'm excited, Kat realised. Worried for Viola, and angry enough to take a chunk out of the groom's leg as he passes. But, for the first time since that vast sheet of rain had blotted out her life, she felt happy.

Whatever happened today the bushranger had made her one quick whispered promise before he'd left.

When this was over, Lionel Nash would die.

'You look beautiful,' said Kat, as she shut the door to Viola's bedroom behind her.

Viola did look lovely, though the white also displayed clearly the darkness of her skin, and the size of the magnificent crinoline also made her look wider than she was tall. Well, Lionel Nash could lump it, every single giggle and whisper about his wife. Kat fingered the pearls at her neck, a gift from the man himself, just as he had given a similar necklace to Titania. Guilt, bribery or simply what a gentleman was supposed to do for those who attended his bride? Kat didn't care. The pearls should fetch at least fifty pounds, and possibly a good deal more.

'And this is from me.' Viola pressed diamond earrings into her hand. 'To keep,' she added. 'Just to keep.'

'I can't take these! You may need the money.'

'I already have all I'll need.' She absently fingered the locket under the dress. Even today she would not take it off. Titania fingered the cameo at her throat, her own gift, with a matching ring. 'We must go,' she said quietly.

They smiled in unison as they went down the stairs — Viola first, her skirt over its crinoline so wide she had to walk in front, lifting her hem, entirely filling the stairway, with Kat and Titania then in single file, each in skirts very nearly fantastic, swaying back and forth against their legs with so much force that Kat nearly overbalanced. Maids trailed behind them. In front, an avenue of the rest of the staff and possibly half the household from the estate too lined the hallway and front steps. Tilson himself helped them into the carriage, an exquisite vehicle hired for the day with matching attendants at great expense, and the grey horses traditionally used for society weddings. Viola faced the driver, her skirts about her. Kat and Titania sat with their own skirts crammed up together on the other side.

For a moment Kat wondered if Marigold was right, if Titania would suddenly give an order to drive down to the docks, not to the church, and leave the groom waiting at the altar while the bride sailed away. But Titania didn't speak to the driver, nor to the footman who closed their door. The carriage rolled along the cobbles, then stopped in the clear space guarded by police officers.

Police also held back the watching crowd, hundreds of them, despite the early hour, men in bowler hats shiny with sweat and fingering, women in dresses washed free of colour, boys with faces of practised innocence, girls sweet and artful who didn't even glance sideways as their fingers reached for brooches, bracelets, fobs and watch chains. Some, possibly, were just there to see the show ...

At last the footmen judged the way clear enough to let down the steps. Titania let herself be helped down first, both height, and today width, making a bulwark against encroachers, then Kat. Viola emerged, somehow managing the vast skirts of the dress that swayed as she moved, her face set and expressionless under the lace veil, her small hand cold as Kat took it.

The crowd muttered in awe, either at the sight of the dress or at the brown arms that showed so clearly between the white sleeves and gloves and even under the thin veil ...

'Caw, look at 'er. Not enough of 'er to fill a snuff box.'

'Brown as a cob nut, ain't she?'

'Ain't she lovely, but?'

'How much you think them red jewels be worth, Harry?'

'Ooh look, her slippers is white too!'

'That's why they put carpet down for 'er, you lushy mollisher.'

'Me, lushy? 'oo was it got floored last night? Ooh, did you get an eyeful of them petticoats? The lace on 'em!'

'It will be right soon,' Kat whispered to her.

'Yes,' said Viola. 'It will be right.'

Titania walked ahead up the carpeted steps, solid rather than stately, coping well with the unaccustomed finery of her whalebone crinoline and silk slippers. Kat felt the crowd would have parted for her, even without the efforts of the footmen. The governor emerged from the church doorway, smiling and in full uniform. Now Viola smiled too, as he walked down the steps and took her arm.

Music from inside the church, something unfamiliar, violins and who knew what else. The wretched major must have hired an orchestra, either because the church had no organ or because that might be the fashion or ... or ...

Kat found she was sweating. She mentally cursed corsets, layers of lace, and petticoats. The governor smiled again at Viola, a signal for her to begin to walk down the aisle. The music changed. The wedding guests stood, craning to catch a glimpse of the bride.

Step, step, step between the crowded pews. Kat could hear the silk of Viola's dress above the music, the whispers on either side, admiration for the dress or simply complaints about the crush. Kat neither knew nor cared. There was Lionel Nash, in a lavender tailcoat and white waistcoat, with two groomsmen, presumably to catch the bride if she tried to flee. And Titania sat in the front row, wonderful and solid, with Marigold by her side, looking ready to attack the groom with her new and most fashionable Japanese fan if he dared to lay a hand too forcefully on his tiny bride.

Viola handed Kat her flowers. She stepped back, to sit beside Titania. The governor put Viola's hand into her groom's. The governor stepped back, to sit in prominence on the other side.

The service began. 'Dearly beloved, we are gathered here in the presence of God ...'

Kat suddenly began to cry. The last wedding she'd been to had been hers and Zebediah's and it had been a mockery as well, but of another kind, and the only treachery had been hers, and not that bad, even if she had carried it out.

'Here, love.' Marigold handed her a handkerchief, not nearly as new as her dress. Kat wiped her nose, quietly, and hoped her tears would pass as a wave of sentiment.

'I do,' said Viola clearly.

'You may now kiss the bride.'

Lionel Nash lifted the veil and bent his lips to Viola's. She accepted them. She even smiled.

That moment of course should be the end, but weddings always dragged on forever after that, signing paperwork — Kat remembered pages of it; she had never quite been sure what.

Back home the early peaches would be ripening. How Zebediah had laughed as he watched her eat her first Australian peach, so fat the juice had run down her chin and even her neck. He had kissed the stain away. Kat wiped her eyes again, then blew her nose, as inconspicuously as possible.

Music, once again. Kat stood, as Viola, still smiling, walked arm in arm with her groom down the aisle. The governor offered Kat his arm too. Kat had not expected that but, of course, he must have precedence, so it made sense to walk with Viola's attendant ...

Down the aisle again, guests murmuring, clearly admiring the couple, the ludicrous extravagance of the dress, laughing, beginning to press behind her.

Viola halted on the doorway as instructed, for the pantograph that Major Nash had ordered to take pictures as a memento of the occasion. Kat stood to one side, as the major's fingers rested slightly too firmly on his new wife's arm. They stood totally still for second after second while the machine under its black cloth recorded the event.

And then the pantograph was finished. Major Nash bowed to the governor. Viola curtseyed. The governor smiled benignly, his duty done. The guests began to shove forwards again, and Titania was beside her.

'Thank goodness that's over,' Titania muttered, moving to one side of the door as guests began to press congratulations on a still smiling, smiling Viola. Her crinoline kept a small private space for herself and Kat against the stone wall.

'Kat! Thank you!' Viola pressed a kiss to her cheek, their crinolines making yet another semicircle of intimacy for the three of them. Viola turned to a woman in pink and peacock feathers ...

Someone gave a short cry of anguish inside the church. Kat hurried to peer inside, along with all the other guests in the vicinity. 'I can't see what's wrong,' she called to Titania.

'Someone must have fainted in the heat,' said Titania, not even bothering to move. 'And no wonder. It's hot enough to cook the birds in the trees already. I'm only surprised the whole lot of us ain't keeled over.'

Kat managed to edge her way just inside the church again. Yes, there was a woman in purple silk, being helped to a pew. Marigold! Smiling up at a man in a top hat, innocent as if she had just left the convent.

Was this why Marigold was supposed to be at the wedding?

Kat turned back.

Viola had vanished.

Chapter 47

KAT

For long moments all proceeded normally, the guests who had shuffled back to look at Marigold turning out to the day again, the crowd of Sydneysiders craning behind them to get a view, greetings, servants taking messages to bring carriages or chairs. Kat was not sure who first asked, 'Where's the bride?'

But suddenly Major Nash was there, what must have been the last few months of strain beginning to erupt in anger ... slightly too much anger and too soon, for such a day. 'Where is she?' he demanded, gazing at Kat and Titania.

'She can't have gone far,' said Kat, gazing around. 'Look for a white dress.'

'I am looking, you fool.'

'I say, sir.' That was the governor, blinking at the insult and the tone.

'I'm so sorry, Major. I'm truly trying to help,' said Kat, managing exactly the correct portion of anxiety.

Lionel Nash managed another of the day's smiles. 'I'm sorry, Your Excellency. Lady Viola has probably slipped away for ... for some female reason.'

Kat tried to think of what 'female reason' he might be referring to. A stocking slipping down? Nausea from her pregnancy perhaps? But the guests would surely have noticed a bride vomiting by the church wall.

His Excellency bowed, a trifle coldly, and moved on. Kat suspected he would not be at this morning's wedding breakfast, despite his role today. That had been for Lady Viola Montefiore's family position, and not for Lionel Nash.

Guests, most unaware of anything amiss, began moving off to the waiting carriages to be carried back to the house. Titania reached for Kat's hand, her face red with sweat. Kat kept her face of innocence. Titania looked worried, but so should any bride's friend, if something went wrong on their wedding day; Kat quickly deepened her look of concern, too. She did not have to assume her surprise or curiosity. How had Mr Smith managed to steal Viola away so soon, and in all this crowd? There was no convenient ridge here or secret valley to gallop along to mislead the troopers. The nearest chair or carriage was out on the street.

Captain Quicksilver had done himself proud with this escape.

Was Viola hidden in plain sight, in the watching crowd? But she would have had to remove the blaze of white and, yes, Kat thought, remembering the design, it was loosely fitted enough for her small form to slide out of — Viola was so tiny that corsets and tight lacing merely made her look like a child in adult's clothes. But then what had happened to all that gleaming white?

'I'll go and search the church,' said Kat helpfully. 'Perhaps Viola felt faint in the sunlight.' If Viola had ducked behind a pew she would make sure she didn't see her, too. She could also kick a discarded wedding dress out of sight.

'Yes, that will be it,' said Major Nash tightly, as if it were possible that about ten acres of white silk over a crinoline could have entered the church and not been seen. Kat discarded her theory too.

But she looked anyway. Nash searched as well, and his two groomsmen and, at last, the vicar.

Titania followed, but only to the shade of the entrance, fanning herself. 'She may already be back at the house,' she said to the major as he emerged again.

'Why the deuce would she have gone ahead of me?' he demanded tightly. 'Very well,' he added. 'I will see you back there too.'

He glanced around at the crowd of onlookers, even more numerous than before, enjoying the show. Word of the mystery had spread already.

'Bolted afore the wedding night, 'as she?' a man in a plain convict cap yelled.

'Didn't like yer ugly mug,' cried another.

The crowd laughed.

Nash turned, in humiliation and anger, obviously longing to be gone. The wedding plan had included bride and groom leaving the church together, in the carriage in which the bride had come. It still waited at the foot of the steps, but he would look conspicuous getting into it by himself.

'You take the carriage,' he snapped at Kat and Titania. 'I'll travel with Phipps and Smithers.' He nodded towards his groomsmen, standing carefully to one side as if to dissociate themselves from this ruckus. 'There's no need for you to wait for the other carriage in this heat.' He strode up to instruct the driver.

It's an order, thought Kat. Nash must have worried that Mrs Boot, so familiar with sea captains and quartermasters, would help his ward escape before the wedding. He was not giving Titania a chance to help her now. Kat suspected the coachman and footmen were being directed to drive directly to the house, no matter what the bride's friends requested.

Kat watched the major hurry off, followed by the groomsmen. 'We go to the wedding breakfast?' she asked Titania.

'Of course,' said Titania. She made her way slowly down the steps, still fanning, taller than any guest, and obviously uncomfortable in the corset and fashionable crinoline she so rarely wore. Kat caught a glimpse of her petticoats as she descended the final step.

The driver slid down from the box to give the women a hand inside — a driver in beautiful livery, but one who surely had never worn it till now, Kat realised in sudden shock, as a familiar face winked at her. She was glad her back was to the guests.

Why had he posed as the coachman? He could not have known she and Titania would make the return journey in this carriage. Had he been going to knock out Major Nash and take Viola to safety? If so, he must be as frustrated in his plan as the groom. But that wink had seemed to say he was pleased with how his plot was evolving.

Perhaps he just wanted to make sure both Kat and Titania were safely in the house before Viola emerged from wherever he had spirited her off to?

Kat forced her face back into its look of mild concern. She managed not to turn and stare at him as Titania mounted the two steps, then draped her skirts about the opposite seat.

Kat sat facing her in silence. The footmen standing behind the coach would be able to hear even a whispered conversation. The journey seemed endless, with so many carriages and chairs on the road. Their own carriage could not get close to the house with such a queue already ahead of them.

'We'll walk,' called Titania to the driver, as they waited in a line that stretched all along the road. 'I can't be melting in this heat.'

It was extremely poor etiquette to leave a carriage and walk to the front door, no matter how long the queue, but Kat didn't care what any of these guests thought of her. 'You go first, Kat,' Titania added, 'then help me down. I feel like a whale dragging an entire ship with it in this dress. How do women stand it?'

'I don't,' said Kat, careless of who might overhear her. 'I never wear a corset at the farm, or even petticoats except in winter. I even leave my arms bare in summer.'

She carefully did not look directly at the coachman as he politely tipped his hat to the ladies. The footmen accompanied them to the house, only slightly resembling gaolers.

Tilson bowed them indoors, his face slightly too carefully betraying no dismay that his master had returned, but not his mistress. Another footman showed them to the drawing room, though the doors to the dining room had already been opened for the breakfast. Kat glimpsed the jellied crab, the asparagus mousseline, lobster patties, sliced suckling pig, magnificently adorned trifles, and all the other luxuries that the four women had planned together in Marigold's kitchen.

Kat accepted a glass of ratafia, but barely sipped the stuff. Guests talked in hushed voices, wandering from group to group as theories and suppositions spread.

'Do you think he …?'

'I wonder if she …?'

'Not quite the done thing, is it, marrying your ex-ward like that …'

'But I was watching her the whole time. I tell you she just disappeared into thin air!'

Those who'd temporarily had their fill of gossip wandered to the dining room and filled their plates instead, even though neither bride nor groom had yet appeared.

The melting iced pudding had been replaced twice before it appeared that someone had sent for the police.

Chapter 48

TITANIA

Titania knew Detective Inspector O'Reilly by sight already. Much of Sydney's police work centred on the docks area, searching ships for convict escapees or smuggling. Indeed, they were familiar enough to each other for him to tip his hat to her while passing, and her to incline her head, though they had not been introduced. She'd heard that he'd been employed from the Dublin constabulary, though that had been some years ago now, before the Irish famine with the harsh winters, crop failures and small revolutions across Europe that had helped lure such a tide of humanity across the world to Australia's gold.

He now sat in Nash's library, a small square man, short but wide shouldered, almost square necked too, with a most pronounced chin and ginger side whiskers. He moved from behind the desk to an armchair, and beckoned her to one of the lower armless chairs created to allow a crinoline to drape. 'Please sit, Mrs Boot.'

Behind her she could hear the orchestra still playing, something light but neither gay nor sombre, the guests subdued now, still forking galantine of duck, pâté en croute, almond bavarois, the claret, burgundy, champagne and punch easing the awkwardness of a social situation never covered by convention, lending at once a hush and an avidity to the conversation.

No one, except the groom, seemed unduly worried, though decidedly curious and delighted to have a front row seat to such a scandal. True, Viola had made no close friends in her years in the colony, but Titania had assumed from the number of invitations that she had issued and accepted that she had been welcomed. Surely, she must have been liked. Yet the talk she had overheard in the past hour had been mostly about the scandal of her birth, with an undercurrent — never openly stated — of 'What else could you expect from a bastard half-breed?'

Titania had also discovered that Nash was still mildly disliked, even distrusted by those who now accepted his lavish hospitality, despite his recent years of affluence, possibly not helped by the knowledge that the money he spent came from his ward's income. There had been several mutters of, 'I say old chap, remember the time ...' and then a cough, as someone whispered, 'Not in front of the ladies.'

She lowered herself uncomfortably into the chair, over six feet of awkwardness plus the bulk of the crinoline, which kept tipping itself upwards as if it had a mind of its own. Of all the stupid fashions to cram a woman into, a corset at one end and a crinoline at the other. Her bulk today would make ten of the detective ...

'You must be worried, Mrs Boot.' The detective inspector sounded almost comforting rather than interrogative.

Titania immediately forgot the annoyance at crinolines. 'I am that. Lady Viola is dearest to me in the world, sir.'

'You have no idea what has happened to her?'

'I have several ideas,' said Titania slowly and truthfully. 'But I do not *know*, if that is what you are asking.'

'What might those ideas be?'

She met his eyes, green, and somehow very Irish. 'The same ideas as yours I imagine. She's bolted, rather than face her new husband, or she's been taken. Either would have been possible if she vanished during this celebration, but not earlier, from a crowd outside the church.'

'Then you do not know where she is?'

'No, sir,' said Titania, equally truthfully.

'You have not booked a passage for her?'

'Yes, sir.' She noticed his surprise. 'I arranged one for next week, on the *Mary Bryan*. I did so at Lady Viola's request last year. She had planned to travel to India as soon as she gained her majority. But that was before Major Nash ... proposed marriage to her.'

'Mrs Boot, I need not tell you that most of Sydney Town's constabulary are searching the docks area and questioning the crew of any ship in port. They will continue to do so until this matter is resolved. We are extremely experienced in finding any convict yet to serve their term, or anyone else not on a ship's manifest.'

'I would hope for no less, sir.'

'Why India?'

'I presume you know the scandal, sir. Lady Viola hoped she might find the man who fathered her.'

'I see.'

Detective Inspector O'Reilly looked at her silently for perhaps a minute.

'You said you had two theories,' he said slowly. 'Have you any basis for either? Was Lady Viola an unwilling partner in this marriage?'

'She was, sir.'

He looked taken aback once more. 'I ... see. No one else has suggested this.'

'Have you spoken to the servants yet, sir? They might tell you she has been in low spirits for several months, and that she even suddenly forsook her home to seek shelter with me. She only returned a week ago, and on the condition I came with her.'

'Then why proceed with the marriage? She is wealthy and since yesterday independent of her guardian's control.'

'I am sorry, sir. I am in Lady Viola's confidence. I cannot betray it.'

'Mmm. I will accept that, for now.'

An intelligent man. She could see him immediately understanding the most likely reason why an heiress should so suddenly and unwillingly marry the man who had been her guardian. She was grateful he did not put it into words.

'Your other theory — that she has been taken?'

Now it was she who hesitated. 'Sir, this is gossip only. But I am a merchant and, as such, hear merchants' gossip. It is said that Major Nash was deeply in debt before he assumed control of Lady Viola's fortune. This house was purchased with her money, but he still had to borrow a considerable amount to buy it. His property on the Hawkesbury is also mortgaged. Even access to Lady Viola's income has not allowed him to repay these debts. He is not a frugal man.'

'He might have disposed of his ward at any convenient time in the past four years if he was inclined to do so.'

'He would not have inherited, sir. To the best of my knowledge, Lady Viola made no will. Until she married, her fortune would have passed to her next of kin: her brother, not her mother's cousin. Alive, Lady Viola or her husband only had access to the income. If Lady Viola dies without a child then her husband inherits the whole of it.'

'You are mistaken, Mrs Boot. Lady Viola's solicitor informed me that Lady Viola made a will two years ago, though of course it has now been invalidated by her marriage. Apart from gifts to the servants, and a bequest equal to three years of her income to Major Nash, she left all she possessed to be divided between you and her friend Mrs Kathleen Markham.'

'What?' Titania stared. 'Sir, I did not know this, nor I am sure did Mrs Markham.' She tried to clear her mind. Who else, of course, would Viola have left her estate to? Yet it had not even occurred to her that she might benefit. 'That does not matter now, in any event. She has married.'

'But if Lady Viola had been killed before the wedding, her fortune would have belonged to the friends she obviously loved, not the husband you say she disliked. That would also be the case ... I apologise if this distresses you further, Mrs Boot ... if she had taken her own life before today. Had that possibility occurred to you?'

'That she might take her own life? Yes, sir, in the past few weeks, but I am sure she has not done so. If she had been ... of ... of that inclination, she would not have gone through with this charade today.'

'Charade, Mrs Boot?'

'I am sorry. A slip of the tongue. I am not one for ... for displays and society, sir.'

'So we are left with a husband disposing of his wife, in full view of the governor and Sydney society? Why not wait for a more convenient time, if he wished to be rid of her?'

Titania sat, silent, uncomfortable among the marble busts, the Roman statues, the wall of leather-bound sets of books.

'Might I put forward a suggestion?' the detective inspector said at last. 'Please excuse my frankness, Mrs Boot. I do so only because I believe you are truly worried about her ladyship's welfare.'

'Please, say what you wish, sir.'

'A man might, perhaps, wish to be seen by as many people as possible — even the governor — during an abduction, so that his role in it would not be suspected. He might well have employed someone else to do the deed. He might also wish to avert the scandal of a young wife abandoning her husband within days or even hours of her wedding, or a child born before it might be expected. Of course he now has another scandal, but in this case either his wife or an unknown ruffian must take the blame.'

'That is possible,' she said quietly. 'But I have no reason to suspect Major Nash capable of such a scheme, nor how he might have procured it. I do not like him,' she added. 'My feelings are more ... pronounced ... even than that. I did not wish my friend to marry him. I have been scared for her, and desperately angry on her behalf. But I have never thought him a murderer.'

'You counselled Lady Viola not to marry him? How would she have lived then?'

'With myself, or Mrs Markham for a time, and then in travel, as she wished.'

'And if there was a child?' he asked gently.

'Sadly, Lady Viola was no stranger to scandal from the moment of her birth. If you know so much about her already, you must know that. Mrs Markham and I would have stood by her. She would even have been free of the stares of society at Mrs Markham's. Her property is isolated.' Is Viola even now travelling there? Titania wondered. Rainbow's End would be searched, but by the sound of the countryside Viola could be hidden.

'Did you or Mrs Markham plan to accompany Lady Viola on her travels? The one she planned before her marriage?'

'We did not plan to, nor did she ask us to. She had asked, and I had arranged, for her to travel with the captain's wife as chaperone. Detective Inspector O'Reilly, Lady Viola seemed childlike to most people, with a most sweet disposition, even an innocence. I think her the most loving person I have ever known, and the most innocent in some ways. But the circumstances of her life, so organised and ordered by others, hid a deep intelligence, a capability and a strong independence of thought as well.'

'In what way?'

Titania tried to find the words. 'I cannot see Lady Viola doing what she believed was wrong, no matter the circumstance. That includes taking her own life, for suicide is both a sin and a crime. She would also have been taking the life of her unborn child. And if Lady Viola had been cast away upon a desert island, like Robinson Crusoe, she too would not just have survived, but thrived. You do know the circumstances of her birth?'

'No, Mrs Boot. I know the gossip about the circumstances of her birth.'

'Then I know no more than you. But whatever those circumstances were, they led to a life where she must fit in with those about her, often without true acceptance. A lonely life, yet I never heard her complain of solitude. She liked the quiet. On board the ship coming here she liked best to stand on deck and watch the sea and sky. Here in the colony, she loved to sit in the governor's public gardens above the cliffs.'

'I ... see. Do you have any further information or suggestions to give me, Mrs Boot?'

'No, sir.'

'Thank you. You have given me a great deal to think upon. Undoubtedly, we will talk again, but I hope your worry is soon eased.'

'As do I, sir,' she said, with utmost sincerity.

Chapter 49

KAT

Kat kept her hands composedly in her lap. 'No, sir, I do not know where my friend might be.'

'Nor how she might have vanished so suddenly?'

'No, sir,' said Kat, entirely without guile.

'Mrs Boot suggested she might have entered this match unwillingly.'

'On the contrary, sir, Viola was determined to do it.'

'Really? Mrs Boot seemed to think otherwise. Do you think her ladyship feels affection for Major Nash?'

'No, sir, very little I believe, but it is not uncommon for women in her position in society — or even my own — to marry for reasons other than affection. Mrs Boot ...'

Kat smiled depreciatingly, exactly as she had practised. 'Mrs Boot is a good friend, who I love dearly, but she is not always au fait with the way matters are conducted in society. Major Nash has proved a competent guardian. He has given his ward whatever she wished and permitted her to see whomever she wished to. Lady Viola gave me no reason to think his behaviour to her would change after her marriage.'

'She seemed happy to you, the last ten weeks?'

'I'm sorry, sir, but until the last ten days I hadn't seen Lady Viola since my own marriage four years ago. I am ashamed to say that in the past eighteen months I even allowed our correspondence to lapse. I owed her many letters. I received a letter from Mrs Boot, about three weeks ago, announcing Lady Viola's imminent intention to marry her guardian and asking that I come to Sydney. I did so as soon as I could arrange passage.'

'So you came immediately?'

'Yes, sir. I admit I was concerned about the urgency of the letter and the speed of the wedding. These matters are usually announced many months beforehand. I also wondered why Lady Viola hadn't written to me herself.'

'Why hadn't she?'

'I didn't ask her.'

'Did she give you any reason why she should marry so abruptly?'

'I think it was Major Nash who wished for the speed, sir. He undoubtedly wished to stay in control of Lady Viola's income. But you should ask him that — I am afraid I am speaking out of turn.'

He looked at her without speaking for several moments. 'So Mrs Boot is the more likely to have Lady Viola's most recent confidences?' he said at last.

'I think so, sir. But despite my ... deficiencies ... in keeping up our friendship, I love Lady Viola dearly. She is extremely easy to love.'

'You would do anything for her?'

'Yes,' said Kat frankly. 'But I did not spirit her away from the church, nor do I know where she is now.'

'Would you tell me if you had, if Lady Viola did not wish to be found?'

'Would I lie to you, to protect my friend? Yes, sir. But I am not lying.'

'And your feelings now?'

'Profound worry for her safety, sir,' said Kat, with utter truthfulness.

'No theories about what might have happened?'

'Only the most implausible, sir: that she was spirited away by ruffians. Possibly a ransom may be demanded. Of course, the "little people" my housekeeper believes in may have magicked her away.' Kat managed a smile, as well as tears, both genuine. She wiped her eyes. 'Viola does sometimes seem almost like a fairy, or an elf.'

'One of Mrs Boot's theories is that Major Nash himself may have arranged for her abduction.'

'What? Titania said that?' Kat shook her head. 'I do not believe it.'

'You think him incapable of such an act?'

'Utterly.'

'He is a man of complete integrity then?'

'Not at all, sir. But he has far too much dignity to employ cutthroats. If he wished to control Lady Viola's fortune, he would instead use the best legal advice available to do so. Which indeed I suppose he has done.'

'Do you like Major Nash, Mrs Markham?'

'I find Major Nash charming, well mannered, well bred and with every intention of providing his wife with a life of comfort and elegance. You may not know that her marriage settlement includes this house, as well as life tenancy of the Hawkesbury estate and a lifetime interest in half the income from her present fortune, the rest to be left on Major Nash's death to be divided among their offspring, according to a complicated set of contingencies I did not bother to follow. I accompanied Lady Viola when the document was drawn up.'

'Mrs Boot was also present?'

'No, sir. Mrs Boot was occupied most days — the wedding was arranged so hastily Mrs Boot hadn't time to get someone to take her place in her business, and so had to attend to matters there for some hours every day. Detective Inspector, I don't know if you are familiar with marriage settlements, but Lady Viola's was far more generous than most husbands would allow.'

'You do have experience with such settlements?'

She flushed. 'Only my own. But there had been several offers for my hand in marriage before I came to Australia, and my father discussed the terms offered with me.'

'Is that usual?'

'I believe not. Most women pass from the hands of father to husband with little knowledge of or voice in their disposal. My father was, perhaps, unusual in this.'

'Why did you refuse the earlier offers, Mrs Markham?'

Kat felt her face grow hotter. 'Is this relevant, Detective Inspector O'Reilly?'

'Perhaps.'

'I had formed no attachment, and nor did I then need to marry for security. After my father's death, and loss of fortune, I did need to marry.'

'So you, like Lady Viola it seems, married for convenience.'

It was difficult to keep her voice steady. 'Not quite. I had resolved, and so had my husband, that we would not stay bound to each other if we were not happy. But indeed, it was the happiest ...' Her voice broke. To her horror she began to sob.

He said gently, 'Mrs Markham, what is the matter? This is not just worry for your friend.'

She could not speak. At last he said, 'Your words were "it was the happiest". You are not happy in your marriage now?'

Kat lifted her face, then blew her nose twice. 'My husband died last year, in the big floods. I ... I felt the loss so keenly I was unable to tell my friends; nor has his body been found. Without that I did not know how to inform ... I could not face ...'

'It is no matter, Mrs Markham.' His voice was quiet.

'I have told Mrs Boot, but not Viola, not so soon before her marriage.'

'You are quite sure your husband is dead, Mrs Markham?'

She nodded, scrubbing at her face with the now-sodden handkerchief. 'I found a man who had seen the building he was in wash away completely. Hundreds of people gone that night, but few bodies, such was the force of the water. I asked every survivor I could find. Sam and Ben died with him ...' Once more she could not speak.

'Your children?'

'No, we had not — it was our young workman and our dog. I'm sorry. My husband is — he was — a magistrate. I should at least have notified the authorities in Sydney, but ...'

'But legally he is lost, not dead. Mrs Markham, I am sorry to have to put you through this ordeal. In months to come, if you will permit it, I will visit you again, informally, and we might discuss the matter of your husband's death. But till then, please, do not worry.' He gave a wry smile. 'You have in fact now notified the authorities, though I will do nothing about the matter till we have talked further, when you are ready.'

'Thank you. You are very good.' Suddenly she could face no more. 'May I go home now? To Mrs Boot's house, I mean. It's in Left Turn Alley ...'

'I know where it is.' He pulled the bell. Tilson appeared, with a swiftness that might have meant he was listening at the door. 'Will you call Mrs Markham a chair, and have one of the footmen escort her? Have you eaten since the wedding, Mrs Markham?'

Kat shook her head. What sort of policeman was this? A kind one, she realised. And also disturbingly intelligent.

'I believe there are no servants at Mrs Boot's home?'

Kat shook her head.

'Please have the housekeeper prepare a basket.'

Tilson bowed. 'Certainly, Detective Inspector. Major Nash's carriage is at Mrs Markham's disposal too. It has just returned from seeing Mrs Boot home.'

'Excellent,' said Detective Inspector O'Reilly.

Chapter 50

KAT

'Mrs Markham?'

Kat paused in the doorway as Lionel Nash came towards her, his face both angry and confused. He hesitated at the sign of her evident tears, resetting once again to the manners of a gentleman. 'I am sorry. You are of course much distressed by all this.'

'As you must be also. Major Nash, please be assured of whatever help, whatever support I can give. The police ...' She shrugged. 'Detective Inspector O'Reilly seems very good.'

'An Irishman,' Nash said dismissively.

'Quite,' said Kat. 'If ... if any of Viola's acquaintances know what might have happened, I am sure they will be more likely to confide in me, or of course yourself. But, sir ...'

'Yes?' The voice was kinder now.

'If she has been abducted by ruffians ... if there is a ransom ...'

Nash stared at her, genuine fear on his face. 'I had not thought of that.'

'But what else could it be? We are in a colony of thieves. Who but professionals could have engineered such a tragedy as this? She was right next to me, sir. I looked away but for a few moments. There must have been more than one villain, to stop her from crying out, to hide her, and they must have been adept kidnappers at that.'

'You may be right,' he said slowly.

'Who would notice half a dozen uninvited guests in all that crush? And there was the crowd of onlookers too, even if the constables tried to keep them back. They may well have let some through who claimed to be servants on an errand, or the members of the governor's retinue, or even police, to keep order among the carriages.'

'That is most true.'

'You will ... you will pay the ransom, sir?'

He pressed her hand. 'Of course. No matter how much, Mrs Markham. You have my word. Thank you — you have given me hope. I would pay anything to have my wife safely with me again.'

'Surely we will see her back, sir, though perhaps the kidnappers will wait for anxiety to build, then send their demand.'

Kat was quite proud of her invention. The idea of suggesting a ransom had only occurred to her that afternoon. She put her hand on the major's arm as he saw her to the carriage door — not the hired wedding carriage, Kat noted with relief, but his usual one — and handed her in. 'Keep strong, sir,' she whispered.

'And you too, my dear Mrs Markham,' he said.

Chapter 51

KAT

Kat knocked on Titania's door, then opened it.

'Is that you, Kat?' Titania appeared at the door to the bedroom. She had undressed already and was swathed in a floral nightgown and vast white cap.

'Yes, it's me. Is Marigold with you?'

'She just left.'

Kat lowered her voice. 'And Viola?'

'Not here. I had the carriage stop at the warehouse too, just in case, but she is not there either, thank goodness. The police will look there and on every ship in the harbour. Kat, do you know where she is?'

Kat stared. 'No. I was sure you must! I thought you would have arranged for her to take passage on a ship that sailed as soon as the ceremony was over.'

'Ships can't sail as predictably as that! They rely on the tide, the wind and the weather, and on the availability of a pilot to guide them through the Heads, too. Any ship might have been delayed by days or even a week. I wouldn't have trusted a captain who agreed not to put her on the passenger list, neither. A rowboat could have taken her, but not far, and she'd likely have been seen. Could Mr Smith have taken her to Rainbow's End?'

'Only by ship, or a journey of weeks over the mountain, where they could be overtaken — and, again, Rainbow's End is exactly where she will be looked for. I hope that isn't where he's taken her to. I could hide her there for a while, but eventually she'd be seen, if watchers were posted. It would be easy for Nash to hire a man to pretend to be a miner and keep the house in view. Titania, did you see who drove the carriage?'

'Mr Smith. He looked pleased with himself, so we must assume he has her safe,' said Titania wretchedly. 'Well, at least we've embarrassed Nash in front of the governor and everyone who matters in society. He can demand her back, if he can find her, but if he does he'll be laughed at as the man whose bride vanished rather than submit to a wedding night with him. With luck, he'll take himself off to Van Diemen's Land, or somewhere he can start anew. But I wish I knew what Mr Smith's plan entailed. We should have demanded more information but I assumed you would know, and you assumed I would ... Do you have any way to contact him?'

Kat shook her head. 'I'm sure he will present himself at Rainbow's End as soon as I'm home. Which can't be soon, as the police will wish to ask more questions. It would also look strange if I left Sydney without finding out what happened to my friend.'

'Mr Smith may be on his way to California by now, with whatever treasure he's accumulated *and* five hundred pounds. I gave him a bank draft for the total last night at Viola's request. I would have preferred keeping half of it, so he must come back for it, but she insisted.'

'Why did she want him paid the whole of it before the wedding?' asked Kat, puzzled. 'Why didn't she at least give him a message for us, to say she's safely away?'

'I wish I knew,' said Titania. 'Oh, Kat, I wish I knew.'

Chapter 52

TITANIA

Detective Inspector O'Reilly arrived while she was at the loading bay two days later, checking an invoice against a delivery docket. No matter what the worry, work must go on.

As she had expected, he barely came up to her shoulder, even in a stovepipe hat, looking almost like a gentleman in his dark, long-tailed coat. At least she was not in a fashionable crinoline today, but her usual olive-green poplin and a small lace cap, with a light cotton overblouse and skirt, to protect her dress from the smuts and grime that necessarily accompanied life so near the docks.

He removed his hat and bowed. 'Please don't let me disturb you, Mrs Boot. I will wait till you are finished.'

'You are very good, sir.' She ran a quick eye down both columns, nodded and added her signature to the end of them. 'That will do, Northwell. Will you come into my office, Detective Inspector O'Reilly? May I offer you tea?'

'Thank you. That would be pleasant.'

He sat while she brewed it, appearing to take in every detail of his surroundings with keen interest. 'Thank you.' He took the cup and saucer, accepted an oat biscuit. 'This is excellent. Your cooking?'

'My receipt. I have little time to do much actual baking, but I've several cooks in my employ.'

'Of course.' He smiled. 'Your reputation precedes you. It has been a pleasure to meet you at last, though I wish it could have been in happier circumstances.'

'Thank you, sir.' She sat. 'There is still no word? No, of course, you would have told me at once if there had been.'

'I am afraid there is nothing. A few guests who no one seems to know, but that is not unusual, I imagine, at affairs like that.'

'I suppose not, sir. I ... I was Lady Viola's companion and her friend, but our social lives were separate.' She shrugged ruefully. 'If I can be said to have a social life at all. She dined with me at my home once a week when she was in town, though I should more accurately say I dined with her, as she supplied the provender.'

'You didn't dine at the Nash residence?'

'No, sir. After my brief time at the house when we first arrived, I was never invited to dine with Lady Viola and Major Nash, nor to a musical evening or anything of that sort. If I had been, I would not have attended.'

'Why not?'

Titania flushed. 'It should be obvious, sir. I am not ... ornamental; nor are my manners those of a ducal residence.'

'I think your presence a great ornament to the town, Mrs Boot.'

'Thank you, sir, but you know what I mean.'

'I do. I gather you dined privately with Lady Viola each night the week you stayed at Major Nash's residence before the wedding.'

'We did.'

'Maidenly modesty before the wedding?'

'No,' she said slowly. 'More a wish to enjoy a privacy we might not have once she was married.'

'Major Nash objected to you?' he asked sharply. 'Was that why you left the position as Lady Viola's companion?'

'No, sir, nothing like that. Major Nash was quite welcoming. I merely wished to start my own business, and Mrs Higgins provided an adequate chaperone in the circumstances. But once Lady Viola and Major Nash were married, well, a husband has right of entrance to his wife's chambers. Lady Viola wished ... a period of quietness.'

'I see.'

She thought that perhaps he did. This man saw a lot.

'You helped her ladyship dress that morning?'

'Yes, sir, though her maid, Alice, was more truly the one who dressed her. Millie the chambermaid also came to help, and Mrs Higgins checked to see the dress draped correctly, then Mrs Markham came to join us.'

'I have spoken to Alice and Millie.'

I'll warrant you have, she thought, and to Mrs Higgins and all the others. No matter how discreet Viola had tried to be, no matter how sly Nash had undoubtedly been, servants saw everything. And Alice, Millie and Mrs Higgins were extremely fond of Viola.

'The dress seems to have been ... spectacular. So much white, and rubies too.'

'It was, sir.'

'Hard to miss in a crowd, so much white.'

'I have thought of that,' she said slowly. 'It would seem so to a man. But a dress is made to fit a shape, and a cloak is made to fit the dress. A hooded cloak over the dress and veil, a man's arm around her forcing her into the crowd, with others blocking the view and her back towards us — it is possible — just possible — that in looking for so much white, we did not notice a patterned cloak. The stonemasons had left several rough paths down to the street from the church.'

'That is certainly possible.' His tone gave her nothing. 'Mrs Markham still stays with you?'

'Yes, sir. Major Nash most kindly offered her the hospitality of his house, but under the circumstances ...'

'Quite. How long does Mrs Markham intend to stay in Sydney?'

'We have not discussed that. Until we have word, perhaps.'

'She is not bored?'

'Kat!' The idea provoked a smile. 'Kat is never bored. She has organised the scrubbing of my house from floor to attic — and my neighbour's too. She has discovered the morning markets and cooked enough yesterday to feed the entire alley, including a luncheon for the children if they stayed two hours to learn their lessons from her. I don't think any in the alleyway will ever forget her.'

Kat had also bought several bushels of last season's apples and early apricots, and was testing poteen recipes, using Titania's kettles and the tubing she had secreted back to the cottage under her pelisse, with Marigold La Belle as an enthusiastic partner in both the brewing and the eventual tasting. But there was no need to tell the detective inspector that.

'Back to the dress. Silk, with silk petticoats?'

'Yes, sir.'

'Silk is a noisy fabric, especially with silk petticoats.'

'Yes. I prefer poplin, or even cotton.'

'I gather her crinoline was large?'

'Yes, sir, the most recent fashion — and a stupid one,' she added. 'It is impossible for a woman to get through an ordinary door. I suppose the size is to show that the wearer only enters rooms with double doors. It was made of starched horsehair. Lady Viola thought that quieter than the creak of whalebone.'

He stood. 'Thank you.'

She looked at him, surprised. 'That is all you wish to know, sir?'

'I believe it is.' He smiled down at her. 'I hope your day goes well, Mrs Boot. I will see myself out. The contents of your warehouse are fascinating.'

She looked up in sudden alarm. 'There is nothing illegal here, sir. I have no hand in smuggling —'

'No, Mrs Boot, I meant nothing but what I said. I find your business entirely admirable and its owner, too. Good day to you.'

Chapter 53

KAT

Kat sat with her feet up on a stool before she tackled the washing up, a task she would not let Titania share, after her full day's work. Kat had cooked dinner for three or even twelve at a pinch, but Marigold had a customer '... and he's an old darling, regular as a morning fart, been seein' me every second Thursday since his wife took up The Poor Children's Small Clothes Committee meetings. Don't want to let him down again.'

Tomorrow Kat would distribute the leftovers to the children of Left Turn Alley, none of whom wore small clothes nor had any wish to, before they were off practising their pickpocketing, or luggage snatching. Perhaps she might ask them to teach her 'dipping' too? It might be fun to pick a pocket. Or at least know that one could ...

She was bored, she admitted, after four weeks in Sydney and a Christmas neither of them wished to celebrate, beyond the church service where both had prayed for Viola's safety.

She wanted her hens to feed, pigs to tend, to fuss over the size of the firewood Black Harry cut for the enclosed stove — he had a tendency to cut it just too big to fit inside the firebox. She worried about Mrs O'Connell alone in the house too, though Black Harry had promised 'the wife' would look in on her.

But at least the plan was working. Every newspaper had a new story daily about the 'missing bride'. By now the scandal would be crossing the oceans to England, India, and the rest of the empire. *Vanishing at the Church. Foul Play Suspected as Heiress Kidnapped.*

Nash would never live it down. Even if he was prepared to outface the sniggers and force his bride to return — if he could find her — he must know that she might leave him again. Yes, a man might legally imprison his wife. But a wife who could vanish before the entire congregation? Public opinion would surely force him to bring charges of desertion. Nash would certainly win the case – and keep the half of Viola's fortune she had not secured — but she would be free of him. But a wife who had deserted her husband would not have custody of her baby, nor even the right to see the child. Divorce could not be the freedom Mr Smith had promised.

She would be glad when they received a letter from Viola saying she was safe. It would not be sent directly to them, but to an address Mr Smith had discreetly arranged with Viola. He had assured Kat her letters would reach them, and they might send letters the same way.

She glanced over at Titania, wearily nibbling the pickled cucumber she claimed aided digestion. Cucumbers were as plentiful as onions in the colony in summer, and thankfully less pungent.

The knock on the cottage door sounded either gentlemanly or official. Lionel Nash calling in for sympathy once again? But that was in the mornings and he sent his carriage to convey her to a tea room, for it would be scandal if he called on Kat unchaperoned, and he knew he'd get no sympathy from Titania ...

... who wearily lifted her legs from her own stool, swallowed the last of the pickle and pulled down her skirts.

'I'll get it,' said Kat. It was probably one of Marigold's customers, wanting to secure her services for tomorrow, and mistaking Titania's door for hers, something that happened at least three times a week. She opened the door. Detective Inspector O'Reilly stood there. For the first time he was accompanied by a constable.

'Detective Inspector! Will you come in. Have you dined?' she asked automatically 'There is plenty ...'

The detective inspector looked grey faced but determined. 'Mrs Markham, Mrs Boot, I'm sorry it is so late. I bring hard news, and an even harder request.'

Titania stood. 'Please elaborate, sir.'

'Please sit down again, Mrs Boot.' He sat himself. The constable stood, because there were no other seats except Kat's, unless he sat on a stool.

'I'll bring a chair.' Kat headed to the bedroom.

'Please stop, Mrs Markham. I must say this quickly. A body has been found. We believe it is clothed in Lady Viola's wedding dress.'

'What?' Kat sat, suddenly, and felt the room's heat vanish. She tried to focus. 'Her ... dress, sir? You did not say you think the body is hers.'

'The person is too badly damaged to easily identify,' he said evenly. 'Again, I must apologise. The height, dark hair colour and age may fit, but there is no way to determine the features. It has been three weeks since her disappearance ...' He stopped, obviously deciding not to say whatever he had been about to add. 'Lady Viola's maid is waiting at the stationhouse with our female searcher — a most kind lady, who acts as special constable.'

'Major Nash?' enquired Kat numbly.

'The major could identify his wife but not necessarily her dress, which he only saw during the ceremony.'

'The rubies,' said Kat, with growing desperation. This couldn't be happening. Viola was free, even if they could not work out how or where. 'Her bracelets, the necklace — there was another necklace she always wore as well. She wore it that day, too, though it could not be seen.'

'There is no jewellery. But that may have been washed away, or stolen before the body was reported.'

'Washed?' echoed Titania faintly.

'I did not make myself clear. The body was found on the beach this morning, washed up by the tide in a cove, some way south. I hoped that Mrs Boot might join the maid Alice in identifying the dress. If you could accompany her too, Mrs Markham.'

'Of course,' said Titania vaguely. 'Please ...' She looked at him imploringly. 'Do not say she did away with herself. I could not bear it.'

Kat crossed the room and hugged her shoulders, hard. 'We will bear it. But Viola would not kill herself. She would hold it a sin. A double sin,' she added, meeting the detective inspector's eyes. 'Her wedding ring,' she added. 'Did they take that? A small gold band of two hands clasped together. I only glimpsed it as Major Nash put it on her finger, but it is most distinctive. If someone has stolen it, it might be traced ...'

Detective Inspector O'Reilly held a hand up to stop the flow. 'I'm sorry,' he repeated. 'There is no sign of a wedding ring.' He breathed deeply then added, 'The left hand has been chopped off.'

Titania fainted.

Chapter 54

TITANIA

She sat, back in her own cottage after a scene she would never forget at the morgue. She would never lose the stench of salt and decay, either, nor the sea- and muck-stained dress, impossible to mistake. The body's face had been covered with a portion of sheet, and the remaining hand covered by its glove, but tangled remnants of hair straggled across the table. Black hair ... Titania's big hands lay empty, idle, for what might have been the longest time in her life, heart and brain empty too.

She had never loved before, nor been loved either, till she'd met Viola. It had begun, perhaps, as love of a mother for her chick, then became a heart friendship, the social distance between them merely underscoring their closeness: they met and shared each other's lives, not for convenience, but simply for love.

'I thought I knew her,' she said softly to Kat. 'I didn't, did I? I never dreamed she might do that. Well, dreaded it maybe, but I told myself it couldn't happen. I thought we'd saved her, too. But we were wrong.'

'Yes,' said Kat absentmindedly. She, too, seemed lost, in this unexpected world that didn't contain Viola, though she seemed to be thinking rather than in shock.

'I suppose Mr Smith took her to the shore, where a rowing boat might pick her up, maybe, to take her to a ship at anchor, which could set sail at once. I didn't want to put it into words before, but that's how it might have been done.'

Had Viola flung herself overboard, Titania wondered? Or had she slipped away and walked to the cliffs in her fine white dress, the cliffs she loved, the slap of waves, the smell of sea, the wild free birds above. Was that where she had ended her life?

But her hand. Her poor lost hand, those fine-boned wrists. Surely no thief would have bothered to chop off an entire hand, when the ring could so easily have been pulled from the finger, or if that was impossible, the finger removed instead of severing the whole wrist. That detail was both the worst to imagine, and the most definite identification. Viola so repulsed by the wedding farce that she had cast even the hand that bore the ring away. Viola pretending to her friends that Mr Smith's 'rescue' would give her a life she could bear, when all the time ...

No, she could not think of how, nor of the instrument used. An axe, it must have been an axe, no, she must not think of that ...

Titania closed her eyes. She, who'd longed for many things — her own life, which she had found; the husband and child she'd accepted she would not — now felt one great conviction surge through every vein and give her life again.

'He'll pay for this.'

'Nash?' asked Kat.

'Who else?'

'Mr Smith. He promised to save her,' said Kat savagely. 'You paid him to save her!'

'He couldn't save her if she no longer could bear to be saved. This is the last thing we can do for her, Kat. Make sure the world believes she didn't die by her own hand. Have her poor body buried in a suicide's plot? Never! Nash killed her, sure as if he wielded a knife. Kat? Kat, speak to me! Tell me you agree.'

Kat was silent, twisting her hands in her lap. All at once she seemed to come to a decision. Her face twisted in what was almost a smile, though a savage one. 'Oh yes,' she said. 'Nash will pay.'

Chapter 55

TITANIA

SYDNEY, 1854

She tried not to think, except of bills of consignment and columns of figures. She ate only bread and cheese and pickles, for their good scent overcame the memory of the fragrance of the morgue. It was the only way she could survive. She could not think of Viola, for if she did, she imagined the poor eroded body underneath the sheet, the agony of mind suffered in the last hours of Viola's life.

She did not think of the funeral to come. Funerals were all-male affairs. She and Kat were not able to attend. Titania could only be grateful that the coroner's verdict had been death by person or persons unknown, not suicide, so Viola might have a Christian farewell.

She carefully did not look at any newspapers, the broadsheets, the pamphlets sold in every street, as each undoubtedly declared *Missing Bride Found Murdered*, *The Bride on the Beach*, *New Bones Found are Not from Missing Bride's Hand*. She only knew the headline of the newspaper that eventually proclaimed *Bride's Husband Arrested* because Kat read it to her.

Who else would benefit from Viola's death? It had come to that. No one, not her friends, nor her brother, far away. Only her husband. Those who had met her, from the governor to the servants, all agreed: Lady Viola had no enemies. A young woman to be loved. No one, it seemed, except her two closest friends, thought it possible that so delicate a young lady would have the desperation and determination and disgust to cut off her own hand. That could only be a crime of passion, and only one man had ever been close enough to her to be accused.

Kat had sailed on the first ship south the day after Lionel Nash was arrested, with no bail granted. No date had been set for the trial, but Detective Inspector O'Reilly had called in to tell Titania that it would be months away, though the police and the governor would do everything possible to speed up a case that was bringing such unfavourable publicity to a former penal colony seeking to remake its reputation.

Kat seemed to relax a little after the arrest — Kat read all the newspapers, even if Titania could not. And Mrs O'Connell had been left alone too long. And the peaches will be ripe, thought Titania without bitterness, and Kat has poteen and a new life to make, and I have my old one, my business ...

And yet, with Kat gone, and no visits from Viola, her life seemed an empty sack, which even Marigold's daily, 'You all right, me love?' could not even partially fill. Marigold's life was easier now, with the annuity Viola had left her. Titania assumed that Detective Inspector O'Reilly knew of the annuity, just as he knew of the bank drafts and properties transferred to her and Kat. He had not mentioned them. Surely those only confirmed Viola's despair and fear of her husband.

The detective inspector had interviewed Marigold, who had told the truth: that Viola had sheltered in her home because she was frightened of Major Nash, and feared he would find her if she stayed with Titania. The annuity must be in gratitude, just as the invitation to the wedding — but not the reception — had been. The detective inspector had seemed to accept this.

Viola's lawyer had confirmed his client had made a second visit, secret from the man she was to marry, and that she had seemed to know exactly how she wished her property allocated.

Marigold now only saw her favoured clients: the luxury of choice. She had bought Chinese carpets for her floors, an upholstered armchair and a chiming clock, whose hourly presence Titania could hear next door. To Titania's surprise Marigold was also paying for lessons in millinery, rather than going through a long apprenticeship, to learn how to create the perfect bonnet or headdress.

Months passed. Titania wanted to call down at the police station, to ask Detective Inspector O'Reilly when the trial would be, but though each night she promised herself she would, by the time daylight came she could not do it, nor even send a message boy to ask. Possibly, probably, the detective inspector too would not know, but had to wait for the colony's judiciary to set a date.

By mid-June — the shadows darker, the rats on the wharves thinner and the wind from the mountains sometimes stinging with a hint of snow — Titania was able to read newspapers again. Suddenly the headlines stared at her from her office desk. Not only was the date announced but it would be soon, as the defendant's legal team had undoubtedly known. Perhaps she should have asked Kat to write to Major Nash, who seemed to think Kat supported him, to see if he had already known the date.

Perhaps, being Kat, she had.

The trial would be by judge and jury, for though Lionel Nash had claimed the right to trial by his peers, he was not a peer. Men drafted from the street would condemn or vindicate him.

Kat came to Sydney for the trial. She and Titania both had been summoned as witnesses: Titania for the prosecution; Kat, for some reason Titania could not fathom, for the defence. Marigold had not been called. They did not speak of the trial, nor even share their memories of Viola. Her loss was still too fresh for Titania to venture that. Just once, in the darkness, she said, 'Nash will be found guilty, won't he?'

'Oh yes,' said Kat, invisible across the room. 'We'll see him hanged.'

They both wore black for the trial, as indeed they both had since Detective Inspector O'Reilly's appearance in Titania's kitchen. Black wool for Titania, black silk, and sadly out of fashion, for Kat, a relic of her mourning for her parents and not remade to suit the wider skirts, the frills and ruffles even a deep mourning gown might now boast. Though Kat had stayed with Titania — the mattresses had been replaced by a proper bed — they must wait in separate rooms down at the court, and not hear any evidence until they gave their own.

Titania waited. She had brought her small account book in her reticule. Figures had certainty — they did not change — but today even the marks on the page seemed to wriggle and she gave up the attempt to balance them.

She waited. The female constable, or searcher, a kind middle-aged woman, brought her tea with bread and butter, the butter too salty but not rancid, the bread edible, at least. At last, the clerk called her name.

The constable walked with her. Titania wondered if it was to stop her if she ran, or support her if she fainted, though she never had but once, and would surely crush this poor woman if she fell on top of her.

The courtroom blurred. Titania could not look at Major Nash, beyond a glance. He had lost weight and had a gaol pallor, but his bearing and his coat proclaimed him a gentleman and he had obviously been allowed to hire a barber. The jury seemed blurred into one man, pink faced, large knuckled, enjoying his self-importance.

'Mrs Boot?'

'Yes?'

The barrister cleared his throat. 'You are Mrs Titania Anne Boot, of Five Left Hand Alley, are you not?'

'I am.'

'You were employed as companion to the deceased ...'

She answered steadily, still carefully not looking but once at Detective Inspector O'Reilly, who sat in the body of the court and so must have given evidence already.

She had thought the detective inspector might have called on her at her office, or even at her home, to give her news as the police case against Nash progressed, but he had not. Why should he? Only her evidence had mattered to him, the evidence she had given last year and gave again now.

'Was Lady Viola looking forward to her wedding?'

'No. She dreaded it.'

'Then why did she agree to take Lionel Nash as her husband, of her own free will, in front of so many witnesses?'

'She felt she had no choice.'

'Was Lady Viola with child, Mrs Boot? A child forced upon her?'

'Your lordship, I object.'

'Sustained. Do not put words into the mouth of the witness, Mr Steadfold.'

'I apologise, your honour.'

The judge peered down. 'For the edification of this court, the jury and myself, was the deceased found to be with child? You are still under oath, Detective Inspector O'Reilly.'

Detective Inspector O'Reilly stood. 'The body was too torn about to be able to determine that, your honour.'

A murmur of delighted horror ran through the court. Titania clutched the rail in front of her.

'A glass of water, Mrs Boot?'

'No, thank you, your honour.' She should have brought a flask of tea, or even some of Kat's poteen.

'Why did Lady Viola agree to the marriage, Mrs Boot?' Mr Steadfold amended.

'I cannot break a confidence. I ... I can only beg you not to ask me to.'

'Very well, Mrs Boot. Had Lady Viola ever given you any hint that she might take her own life?'

'None. On the contrary, I knew her as a woman of deep faith and integrity who would never have committed such a sin.' I truly did think so, thought Titania, so this is not a lie.

'Do you know of anyone who had a personal grudge against or enmity with Lady Viola?'

'None at all.'

'Or any reason to wish for her death?'

Titania hesitated. 'I cannot say,' she managed at last. 'All I could give would be supposition, which is no more than anyone else here might give.'

'Perhaps not *any*one,' said Mr Steadfold, with the briefest glance at Major Nash. 'Did Lady Viola ever ask you for a professional service beyond that of companion?'

'Yes. Some months before her disappearance Lady Viola asked me to find her a passage on a good ship, preferably with a captain's wife on board who might act as her chaperone, leaving for India as soon as might be after she attained her majority. She wished to travel. I made such a booking for her, on the *Mary Bryan*, but I cancelled it at Lady Viola's request when the ship came into port a week before her wedding. Lady Viola insisted on paying the full fare, in case her place might not be taken at short notice.'

'Had she informed her guardian of her intention to travel?'

'I have no knowledge of what she told him, but she informed me that she wished it kept secret from him until closer to the date of sailing.'

'Thank you, Mrs Boot.'

Mr Locksley stood. He was the lawyer defending Lionel Nash. Kat had mentioned that a prisoner's right to a full defence had recently been established in law, but Titania had not asked if that meant last year, or last century.

'Did you ever hear Major Nash declare his deep affection for the woman he asked to be his bride, Mrs Boot?'

'Yes, several times in the week before the marriage.'

'He seemed sincere?'

'I cannot tell.'

Mr Locksley frowned. 'Did you, of your own observation, ever see him do her an unkindness?'

'Not of my own observation, no.'

'He was always kind, gentlemanly and considerate of her to the highest degree?'

'That is what I saw, sir.'

'Did Major Nash ever invite you to dine, Mrs Boot?'

'No, sir.' Titania wondered at the question.

'Or to any social event held by him, or by his ward?'

'No, sir, only to their wedding.'

'You had been Lady Viola's companion, Mrs Boot, though you were not her social equal, were you?'

'That is correct, sir.'

Mr Locksley raised an eyebrow. 'Did you not feel slighted by Major Nash that you were not on their guest list, when in this colony even an ex-convict may be invited to Government House?'

'Not at all, sir. I asked Lady Viola to excuse me. I felt guilty at abandoning her on social occasions at first, but she assured me she had no need of my company. Sir,' she held up her hand as he began to interrupt her, 'I never knew Major Nash to deny his ward anything she wished, except possibly her freedom. I am sure that if Lady Viola had asked him to include me in any invitation, he would have agreed.'

'These are not the wistful imaginings of a neglected employee? You have not, perhaps, concocted the story of an unwilling bride from malice?'

'No, sir. Lady Viola dined with me at my home weekly and gave me every indication of her affection. I felt no neglect, only love. It is with the strength of that love I stand here today.'

Mr Locksley flinched as if she had bitten his leg. 'I have no more questions, your honour.'

'You may stand down, Mrs Boot.'

The constable found her a seat in court. Tilson, a dignified witness. Yes, his mistress had not seemed herself for some months. Yes, she had vanished before without leaving a note, six weeks before the wedding, on the afternoon they had returned from their Hawkesbury estate. To the best of his knowledge there had been no word from her except a single letter, and she had not returned until a week before the wedding, accompanied by Mrs Boot. Yes, Major Nash had seemed surprised, angered and worried by her absence.

'Do you know what attempts he made to find her?'

'Major Nash ordered the grooms to watch Mrs Boot's home and workplace, sir.' Tilson spoke with the slight distaste of a butler whose underlings should not be expected to perform duties of a non-domestic nature, especially spying on a lady. 'I believe Major Nash had an arrangement with … other parties … to trace her too, but they did not give their names.' One of the great sins in a butler's world: *they did not give their names.*

'Did they find her ladyship, Mr Tilson?'

'To the best of my knowledge, sir, her ladyship's whereabouts remained unknown until she returned to the house, though her letter to Major Nash outlined certain wedding preparations.'

'Were you fond of Lady Viola, Mr Tilson?'

'Extremely fond, sir, as were the entire staff. Her ladyship was everything most kind in a mistress and so very much a lady.'

'Have you ever had any reason to think Major Nash might wish her ladyship ill?'

Tilson paused. The courtroom sat silent. Not even one of the ragged ex-cons in the back seats scratched a louse bite. 'It is not my place to say, sir,' Tilson said at last.

The courtroom sighed, almost as one person. Major Nash winced.

Mrs Higgins, in a new black silk dress with jet embroidery and matching cape and black lace cap, made a reproachful witness. It was not her place to judge her betters nor her employers. Her ladyship was all that was gracious at all times, and Major Nash invariably a gentleman. She had seen nothing to the contrary. No, her ladyship would not commit violence to herself! The very idea!

'As gentle as a lamb she was, the poor darling.' Mrs Higgins dabbed her eyes with a black handkerchief. 'I'm sorry, your honour, I should not speak that way about my betters, but you could not but feel for Lady Viola, all alone in the world.'

'Except for Major Nash,' said Mr Steadfold smoothly.

'Well, yes,' said Mrs Higgins, too carefully, and not meeting her employer's eye, and with the certainty of a servant who would have her choice of employers when this scandal had run its course, and knew that no matter what, Major Nash would not be one of them. 'Except for Major Nash.'

'Was Lady Viola happy at the prospect of her marriage?'

'It is not for me to say, sir,' said Mrs Higgins primly, then immediately followed it with, 'but I could see she was frightened about something when we were out on the master's estate. She asked me to sleep in her room with her, as she felt ill, but the master sent me back to Sydney that very day.'

'How did she seem when she returned from the estate, Mrs Higgins?'

'Not herself, sir. Oh, she smiled, poor love — I'm sorry if that's disrespectful, sir, but she had a way of making you love her. I could tell she had been crying. She looked so pale too. And then she left for a charity meeting and didn't return, not a word from her till the letter weeks later.'

'Did you read the letter, Mrs Higgins?'

'No, sir,' said Mrs Higgins regretfully. 'Just the menu what was in it for the wedding breakfast.'

'Did Lady Viola confide in you after that?'

'No, sir,' said Mrs Higgins, even more regretfully. But the look she gave her former employer was eloquent.

Alice, an excited witness. Yes, that had been Lady Viola's dress! The thief who took the rubies had not known to take the pearls embroidered on the cloth. Yes, her ladyship had become suddenly most distressed nearly three months before the wedding. Alice had first noticed it one morning at the Hawkesbury estate: she'd been bright as a button the night before, but when Alice brought in her tea in the morning she'd been crying. She'd never known Lady Viola to cry before. She asked Alice to sleep on a trundle bed in her room, but after that the master gave Lady Viola a sleeping draught each night, and said no company was needed. Yes, she had seen the master give Lady Viola the sleeping draught several times. The poor lady didn't want to take it, but he insisted. No, the sadness did not depart, but continued to grow to a malaise. Alice had offered beef tea, and chamomile. She would have done anything to help Lady Viola, but could think of nothing more she might do …

'How was your mistress the week before the wedding?'

'After she returned from Mrs Boot's? Except of course the whole house knew she couldn't have been at Mrs Boot's like the major said because James and Charlie had been watching, oh, sorry sir, that week? Well, her ladyship was vomiting each morning.'

Alice waited with barely suppressed delight for the slight hubbub to die down in court. This gossip would make her the most sought-after lady's maid in Sydney. 'Mrs Boot removed the chamber pot each morning, but I could smell it, vomit being a stink you don't mistake.'

No, it was not Mrs Boot's job to remove the chamber pot, nor Alice's neither, but Millie, the chambermaid's, and Billy to scrub them. Yes, her ladyship was most particular in her prayers each morning and evening and before she supped, even in her chamber. Lady Viola would never commit such a sin. Major Nash? 'Why yes, a proper gentleman, but he deserves everything he gets in my opinion, because a sweeter kinder more loving mistress you could not have and anyone who laid a finger on that poor child deserved … Yes sir, I will be silent.'

Mr Locksley discreetly wiped the sweat from his forehead, despite the coldness of the day.

Kat, a Kat Titania had not seen, quiet, elegant, the Kat who had been courted by a viscount, a squire's son and several gentlemen of considerable ton before the tragedy of her parents. Yes, she was Mrs Zebediah Markham of Rainbow's End, in the County of

Gracemere, New South Wales. Yes, she and Lady Viola had been close friends since they had adjoining cabins on the voyage out. No, she and Lady Viola had not met in England, but she believed their fathers had both attended the same school, Eton, though in very different years, and she had once met Viola's brother at a balloon ascension. That was to her knowledge the extent of the family connection.

'Was Lady Viola happy about her approaching nuptials, Mrs Markham?'

'Lady Viola at all times stated she wished the wedding to go ahead. She was quite definite on the subject. I always found Major Nash to be a gentleman on every occasion, polite, considerate and sparing no pains to give his ward comfort, pleasure and entertainment.'

'Thank you, Mrs Markham.'

Why is Kat playing at being Nash's friend? wondered Titania. It had made sense to do so soon after the wedding to find out what he knew. But now?

Yet she was sure Kat was as determined as she was to see Nash pay for his crime.

Mr Locksley rose. 'Did you ever invite Lady Viola to visit you, Mrs Markham?'

'Yes, several times. Lady Viola was unable to make the journey.'

'She wrote to you regularly?'

'She wrote every week. She was a most faithful and loving correspondent.'

'She showed you every sign of close friendship?'

'Yes, she did indeed.' Kat silently fingered a black silk handkerchief.

'Did Lady Viola give any reason why she should not make the journey by boat and horseback to your estate?'

A hesitation. 'No, she did not. She stated she was merely unable to accept. It is an arduous journey by sea and horseback, involving a night on board ship, and a long and often dangerous one across country.'

'Might her guardian have forbidden it?'

'I have no knowledge of what might have happened, sir. Lady Viola never gave me any reason to think her guardian had forbidden a visit to her closest friend.'

'You were her closest friend?'

'I was, sir.'

'Was not Mrs Boot closer?'

'Mrs Boot is my dear friend, too. I do not see Lady Viola choosing between us. Mrs Boot, however, had the privilege of seeing Lady Viola every week. Mrs Boot, too, has been a most kind correspondent. She told me details of their meetings and all they had discussed ...'

'Quite. Do you believe Lady Viola capable of taking her own life?'

'No, sir, I am sure that she would not.'

'How did she seem on her wedding day?'

'She smiled at her new husband as she walked down the aisle,' said Kat quietly. 'All of Sydney Town's society saw it.'

'Have you any opinion about what might have happened to Lady Viola, Mrs Markham?'

'I am sure I know just what happened to her, sir,' said Kat eagerly.

'Could you share that knowledge with the court?'

'She was kidnapped by ruffians! They wrapped her in a cloak at the church to carry her off, and kept her prisoner. They must have kept her in a cave along that beach where she was found. They meant to ask for ransom, but then when she escaped ...'

She might, thought Titania, but you know full well that wasn't the way of it. What are you playing at, Kat?

The judge coughed. 'We are not here to listen to your opinions, Mrs Markham, nor to a romantic novel. This court is concerned only with facts. Do you, as a matter of fact, know what caused the tragic death of Lady Viola?'

'No, your honour. I do not. Only what ... what is the only way the tragedy must have happened.'

'Quite. You may stand down, Mrs Markham.'

The female constable found Kat a seat, tactfully on the other side of the court from Titania.

'Your honour, Mr Sorenson-Weatherby was to give evidence as to the good character of Major Nash, but is unfortunately indisposed. It seems he will be indisposed for some considerable time to come and begs to be excused. There are no more witnesses.'

The Sydney Morning Herald, and others, reported that at that moment the accused man placed his hands over his face and seemed to weep.

Titania had expected the trial to continue for days, a spectacle and entertainment for newspaper readers and those to whom the newspapers were read across the world. But it seemed Nash's influence or, more likely, that of Viola's brother, the duke, had ensured the trial would be short. His sister had caused scandal enough for the family. Let this one at least be brief.

The jury was dispatched after the most brief summing up. They returned a bare twenty minutes later.

Guilty.

Titania found her dress wet with sweat below her hands.

'As there is but one sentence open to me, I see no reason to further deliberate on this most unfortunate matter. I sentence the prisoner at the bar to be hanged by the neck until he is dead. May I also express the gratitude of the court to the witnesses who have spoken so courageously today, and give my profoundest sympathy to all the family and friends of the late Lady Viola Nash.

'Court adjourned.'

Chapter 56

KAT

The corridor of Darlinghurst Gaol was dank. It smelled of urine. Kat lifted her skirts as a rat brushed her feet. The creature didn't even bother to scurry. The lock creaked as the warder turned the key, the bribe Kat had given him safe in his knife pouch. She had bribed the constable at the desk too, and several others, to be here this afternoon.

'I'll be 'ere if you need me, missus.'

Kat nodded. Nothing the warder heard could matter now.

Major Nash stood as she entered. Even in the two months since the trial, as his lawyer and men of business appealed the verdict, he had changed almost beyond recognition. It was not just the faded convict suit, the boots that did not fit, the grey beard that had grown shaggy since he lost the privilege of a barber. Even his face seemed to have turned to slate.

He held out his hands, ingrained with dirt, the nails filthy. 'Mrs Markham, you at least have stood my friend. Even my solicitor …' He stopped and dropped his hands, as Kat continued to stare at him.

'You know they hang me tomorrow.'

'Yes.'

'I have asked that they ring the church bells for me, as they do at home when a man dies, one peal for a man and forty-three for my age.'

'The bells will ring for you as you walk.'

'Thank you. You ... you are very good. Mrs Markham, please make one final attempt to convince the governor. He can still pardon me, despite the court, or at least have me sent to England to be tried by my true peers. I swear upon the Bible, I did not kill my wife.'

'I know,' said Kat.

'You have a heart of gold, Mrs Markham, just like my dear wife.'

Kat considered. 'No, I don't think Viola had a heart of gold. Gold glitters, but it's too soft to trust. Viola was loyal forever.'

He gave a tattered, frantic smile. 'As you have always been loyal, too.'

'I am still. Loyal friend to the woman you married, the woman you didn't kill. Kill her on her wedding day, with half of Sydney watching, wondering, asking how and why? You would not have been so stupid. You'd have waited another few months, at least, to kill her.'

He stared at her in the dimness, not even noticing another rat scuttling across his boot.

'You'd already taken her innocence. What use did you have for her after that, except her money? You would not even have waited till her child had been born, of course, not with part of her fortune entailed upon her offspring. Though there are ways to bring about a miscarriage. Was that what you were planning? Or did you decide to wait till your son was born and kill her in a simple burglary gone wrong? Or make it seem mother and child died in childbirth, if it was a daughter?' She shrugged. 'I am no more than curious. It cannot matter now.'

'How dare you?' He glanced at the warder, mouth open, listening in the doorway, showing scattered yellowed teeth. 'This is a plot to incriminate me.'

'You are already incriminated. I could not tell Lady Viola, of course, or even Mrs Boot. But from the moment I learned you only wished to lie with young innocents, I knew you planned to kill your wife eventually.'

'You are wrong!' he yelled. 'I loved her! I would always have loved her. She had the kind of innocence that never fades. And I would have welcomed a son. Deuce take it, woman, I would have been my son's guardian till he was twenty-one, and still in control of all the income.'

Kat regarded him in cool surprise. 'You think you loved her?'

'Of course I did, you damned fool. I trusted you, Mrs Markham! Viola was the only woman I have ever loved, or ever could love, one who'd be forever sweet and childlike.'

'Lust is not love. You never truly saw her.'

'I lived with her for four years, which is more than you did.' He sat on the bunk and covered his face with his hands. The nails were long and yellowed. 'I always planned to marry her. Why shouldn't she marry me? A half-caste, a bastard! At least my blood is pure. She should have been grateful! I did not plan to love her, but I did.'

'You raped her.'

'Rape? Nonsense. Rape is a violent crime! I could never have hurt Viola. It was ... unpleasant ... for her, I admit, but good women do not find that side of marriage pleasant. It is necessary for children. It was necessary then, to convince her that she would be happiest, safest in marriage and with me. She was so young, so innocent. She didn't understand that marriage is a woman's natural state.'

'She understood far more than you. And so do I,' said Kat flatly.

She saw the moment he realised. 'You know what really happened to her, don't you? Tell me! She would not have run from me. I know it! She smiled at me as I put the ring on her finger!'

'Viola smiled often, and usually to hide her feelings. Anyone who truly loved her would have noticed that. Major Nash, I am one of four people who believe you did not hire men to murder your wife that day. I will even accept the possibility you did not intend to kill her after you were wed. But nonetheless I know you guilty.'

She met his eyes. 'Viola could not live with what you had done to her, what you would do again. You assaulted her, drugged her, blackmailed her, kept her your prisoner —'

'You have been a guest in my house!' he shouted. 'You know the comfort in which she was kept, the luxury. She wanted for nothing!'

'She wanted safety. Her own life! To decide what was done to her very *person*! Why should she not? You killed her will to live! And in her shame of the sin you had forced upon her and her despair at a life that must be spent with you, she killed herself, flung herself upon the rocks.'

'You ... you cannot know that. You saw her smile!'

'Many people saw her smile. I believe she smiled because it was at that moment that she chose to be truly free. And for a woman in the trap you had set there was only one path to freedom.'

'Then how ... how did she do it? It is impossible! Viola was too ... too gentle, too compliant to do anything like that.'

'You have not said it was impossible that she should want to.'

He stared at her, suddenly speechless.

'I came this afternoon so you would know in these hours before you die that Mrs Boot and I have always known that you caused Viola's death. Mrs Boot and I remained silent, for we would not shame a friend by telling of the degradation you inflicted upon her, or letting the world believe your actions drove her to kill herself, and her child as well.'

'It ... it might have saved me,' he whispered.

'If you had admitted to being a rapist, a fortune hunter, a predator of the worst kind, who drove a young woman to suicide? Would you admit it now, to save your life?'

He gazed wildly at the slip of light that came from the high window, the slice of sky, the only freedom he would ever see. 'I do not know. Yes ... yes! Go to the governor, you and Mrs Boot. I will confess to everything, explain how I meant it for the best! I will go abroad. Change my name.'

'You would be a free man then. And a wealthy one. Rape or not, your marriage was legal.'

'I will reward you. Whatever sum you name.' He reached for her hand again.

She did not take it. 'You are a murderer, Major Nash. Twice over a murderer, and one who has not even begged forgiveness for the lives you have destroyed, or understood that it was needed. How many other girls' lives have you maimed?'

'Other girls?'

'Girls you bought for your own lusts.'

'You mean whores?' He looked puzzled. 'Whores do not feel as gentlewomen do. It is unwomanly of you even to know of such things, much less speak of them. I tell you, I have never been a rapist, a brute forcing a woman in an alleyway. I paid well each time!'

'Now you will pay in another coin.' She looked at him, considering for a moment. 'I think perhaps I have a heart of flint, one that sparks fire when you strike it.' And a heart of flint can't be broken, thought Kat with a wisp of desperate longing for Zebediah, just chipped a bit. 'I can't have you burned, but I'll rejoice the moment that they hang you.'

Kat stepped back, towards the warder, then took another guinea from her reticule and handed it to the man. He took it, staring at it numbly and then at her, then at the prisoner.

'I will not ask you to say nothing,' said Kat calmly to the warder. 'That would be unreasonable. But if you say nothing until after the execution there will be three guineas for you, if you call at the Boot and Anderson warehouse, down from Campbell's in The Rocks.'

'I know where that be.' The warder's fist closed over the guinea.

'Good.' Kat turned again. 'I promise you this, Major. I will say nothing of my friend's shame, nor mention to anyone again that she might be guilty of the crime of suicide. I promise you this, too. From this moment, all through your last night on Earth, to when you stare out from the gallows tomorrow morning, in those final moments of your life, you will see Viola's face before you. You will see her terror of you, her hatred and contempt. You will see it forever.' She lifted her skirts to go.

'Mrs Markham, wait!'

'What is it?'

'I loved her. If only she had loved me back, been sensible, she would be alive and happy. I love her still.'

'You do not. Though indeed she was born for loving.' Kat stepped through the doorway and nodded at the warder. She heard sobbing from inside the cell as the man locked the door.

Chapter 57

MAJOR NASH

He did not sleep. He could not sleep. At times, during that long night, he even longed for the oblivion of death the next morning. But Mrs Markham's curse lingered. Each time he shut his eyes he saw his wife's small face, pale, accusing. He saw other girls, scared, trembling, but surely that had been pretence. They had been coached to show the emotions of their betters! They played a game, and were given gold for it. Some, he was sure, had sold their virginity four or five times at least. He even tipped his favourites, twice the quoted cost.

Why did they accuse him then? The night was full of ghosts. This time tomorrow he would be one of them.

Someone, his solicitor perhaps, possibly the chaplain, had arranged a gentleman's breakfast at dawn for him the next morning, or the best that could be had: a pewter plate, a hunk of bacon and what smelled like a game pie. He refused them, determined not to vomit his guts up in front of the crowd. He drank the measure of whisky though. It settled him somewhat. Viola's face vanished, and the girls whose names he had long forgotten, if he'd ever known them. At least public hangings had been discontinued two years before, though he had heard that a good many private invitees would throng the courtyard.

They manacled him before they took him out, a warder on each side and one in front and one behind. Did they think he'd try to fight and run? Down the corridor and then the steps and climb the iron gate?

There would be a new rope. They would not trust an old one to hang a gentleman.

Down more steps, into the light, so bright, so sudden, he could not see. A blessing. He did not want to see the oafs, the brutes, the inmates of this colony who thought a hanging sport. He could hear, though, the jeers, the cheers, the yells of 'Shame!' Peasants, friends of the warden, perhaps, who probably beat their own wives half dead, wives who sold themselves to other men, judging him, who had no right to judge him. He was a gentleman ...

And then the bells. One solitary ring, and then the forty-three, the chimes of his childhood, just as Mrs Markham had promised. He'd thought that the bells might comfort him. They didn't.

Up the gallows stairs. He heard the chaplain's mutter. He shook his head, as if to ward off pigeons. He could not think of God. Why now, when he had never bothered to before?

He felt the rope around his neck. He stood straight as his vision suddenly cleared, and stared out at the crowd. He yelled, 'This is a travesty! I call upon all here to witness it. I am not —' He saw her face and stopped.

She wore a travelling cape and a shawl draped from her bonnet around her neck, for the wind from the water breathed chill. But he knew her eyes. Dark eyes, skin even darker than he remembered. She looked up at him. Their eyes met. He thought he saw shock on her face, alarm, not the night's accusation from her ghost. If only he could see love, he thought desperately. Suddenly that was all that mattered, that one person, that small person, might look at him with love, might hold out her hand towards him ...

The floor dropped below him. He struggled, his legs leaping as his fingers tore at the rope. Pain, blackness, and still more pain. But not for long.

Chapter 58

CONSTABLE JOHNSON

He was trying to get the log book up to date when she came in. Constable Johnson never had no book learning, naught but Sunday school a few hours a week till he could write his name, just.

He'd learned a bit since then, enough to scribble down each prisoner's name on a scrap of brown paper, then copy it out laboriously into the ledger in the quiet times, like now, when all were up at the hanging or the market, or if they wasn't, was sleepin' off what they done the night afore.

He looked up as the door opened. She was a lady, no question about that. Despite the darkness of her skin she didn't have the features of a native, nor of them blacks what worked upon the Yankee sailing ships, and her cape was embroidered at the collar and edges, with a flash of a blue dress underneath that matched the blue ribbon on her bonnet.

She looked tired and shocked, and upset too. A nice-lookin' young lady. Constable Johnson was used to those who came into the police house lookin' upset. An older woman in a black dress and cap who must be her maid walked behind her, carrying a valise in one hand, a shawl in the other.

'Excuse me, officer?' The young woman's voice was quiet and tentative.

He stood a little straighter. 'Yes, ma'am?'

'I am in some distress. I am not sure what I should do. I tried to speak to the warden at the prison, but I had no appointment. I ... I hope that you can help me.'

He borrowed the detective inspector's accents and puffed out his chest a little. 'I'll do my best to help you, ma'am.'

A smile of gratitude flashed for a second, sweet as honey he described it later, with a burst of poetry he hadn't known was in him and a waft of orange blossom scent, as if angel wings had fluttered past. 'Thank you, Constable. My name is Mrs Major Nash. I ... I may be mistaken, but I believe I just saw my husband hanged.'

Chapter 59

VIOLA

'But you're dead, miss!'

Griggs snorted behind her. Griggs had been maid to two successive memsahibs in India and brooked no nonsense. 'As you can see Mrs Nash is most assuredly alive.'

'But I am also extremely concerned.' Viola heard her voice tremble now. The journey had been long, and the last leg up the coast from Twofold Bay had been rough. For some reason the boat had been in port there for a whole week for supplies, instead of heading to Sydney and resupplying there. Nor had there been anyone to meet her at the wharf, as she had expected, except a footman in no livery she was familiar with, who had ushered her into a chair.

She had thought she would be taken to Titania's, or her office or possibly an hotel. It had been frightening to be carried through the prison gates. The chair carriers had left her there, denying all knowledge of who the liveried man had been, nor why they had taken her to a prison courtyard, where a gibbet hung. And then ...

She found her voice again. 'Those in the crowd this morning informed me that Major Nash, my husband, was being hanged this morning. The unfortunate man this morning did not look like my husband, and then I saw his face ... I could do nothing! Please, tell me if that man was or was not my husband.'

'Mrs Nash ...' He stared at her apparently unable to choose between offering her a mug of ale or other restorative, or calling the surgeon to attest that she was alive. He seemed to come to a decision. 'I ... I must call Detective Inspector O'Reilly.'

'And I must know the truth about my husband. Is he alive or is he dead? I have a right to know.'

'I ... I do believe that he is dead. Ma'am,' he added, clearly suddenly remembering the sergeant's lessons in how to address gentry, if by any chance a female of that species needed to be spoken to.

'Hanged? This morning?'

He gulped visibly. 'Yes, ma'am.' He hurried to place a chair under her.

'On what charge?'

'Murder, ma'am.'

She sat, felt the hairs raise on her skin. 'Murder?'

The constable reached under the counter and offered her a jot of what must be his own personal supply of rum. But before he could offer it Griggs had waved a bottle of smelling salts under her nose. Viola waved it away, fingers of inevitability gripping her. 'Thank you, Griggs. Who ... who did Major Nash murder?'

Her mind shuddered. Nash was a man of temper, despite his ability to channel it into what the world deemed to be duty. Had Kat — it must be Kat — provoked him into striking her, beating her so badly that she died?

She sat entirely still, so that nothing showed on her face. And then she realised. The constable had said, 'But you are dead.'

Her mind grew cold, and then her body. She was free. But at what cost?

Chapter 60

VIOLA

It seemed there was no suitable place at the Sydney Police Station for a lady — especially not one sitting with her handkerchief over her eyes, her shoulders shaking, from confused emotions rather than sobs, but the constables did not know that. Griggs hovered, offering sal volatile, dabbing her forehead with lavender water, fanning her with the peacock-feathered gift from Yasmeen.

Yasmeen and the quiet courtyard with its laughing women seemed so long ago, the pop of mustard seeds, frying for the mid-morning snack of jalkhabar, deep-fried cauliflower pies in strange pastry, sondesh sweet with jaggery ...

Calcutta seemed even further once Detective Inspector O'Reilly, summing up the situation in a glance, suggested they repair to her house — for it seemed somehow Major Nash's residence was now *her* house — sending the constable to ensure that it was open to her — she hoped that did not mean breaking down the front door — with two more constables in their drab uniforms accompanying them.

The constabulary did not keep a carriage. She and Griggs had to stand in the street while chairs were fetched. Viola tried not to shiver at the crowds, the stench, after the clean winds of the sea, and her months in India.

Calcutta could not be described as a clean city — she had indeed been startled by the quantity of bloodstains on the street till a man herding a flock of skinny goats shot an arrow of red fluid from his mouth that dripped gore-like down the wall opposite the alley — her first acquaintance with betel.

But Calcutta had colour, from the wide baskets of reds and golds, greens and black spices to the garlands of marigolds, the bundles of cane, the tables laden with small yellow grapes from the North-West Frontier, the blue and red of carpets, the brilliant white and flaming reds and blues that even the poorest beggar could sport that a gentleman would find hard to imitate here. And its scents ...

Sydney was drab, its colours faded, except for its sky. It smelled of long-dead mutton, with no spice to sweeten it. She moved quickly away from a stray pig, its beady eyes examining who to charge or bite, avoided a malodorous pile of cabbage leaves and nameless guts, Griggs hovering, trying to shield her with a parasol.

'I apologise, Mrs Nash.' Detective Inspector O'Reilly did not say for what. For the noisy street? The lack of carriage? The death of her husband for a murder he had not committed? Detective Inspector O'Reilly gave a quick whistle. Two chair carriers sauntered over. She climbed into the chair with relief as the detective inspector signalled for another one for Griggs.

'Is the house still open?' she asked tentatively.

'It is, Mrs Nash. Your brother sent orders as soon as he knew of your disappearance. He asked that the house be kept in readiness for tenants in case ... in case of events like today's.'

'My brother?'

'It seemed likely you were dead, Mrs Nash,' he said baldly. 'Or soon would be. If you were dead, and your husband dead too, your brother would inherit your estate. He would also inherit Major Nash's estate, as Major Nash's next of kin, after you, and the major's will left you everything, unless there was a child to share the inheritance.'

'But ... but I am not dead! How could anyone believe that he had killed me?'

'That is what we must find out, Mrs Nash,' he said grimly. 'But not here.'

In Calcutta the carriers would have trotted, proud of the stretch, their turbaned heads erect. Here the men sauntered, feet squishing unconcerned in filth. At last they came to the familiar street.

The house looked much the same, though the stairs had not been whitewashed nor their edges trimmed, presumably since Major Nash's arrest. But the door stood open, still on its hinges too. Someone had even lit a fire in the drawing room, pulled the curtains and removed the dust covers from the furniture.

'Your ladyship!' Tilson stared, forgetting to bow for what was probably the first time in his life. She could see other servants peering, heard the whispers. 'It's truly you!'

'Yes, Tilson. It's me. There ... there has been some terrible mistake. Is Mrs Higgins here?'

'No, your ladyship. She took other employment, and Alice too. I chose to stay with the house. A Mr Whistlewhite and his family are expected next week. They will bring their own housekeeper and kitchen staff ...'

'Then they may come,' she said tiredly. 'I do not wish to stay here.'

She let Griggs remove her bonnet and cape, then sat in her accustomed chair. 'Griggs, would you mind bringing tea?'

There would be tea, at least, for one of her trunks, which she had glimpsed in the far shadows of the hall, held excellent Darjeeling and even a crystallised pineapple cake, one of a dozen pressed on her by the captain's wife and still not eaten.

'Please sit, sir.' She was not sure how one addressed a detective inspector. Should one ask constables to sit as well? She imagined no finishing school covered the etiquette of being interviewed by colonial police. But the constables vanished, possibly to question Griggs and whatever staff remained here.

Detective Inspector O'Reilly opened his notebook. She waited for him to suggest that she might like the support of a friend. He did not.

'I am sorry to distress you, Mrs Nash.' She noticed he did not call her 'your ladyship', though she kept the title with her marriage. 'But as you have already discovered, your husband was hanged this morning, and for your murder.'

She felt his eyes on her as she looked at her hands, slowly stripping off her gloves, revealing a left hand with its wedding ring upon it. 'No one has told me that directly, but I ... I assumed that must be the case. Why else would your constable be so shocked I was not dead?'

'Why aren't you?' he asked directly.

She blinked at him. 'Because there is no reason why I should be. No one has attacked me or kidnapped me or sought to harm me in any way.'

'Yet your body was discovered in its wedding dress, a week after you vanished as you left the church. The colony has buzzed with the mystery ever since.'

She stared at him, wide eyed. 'It was not my body. Indeed, I cannot account for it.'

'The wedding dress?'

'That, perhaps, I can account for. I cast it off as soon as I left the church. I wore another dress beneath it.'

'Why did you do that?'

'So I could escape straight after the marriage service, sir. I kept the jewels, of course, though I have since given them to relatives in India.'

He took a deep breath. 'Mrs Nash, perhaps you could tell me what did happen on your wedding day.'

'I did not want to marry Major Nash but felt ...' Viola closed her eyes again. How could she say this to a stranger, and a man?

'Would it be easier if I told you I know you were expecting his child, Mrs Nash?'

'No, sir,' she whispered. 'Not easier, but true.'

'What happened to the baby, Mrs Nash?'

'I miscarried, two days after the wedding. I ... I do not know if the upset caused it or if I am not formed for motherhood.' She brushed the tears away. With every skerrick of her being she had not wanted Nash's baby, but with every kernel she had already loved it. How could any man understand the tempest of grief, guilt and relief?

'Mrs Nash, you vanished before the whole of Sydney society. How could that be?'

She met his eyes. 'I can't tell you how they did not see me, sir. I can tell you that I walked on my own feet to a carriage, where I hid under an upholstered seat, and later changed my dress. That carriage eventually took me to the far north of the city, a long journey, to a beach with a rowing boat, and at dusk I was taken to a ship anchored offshore.'

'Why the secrecy?'

'For the obvious reason, sir. I needed to marry to have my husband's name for my child, but also needed to be free of him. I boarded the ship as Mrs Green.'

'And who arranged this?'

'A man I knew as Mr Smith. I paid him five hundred pounds.'

She could see Detective Inspector O'Reilly had not expected this. 'Where is this Mr Smith now?'

'I have no idea. I have never had his address nor, I am sure, is Mr Smith his real name. He was a chance acquaintance of a friend, who happened to be there when I needed help.'

'The friend's name?'

She met his gaze. 'I prefer not to give that, sir. But I do not think my friend knows any more than I do about Mr Smith. The arrangements were kept private between Mr Smith and myself. I did not want to involve anyone else in what ... what must be an unpleasant aftermath.'

'Unpleasant! Your husband was tried and hanged for your murder!'

'But not by any intent of mine!'

'What did you intend then?'

'Once I was safely far away I wrote my cousin a letter. I could not use my own name nor let him know where I was, so Mr Smith suggested I enclose a letter to Major Nash in one addressed to J Smith esquire at the Four Boars Inn down near the docks. Mr Smith would make sure my husband received the letter. I offered Major Nash all but a small portion of my income if he would divorce me for desertion. I ... I meant to embarrass him, Detective Inspector. That's why I left dramatically, rather than wait till after the reception when I might leave so discreetly that he could hide my absence for weeks, or even months. My cousin expected me to give up my life, my body and my child, not just my money. He even believed he did this for love of me, and that he had committed no sin or crime. I had tried to convince him otherwise, but had failed. I now hoped — expected — that scandal and so prominent a mystery would be enough for him to decide to be well rid of me, and even to repudiate the child, for ...' her voice broke for a moment, 'for the child would have been born only seven months after my marriage, so I could have threatened to claim it was not his, embarrassing him still further.'

'Did you get a reply to this letter?'

'No, sir, I did not. I've had only one letter since I have been away, and that was from Mr Smith, the man who helped me escape. I wrote to my friends as well. I ... I think they must not have received the letters. Probably Mr Smith did not give my cousin his letter, either, or he would have had proof I was alive.'

'I think that must be the case too,' the detective inspector said grimly. 'Your friends have not mentioned any letters, and I am quite sure Major Nash at least would have done so, as it would have saved him from the gallows. Where have you been then? The whole world has probably been buzzing with the discovery of your body and your husband's trial. How did you not hear of it?'

'I did hear something,' she said slowly. 'But not in a timely manner. The ship I met offshore was a whaler. They set me down at a settlement near the Canterbury Plains in New Zealand. The community there did not get any newspapers, of course, so I missed the accounts of my so-called death. I stayed in New Zealand for two months, living with a farmer and his wife, then was finally able to board a ship for Calcutta. It was where I had planned to travel before there was any talk of a wedding. Once I arrived in India I ... I saw the newspapers there, with headlines about my disappearance, about a body being found that was assumed to be me. No one connected me with the case, as I called myself Mrs Green. Of course I wrote to my friends again as soon as I heard, assuring them once more of my safety. But there had been no letters back from them, nor any mention in the newspapers that my cousin would be sent to trial when I received a letter via the embassy from Mr Smith. He said that I should journey back to the colony, so that the divorce could be finalised ...'

'I don't think a deserting wife needs to be present for a divorce. Nor is desertion so quickly determined.'

She stared at him. 'I did not know. How could I know? I obeyed Mr Smith ...' As she had obeyed the man who had once called himself her father, obeyed her brother and then Major Nash. It had not occurred to her not to obey, when what seemed a proper course for her life was laid out.

I must not make the same mistake again, she thought. But now there was no man to order her life, except her brother, far away, who she knew would not bother with the scandalous sister once it has been established that it was truly her, and not an impostor.

'How long did it take you to return to Australia, Mrs Nash?'

'More than four months. It was a trading ship, that travelled between the islands, where there were no newspapers less than ten years old, kept for curiosity, not news. But that ship too had a captain's wife on board, a most pleasant woman. I was even grateful to Mr Smith for choosing that route back to Sydney. The islands were beautiful, and I could rest from worry. I did not know what was happening in my absence. Truly, I did not know!'

'I believe you, Mrs Nash,' he said gently.

'My cousin's crimes might have warranted a trial,' she said quietly, 'but believe me, sir, I could never have imagined Major Nash was to hang, nor did I ever wish or intend it.'

'Surely you felt anger and bitterness towards him.'

'Yes sir, I did. But did I feel him so irredeemably evil that he must be killed? I cannot easily divide the world into those who are pure, and those who are bad. If it was as simple as that, we could remove all the evil people, and the world would be filled with goodness. You, of all people, know that isn't possible.'

He looked at her with a kind of wonder. 'I do know it, Mrs Nash. But if I had suffered as you did, I do not think I would be as philosophical.'

Her face twisted in sudden pain. 'There have been times when philosophy was my only security, sir, and all else like sand washing about my feet. Have you read much philosophy, sir?'

'Only the little they tried to drum into me at school, with a measure of ancient Greek and Latin.'

'Then perhaps you can understand. My cousin was created by a society that is neither good nor just, but based on the worst of human emotions, on envy, and vanity, and lust, and the belief that money is of greater value than love, or truth, or beauty. How can we condemn my cousin for embodying what is so common?'

'Maybe to try to make actions like his less common,' Detective Inspector O'Reilly said dryly.

She nodded slowly. 'That is a good point. You are a man whose work is restraining the worst in our society. But even if Cousin Lionel was an evil man in a good society, I must forgive him. We pray to God to forgive us our sins, not just the ones we have understood and repented.'

He smiled wryly. 'You are ... unusual, madam. I can see why Mrs Boot helped and defended you.'

'Titania is a truly good woman, the best of friends. I could not have survived without her comfort. Knowing that a person of her decency and integrity exists has been enough to keep my faith in goodness.'

'She is indeed an excellent woman,' said Detective Inspector O'Reilly.

Tea arrived then. Griggs sat too, without invitation, obviously to protect her mistress, though she did not take a dish of tea. Tilson lingered at the doorway, and Viola thought not just out of curiosity. Would he protest if the detective inspector tried to arrest her for ... for whatever crime had been committed in her name? Perhaps Tilson would refuse to give him back his hat till she was free.

More questions. She explained about the ship tarrying down at Twofold Bay the last week, the man in livery this morning, the waiting chair that had conveyed her to the prison, how she had tried to see the warden though she now realised there had been no point, for a hanged man remained hanged ...

She did not want to think about her cousin's face. She knew she could not forget it. She did not want to shoulder the guilt of his death, either, nor the horror he must have been through before it. But this had been done for her. Even if she had not willed it, she was the cause.

She had to bear it. She had to get through this day, and then another and another. She had to make sure neither Titania nor Kat was implicated in the deception, because a man had died for a murder that had not happened, and so surely a crime had been committed, though she did not know exactly what.

The detective inspector looked at her without expression as she finished her story. 'You expect me to believe this is the entire truth, Mrs Nash?'

'It is the truth, sir.' Though not, of course, the entire truth. But she was not sure that mattered.

She leaned forwards earnestly. 'Detective Inspector, there is one piece of law I do know, most commonly mentioned in the newspaper accounts of murders. No one can be charged with murder unless a body is found. It is one of the most deep-rooted of our common laws. It never occurred to me that my husband might be charged with my murder, because I wasn't dead.'

'Someone was. In your wedding dress.'

'Anyone might have found the dress — I certainly did not take it aboard ship. It was valuable. I can only think that some poor wretch wore it and had an accident. Detective Inspector, if I had plotted to have Major Nash hanged, I would have stayed away far longer. If I had arrived even an hour earlier, he would be alive now.'

'And yet conveniently he is dead, and it is all the fault of this unknown Mr Smith, who so usefully cannot be found and questioned. He appears to have wanted Major Nash dead, for some reason best known to himself, and humiliated before the world, too.'

'I cannot help you there, sir. I met him only twice, the day he planned my escape and gave me my instructions, and the day of my wedding, when he left me at the beach.'

'You seem to show very little grief at your husband's death. Shock, perhaps, and regret, but not grief.'

'I don't grieve for my cousin. I am even relieved that I will never have to see him again. But I am sorry for whatever he went through before the hangman put the noose around his neck. I grieve for …' She tried to find the words. 'I grieve for a man who was unable to see that what he did was wrong. I … regret that he died for a lie, not his crimes.'

'Then what crimes was he guilty of?'

She did not answer. Would not answer. She did not think the detective inspector needed an answer, either. Nor, to her relief, did he press her for one.

'Ahem.' Tilson gave the bow he had forgotten before. 'Will I order luncheon, your ladyship, and your room made up?'

'No thank you, Tilson. We are not staying. Will you arrest me, Detective Inspector, for wasting police time? Or plotting to have my husband killed?'

'I do not think you did,' he said slowly.

'Then I am free to go?'

'Not entirely, not yet. I must make my report to the superintendent of police, and I expect him to go to the governor.' He gave a wry smile. 'It would be easier if you'd simply vanish again.'

'I cannot until my husband's estate is settled, and my own affairs. I imagine that may take some time.'

'I do not think you will be arrested, Mrs Nash. But I must speak to my superintendent, as I said, and probably to the governor, who will want to speak to you, too. Luckily, he is in residence. If you wouldn't mind waiting here for a short while, I will ask if a carriage might be sent for you. His Excellency might wish you had taken him into your confidence, ma'am, as he was the one to give you away.'

'Once I was with child, can you see any way even His Excellency might have saved me from either shame, or a forced marriage?'

'No, ma'am. I cannot.'

'Then you have my answer. I will wait here until you send a message, Detective Inspector, in case the governor wishes to see me.'

He stood. 'I expect he will. I also expect your friends will be glad you are alive.'

They had thought her dead. All of Sydney — even in England — they had thought her dead. The scandal she had embodied since childhood had been compounded a hundred times now.

And she must live with it.

Chapter 61

TITANIA

Titania was trying to order more cabbage, but the nib of her pen had broken twice because she had pressed it so hard. She had heard the church bells, just as Kat had promised: one solitary clang, and then the peal that gave his age.

It was done at last then. Viola gone, and now her destroyer gone too. Impossible for her to have watched the hanging. Even Kat had not wanted to see his final agony. Titania had half thought to spend today with her, up on the cliffs Viola had loved, perhaps. But she didn't want to celebrate Viola's life with Nash's death. They would wait till next year, on Viola's birthday, and throw blossoms into the sea for her then.

Kat had left on the previous night's tide. Her boat would be halfway down to the river mouth now. She said a village had grown up at the south coast harbour, supplying whalers and sealers and fishermen, so she was going to arrange permanent stabling there for a horse. She had even commissioned a sulky that could manage the new track along the river, and which would be shipped down for her to collect in a month or two. The valley was not a major goldfield any more, nor would it ever be with the gold-rich sand and gravel now washed away, but a few dozen claims remained, and farms too, to supply the needs of the remaining miners as well as the ships that called at the harbour, so there was enough traffic along the track to keep it cleared.

Titania's office door opened. Her room was not a library, for it had no books except the shelves of ledgers, and nor was it a study for she didn't study here. She worked.

'Detective Inspector O'Reilly to see you, Mrs Boot.'

Suddenly she was glad she would not spend the day of Nash's death alone. 'Thank you for coming, Detective Inspector. Porter, could you ask Cook to bring us tea, please, and whatever she has baked today?'

'I'd prefer ale, and cold meat, cheese and bread and pickles, whatever is handy. It's getting near to dinner time and I've had naught but a piece of cake since morning.' The detective inspector stood by her desk, his hat in hand, that tall hat that proclaimed he did not have to wear a uniform.

'Of course. Please see to it, Porter. Your constable is not with you, Detective Inspector?'

He shook his head as the door shut. 'No. I don't need a witness for this.' He took the hard chair opposite her desk. 'Hard at work?'

'Ordering cabbages.' Half her life, it seemed, was cabbages these days, and the other half was turnips. 'What is best done without witnesses, Detective Inspector?' Surely it is all over now, she thought, the half-truths and the waiting, the hoping and the loss.

'Her ladyship has returned,' he said expressionlessly. 'You left it a bit fine, didn't you? A day earlier, even an hour, and someone would have told the governor.'

'I don't understand,' Titania said shakily.

'Mrs Nash is safely back in the colony. She's explaining everything to the governor now, but no doubt you will see her before evening.'

The air seemed to shimmer in front of her. 'No! She ... she can't be. We saw her body!'

'Ah,' he said gently. 'So you didn't know. I wondered about that. I couldn't know till I saw your face when you heard the news.'

Titania refused to sob. She pressed her fingernails into her palm to distract her body from such frailty. 'She is truly alive? And safe?' How could a closed door open so quickly?

'I imagine Government House is as safe as anywhere in the colony.'

'She is quite well?'

'Quite well, if somewhat shaken by what happened this morning. No doubt she'll tell you the rest when you see her.'

'I ... I must go to her. Of course this will be the greatest shock to her. To be thought dead and then alive. To know her husband has been hanged! She mustn't face this alone.'

'You won't gain admittance to Government House. Besides, she told me she would come straight to you from there.'

'Here, or to my cottage? And with her maid?' Titania frantically thought of sleeping arrangements. A respectable maid would not agree to sleep at Marigold's. And the baby. She must find a cradle, or perhaps a well-padded drawer would do ... 'Is the baby a boy or girl?' she asked eagerly. Oh, to have a baby in her cottage, a baby to hold in her arms ...

'She lost the baby, it seems, soon after she left. A tragedy for her, both its loss and its begetting.'

'Yes,' said Titania in a sudden gust of new grief. 'A tragedy.'

'Calm yourself, Mrs Boot. It's all worked out, and will soon be even better. I'll warrant her ladyship will be at your cottage door by teatime, and without her maid, for the woman came to Sydney to live with her sister, though she'll return to care for her ladyship as needed.'

'I can hardly believe it. Viola is safe, after all this time ...'

But he was continuing. 'There's not an ounce of cunning in Mrs Nash, but somehow she is always looked after. Oh, there'll be questions, and some things will need checking, but it seems she was long gone afore the body and the wedding dress were found. Unless someone confesses that she paid them to arrange that, there is nothing she can be charged with.'

'Viola would never do such a thing!'

'Nay, lass. I believe that you are in the right with that. She says she merely wanted to embarrass Nash enough so he would divorce her, and have the world doubt the babe was truly his.'

Titania nodded. 'That ... that was what we decided.'

'Ah, so you were party to some of it. I thought that is how it must be.'

Titania looked at him. But unless he positively accused her she must still play this out. All women learned to be actresses, to play the roles men had assigned them, wife or daughter, lover, meek but capable businesswoman.

She had never been much of an actress, though, which was probably why she had failed as a wife. She'd never had to pretend to be a good companion, and the business part only required that she should assume a little meekness over a core of granite. 'What do you mean, some of it, Detective Inspector?' She tried to sound indignant.

'Well, Mrs Nash says,' he paused, to let her see that 'says' was not the same as 'truth', 'that she walked down to her carriage and the carriage took her to a boat that took her to a ship. She didn't have any idea her husband might be hanged for her death, nor even that she might be thought to have died. She was telling the truth about that,' he added. 'She didn't like the thought at all. In fact, I don't think she told a single untruth. She didn't tell all the truth, of course. But people rarely do. I am fairly good at sniffing out omissions.'

He smiled at her. 'Such as all the truths you chose not to tell me.'

'You ...' Titania chose her words carefully, still half in a daze. Viola was alive! The child unborn! 'You always knew how she had escaped the church?'

'Oh, yes.' He grinned at her. 'You're a fine figure of a woman, and she's just a dab. She drew the eye that day, in her big crinoline. But I've arrested women in crinolines before, and been there when the searcher frisked them. There's nothing to a crinoline, if you twist it the right way. That fainting in the church was a bit too convenient, as well. Her ladyship walked down to the carriage, just like she said. What she didn't say was that she'd ducked under your skirts and was hidden there. Your skirts were a fair bit bigger than hers, and hers could fold right up, and she could fold herself up too. A crinoline is vast, but it's naught but ribbing, a piece of cloth, and lots of air.'

Titania said nothing. What was there to say? Viola was alive and she should be rejoicing. A policeman had discovered her fraud and she might be arrested and charged with perjury or worse.

'You played it well, both you and Mrs Markham, but there wasn't enough shock in either of you after the wedding, though I saw grief and wariness. You knew she was gone, and gone safely. The shock came when we found the body in the wedding dress.'

He looked at her thoughtfully. 'You assumed then that Lady Viola was dead. I'm not sure Mrs Markham did, nor me either. Too convenient, a dress like that, with the body in it appearing too disfigured to tell who she was. Some young woman, a girl perhaps, and maybe a native. Well, at least she has a decent grave now, though the name on the stone will need to be changed.'

Titania nodded dumbly.

'Who helped you?' he asked gently. 'It wasn't your mind that came up with a plan like that. Mrs Markham might have, but she had no chance to arrange the body in the dress, and I'll warrant she was as shocked as you at the sight of it.'

It could do no harm to tell him. 'A man called John Smith,' she said, suddenly leached of emotion. 'But whatever his name is, it's not that, and nor do Mrs Markham or I know it. I believe he is a thief and a highwayman. Mrs Markham met him by coincidence just when we needed help. Viola paid him five hundred pounds to help her escape. But I am sure she never dreamed of letting us think she was dead.'

'I'm sure she didn't either. The poor lass was rocked to the core. She'd sent you letters that it seemed this John Smith never passed on, nor her letter to her husband, either, offering him a divorce. What does John Smith look like?'

'In his twenties. Brown hair. Whiskers. Laughs a lot.'

'No identifying features? A tattooed mermaid? Scar on his face?'

'No. You truly thought Viola might be alive all along? But it was you who told the court that he was guilty,' she said slowly.

'Oh, he was that all right. I saw that from the first, too. Not guilty of what they hanged him for, but guilty enough to face the noose. Justice is done.' He stroked his hat absentmindedly. 'I'm done, too. I'm resigning from the police force.'

'Because of this?'

He hesitated. 'In part. There's nothing more to be done with it, and I'm glad, but I'm concerned that I'm glad, too. It's the first time I've let justice win over the law. Mrs Nash had me thinking maybe that's not something a policeman should get used to doing. Not good for my career, either, something like this, embarrassing the governor. But mostly it's because I've found I want more than policing.'

'What will you do?'

'It depends if you'll marry me.'

She stared at him in shock. 'Or you'll arrest me for perjury?' She couldn't separate this from Viola's arrival. She closed her eyes briefly. How was she supposed to combine joy at Viola's return, and shock and wariness too, with a question like this?

'I'm not arresting anyone,' he said patiently. 'I just told you, I'm resigning this afternoon. It's been my case, and it will end with me, and Lady Viola's return. I'll warrant the governor wants it all hushed up soon as may be, and her brother too. But I've saved enough to buy my way into a business, someone else's if you won't take me into yours. I want to marry you because I love you.'

'You ... you could have waited till tomorrow!'

'I could have,' he said a little ruefully. 'Perhaps I should have. I've made a rum go of this, haven't I? But I've been holding my tongue for long enough. I had to wait until the case was over.'

He reached into the pocket of his great coat and pulled something out. It took her a moment to realise it was the remnants of a bunch of wattle, the flowers fallen off. He looked at them. 'I picked them down at the governor's gardens. Must have squashed them on my way here. I've never given flowers before, you see.'

'Nor have I ever been given them.'

'I'll give you a bunch every day if you say yes,' he said hopefully.

'And if I don't?'

'Then mayhap we can be friends. I'd have asked you long

before, but it would have looked suspicious if we seemed to be on more than nodding acquaintance when Lady Viola turned up, as I thought she would, one day. Now, well, she's not going to find it easy, but my part in it is done.'

The world had suddenly changed direction once again. Or maybe she was looking exactly the same way, but instead of one new door opening it was two, or maybe fifty. And yet I have spent the past four years building up a business, she thought dazedly. It was insanity to make all she had over to a husband, by signing her name as his wife. 'You said you loved me,' she said slowly.

'I do, and very much.' His eyes lit up. 'There's a lot of you to love. You ain't said no.'

'I haven't said yes.'

'Don't trust me, then? Surely you should trust a police officer.'

'You're resigning,' she pointed out, trying to hold back a glint of a smile.

'That I am. Perhaps we'd best not be formally wed then till you've come to trust me a bit more. The colony ain't like London — I doubt many will pay it much note if we live together without a ceremony. But I'd like you to wear this.' He held out a ring, a thin gold band, carved with flowers.

'Where did you buy that?'

'I had it made. Commissioned it two weeks after meeting you and you can check that with the goldsmith if you like, for I'm not gammoning you. And now you'll want to go to Mrs Nash, but I'm hoping you'll put my ring on first.'

'I ... I don't know. Have you any knowledge of the business?'

'None,' he said promptly. 'I think that will suit you, as you won't want to be handing over the reins. But I'm a good judge of character. You'll find me useful.'

'Children,' she said desperately, because what if she said 'yes' and he changed his mind tomorrow? 'I am too old to have children.'

'You don't want them?' He looked surprised. 'The children in Left Hand Alley say you give them candied peaches. I'll warrant you are no more than thirty.'

'I'm nigh on thirty-six.'

'I'm nigh on forty, so we may manage to squeeze out a few young'uns yet, assuming you want them.'

She wanted them. Children to hold. A home that was more than two rooms. Someone to talk to in the evenings.

'If no young'uns come along there are plenty who'd like a good home. I like pickles, too,' he offered. 'Nothing like a good strong pickle. I'd even rather have a chutney than a jam.'

He knew that she liked pickles. He must have watched her, just as sometimes she'd watched him. Well, every time she saw him, if truth be told, for the last four years on the waterfront. He'd looked ...

Businesslike. Just as he said, he was a useful man, just like she was useful. A useful life together.

She slipped the ring on her finger just as Porter brought in the tray with ale and bread and sliced mutton, and half of a cold chicken, and a pot of mango chutney as well as a plate of pickled cucumbers. Titania put her hand quickly behind her back. 'Thank you, Porter.'

'A pleasure, mum.' Porter backed out, with a last curious glance at the detective inspector.

'Well,' and this time the detective inspector's voice was amused, 'I'm detective enough still to see the ring fits. Going to kiss me afore you go home to wait for her ladyship?' He gestured at the tray. 'I'll be fine with this.'

'Not engaged a minute and you've got your feet under my table already,' she said resignedly, but with a smile that seemed to come from her whole body.

'Nay, lass, this is a desk, though I will admit I'm hoping for an invitation to dine this evening. Now about that kiss ...'

'I'm not good at it,' she said quickly. 'I don't know what you're expecting ...'

'This,' he said. He stood. She stood as well, suddenly awkward as he stepped towards her.

Then he kissed her.

Chapter 62

TITANIA

Dinner with Viola and the detective inspector who'd investigated her death could have been embarrassing or tragic. Thanks to the detective inspector it was neither.

Titania realised she didn't even know his first name, as she sent Porter to fetch a fish course up to her cottage, and beef steaks to serve with a curry sauce, to go with the duck and green peas and apple pie and cheese, as well as pickled onions, which went wonderfully with apple and cheese. One good thing about being in the trade — there was always a case of good wine to broach and nuts and sweet meats too.

She arrived at the cottage just as Viola's chair arrived: the governor obviously hadn't offered her his carriage, a sign he was seriously annoyed, but Viola was here, and without a constable, which meant the governor had accepted her innocence and probably hoped the matter would be forgotten as soon as possible.

Which would be a very long time indeed.

'Titania? I didn't know. Truly I didn't ...'

'Me either, love. Not at all.'

And they were both crying, embracing, then Viola had her feet up on a stool with Mr Tom purring on her lap, almost like old times, while Titania served her tea and toast then prepared the ingredients Porter had fetched, while Viola sipped and watched and looked less whey faced with every moment of the quiet kitchen routine.

Just what she needed, Titania thought, a kitchen cup of tea instead of melodramatics, and Mr Tom expecting to be stroked. There was much that was comforting about a cat.

It was good to have her hands cooking again too, instead of ordering it done. Mrs Anderson poked her head in to offer to help — amazing how the news had flashed around the wharves — and there was no chance to talk, except when Mrs Anderson had gone, the cream setting in the larder and the duck roasting in the oven and they'd both changed for dinner, high necked, of course, for this was a cottage not a mansion.

But one day, she thought, I will change for dinner in my own home and show my bosom too. It's not like I lack the quantity.

'You are truly going to marry him?' Viola asked abruptly, arranging her old necklace with the locket, now the only jewellery she wore, except for her wedding ring. Titania supposed that must be kept for respectability. Though, when she glanced at it again, it seemed somehow thinner than the ring she had barely glimpsed last year. Had Viola substituted another? She would not ask.

'I think so.'

'Make sure a good lawyer draws up the settlements first.'

'I will.'

But she wouldn't. There would be no settlements this time. If she did not trust him, she should not marry him. She wanted no dialogue of money between her and her husband. She'd had a settlement once, and it hadn't saved her. Never again.

Titania did not know if she was doing the right thing marrying him, but she knew that if she did not take this chance she would regret it always. She would not live in the land of 'might have been'. Nor would she let the law bind her to a bad marriage, either. But the detective inspector knew that about her already.

The dinner was amusing, Mr O'Reilly coaxing Viola to speak of India, its architecture, the Mogul palaces, the climate. Viola relaxed as she spoke of thin dogs with yellow eyes, and wandering cows, and markets with a thousand fragrances and colours. Titania found herself smiling as her body relaxed too, well fed with food and love and hope. Had she ever smiled like this before?

Yes, she would marry him. And in a church too.

'Another slice of pie, Detective Inspector?'

He peered at her over his plate. 'You might call me by my Christian name, if we are to be wed.'

'I might, if I knew it.'

'Ah, there's the rub.' The detective inspector let her help him to more pie, took a good forkful, then selected a pickled onion himself from the plateful. 'You might not marry me if you know it. Perhaps I should keep it to myself till after we are married.'

'I could call at the police station,' Titania pointed out. 'I am sure they have a record.'

'You might at that. I'd better let the secret out.' He grinned at her. 'It's Oberon.'

Viola gave a choke of laughter. 'I don't believe you.'

'That's what's written in the church register and what me parents called me till I left old Ireland's shores. My da had a love of Shakespeare, you see.'

'So did mine,' said Titania briefly.

Viola clapped her hands. 'You have already been married then for hundreds of years.'

'About time we made it official in that case.' Oberon O'Reilly slipped the pickled onion into his pocket and looked regretfully at the remnants of the pie. 'I think you both will wish to talk and you need your sleep too. Will you see me out, Titania?' It was the first time he hadn't called her Mrs Boot.

She blushed. 'Of course.'

She handed him his coat and hat, then slipped out the front door to say goodbye, but he said nothing about the case. She was suddenly sure he never would. It had brought them together. That would be the most important thing about it. The rest would fade away, but never that.

He stood on tiptoe to kiss her, until she bent to him. He pulled her closer. 'Aye,' he said softly, 'you're a might too tall.' She was about to pull away when he whispered, 'Until you're lying down. You'll be the perfect size then.'

She blushed again. 'You deserve a slap on the face for that.'

'I do,' he said agreeably. 'But you'd never hit a man smaller than yourself.'

She laughed. 'Don't be too sure of that, Oberon O'Reilly. I might just have a rolling pin in my hand too.'

'A shrew,' he said regretfully. 'I've tied my troth to a veritable shrew. Ah, well, too late to pull out now. A policeman knows full well the trouble a breach of promise suit can bring. I'll have to make the best of it.' The laughter faded slightly. 'Your Lady Viola is tough as a bullock hide.'

'She is kind and gentle and loving.'

'Did I say she wasn't? But if push comes to shove another time it might be you who was hurt. It never will be her. Next time, if there's a roundabout you come to me to sort it out. Agreed?'

'Of course I will. What else is a husband good for?'

He winked. 'I'll have to show you, won't I? Take care, my love. I hope your dreams are sweet.'

No one had ever wished her sweet dreams either. If you were big they assumed you could fight off nightmares too. She watched him walk down the street till he reached the gaslights that had been a birthday gift for the Empress of Australia, as if Queen Victoria knew or cared about the light given in her name across the world.

Perhaps she even did. At last, Titania closed the door and pulled the bolt — no one with sense in a colony that was still half composed of thieves and the other half none too honest would leave the door unbolted for even ten minutes — then turned to find her apron and do the washing up. But Viola already had it stacked and even wore an apron too.

'Will you have a cup of tea first? It's Darjeeling, from high up in the Indian mountains. I think you'll like it.'

Titania sipped. It was all right, better than Chinese, but give her a strong Ceylon brew any time. 'I still keep having to pinch myself. What a day. A wonderful day.'

Viola nodded, still scrubbing a pan, then her face suddenly clouded.

'What did the governor say?' Titania asked abruptly. But they had to speak of this if they were ever to put it behind them.

'He gave me his hand and his condolences. A tragic accident.'

So that was how they were going to play it. Titania wondered how the detective inspector had pitched the story. How much had he told Viola, too? Did she know the horror of that poor decayed body? She could probably imagine it. Titania hoped desperately no one had told her about the missing left hand.

Viola stared into her teacup. 'It's not as if poor Lionel had any close relatives, or even friends who would take up a petition to exonerate him posthumously, or write letters of complaint to England. His Excellency's last words to me were, "It will all be forgotten in a year."'

'Viola, I'm so sorry about your child.' She had wanted to say that from the moment she saw her, her arms empty, no nanny behind her.

'I lost it soon after I left ...' Viola closed her eyes, and for the first time Titania saw tears. 'So it was all for nothing.'

Titania budged her chair over, to hold her close. 'No, it wasn't. You're free. You're here and you're safe and that's all that matters.'

Viola looked up at that, wiping the tears with her fingers. 'And I found my father!'

'Don't tell me he's really a maharajah?'

Viola looked at her a moment, as if considering how much to say, or possibly how to say it. 'His name is Jagadish Basu. I went by the name of Mrs Green, but it seems he had been expecting me to come, as soon as I was of age. He knew all about me, it seemed, or at least until my mother's death. He showed me all her letters. They — they were wonderful. But I suppose it wasn't safe for her to keep his to her. He wrote care of an old friend of hers.'

'How did they ... meet?' Titania couldn't bring herself to ask how they'd conceived a child together.

'He worked in the company's library, transcribing scrolls. My mother was interested in Indian history and had learned a little Hindustani ... then one day he seemed troubled and, when my mother asked him, he said his youngest daughter was ill. So she arranged for the English doctor to visit his home ...'

'He was married?'

'Oh yes,' she said. 'He didn't tell me how I was conceived of course. But he said he loved her. She must have been afraid that if she told me openly I was not her husband's child then I might announce it to the world. He knew all about me, but of course he had heard nothing since my mother died. He had always hoped that one day she might return and they would meet again. But her illness meant that she never had even the freedom of widowhood. They were so happy to see me.'

'They? His family?'

'Of course. He has four sons and two daughters. He is quite enlightened about his daughters. They have been well-educated by governesses, and his eldest son is training to be a doctor and another an historian. The youngest are still in the nursery.'

'They all accepted you?' Titania felt slightly stunned at the calm affection in Viola's voice, the matter-of-fact way these strangers had lived so ... unconventional ... a story.

Another hesitation. 'Yes, they accepted me and with no bitterness at all. They forgave me entirely.'

'For your mother's ...' Titania found it hard to say the word '... adultery?'

'That was for my mother's husband to forgive. No, they forgave me for being English.'

Titania had not expected that. 'They are ... critical ... of mixed blood, too?'

'Not that at all. The English are ...' Viola seemed to choose her words carefully and arranged her face into blankness too. 'Much disliked, and feared. But the family treated me as one of their own.'

'You stayed with them?' Titania found herself faintly scandalised.

Viola looked at her strangely. 'No. I wear English dress and bear an English name. There might have been ... trouble ... for the family if I had stayed with them. Mrs Hamish McDermott was kind enough to offer me the hospitality of her home.'

'What kind of trouble could come from being English?' demanded Titania indignantly. The sun never set on the British Empire.

'I'm not sure. Calcutta seethed, oh, with life, with noise and with a thousand smells, and with anger too, and I understood none of it, except that sometimes I was ... ashamed to be called English.'

'Viola!' This verged on blasphemy.

Viola met her eyes. 'I am going back there.'

'To live?'

'I don't know. I know I am not Hindu. To see more of India, perhaps. I would like to see Kashmir and Kerala ... perhaps just to stay long enough to understand.'

'You could live comfortably here. With Kat, perhaps, till the scandal dies down.'

Viola stretched. 'While I live I will always be just a little scandalous. Someone will say, "Do you remember?" And, Titania,' she hesitated. 'I found that I very much enjoyed not having the only brown skin in nearly every room. I ... I think, perhaps, it is impossible for you to understand. The division between brown skin and white — I have met so few people with white skin who have been able to ignore another colour skin, and all that it implies.'

Titania could only realise it was even worse than being tall and plain.

Viola met Titania's eyes. 'I don't want to talk about what happened at the wedding. What I saw at the prison today.'

'What! You ... you weren't *there*?' replied Titania, horrified. Oberon O'Reilly had not mentioned that.

'I was. A chair was waiting for me at the docks. It took me to the prison.'

'No! That is terrible,' said Titania, aghast. 'Mr Smith?'

'Who else? I don't think he meant to be cruel. Probably,' admitted Viola. 'He was most likely trying to give me revenge, the certainty I was safe.'

'He shouldn't have done that,' said Titania helplessly. She hugged her, dish wet hands and all.

Viola allowed it, then stood back. 'But I have been safe all my life. There has always been a refuge. I have been safe these past five years, because of my two friends. I must write to Kat, unless Mr Smith has told her.'

Viola suddenly seemed to realise what she had said. 'You don't think ... could Mr Smith have told Kat I was alive? Surely Kat could not have let Cousin Lionel go to his death, knowing I was safe?'

Titania was silent. Oberon O'Reilly had guessed that the wedding dress had been a trick. Had Kat guessed too and never told her? What had the bushranger shared with Kat, and not with her or Viola?

She should be ashamed of even thinking it. But Kat ... yes, Kat might have guessed. Mr Smith might even have told her — no, not that. She could never believe Kat would have known and not told her.

Viola stood and kissed her hair. 'I'm sorry. I believe I'm tired. I'm not saying the right things at all. India has changed me, I think. It's made me question things I never doubted, made me wonder how much to doubt. Thank you for taking me in. Thank you for everything.'

Or not quite everything, thought Titania. And changed or not, it seemed the detective inspector had been right. Viola would slide through this, leaving the memory and guilt to them.

Chapter 63

VIOLA

A shadow clung to her. Perhaps the guilt would always be there. But she could not let Titania see it, for Titania was of that compassionate breed of woman who would share the anguish too.

Viola lay in the narrow bed, though no narrower than her berth at sea, and tried to piece together the story of what had been done in her name, allocating blame and shame, including her own, for surely you were responsible for what had been done for love of you, as well as all you had approved without worrying over the consequences.

And yet a pattern would not come. Memory seeped into her mind instead: a story of other bad deeds done for what seemed good reasons, and lies that had become truth, with deadly consequences. It was a story of her past too, or at least her family's past. Yet until recent months she had never known it.

She had been sitting with her father, just as she had sat with him each day, in the sunlit courtyard that was washed and swept each morning, on a blinding white sheet placed upon another sheet, just as white, shaded by a tree whose name she did not know, and perhaps it had none, only an existence: the tree of my family courtyard.

The courtyard smelled of the spices of a thousand meals, and the cigar her father smoked. He wore his usual white. Even his cap was white.

'But what do you do, Father?'

He smiled. He was little taller than her, though not as fine boned. His wife and other children were twice his size, and with lighter skins than hers, too. 'I did what I was born to do, and my father and ancestors before me. It was ordained that I record. I recorded the business of the company, until the pension arrived from England. Then I could record what matters, and not what businessmen desired. Our family has always recorded. Almost a hundred years ago your great-great-grandfather recorded what the English call the Black Hole of Calcutta. Ah, you have heard of it.'

'Of course.' The horror of the Black Hole of Calcutta had been the crucial act that had convinced the British government to make India part of the Empire, and not leave its governance to businesses or natives.

Viola had read Mr Macaulay's most tragic book about the Black Hole of Calcutta too. During the Nawab's rebellion against the British East India Company, which traded in India, the company's Fort William had been overrun. The Indian troops had imprisoned over a hundred English men, women and children, soldiers who had surrendered, civilians desperately seeking shelter in the fort.

They had all been crammed into a room barely six yards long and four yards wide, so tiny that women and children were layered, one upon another to fit them in. All that night they had screamed for water, for help, but one by one their cries grew silent as they suffocated from the pressure of the bodies and the lack of air, and their captors laughed and poured the water the prisoners longed for onto the ground to torture them.

At dawn over a hundred bodies lay crammed within that desperate cell. Only twenty-three survived and, of those, many died of the experience afterwards.

'How was my great-great-grandfather there?' she whispered.

'He worked for the company at the fort, recording transactions just as I did in my youth. When Sahib Holwell surrendered, your ancestor and all who worked there surrendered too.'

'He was put in the Black Hole?' Please, she thought, let him have survived.

'No, but he saw what happened and he recorded it. I have his diary, though as it is in Hindi not English it would take you time to learn to read it.'

'He saw all that devastation, all the horror?'

Her father looked at her steadily. 'He saw an inexperienced Sahib who had been a lawyer, not a warrior, try to defend a crumbling fort and fail. He saw an honourable surrender honourably accepted by the Nawab. But nine English soldiers did not follow the rules of surrender. They kept killing. Eventually they were captured, some wounded, and the nine were placed with great anger in a cell meant for two men only, with two small slits for air. When the Nawab heard the next morning he was angry that those to whom he had offered protection had been so treated, despite their treachery. He had the men released. Three had died of their wounds. The others were cared for and lived. That was the Black Hole.'

'But the women, the screaming children?' Viola asked, puzzled. Behind her, her stepmother and half-sisters began chopping vegetables, fragrant mushrooms of a kind she had never seen before, okra, grinding spices in big mortars, with the soft chatter the work required.

Her father nodded slowly. 'Your great-great-grandfather recorded what he saw. Later, the man they would call Clive of India laid siege to the fort and finally it fell, and then the British government took control from the company, and when your grandfather began work it was for them.'

'You believe this is true?'

'Our family records what we see. I never knew my father, nor my grandfather, to err by a single day in a report; nor would my father praise the beauty of my mother's neck, for it was too short, though he often gave her compliments on the sweetness of her skin.'

'Someone lied,' she said softly.

'Yes. I cannot believe that it was your great-great-grandfather, and his report echoes whispers from my grandfather's friends. But only whispers, for we were servants of the British King.'

'Then who did lie? Mr Macaulay?'

'I do not know him.'

'He wrote a book, but it has not been published long.'

'Then he did not see what happened and so, perhaps, he does not lie but writes what he thinks of as the truth. A great convenient truth Britain could take into her heart, for it gave her all the kingdoms of this continent, one by one.'

'Where did the lie come from then?'

'I do not know.'

'No, but you can deduce.'

He smiled. 'My clever girl. I do not know, but I deduce, perhaps, that Sahib Holwell created the report to divert criticism of his most great incompetence, both in repairing the fort and in trying to hold it. But did he lie? One of the nine men, perhaps, told him how so many had been crammed into the tiny space, sweating and crying for air and water, and the Sahib saw more in the pages of his mind than fate had written. Then as he told it each time, and horror in England grew, his story grew as well. Perhaps he thought, I have a tale of treachery, how natives took the company fort. They will not understand the perfidy of natives here in England, but the screams of dying children will echo in their ears. But this is your word, deduction. It is perhaps the truth. The truth is also that I do not know.'

They sat silent in the courtyard as she tried to absorb, to understand. I am of two races, she thought, and I have heard two stories. Am I English? Do I hug the English story to me, the one I have believed? Or am I the daughter of my father, who believes that his ancestors, my ancestors, could not, would not lie?

Yet there was a third option. What *exactly* had her great-great-grandfather seen? Had he sat all evening, night and morning by the cell, counting and recording? Had other prisoners been shoved in, and their bodies taken out, that he had not seen, and so did not record?

Had Mr Holwell only heard the tale from a man who had indeed been tortured, body, mind and soul, and had magnified the treachery, and Mr Holwell saw the greatness of that man's horror, the desperate dishonour of a man defeated and humiliated by the natives, and wrote not a lie, but what he thought he heard?

That was deduction too.

Her father's wives and other daughters laughed as they scraped out the small sour gourds to fill with savoury native ragout for lunch. Frying spices popped and filled the courtyard with a new fragrance. I am no race, thought Viola, not truly English but not Hindu.

At last Viola said, 'It has been twenty years, perhaps, since you stopped recording for the British.'

'Nineteen. It will be twenty in September.'

'What do you record now?'

'I write what I see and what I can deduce. I like that English word. Deduce. I see the world around me and seek the mind of God.'

'Which God? Do you not believe in many?' In England she would have thought `pagan'. But this was not England, nor was she the girl who'd knelt in church there. My beliefs haven't changed, thought Viola, just widened.

'I ... deduce ... one God with many names and many aspects, but I can see Him in the miracle of a drop of rain which contains more colours than a man can count, or a mountain that changes shape and colour from every angle and every day a man may look at it, or even in size, as an ant adds a grain or the wind blows a grain away.'

'May I read what you have written?' she asked humbly.

The smile again. 'You may read it. The records of our family are just that — to record, and records should be read. But you must read Hindi to be able to.'

'It can be translated.'

He shook his head. 'How many languages do you speak, Lady Daughter?'

'Two, English as my mother tongue, and French quite well.'

'I speak seven languages and I tell you this as truth, not as deduction. Some truths cannot be translated. Oh,' as she began to protest, 'most things of the world can be translated easier than a juggler catching two balls. The oil is in the pot. The oil is hot. But to be precise this works only if you know which oil, which pot and how hot the oil must be to cook paratha. And that is something you must ask my wife or your aunts, for I cannot give you a true answer.'

'I think,' she said slowly, 'I must learn to see, and to deduce.'

'You might imitate the trees, too. They sit and watch and see all change and know that nothing stays the same for long, not even pain.'

'But trees don't understand.'

'Perhaps trees know that the view that one tree sees is not another's and so each accepts the limits of its understanding. They learn the limits of their reach, too, and enjoy their journey upwards and do not weep if their branches cannot touch the sky. You might learn Hindi, Daughter.'

From somewhere came a thought, even a deduction: If I learn Hindi and read the records I cannot go back to being a memsahib, or ever balance between one family and another, two cultures and two countries, or three, for she was bound more to New South Wales now than England and she must go back, and soon.

Now she had returned. But even here she had found lies, a past rewritten, a man hanged for a crime that hadn't happened, and all for her. A man she'd feared and hated, at the end. A man who might have been hanged anyway if she'd had the courage to say, 'He forced me. He blackmailed me.' That would have been truth. Not this.

They had done it all for her. She wondered if the guilt would ever let her go.

Chapter 64

KAT

Kat swung her valise as she turned into Left Hand Alley. The three of them would be a squeeze at Viola's, but how wonderful to be together again. Viola must be rejoicing at her freedom, at the destruction of her assailant, too.

Kat had hoped to find Titania at her office on the wharf, but Mr Porter said she had gone to see houses with Detective Inspector O'Reilly. It was indeed time for Titania to think of a larger home, one with two bedrooms at least, but why did she need a detective inspector to help her do so?

Perhaps Marigold will rent me her room, Kat thought. She might finally learn the business of Scarlet Womanhood, even if the ambition to be one was long gone. She knocked on Titania's cottage door, above its freshly scrubbed and whitened step. The door opened.

Viola looked even smaller than Kat remembered, and her skin was darker too. She must not have worn a bonnet or sheltered under a parasol on the voyage. She wore a plain pale yellow cotton dress, which showed her wealth more than any sprigged muslin. Plain cotton cloth was almost impossible to obtain, as it must be washed so often and its colour faded quickly with each washing, while a darker pattern would keep some semblance of decoration for years.

'Viola!' Suddenly Kat could find no other words.

'Kat, how pretty you look. That colour suits you.'

Kat did not say the fine wool walking dress (with six hem ruffles, six arm ruffles and six ruffles in a deep V at the front to below her waist in her favourite shade of green) had been placed on the late Major Nash's account in their flurried week of ordering at Madame Lucie's before the wedding, even though the dress itself had not been delivered till a month later — by which time she was in black. This was the first day she had allowed herself colour. She moved to kiss Viola's cheek, then stepped back, as Viola accepted the kiss, but did not return it.

'Viola darling, what's wrong? I thought I'd find you free and happy.'

Viola's expression was impossible to read. 'I'm sorry. I didn't expect you so soon. My letter can't have reached you yet. Will you come in?'

Kat stepped into the room. 'Mr Smith called in three days ago to say you were alive, and back in the colony. Mrs O'Connell and I opened a bottle of elderflower champagne, and as soon as we'd drunk it I set off for Sydney. I probably passed the ship with your letter on the way and I wasn't even sea sick! It must be from joy. Viola, it is so wonderful to see you.'

Kat waited for a proper embrace, which did not come, and for gratitude, which seemed missing as well. She sat on a kitchen chair, it being the only thing she could think to do, and took off her gloves and bonnet. 'Will you rent another house?'

'I'm content here for the moment. The estate is still confused, and the police naturally want to check my story. It will all be resolved eventually. I must remain in Sydney till it is and, given the unreliability of mail to and from England, that may be two years perhaps. I must ensure that the estate is properly secured and my brother in full agreement, and that other matters will be well looked after before I leave again.'

'You're leaving again? Are you going back to India? I am longing to hear how you found it —'

'Kat, please listen. I am so sad about Zebediah — Titania has finally told me.'

Kat's face lost its eagerness. 'I am so sorry I couldn't tell you back then. I ... I couldn't tell anyone for a while. I meant to explain to you both in Sydney, but you were so distressed. I couldn't add my grief to yours.'

'It is I who must apologise for not realising something had happened, for not being with you to help and comfort. I am also more grateful than I can say for all you have done for me. You saved my life, by giving me the chance to have the life I choose freely, instead of one imposed upon me. But, Kat, I cannot face you now. One day I will, but not for a while.'

'I ... I don't understand.'

'You knew that I was alive all along, didn't you?'

Kat stared. 'How did you know?'

'I didn't; I guessed. Tilson told me about the trial, you see, and how you appeared to be Lionel's friend and testified in his defence. Tilson thought you had betrayed me. But you wouldn't have testified for Lionel if you'd believed I was dead. You would have been as angry as Titania. Angrier, blazing with revenge.'

'That *was* revenge,' said Kat fiercely. 'The best revenge I could contrive. And I didn't *know* you were alive. I hoped, when the body in the dress couldn't be identified. No more than that. I wanted to give Nash hope too, that there was one person who believed in him, would try to free him. I let him believe that until the end, then I dashed the hope away.'

'Why not tell Titania what you thought? To give her hope too, instead of grief?'

'She had to appear grieved and beyond hope you were alive,' said Kat flatly. 'We both did, if Nash was to be condemned.'

A memory returned: Captain Quicksilver telling her, swiftly, quietly, that first evening outside Titania's cottage. 'No matter what you're told or shown, Kat darlin', don't worry. She'll be safe. But don't tell Titania. She ain't got an ounce of deception in her.'

'And I have?' Kat had asked.

'Of course you have.' He'd grinned. 'I couldn't tell your friends that you're the best liar in Australia, could I?'

'Kat, you had a man hanged for a murder he didn't commit.'

'Nothing I did made any difference to the verdict. Even if I said I thought you were alive, the dress had convinced the police that you were dead. They would have assumed I was deluded. And Nash was *not* innocent!' Should she tell Viola about 'Nanny' Nash? No, she thought. Viola should never know that she had been desired simply because she had been childlike. Nash's love of her money meant nothing. His lust for her body defiled the whole time Viola had been in his care.

Viola sat with her hands neatly in her lap. 'Lionel was innocent of the crime of which he was convicted, and guilty of no more than many men assume to be their right. He was not a morally sophisticated man.'

'He was guilty of a crime that carries the same sentence as murder, Viola. You would never have been free while he was alive. Nash would never have divorced you! He'd have written to say he would if you came back to Sydney and you would have obeyed, just as you obeyed Mr Smith when he wrote to say you could return. Nash would have killed you so he could be a grieving widower, not a deserted husband.'

'Do you truly believe that?'

Kat hesitated. 'I ... I did then. I'm not so sure now. But I am positive he still would never have divorced you.'

'It would not have mattered. I had got far away, under another name.'

'He'd have found you and brought you back.'

'And lived with me after the scandal I put him through?'

'Perhaps. That might have been his revenge. To keep you shut up and whipped each day.'

'No. Lionel was too ... conventional for revenge. Even his attack on me was conventional. Once I had left him in full view of society, and once he had no child to threaten to take, I was free. I would never have returned if I didn't believe that after that humiliation he'd have agreed to divorce me, or even have the marriage annulled, as after I lost the child there was no time for the marriage to have been consummated. A wife who'd fled, and a marriage that had not been consummated — he would have been the butt of jokes across the colony.'

'Mr Smith told me you'd lost the baby. I'm sorry. So sorry. I lost a baby. Not far along but enough to hope, to plan —'

Viola held up a hand to interrupt her. For the first time since they'd met Kat felt she was in the presence of an aristocrat, one who assumed her orders would be carried out. 'Kat, I have to know. Did Mr Smith plan for me to witness Lionel's death? I know it was well meant, but it was cruelty, Kat.'

'What? You saw him hanged! I had no notion he planned that. Except ...' Kat hesitated again.

'Except what?'

'Back when we were planning this he told me to tell Nash that your face would haunt him forever. I thought that was just to remind Nash of his crime, not ... not that you would see him hanged! Abominable.'

'But you did plan that my cousin would die for a crime he had not committed?'

'I wanted him to die for the crime he *had* committed,' Kat said at last. 'Your marriage would have licensed him to assault you legally *for your entire life*, Viola. You couldn't accuse him — of course you could not! You *know* how trapped we were.'

Viola looked angrier than Kat had ever seen her. 'Have you and Mr Smith been plotting together all the time I was away? I wrote letters to Mr Smith, but no one seems to have received them. Did you?'

Kat met her eyes. 'No! I promise. I only saw Mr Smith again a few days ago, the day after ... after Nash's death. That was the first time I knew for certain you were alive. Mr Smith must have kept your letters so we would keep playing our parts in his revenge. But, yes, I wanted Lionel Nash to die for what he'd done to you, right from the first. I wanted him to suffer, as you had suffered too. He tried to steal your life when he raped you, and he tried to steal your life a second time with marriage. Surely you can see that a man who could rape one woman would do it again, and must be stopped? Mr Smith knew exactly how I felt. He should never have made you witness the death — a horrible thing — but he probably saw it as our final revenge on Nash, and that you'd want the revenge as much as I did.'

'Then the revenge is on your shoulders, not on mine.'

Kat put her chin up. 'If you wish it to be. I am proud to bear it, for my friend, even if she blames me for it.'

'You don't understand. I don't blame you,' said Viola quietly. 'I simply cannot bear that I was the cause of it. Not yet. It should have been my choice, Kat, not yours. I was the one wronged. It is my right to be the one to choose revenge, or have the gift of forgiveness.'

'Forgive?! How could you, after what that monster did?'

'The greater the sin, the greater the gift of the chance to forgive.'

'Viola, that is sentimental rubbish. Even on that last day, Nash didn't repent about what he'd done. He kept giving excuses, *horrible* reasons why he was justified ...'

'In the Bible, Jesus forgave Peter for betraying him three times in one night, long before Peter repented. Kat, I told you that first day that I didn't seek revenge, only safety, and freedom if it was possible. I had both. I could bear Cousin Lionel being hanged for the crime he was guilty of, even if it meant my humiliation. But he had the right to be condemned for the crime he had committed, to have to face it, perhaps even repent. Instead he knew he died for an injustice.'

'Do you blame me for losing your baby?' asked Kat suddenly. 'You think that the ... strain ... of your escape led to the loss?'

'No.' Viola's voice sounded slightly less composed. 'I had felt slight pains for several days.' She shook her head. 'Another "might have been". If I had postponed the wedding for another week, I might never have felt the need to go through with it. Kat, I have to know — who was the poor soul who was mistaken for me?'

Kat closed her eyes briefly. It was the question she had asked the bushranger the morning he had arrived on her doorstep, eyes gleaming with laughter and triumph as he waited for her gratitude, her questions.

'I don't know. Nor did the man who calls himself Mr Smith,' she added hastily. 'It seems he has a wide ... acquaintance, including those resurrectionists who deal in the sale of the bodies of the unclaimed poor for anatomy, taken from hospitals or the workhouse. I suppose one must meet all kinds of people, disposing of stolen goods. The young woman was a nameless pauper, probably a native girl, who was to be buried in a common grave. Mr Smith said you gave him the dress.'

'I never wanted to see it again, but the cloth was valuable. I thought he might know someone who could use it. I am grateful to him, too, Kat. But it isn't possible not to feel revulsion with that part of his scheme, as well as what he put Titania through, and you, and even Mrs Higgins and others who had known me. The whole colony — half the world perhaps — has been feeding on the scandal. Some scandal was necessary but Kat, the drama of it — that poor mutilated body, and having me witness Cousin Lionel's death. He saw me, Kat! At the last second, he knew I was alive! None of that was necessary, simply melodrama and cruelty to a man who was going to be hanged anyway, as well as the added callousness to those who cared for me.'

For the first time Kat understood a little of Viola's anger. Because part of her *had* enjoyed the challenge, and the deception, and yes, the melodrama, despite her worry and her grief.

'I suppose you have hated the pretence the whole time,' she said bitterly.

'Oh, no. I enjoyed it,' said Viola surprisingly. 'I loved the voyages, the time in India, even the escape from the church. I always envied my brother's freedom of movement, of thought and expression, the chance for adventures. I regret nothing I have done the past year, except my part in the shock and grief to those I loved, and the cruelty to a man who should be pitied for his lack of heart.'

'It was justice,' said Kat stubbornly.

'Perhaps. But if we all dispensed such final justice, who would escape hanging? Is there one of us who truly has no guilt to stain their soul?'

'No decent person has a stain like Nash's! I can't believe you would forgive him.'

'Don't you see? I *can't* forgive him yet! But I have to try. I do not forgive myself either. I should have spoken up, no matter what the cost, and accused him openly, instead of bowing to convention. I should have had the courage to bring up a child and give them the love and confidence they needed to face being illegitimate. I should have questioned Mr Smith further, but I thought the game was finished with my escape. Kat, was your revenge just for me? Fooling Lionel to think you supported him, that there might be a chance of escape?'

'I don't know,' said Kat honestly. 'The fury that drove me was all for you.' Or was it? she wondered, remembering the nightmares where Nash's face and her father's mingled, and even Zebediah's, because by dying he had left her, betrayed her.

And she had enjoyed the game. She had known Captain Quicksilver was quite capable of faking a body as soon as the dectective inspector had told them about the dress. His very insistence on the remarkable white dress had suddenly made sense as soon as she saw it on the poor rotting corpse. She had laughed at his trickery, when she'd got home, becoming more and more hopeful — even certain — that the dress had been part of the bushranger's misdirection.

But she would not say those words to Viola. Viola already knew. Mr Smith had enjoyed pulling strings and tricking the whole justice system of New South Wales. And Kat had, too. It was not her actions that condemned her, but her pleasure in them.

Nash was a monster. But Kat had now absorbed enough of Viola's philosophy to realise that one sin does not excuse another.

'You will cut me off entirely?' she asked in a small voice. 'Will Titania abandon me too?'

'Ah Kat, no! I will write. I promise I will write. And you must bring yourself to actually put pen and paper together with the ink sometimes. I haven't told Titania that you guessed I might be alive. I will never speak of that again. Kat, there will come a time when I long to see you again. But just now all I see is an adventure out of tragedy, even if the adventurers thought it was for the best of reasons. I see Cousin Lionel's expression, as he saw me in his final moment. I saw his face … Kat, have you ever seen a man's face, after he has been hanged? I have to find a way to forgive him, Kat, or I will go mad.'

'I understand,' said Kat, ignoring the tears on her cheek, and Viola's too.

Kat understood too well.

Chapter 65

KAT

RAINBOW'S END, 1856

The sky echoed with cicada cackling. A branch dropped, unwanted by its gum tree in the heat. Kat sat in the shade of her verandah, the dog who was Not Sullivan panting at her feet, reading the mail that had come with the last delivery from Sydney.

Kat could afford a regular monthly order from Boot and Anderson now, brought down by boat and up the track along the river: flour, salt, sugar, tea, syrup, lamp oil, linseed oil to make putty or polish, isinglass for storing eggs and whatever else her extended household might need, as well as the month's collection of mail and newspapers and magazines.

She had returned from the last harsh journey to Sydney eighteen months earlier to find one of the cottages inhabited by a bag of hair and bones called Cranky Nick.

Cranky Nick was sewn into his clothes and muttered about flying cockroaches sometimes, and turned his back rather than face a woman, but he liked a solid roof above him and three meals a day left for him at the back door. He kept the wood box full and the fences mended, and was no trouble as long as you never tried to look him in the face and ignored his occasional shouted arguments with the cockroaches.

Like Mrs O'Connell, Cranky Nick worked compulsively, as if

unsure what to do if not splitting wood or strengthening fence posts. With the existing fences all mended he was even extending them to new paddocks, as if trying to enclose an unpredictable world in the orderliness of rectangles.

Cranky Nick's contributions left Black Harry to his vegetable growing, using Kat's horse and plough for paddocks of Indian corn once again, mangelwurzels for winter fodder, ridged grey pumpkins that lasted through the cold months too, as well as potatoes, onions, parsnips, cabbages, cauliflowers, carrots and the less common vegetables whose seed Kat ordered from a Sydney catalogue: globe artichokes and oyster plant, nasturtiums and as many lettuce varieties as he could be persuaded to try, as well as a large bed of asparagus. The enterprise had proved profitable to them both, not just in vegetables but in the coins Black Harry handed her each month — her share of the crop sold.

Six months after her return, the Ribonis trekked up from the valley, finally tired of life under canvas and envying the empty cottages above them on the hill. Mrs Riboni spoke little English, but made excellent cheese, if not the kind Kat was used to, as well as a dense salty ham and what Kat assumed was the Corsican equivalent of bacon. Mr Riboni and Mrs O'Connell talked longingly of revolutions sometimes, but as the revolutions they dreamed of were for countries far across the world Kat wasn't worried.

Titania sent her two Irish maids, straight off the boat, and both believing in leprechauns as strongly as Mrs O'Connell, who consequently approved of them. Within months they both acquired not quite husbands, ticket-of-leave Irish rebels, which warmed Mrs O'Connell's heart and made her discussions with Mr Riboni all the more interesting. Kat had discovered that the best way to attract good farm hands was to give them happy wives.

She had six wide-hipped Jersey cows now, a bull who liked carrots and his nose scratched and, down in the pig sty mud, Bacon, Ham, Roast Pork, Sunday Dinner and their kin rooted fatly. The Oriental hens were laying even better than expected.

The Oriental–Dorking cross did, indeed, at times lay almost an egg a day. She hadn't sold any, partly because she wanted to keep them but also because, as Mr Smith had suggested, the price had dropped as quickly as it had risen just as the bubble had burst for her father's railway shares.

The latest batch of poteen was maturing in its flagons, though not for long. Sunlight, unlike wine or even whisky, was best drunk fresh. Soon it would go to the wine merchant Titania had reluctantly found for her, who was willing to pay an increasingly handsome price for the bottles discreetly stacked in the walled-up room at the end of her dairy.

The five hundred guineas — and interest — had not yet been needed. Kat's poteen money paid for the deliveries from Sydney and wages. The money made from Mr Harry's vegetables paid for items from Mr Wehby's draper's cart that now toured the district twice a year. The small fat man from Lebanon carried everything from bolts of gingham or fine wool cloth to needles and thread to ready-made boots. Mr Wehby would even take an order if a fussy client wished their boots to fit them.

Kat scratched Not Sullivan's ears, then his chest as he rolled over, took a sip of tea, given just a touch of body with poteen, then turned back to her letters. Usually she only touched poteen of an evening, a fraction of a sherry glass after dinner, taken with Mrs O'Connell in the kitchen, and sometimes Mrs Riboni too. But mail ...

Mail deliveries hurt, even though Viola had kept her promise to write often or perhaps because of it. Titania wrote each fortnight too. But there had been no invitations to Sydney, not even to Titania's quiet wedding to Oberon O'Reilly. That hurt, a little, despite Titania's assertion that only witnesses had been present. Perhaps Titania was worried that her ex–detective inspector husband might ask questions, even though the case was over. Maybe she had not wanted to court the possible publicity of having the three of them together, with the detective inspector who had been in charge of the investigation too.

Titania now lived a most bourgeois life in peaceful Paddington. She and Oberon O'Reilly took the horse-drawn omnibus each morning to the office on the wharf. Her letters were full of housekeeping details: the virtues of filling a fireplace with a vase of bright-dyed feathers in summer, lest it look drab and empty; the best way to keep lace curtains white and drive beetles out of carpets.

Viola had rented a small house near the cliffs she loved so much. She avoided society. Her letters consisted mostly of descriptions of the birds she saw on her morning and afternoon walks, and reflections on books she had read. They all seemed of the improving variety, with a decided bluestocking and philosophic bent.

This last letter though was full of disturbing news from her father in India. Anger at the British was growing, Viola declared, though Kat found it hard to imagine why the Indians should be angry. Surely the English had brought order and civilisation? She must ask Viola in her next letter ...

'Your money or your life!'

Not Sullivan barked, embarrassed he'd been so lax as a guard dog. Kat looked up, startled, then laughed as Captain Quicksilver pointed his pistols at her. It had been six months since she had seen him. It was only his fourth visit after the one she preferred to forget, when he had explained the whole of the plan that had led to Nash's death. She had been delighted then, not just by the confirmation that Viola was alive, but in each detail, as well as its stark conclusion.

She had never reproached him afterwards with Viola's shock at seeing Nash hang; nor had she let him know that Viola's repulsion at that sight was at least in part responsible for her estrangement from Kat. Captain Quicksilver had risked his life for her. If he'd been recognised driving the carriage, if anyone had given the police the tale of a man who'd bought a body or seen him take it out where it would float to shore, he would have been arrested at the least for deception, and possibly hung for Viola's murder instead of Nash.

She was still not sorry for anything they had done to Lionel Nash, she concluded every time she turned the events over in her mind, awake at two am. She would kill a snake on her verandah without compunction, for the harm it might do. Lionel Nash had done evil and would have certainly done more.

She pushed the thoughts aside. 'I hope those are not loaded. You might trip.'

'And shoot you accidentally? Never.' He slipped them back into his belt.

'I was going to say, "and shoot your big toe if you could manage to hit anything at all".'

'What a barney to say to a bushranger!'

'Not at all. By your own admittance you have never shot a man.'

'I've shot ducks and quail and, let me tell you, that takes more skill than aiming at a seated man.' He casually climbed the stairs and sat in the chair next to her. 'The valley is growing green again.'

'It is indeed. The wattle trees seem to squeeze their roots right into the rock, and the thorn bush thrives on pure clay. I suppose you've come so far from the coach road to see if the poteen is ready for a tasting yet?'

'Not quite. I've got some news for you.' He grinned at her.

'Well, spit it out, man, instead of sitting there like a jackass.'

'You'll never have to work again,' he informed her.

'I'm not working now,' she pointed out. Though she would be soon, for it was time to put dinner on. She supposed he'd stay for dinner with her and Mrs O'Connell, though he had never asked to stay the night, either in her room or the spare room where he'd slept before. It seemed he guarded her reputation now there were so many who would observe it.

She was about to tell him the dinner menu — mutton shoulder stuffed with thyme and lemon, and roast potatoes and pumpkin, and a spiced pumpkin pie from a receipt Titania had sent her that she'd been wanting to try, when she noticed him glancing down meaningfully at the date on the newspaper on the table by her chair. 'What's so interesting in the newspaper?'

'Ah, I see you haven't read it yet. Some bounder has held up the gold coach from Tumble Mountain.'

'What a dastardly crime,' said Kat comfortably. 'No man nor his dog is safe these days.' Not Sullivan gave a slight growl of agreement, though that might have been because the bushranger's boot was scratching just above his tail.

'Seems the villain made off with more than six thousand pounds in cash and a strong box of gold bars.' Mr Smith stretched out his legs and tilted his hat over his eyes. 'A man could doze his life away with that kind of money.'

'You and Jimmy stole six thousand pounds!'

'I stole six thousand pounds and the gold bars,' said the voice under the hat. 'Jimmy helped me get away, but I'm the one that faced the danger. Jimmy will have a share, but not the half of it. I already have near two thousand pounds in the bank in Sydney, and now I have a treasure buried in the mountains.'

He sat up, and looked at her, his eyes gleaming. 'I'll go no more a-roving, Kat, me darlin'. I'm going to be a gentleman.'

'Won't people wonder where all your money has come from? Your stepfather too?'

'Ah, that's the beauty of it, Kat. If you marry me everyone will think it came from you. Clever lad, marrying the heiress. If we don't go splashing the fancy too much no one will ever guess. Well, me darlin', will you marry me?'

She stared at him. She had sometimes wondered if Viola's rescue had been his idea of courtship, as well as the gifts he sometimes left unannounced. But bushrangers were known for rewarding the small farmers who protected them.

'I can't marry anyone,' she said tightly. 'My husband has not been declared dead.'

'So we can't tie the knot in a church or courthouse. How many in the colony bother with that?'

Not many I care about, she thought. And the few who cared — like Titania — might believe they'd just married quietly if Kat told them so.

'Kat, I do love you. Even if you say me nay, I'll still go straight. Find myself a nice plump blonde down in Victoria maybe, who can cook as well as you.'

'I don't even know your name.'

He lifted up his hat and grinned at her. 'It's John Smith.'

'It isn't. Is it?'

'Almost. I'm a John, John Henrickson.'

She nodded, unable to find words, or even a coherent thought. She gazed out at the valley. The first vivid greenery had been weeds. Now, finally, she could see the long shapes of trees, probably bound to be cut for firewood or fence posts as soon as they were larger but, just now, the promise of life.

Life continued, even if you didn't join it. Titania married. Viola, lost to her, or as good as, but safe. Perhaps Kat's true match was a bushranger, one who had no compunction in using a dead body, for the soul that had inhabited it needed it no longer, who had carefully timed Viola's arrival so she'd see her husband killed and know that she was safe from him forever.

Ah, that was it. The rest she was content with, but not that, she realised. It was that memory that snapped her awake at nights: the moment when the adventure itself became the purpose and not rescuing the woman in peril, a woman of sensitivity and deep moral sense whose only reaction had been horror and guilt.

She and this man were well matched in many ways. But he had brought out the worst in her, as Zebediah had found the best. Viola and Titania had each learned to follow their own moral path. But Kat's charge through life meant she needed others to help her see the implications of her actions.

'Kat? It's common for a woman to answer when a man asks, "Will you marry me?" Even if we can't say the words in a church till we've a couple of brats in our arms, we'll be together.'

'Don't answer him, love.'

For a moment Kat thought the voice behind her was Mrs O'Connell's, for it had the same Irish lilt. But then a young woman hoisted herself over the side rail of the verandah — definitely a young woman despite the men's trousers, shirt, waistcoat and boots, and the cabbage tree hat as well. Her voice might be from Ireland, but her skin was darker even than Viola's and by her features she was a native.

The man at her side leaped to his feet. 'Jimmy! What the flaming hell are you doing here?'

'Giving you fair warning, Johnny. The traps know your name and your direction. I'd say you have about four hours' start on them.'

'What? Where are they coming from? How the deuce do they know ...?'

'They're comin' from Bathurst, and they know because I told them. A hundred pound,' the girl spat. 'Who do you think you are, Captain Flash, leavin' me a hundred pound?'

'A hundred pounds is more money than your family will see in a lifetime.' It was as if Kat wasn't there, nor Mrs O'Connell's face, which Kat glimpsed peering through the window.

'And that's all I've been worth to you? Saved your bacon a hundred times and even brought you here when you were hurt? "Ooh, no, Jimmy, she's just a kind lady," you says. "I owe her, Jimmy, just calling in on a friend." You been selling me a dog all along, ain't you? You planned to do this.'

'You get out of here.' Kat had never seen his face in fury. 'I told you it was over. You have no right —'

'No right? I am your wife.'

'What?' Kat found a word at last.

The young woman turned to her. 'I'm sorry, Mrs Markham. You're a good woman. I've watched you. I've watched the both of you, each time Johnny's come here. You don't know him and you don't deserve the likes of him. And he certainly don't deserve you.'

Kat turned to the man at her side. 'Is this true?'

He shrugged. 'There was a ceremony. But she's a native, Kat. It doesn't count.'

'It was Father Michaels,' said Jimmy coldly.

'It was me mate Blarney Murphy, Jimmy, down from Sydney, in a robe and collar and spouting hokum. A wife is someone who you take to your parents.'

Jimmy stared. 'You said your step-pa wouldn't accept me. You said we'd buy a farm together, one that stretched from mountain top to mountain top.'

'You know full well what Pa would have said. He wouldn't even have a native working in the house.'

'Your step-pa don't object to me going off as your servant.'

'He assumes you're my mistress and doesn't like that either, though he accepts it. A man don't marry his darkie mistress.'

'An' you sayin' you loved me, an' all the rest of it?' The girl spat on the ground. 'It was just words, wasn't it? And words don't matter? Well, I gave words to the troopers too. Let's see if they matter now.'

'I don't believe you,' he said uneasily. 'Jimmy, we had a good run, but it's time to settle down, the both of us, and not with each other.'

'Only place you'll settle is in a prison cell,' said Jimmy flatly.

He changed. The look of vague worry became a grin. He turned to Kat. 'Then it's California, not a gentleman's life at Rainbow's End. What do you say, Kat me darlin'? Will you come to California with me and eight thousand pounds? We can do anything you'd like there, buy a farm or a hotel on the goldfields for a bit of spice in our lives ...'

'You ain't got eight thousand pounds,' said Jimmy, calmly. 'Because I've got the six thousand, too. If I can hide you, I can follow and find your stash. You think I'm a gigglemug?'

The grin slipped from his face. 'You bitch! You'll never get away with spending it. How can a native buy a farm with that kind of money?'

'The troopers will be here soon,' said Kat, suddenly empty.

'You need to go. I don't have much money here,' she added. 'Maybe five pounds in coin. I'll go and get it.'

'No,' he said tightly. 'I've got cash enough with me, and the money in the bank in Sydney. Kat, I'll write. I'll —'

'Don't.'

'Kat, you can't say that after all I've done for you, after all we've been to each other. I saved your friend!'

'You had an adventure and were paid for it.' And it didn't even occur to you who you might hurt, thought Kat. Not Viola, me or Titania, nor Jimmy either. And I should have seen it long ago.

'Kat, you have to believe me. You can sell this place and we'll still be set up for life!'

She stared at him incredulously. 'This *is* my life.'

'If you aren't goin' now, you varmint, it won't be the troopers who'll have your head.' Mrs O'Connell appeared, warming pan in hand. 'I got this full of red-hot coals and by Jesus, Mary, St Joseph and St Patrick, I'll slap it against your ugly mug if I'm still looking at it as soon as I take another breath ...'

He stepped backwards down the steps and stared at Kat. Then he was gone, striding towards the paddock behind the house where she assumed he'd left his horse. He didn't look back.

'Sit down, the pair of yers, and I'll fetch tea,' said Mrs O'Connell, as calmly as if she'd taken a rat from a trap and disposed of it.

'I think we need something stronger,' said Kat.

'I'll be bringing that too. Men. They're always rogues. Only known one that wasn't.' She left, muttering.

'I wonder who he was? The one good man,' said Jimmy, her voice shaking now. She sat and Kat sat too.

'Probably Zebediah. My husband.' As soon as Kat said the word she knew it fit. Zebediah *was* her husband, the only man who'd ever fit that word. 'He was too big for any man to match his shadow. He was the best man I've known and the kindest and the most honest. I wasn't going to say yes just now, you know.'

Jimmy sat slightly warily beside her. 'I didn't think you would. That's why I interrupted when I did. I want him to spend the rest of his life thinking you might have married him.'

'Are the troopers really going to come here after him?' Kat hoped no one else had seen him visiting. She had never cared much for her reputation, but the man who had just left was not worth its loss.

'Not yet. I just sent a letter naming him and I told them where to find the stash. Or some of it, anyway, and the chest it was stolen in too. Yes, I can write,' she added, at Kat's look of surprise. 'My mam used to be maid at a neighbour of Johnny's ma — old Mrs Kitterson didn't mind the colour of my skin — but I liked life on horseback better, like my brothers. And I loved Johnny.'

'He might turn you in too,' said Kat. 'Especially if they catch him.'

'He might. I don't think he will. He's not a good man, except when it suits him, but he's not a bad man neither, except when there's something he wants. Mam warned me he'd never take me to wife.' Jimmy shrugged. 'It doesn't matter if he squeals on me or not.'

'Why not?'

"Cause the traps got to find me first, and I don't think they will. Jimmy ain't my real name, and Johnny doesn't understand native names, so he won't know what other to give. He's right about not being able to buy a farm with the money, but there's no need for my da and uncle to work for his step-pa any longer, neither. Penny-pinching old scragger he is. We can all of us leave now.'

'I'll buy you a farm,' said Kat. 'If you'll trust me with the money to do it. Better make it somewhere far from the roads, and over several titles, not just one. That way if someone claims a native can't own one of the pieces of land and wins, you'll have the others. There's a family doing just that about forty miles from here,' she added. 'No one in the land titles office seems to have twigged that they're natives, or if they have, there's been no objection. But you'll need to trust me with the money.'

The woman who wasn't Jimmy looked at the ground for a time. At last she nodded. 'I trust you. I trusted you with me husband, didn't I, when he got hurt? If you say you'll do summat, you do it.'

'We'll find you that land. I've had a bit to do with land titles now and this area has all been surveyed. Would you settle for a place near here? Not too far away, either. It's time I had more neighbours. Zebediah promised we'd visit with five families and I haven't had a single one yet, except those who work on the property.'

'What would your husband have thought of you visiting black neighbours?'

'Zebediah?' She thought of Summat Sam, the scars on his back. 'You married properly, with a priest, didn't you? Or a man you thought was a priest. Your family is as nice as you?'

'Better. And with more sense,' she said shortly.

'Then he'd say you are a young woman of good family and would be delighted I might have friends,' said Kat, as Mrs O'Connell brought out the tea and a flagon too, and the pumpkin tart that had cooled on the windowsill.

Chapter 66

VIOLA

SYDNEY

Viola sat on the weathered seat overlooking the harbour, watching the sea crush into waves and froth against the rocks, listening to the high screams of the seagulls, the echo of a ship's bell: attempting, as she had every day for the past few months, to see and hear directly, and not translate the world to words.

Every time she reduced an experience to words she knew she changed it subtly. A wave was a cliché white-topped semicircle of water, not the scene below her. Yes, that reduction was necessary, often — one could not survive without taking most of the world for granted, think 'This is a brown animal with four legs and hooves and pricked up ears that is galloping on a cobbled roadway' before that horse trampled you if you didn't get out of the way. But she had spent too much of her life living in the world of words, the books and essays of philosophers. If she was to find out who she was, then she had to go beyond those words. Perhaps, as her father had said, she must learn to be a tree.

Socrates said it was impossible to understand the soul without comprehending the universe. She smiled suddenly. She couldn't comprehend the universe while sitting on a seat on the cliffs, nor confined by the society of those who would always see the scandalous Lady Viola, not whoever she really was.

Yesterday's mail had brought the final document settling her affairs after Lionel Nash's death. It was time to travel, to places she had never seen, and where people had never heard of her.

She stood, truly free for the first time in her life.

Home was a short walk across the headland. Viola lived simply. Mrs Higgins had given up the new glory of a house with ten bedrooms and a master who'd made a fortune in gold nuggets to do the simple cooking her ladyship and the household desired, with the help of a kitchen maid who came in each day, and a woman to do the scrubbing. Alice and Millie, too, had proved loyal. The only other staff was a man to do the garden, the boots and the firewood. Viola did not even keep a carriage.

'You've a visitor, your ladyship,' said Mrs Higgins, taking Viola's pelisse and bonnet. Her voice had the slight hesitation that told Viola exactly who was in the drawing room.

'Marigold, you look beautiful!' Marigold was now the highly successful proprietor of La Belle Millinery, and employing three women. She carefully copied Viola's intonations when she spoke. Viola had been teaching her French, too, the phrases a society milliner might casually drop into conversation.

'I needed a rest from assuring plain ladies that a bonnet trimmed with seven ostrich feathers dyed puce is exactly what they need. Which it is,' said Marigold frankly, 'as everyone looks at the feathers, not their faces. Besides, I have made you a gift.'

'A bonnet?' Viola took the hat box with misgiving, and a determined smile. She disliked the silk, lace false flowers and furbelows of the creations so loved by Sydney society, but would never say so. She opened the box, and lifted the hat out.

It was of French straw, totally plain, finely woven, the narrow brim drawn upwards. Viola stared at it. Every other milliner had created bonnets for her that cradled her face, hiding her face as well as protecting her skin from further tan. This one, she thought, was the first that would emphasise her features, not disguise them.

'Do you like it?' Marigold asked anxiously as Viola stayed silent. 'I can add ribbons and ruching if you like, or a satin under-trim ...'

'I love it,' Viola placed it carefully on her head. 'I may never take it off.'

Marigold laughed. 'You'd better, before you go to bed or have a bath.' She sobered. 'I owe you everything, you know.'

'It's I who owe you. You offered me help, and shelter. All I had to give was money.'

'You gave me more than that. Right from the first you knew who I was, and what I did for a living, but you forgave it all, and gave me your friendship anyway.'

Viola sat silent. It had never occurred to her to judge a woman who had so unstintingly given a stranger aid. And yes, they had been friends from the first, just as it had been with Titania and Kat.

She had a fair idea of the moral compromises and struggles necessary for a New South Wales whore to survive. But who was she to condemn her? What had her father said? 'Perhaps trees know that the view that one tree sees is not another's and so each accepts the limits of its understanding.'

Why had she never thought to judge Marigold, but had not forgiven Kat?

Because Kat did what I did not dare, physically or morally, she thought. Because I was glad that she and her bushranger had freed me, as I could not free myself. Placing her at the scene of her husband's execution had been unthinking cruelty. But that had been John Smith, not Kat. And if Kat had enjoyed the deception and the revenge? Well, that was for Kat's conscience. Viola admitted that here, too, she knew too little to judge.

'Viola? What are you thinking?'

'That a friend is someone you forgive, over and over. And that I need to write to Kat.'

'I'm glad,' said Marigold simply.

It was as if the sea wind had washed into her drawing room. 'Yes. I'm glad too.'

Chapter 67

KAT

RAINBOW'S END

My dearest Kat,
This is a hard letter to write, for I do not have the words to say how much I have wronged you, or to express my heart-felt hope that you may forgive my coldness and my separation from you.

I owe you not just my life, but my freedom, and whatever life I forge from here. The anger that I directed at you was more truly anger at myself, for being so helpless that my friends were forced to such lengths to protect me. That anger has vanished, as have the shock and confusion I felt that last day we met. All that remains is gratitude and longing for the laughter of my friend again, and sadness for how I must have hurt you, to whom I owe so much, and to whom I truly owe the gift of Philia, the love of deepest friendship, as well as Pragma, long-standing love. No matter what, through all that has happened, love has connected us. It always will.

This letter is also to let you know that I plan to sail to Calcutta on the Mary Bryan, due in Sydney Town within the next two months and leaving perhaps three months after that. I have grown worried about the reports of unrest in India. I cannot know if my presence would endanger my Indian family unless I see them — it is quite the conundrum. I have decided to risk visiting them. If it causes trouble I can be quickly away again.

I also believe I am now ready to begin the next part of my life, to travel further, and see where it may lead me, but I cannot do so until I am sure they are safe and do not need my help.

It is my most sincere wish that you might come to Sydney and stay with me for as long as you can spare before I leave, and that in friendship we can be together in person, as we will always be within each other's hearts.

With love always, to my most dear friend,
Viola

Kat looked at the neatly written letter in her hand as she sat on her verandah, the other mail and newspapers that had arrived this morning scattered over the table. You have not said that I was right, thought Kat. Nor will you ever say it.

But Kat *had* been right, if not for all the right reasons, just as she was right to refuse to marry the bushranger too. When a man feels entitled to use one person there will have been other crimes committed in the past, and more to come. Viola presumably still knew nothing of Nash's other evils. Kat did not regret his death.

Yet Viola had been correct as well. The melodrama of that severed hand had not been needed, nor the vengeful torment of a man about to lose his life. She had been seduced, not by the bushranger's body, for she was still bound to Zebediah, but by his mischief, his defiance of convention, his games against the law in which she'd found distraction from her grief. She and Viola had both been right, and wrong too.

But this letter was enough.

She could travel to Sydney with a clear heart and mind now. The McDonalds (a fine, respectable name, a name no one would question, for the family of the woman who had been Jimmy) had a friend of a friend who was a stockman too, who knew another man, a shepherd from Saxony who'd given up panning for gold when the cold took four of his fingers one winter. He had become

Kat's foreman, with four new men in the barracks now to work with him, all men she trusted, and who enjoyed working on a property that had become their home.

Labour had become plentiful again with not just starving Irish but the hungry from all across the world having reached Australia in the hope of the pot of gold at the end of the rainbow, and some of them glad to find a cottage, comfort, security, and a wage and all the butter they could eat at Rainbow's End instead.

Jimmy had become Jane, and somewhat unwillingly taken to wearing skirts. She rode over once a month at least to make sure the new foreman was doing his duty — they could buy good horses with over a thousand pounds left after they'd bought the land — and to eat apple dumplings on Kat's verandah, and for she and Kat to carefully not talk about a man they'd both known, though sometimes Jane smiled as Hans Sixfingers presented her with a basket of the lamb's tails that Kat had expected would be grilled for her dinner, as well as flowers, fleece, and other gifts the shepherd thought suitable for courtship.

The sheep agisted at Nash's Hawkesbury property had been returned, four times as many sheep as had left, which Viola said was only to be expected with sheep breeding as sheep do. The Hawkesbury estate had been sold, for Viola had no wish to manage it. Her brother had formally renounced all interest in her or Nash's property.

Rainbow's End was a farm again, its orchards tended, its cottages filled, and Kat slept soundly in the bed Zebediah had built, with Not Sullivan snoring on the rug nearby.

But she would enjoy Sydney and old friendships, too.

Sheep, it seemed, were not the only things that bred. Kat stared at the scrap in Titania's arms, having found her and Oberon O'Reilly sitting in Viola's small front room when she came down after changing for dinner on her first night there. Outside the waves crashed on the cliff's edge and woodsmoke sifted into a star-dappled sky.

'What ...?' began Kat.

'It's a baby,' explained Oberon O'Reilly.

'I know what a baby is! But why didn't you tell me you were breeding?'

'I didn't know,' said Titania, half embarrassed, half besotted, as she looked down at the baby's face. She stroked his cheek with one large callused finger. 'I was getting stout, well stouter, and as for the rest, well, what did I expect at my time of life?'

'Not this,' said Oberon, beaming with pride. 'You should hear the lungs on him.'

'I'm sure we will again, quite soon,' said Viola dryly.

'Then I had a stomach ache and went to lie down, and next thing I know there was a mess and him, without even time to call for a fingersmith. I don't know what all the fuss is about, having babies,' Titania added.

'Not all ladies have your figure for it, love,' said Oberon O'Reilly.

'Are you going to call him Puck?' asked Kat, grinning.

'His name is Anthony Patrick O'Reilly,' said his father.

Anthony Patrick O'Reilly burped.

A happy time. An unexpected time: weeks of memories, and gossip about memories.

A time to treasure. A time of things unsaid, too. Lionel Nash was never mentioned, or John Smith, or whatever his name might be now in California.

He spoke to all that was wrong in me, Kat thought. He made me think just as my father did: that other's lives were mine to judge or take. I was wrong, quite wrong.

She did not say it. It would hurt them both too much. (Later, she thought perhaps she should have said the words. One day she would need to write them down and tell Titania too.)

They did not even talk of India, where it seemed from the newspapers that things had settled enough for Viola to travel there and her friends not to worry more than you would for anyone you loved who sailed in peril on the sea then faced the unknown on land as well. But to Viola, Kat supposed, it was not quite unknown any more.

Nor did they talk of the future, except of the new wharf Titania and Oberon had planned, beyond the present overcrowded portion of the harbour. Just once Kat asked, 'Have you chosen where to travel after India yet?' and Viola answered, smiling, 'I will let you know when I have reached it,' and said no more.

She, who had known so much of Viola's life, now knew almost nothing of the past few years nor of the future she had planned. She even, Kat realised, knew almost nothing of who this woman had become.

But Viola was still, of course, such an easy woman to love.

Marigold joined them at church each Sunday, and came to dinner too, dressed in frilled green satin and with a matching toque with gold trim, bringing a broad-brimmed hat with blue ribbons and pleated muslin lining for Kat, to attempt to stop her ruining her complexion with too much sun.

'You look happy,' Kat told her.

'I am at that. I get more sleep and better gossip making hats,' Marigold said complacently. 'I know who's in the family way before the fathers do, and what sprig of fashion's keeping a lightskirt on the sly. Besides, there's only so much you can do in bed, but no end of invention with a hat.'

She, Mrs Higgins, Millie and Alice came with Kat and Titania to say farewell on the dock as the *Mary Bryan* prepared to sail. The captain offered Viola his arm up the gangplank. She stood on deck, small in her dark blue dress and Marigold's bonnet, already at ease with the captain's wife, who had dined with them all the night before.

Kat and Titania waved as the ship cast off, the sails creaking, flapping, seagulls yelling, the south wind spitting iced salt into their faces, with Master Anthony warm indoors with his nanny, so as not to catch a chill. And then the ship turned, and vanished except for the water heaving behind it, then even that grew still, for a little while, until another vessel came to disturb it.

Master Anthony Patrick O'Reilly needed to be fed. Kat needed to walk.

At home, where she was no longer always busy scraping a living together, she'd have walked up onto the ridge with Not Sullivan, to sit on the lichened rocks as she had done so many times with Zebediah. Sometimes she even imagined the wind sang his song, or that she felt the warmth of another's body beside her.

This morning she walked along the docks, and through the governor's public gardens, then along a street of workshops that had grown up on the other side, her shawl over her head in the sharp breeze, ignoring small boys wheedling for a penny, careless of pickpockets, for she hadn't bothered taking any money or even a reticule, so had nothing for them to dab, somehow not hearing the hammering of wheelwrights, the thud as a cooper tried the soundness of a barrel, the old woman hawking oysters and another with bunches of lavender.

She would stay one more night in Sydney, for the cottage on the cliffs would be kept open indefinitely. Viola would not leave her servants homeless, and the cottage was as much their home as hers, or more. It was understood that Kat would use the house when she wished to come to Sydney, and that would be often enough to keep the staircase dusted, the front steps white, and not just for a mistress who might never return.

But Kat was heartsore for home now. Shearing next month — she'd need to get more maids to help with the cooking and dishwashing, Irish if possible. Mrs O'Connell could put her feet up in the kitchen and direct her new girls properly and hear the accents of her home.

Kat needed to hear wombat's dig and lyrebirds sing. Every time the big male in the gully sang she almost imagined it still echoed Zebediah's ballad in its tune.

'Oh Nancy mine, I'll meet you in the flower time,
Oh Nancy mine, I'll meet you in the glen

Oh Nancy mine, I'll kiss you in the flower time,
I'll hold you close, oh Nancy mine and then ...'

Kat stilled. Someone *was* singing it. Not 'some' one. As soon as she heard the voice she knew.

She found him in a workshop down the alley, a cabinetmaker's, of course, smelling of sawdust, wood shavings and linseed oil and the slight flinty scent of sharpened tools. She stood in the doorway and watched him, humming now, as he sanded a tabletop, by touch, for one eyelid was closed over a sunken socket, and the other eye was white. A purple scar slashed his forehead.

None of which signified in the slightest.

A shadow appeared behind her. Kat didn't even turn around. 'Can I help you, missus?'

'No, thank you. I have all I need,' she said. The man walked on.

The humming stopped. 'Kat.'

His voice was quiet, uncertain. He repeated more strongly, 'Kat?' He stretched out a callused hand.

She walked towards him steadily, and took the hand, feeling no shock because she had known, had always known ...

No, she'd believed that he was dead. Totally believed it. Maybe.

Perhaps she'd simply not had the courage to hope.

That didn't matter now. All that mattered was his hand, grasping hers, the utter familiarity of it. She didn't feel she could ever let it go.

'Why didn't you tell me?' She found her voice was steady. In a strange way it was as if they had taken up a conversation dropped four years ago.

'I didn't know myself for months.' He touched his head with the hand that wasn't in hers. 'They found me on the beach, they say. I've no memory of how I got there, or anything beyond leaving you that day. The people who run The Harbour Inn, the Harrisons, took me in, and others who'd been injured too. Good people. I owe my life to them and this job too, though luckily the workshop was so shorthanded back then that they were prepared to take even a blind man on, till I showed I knew what to do.'

'You ... you didn't think of me then?'

'I ... I thought of almost nothing else. I managed to find out that the house and farm hadn't been damaged in the flood, that you were safe.'

She gave his hand an angry squeeze. She was not going to let it go, 'You couldn't even have sent a message to me? You let me grieve, and all the time you were just down the river ...'

'Kat, I was blind, scarred, not even able to work for almost a year. I couldn't harness you to a cripple. I'd done too much to you already.'

'What do you mean?'

'I offered you a home as a gentlewoman, comfort, safety, not a farm of mud and stench. You came to find a man who could be a proper husband to you ...'

'How dare you, Zebediah Markham! You are my husband! No matter what, you are mine to love and cherish. You had no right to decide I wasn't!'

He was quiet a moment, though he, too, didn't release her hand. At last he said reluctantly, 'Just as I was beginning to know myself again Nobby Harrison read me bits of the newspaper. There was an article about troopers hunting a Captain Quicksilver, and how many magistrates had promised their help. It said that Magistrate Markham in particular had offered all the help possible in watching for the miscreant, and that he and his hospitable wife had kindly entertained the officers of the law.' His face carefully expressionless.

'You thought I'd replaced you,' said Kat flatly, grabbing his other hand as well. 'One day I am going to skin you alive for that. But not today. You should never have believed it.'

'It wasn't true?'

'Of course it wasn't true. The man they took for you *was* the bushranger. Mrs O'Connell and I dressed him as you. He was injured, and Mrs O'Connell thought he was like some ancient Irish rebel who fought the English — I'd never guessed she was a rebel too — so we looked after him and, yes, I enjoyed the adventure, but that was all there was to it and then he left.'

It was the truth, too. One day she'd tell Zebediah the rest, and be glad there was nothing she was ashamed to tell. But not until she'd made sure he knew he was her husband, and always would be, and given him several tongue lashings for ever doubting her.

'There's more Kat. It wasn't only that. Just as I was learning my way about, and had begun this job and thinking that maybe I did have a life to go on with, you were in the newspapers again, after Lady Viola went missing,' he said, his voice reasonable, though holding her hands as if it were a jetty and the flood was all about him again. 'They called you the wife of a magistrate, not his widow. I assumed whoever had taken my place was still there. Kat, I didn't blame you. I'd been a poor husband to you. I should have taken you to another home as soon as things got bad. If I had we'd not have gone through all we did.'

'You were the best of husbands,' she said unsteadily. 'And Rainbow's End is my home and not even you, Zebediah Markham, are going to persuade me away from the home you built, that we worked on together. I just couldn't bear to tell people you were dead. You weren't officially. I mean you aren't. You have to be missing for seven years. I only told the police — Detective Inspector O'Reilly, he's married to Titania now — after Viola vanished. I wrote to tell Lettice about the flood then but I ... I couldn't tell her you were dead.'

'I ... I had never wished for my eyes more than when I read you were in Sydney for the trial and when Lady Viola turned up again. The whole street was talking about it.'

'Half the world talked about it, maybe. Viola sailed away once more an hour ago. I don't know if she's ever coming back.'

Another silence. He slowly drew her too him. They stood for a while, his arms about her waist, her head on his shoulders. At last she said, 'I'm still considering feeding you to the dingoes when we get home. Or the dog. We have a new one now.'

'Kat, once I knew the house was safe, and the area around it, I knew you'd be all right. We had money enough in the bank, and coin and gold enough buried so you didn't have to farm —'

'I had no idea how much you had in the bank. I never thought to ask.'

'What? It was nigh on seven thousand pounds. I haven't drawn on it — I left it all for you.'

'I didn't know,' she repeated. 'You weren't declared dead anyway. You can't be declared dead without a body.' For a moment she glimpsed again the poor decayed shape in the wedding dress, and repressed a shudder. 'I couldn't have drawn money from your bank account unless I was a widow, and if you'd left a will leaving it all to me.'

'Of course you could. I made you co-signature the day we were married. I made a will leaving everything to you, too, and you signed one leaving any property to me among children we might have. Don't you remember signing the papers?'

She shook her head. 'I signed so much that day I had no idea what was in most of the papers. We were in such a rush to sail. And I'd never even held a bank book before. I didn't even think to draw on my own five hundred guineas until I didn't need to any longer.'

'Kat ...' He shook his head in distress. 'How did you manage?'

'That's a long story and we've time enough to tell it. All our lives. There's more money in the bank than there ever was, and we have a farm again. It's running extremely well, with people we can trust, not those ruffians you had before. Not as many sheep yet, but a good income.' This was possibly not the time to tell him about the poteen.

'I think perhaps my wife is a miracle.'

She would not cry. 'I think, more like, a miracle has given me back my husband. You're coming with me now. I may not even let go of you till you're back home in case you disappear again. And you're too thin. Much too thin.'

'I've done well enough. Kat, are you sure? You deserve far more than a blind husband.'

Perhaps a heart of flint was not what she wanted, after all. 'I deserve the best husband in the world, and I intend to make sure I keep him this time.'

'Truly? I have a life here. You needn't take me out of pity.'

'Say that again and I'll skin you twice over and nail your hide to the fence. Or make new boots with it. Are you sure you want a wife who shelters bushrangers, brews poteen in the dairy, and has been mixed up in the colony's most notorious scandal? Because if you don't there's more than enough money for both of us to be comfortable.'

'Poteen?' A grin began to appear.

'I didn't mean to tell you about that yet.'

'I think,' he said slowly, 'that I have exactly the wife I dreamed of, one with extremely interesting conversation of an evening, and who I could never, ever find boring.'

'It seems we are well suited then, Mr Markham, and for the second time.' Her face was wet, but she kissed him anyway, a gentle kiss, that then grew longer. 'Come on my love. Let's go home.'

Chapter 68

KAT

The Sydney Morning Herald, Friday 11 September 1857

The intelligence recently received from India from last July is of an alarming character as regards the progress of the mutiny in the Bengal army. At the latest advices, about 12,000 of the mutineers, after killing their officers, had obtained possession of the city of Delhi. An overwhelming force of European troops were concentrating around that city, and the next mail will, it is hoped, bring intelligence of the suppression of this fresh outbreak, and the chastisement of the leaders.

The brief shower had passed in a wavering veil, leaving the rainbow hovering pale over the valley, one end above the handful of bent-backed men shovelling a deep vein of gravel, still hoping for leprechaun gold. Violet and red light spilled in pale radiance over Rainbow's End's new stone workshop. And then it faded.

Late afternoon sun poured over the ridges. The valley cupped the light and seemed to breathe it out, the air a golden haze. Cicadas sang, their song so constant under the pure blue sky it vanished into the hush of summer, when only humans made a noise and animals slept.

Two such people and a dog sat on the verandah, though they were quiet with it, the dog dozing, a pile of mail and newspapers months old and only recently delivered weighed down by a jug of lemon barley water and two glasses, the women gazing down upon the valley that had changed so much. Trees hid the piles of rocks that even the flood had not been able to remove. A river snaked silver under the branches. The land below would seem untouched if you had not known what it had been before.

As with the two of us, thought Kat. Titania's brown hair was still parted in the middle and drawn back, without a hint of grey; her brown dress was unadorned as always, despite her wealth in granaries, and the warehouses and pickle factory that Oberon supervised these months while his wife was away. Kat doubted Titania had ever even thought of wasting good investment coin on golden necklaces.

And herself? Nine months' pregnant, a woman who had gone through more dramatic changes than a caterpillar butterfly but who had finally found the bedrock where she fitted best. Just now she felt almost as large as the Pigship, and needed to widdle every few minutes. But that would pass.

Down by the creek Titania's three children laughed and splashed with nanny. Childbirth was as easy as spitting out a grape seed, Titania had assured Kat, for she'd had the twins with as much ease as she'd had Master Anthony, though she daily thanked providence for nannies and nurses. Kat was not so sure, but had no qualms about the baby she expected any day now. Titania would be with her, and Mrs Riboni, and as soon as the green flag was hoisted as a signal Black Harry would ride to fetch Jane and Mrs McDonald. 'Mrs McDonald' spoke little English, but Jane assured Kat that she was an expert midwife, the natives being more skilled at that art than any white woman.

'Jane McDonald' would marry Hans Sixfingers next month and occupy the new manager's house. Three more cottages had been built that year. The main house had been extended too. Thanks to the futility of the gold rushes for most of the dreamers, there was no shortage of men seeking work now in the colony, or women seeking Australian futures more secure than the damp harvests of Europe could provide.

Soon Kat must hire a nurse, nursery maid, another kitchen maid, and, probably, she admitted, a cook–housekeeper too, and eventually nannies, governesses, tutors, even probably a boot boy, but not a butler, definitely, and she would never give a dinner where a corset, crinoline and evening gloves were required.

The household had become a village of its own peculiar character, cottages scattered up the hills and gorilla whiskers more common than the milkmaid cheeks of England. The compound was filled with more bustle and certainly more laughter than the remaining mine workings below.

Most of the races once built for puddling and panning were now used to water vegetables or sheep instead, though down in the valley some stubborn individuals still burrowed like wombats, hoping to find the reef tomorrow, or next year. Perhaps men would still be stubbornly reaching for gold in a hundred years' time, just as there seemed to always be a wombat enlarging or repairing the burrow under what had been the front steps.

Sometimes when Kat woke she thought that if she didn't open her eyes the lagoons might still be down in the valley, the clouds of ducks spearing upwards into the mist, waterlilies spreading in islands of flat green leaves and white flowers, the smoke from the natives' campfires twisting endlessly into a sky that gave only the rain the land could cope with, and then broke into a thousand colours, most of which could only be sensed, not seen. She could even hear the native chanting in the wind, the stamp of bare feet in a dance, the triumphant laughter of dark-skinned children hauling mussels or twisting yabbies and for a second feel that she and Zebediah were a world of two within the stones of the house except for Mrs O'Connell, silent as she'd been back then.

But the present was good and, anyway, this is what was. Best to eat the cake you had, and think of the ones you'd make tomorrow, and not repine too long on the one lost in the ashes. That was the way to anguish, and after all, the loss was far greater for Jane and all her people, an agony so vast and deep that Kat knew she could never truly understand it. How could you comprehend the theft not just of one's land, but community and nations, and in the loss of land lose so much richness of memory, and every certainty that had once held their future?

And for what? All that most of the newcomers had found was that unfed dreams would starve the belly. The gold rushes had brought more slums than fine buildings. The colony's brief romance with gold had been replaced by a heart of wool, and a growing trade in beef and mutton.

Hadn't one of Viola's enigmatic pronouncements been something about living only in the world of now, aware of the beauty around you, the mutter of frogs after the rain, the thud as Black Harry slit more wood for the kitchen fire, the breathing of the friend beside her. 'It might have been different' was useless, unless, perhaps one used the knowledge of what might have been to help create future.

Kat listened. She could just hear a rhythmic sanding as out in the workshop Zebediah was putting the finishing touches to the rocking horse, adorned with real horsehair for mane and tail, that their baby would not use for at least a year. Zebediah Markham had already become something of a legend in the colony: the blind man who could make his way about his property with no one to guide him, who could build a rocking chair and even shear a sheep, as well as judge the best ram for the sheep that had gained an excellent reputation too.

All of which was true, though like legends everywhere it ignored the details: Kat had fixed ropes of differing textures and thicknesses across the farm and even up to the rocks on the ridge for Zebediah to follow. Sheep shearing and carpentry were as much about touch as sight, especially for a man who'd done both so long, though these days Zebediah shore only one sheep, purely as a demonstration to the men that the master knew his business. Any farmer, blind or not, judged the worth of a ram by the feel of its testicles, and the staple of a fleece. But it was true, too, that

Zebediah's skin seemed to understand the warmth blowing from the valley or the tang across the ridges from the sea so that at times he hardly needed the ropes' guidance.

Zebediah knew his land from the smell of hot rocks from down the valley, the fragrance of she-oak trees, the scent of roast mutton from the kitchen and Mrs O'Connell's lavender furniture polish. He knew his wife by the sound of her footsteps, the fragrance of where she'd been, or the way the air moved about her body, and the touch of her skin against his.

He had taught Kat to see the valley with every sense now, too, to know the scent of native cat or black snake. He relied on her descriptions of the seedlings' growth, the numbers of lambs born overnight. They had lived in partnership from the first months of their marriage. This was a deeper partnership, far richer than gold.

Sometimes she wondered if these days she occasionally saw with a sense of time as well, blessed with the glimpse of the land she'd had before gold possessed men's dreams, where she'd known what that dismissive phrase 'the bush' could truly be before the teeth of sheep began to turn forest into pasture. At times she even heard the laughter of children yet to come.

But surely the visions of generations of her family here were pregnancy fancies, abetted by Mrs O'Connell, who was sure a guardian angel had taken up residence to protect them all, and who polished the new cradle every day, humming old bedtime songs from Ireland. 'For I'm sure I've been waiting all me life to be a grandmother,' she'd said to Kat. 'I hope you have a dozen chillun, Kat me heart'.'

Mrs O'Connell sewed and knitted, too. These days her work was almost solely sitting to supervise, instruct and criticise the scrubbing, polishing and dusting of maids who would never meet the standards of the convent. The sandalwood chest in the new nursery had enough matinee jackets and booties and cradle caps as well as smocked nightdresses, to dress quintuplets, if by any chance Kat happened to produce them.

'Teatime,' said that woman now, hefting a tray holding a brown pot and a plate of mutton sandwiches with chutney, a bowl of Boot, Anderson and O'Reilly's best pickled walnuts, and another of scones and apple tarts which luckily one of the Irish maids could make, for in the past weeks Kat had found rolling pastry was difficult when you couldn't reach the bench. 'There, look at that now, a spread I'd be proud to serve St Patrick himself. And I'll just be taking a tea tray out to his lordship.'

'And buttered scones too?' Zebediah had put on weight, even a small paunch, but Kat still felt the need to fatten him, as if by keeping him more solid she could prevent him vanishing again.

'I'll be making sure he has enough food to feed the English army, bad 'cess to 'em,' said Mrs O'Connell, with a quick assessing glance at Kat's belly as she unloaded the tray. 'And there's more scones in the kitchen for the chillun and their nanny too, when they come in, as long as they wipe their feet proper. I'm not having mud on my good floors again. Not to mention tadpoles in the wash tub.'

'Will you come back and join us then?' Kat had noticed enough cups for three.

'I might, if them maids is doin' as they aught.' She took the tray back in to what was still the best polished hallway in the colony, followed by Not Sullivan, who had learned that a dog might help with the washing up by being there when the dishes were scraped.

Titania poured, waking from the daze of peacefulness in which they'd both been sitting, and took a sip of tea. 'This is delicious, Kat. Your tea always is. It must be the water from the stream. We can never get it so pure in Sydney.'

'Probably,' said Kat lazily, listening to the rooster crow, except the sound came from the gully and so was a lyrebird, copying the noises of the farm.

Titania took another sip of tea, then reached for a sandwich and a pickled walnut. 'Read Viola's letter out again, Kat. Strange she knew to send it to both of us here.'

'Maybe she only had time or paper to write one letter.'

'I wish she hadn't gone to India again, of all places, with all the trouble there. Do read it, Kat.'

Kat obeyed, as if hearing the words might give them more insight not just into what their friend had seen, but where she might be now so many months after it had been written.

My dearest Kat and Titania,
I write this quickly, and will send it by the first reliable ship, to reassure you that I am Safe and Well and have survived what Newspapers call The Sepoy Rebellion, but which is far more profound, though I do not have a better name to call it.

In Truth I Do not know what this Year has been in India, nor what to call its battles. It began with Portents, Men running swifter than Serpents bearing Chapattis in their Turbans from Village to Village, yet what they carried held no Message and no Mark. Sometimes they bore Lotus Blooms or Goat, yet none of the Runners knew What they Carried nor why Swiftness was so Vital, yet Run they must. The British blamed the Natives and the Hindu and Musselmen the English, and yet I think none were to Blame, but the Wind of History heralding the Storm.

The storm broke like the Monsoon, but Built from Years or decades not merely Months. Despite the many Accounts I do not regard it as an uprising of Sepoys, for in places whole Towns and Villages rebelled, yet many or even most Sepoys kept to the Duties of their Regiment. What comes Now I do not know.

The Injustices of this Land are Great, yet as we three know the Injustices of England and Colonists are Large as well. What Hand can weigh the two?

I sheltered in the House my Father has built outside the town. When the Sepoys came I was his Hindi Daughter, with my eyes downcast, and when the Red Coats battered at the door a Memsahib greeted them. To you, my friends, I can say this: when the Time of troubles ended I was neither Daughter nor Memsahib, and nor do I know who I have become, or perhaps have ever been. I think I see the beginning of the path now that I must walk to

*find the answers. Books and good friends and my father's wisdom
helped me see the way's beginning, but what I seek now can't be
encompassed in words.*

*Trust that I am well in Body, Mind and Spirit. I stay in
Calcutta only long enough to ensure all who have given me
Kindness remain safe. I intend to travel, and would accept with
Gratitude if Mr O'Reilly would arrange Drafts upon such Banks
as may become available, but for now my Needs are Scant. Do not
fret if you do not hear from me, for Mails may be uncertain in places
where I travel. I am not sure of my Destination yet, but know the
Journey will be Full.*

*My love will be with you always, as constant as a Rock no Tide
can wash away,*

Viola

'What does she mean, "the journey will be full"?' fretted Titania, spreading a thick black foundation of pickled walnut on her mutton sandwich. 'Why not say where she is bound, either?'

'Perhaps she is waiting for passage on a good boat,' said Kat. 'To Rome maybe? Or Venice.' Somewhere the names Lady Viola Montefiore or Lady Viola Nash have not been heard, Kat thought.

Impulsively she said, 'Titania, I need to tell you something. I'm so sorry. I guessed that maybe she was alive all the time she was away. Mr Smith didn't tell me, but the sea-battered body, that severed wrist ... it all seemed like things he'd do. Not Viola.'

Titania raised an eyebrow. 'Did you now?'

'I've been too ashamed to tell you before. You're not angry?'

'For not sharing a guess? I'd have worried as well as grieved then. And maybe Oberon would have caught that I was holding something back. He guessed the same as you, but never told me either, just as I've never told Viola that Nash liked them young. And I never dreamed that a man with his place in society ...'

'There's as much crime in society as in a flash pad,' said Kat dryly. 'Not so many pickpockets, that's all, but maybe even more captain sharps.'

'That's as may be. We're well out of it, me and the family.'

'Do you ever dream of sailing on the ships you provision, Titania?'

'No,' said Titania, with complete certainty. 'Nor Oberon either. We've reached our journey's end.'

Kat smiled. Why travel anywhere when there was friendship here, and children, plans to make at breakfast and love and warm arms in the night?

And in the small space between the new 'rough shop' where Zebediah planed and sawed and sanded, and the workshop where the furniture was polished, stood another room, its doorway hidden by shelves, sharing its chimney with the workshop. Unlike the shallow space she'd had bricked in at the end of the dairy when she was making her start, this one was big enough for a still and fifty jugs. At the other end of the compound was a storeroom of barrels of apples in sawdust, baskets of peaches in season — and what was suspicious about that for a community their size?

It wasn't just the money any more, though Kat had nothing against money. Money was as useful as water though, just like water, if you longed for money too much you might drown, like the man who'd been John Smith: still in California possibly, for Captain Quicksilver had never been heard of again. The poteen meant knowing that in a small way she and those she loved still slipped between the laws and lores made by pale men now mostly dead, and laid upon a land they'd never seen. It was a way of linking the joy-filled girl that she had been with the fulfilled woman she was now.

She smiled and lifted the teapot and filled the cups again with the smooth liquid which was not only tea.

Some girls were not born to be good.

Chapter 69

VIOLA

1860

The knife blade flickered in the firelight, then thrust towards her. Viola inclined her head politely and, using her right hand, plucked the hunk of roast goat off the point that was offered to her. Yet the pronoun 'her' did not quite fit, nor did the name Viola now.

To the young cameleer whose hospitality she shared tonight she was Nur, a seeker after knowledge who trudged these roads from the far east of the subcontinent, where assuredly they had strange ways, that explained all the strangeness in this young man as well.

Next year the person once called Viola might be Hindi or Musselman, might be man or woman, or rather neither, a person without desires, not for intimacy of flesh nor a child within her arms, or for a land or people or even language to tie you to their form. She was a tree, content with the journey to the sky, even knowing she might never reach it. She was a stone, that allowed the accretion of lichen and small creatures around it. She was a moth, driven as much by the wind as its own decision. Just now the world was the soft breath of night, the sword leap of the flame, the scent of the discs of dung and straw it burned, the pungency of goat and the flat bread with which she caught its juices.

Tomorrow's light would show a land of dust, but dust can be fruitful when it carries seeds, or when the white tops of the mountains on either side droop in spring and turn to water. A person, too, might change, just like a tree, its leaves unrecognisable in the seeds that stored them, or the stone, slowly eroded to new shapes, or the moth, emerged from its cocoon. Nations, peoples, changed as well, though few sat quietly enough to see it.

What might a woman become, or a man, or even the lands she had passed through? Permanency was illusion. All was change, even friendship, even love.

The girl Viola thought that she had known it. She had not.

But love was there. She glanced up, and saw beyond the gaudy gold of moonlight the endless wheeling stars, like strangers to be met upon the road.

Whatever paths she followed, there'd be love.

Author's Note

This was inspired by the history of the valley where I live, but not based on it. The valley's history is far more complex than one book allowed — nor are any characters here based on any one historical person, but are composites of those who lived and worked in those times.

Women in colonial history are often dismissed as having been merely wives, mothers, housemaids or harlots. Instead a large number were successful businesswomen in their own right. Others, like Elizabeth Macarthur, managed the large estates of their husbands with great success, or were botanists, philosophers, philanthropists or dreamers, and any number of combinations of these.

According to official police history, there were no female constables till the twentieth century. The police wage books, however, state that in 1853 they were being paid twenty pounds a year. Like so many women, these constables or 'female searchers' have been almost entirely written out of history. Readers might find what they think are a few other anachronisms in this book, like the concept of 'being in the now'. Philosophic visions — like those of Kierkegaard that Viola read — may take many generations to permeate popular thought.

Others come from the inconsistency of history — once something is invented, or a process changes, it may take months, years or decades to be adopted. Voyages from England to Sydney might take as little as 100 days in perfect conditions. They might also take eight months with storms, broken masts, a non-lethal encounter with an iceberg, becalmed in the doldrums plus the time taken for repair, restocking or simply commerce at ports along the way. It wasn't until the steamships and improved sail designs that became common in the late 1850s that a voyage's length became somewhat more reliable, and improved quarantine made the arrival at Australian ports safer.

But the voyage to Australia from Europe remained long, and far more expensive than the closer Canada or United States of America, which was where the majority migrated. Those who chose Australia either had a professional or family reason to come here, were adventurers, or needed to get as far away as possible from their pasts. Even during Australia's gold rushes, the Californian goldfields were a cheaper voyage from Europe. Prospective miners had to get from the east coast to the west, but in 1842 this only took between forty-two and fifty-three days if the travellers crossed the Isthmus of Panama. California was even a relatively easy journey from China.

The gold rushes and subsequent clearing to support a fast-growing population destroyed much of Australia's ecology. This destruction still continues at an even faster rate. Few Australians have seen or even dream of the almost paradisal beauty and extreme generosity of this land before colonisation.

I'm lucky enough to have known places like Surfers Paradise when it was sandhills and river, and Grandma and I could catch enough fish for three meals in an hour, gather pipis, edible greens, catch crabs, or eat our fill of oysters armed only with a stone to bash the top shells at low tide. Much of the land above my present home is so steep that its suspended valleys remained pristine until the careless local introduction of feral goats, and the deliberate introduction of feral pigs and deer. Even now, it is impossible to walk a step without encountering a food or medicinal plant, though the clouds of ducks, so thick it was said you could fire a shot in the air and three would fall down, have gone, as has most of the wildlife, large and small, even in the half century I have been here and trying to keep the land protected. The valley's lagoons of waterlilies, the stems, leaves and flowers eaten as a vegetable and its pollen to make cakes, vanished within the first weeks of the gold rushes.

But enough still exists here, in life and in memory, for me to reconstruct the days when the provision of magnificent food and adequate shelter, not to mention the luxury of possum skin cloaks and rugs of a softness and warmth almost incredible today, took less than an hour a day, and the rest was laughter, fun and friendship.

THE SEPOY REBELLION / FIRST INDIAN WAR OF INDEPENDENCE

A full chapter in my third-year reader at school was devoted to The Black Hole of Calcutta, with a graphic illustration of screaming women and children, though the incident seems to have vanished from the syllabus now. I assumed it was true until a few months before I wrote this book, even though by the age of five I knew from my grandmother's stories of the women in our family that much of what we think is history is not just partial and biased, but entirely concocted. But the most unlikely events in this book, from the scam that created a genuine gold rush to the flood that washed one goldfield away, are based on fact.

BOADICEA

This was the way the British rebel queen's name was mistranslated from about 1782 when William Cowper wrote an ode to her. She is more commonly known now as Boudicca, or similar variants on that name.

Acknowledgements

This book owes its beginning to a PHD on the history of banking in New South Wales, accidentally read perhaps a decade ago while googling something else. I haven't been able to find the work again, nor did I make a note of the author, but it showed that women in the early colony had bank accounts in their own names, and businesses prosperous enough for their accounts to grow. My apologies and gratitude to the author.

It is impossible to thank incomparable editor Lisa Berryman enough for her part in the inspiration, creation and the inevitable many revisions of this book, including a superwoman endeavour to find a title. Will the Elf of Perfect Titles please visit this valley at her/his earliest convenience, preferably before we have to decide on the title of the next book.

Kate O'Donnell gives her heart to every work. I treasure her comments and criticisms. Like Lisa, Kate is invariably correct, or at least it is reasonable not to question her opinion of a manuscript. I love Kate's outrage and fury at events both real and fictional, and her passionate adoration of various characters even more. It is a total joy to be edited by her.

As I write this Angie Masters will be wrestling with my illegible last-minute changes to the page proofs, and possibly eating the chocolates I sent as an apology and bribe so that she'll keep coordinating my work. She's been wonderful. I've been trying to write legibly since I was five years old, but sadly the scrawl has only been deteriorating since I left Miss Davies' Year Two class, despite every effort to write even a shopping list my husband can interpret without translation. Gratitude, too, to Angela Marshall who has turned all my books from misspelled gobbledygook into the text I send to HarperCollins, and to fabulous proof reader Pam Dunne.

The cover of this book, and that of *The Angel of Waterloo*, was created by brilliant designer Mark Campbell, based on the sublime portraits by Mary Jane Ansell, whose genius stuns me every time I look at her website. I deeply hope that one day I might see the originals of her work. Lisa emailed me seconds after she discovered her magic — I wish Mary Jane Ansell could know our joy when she agreed to let us use her work. The face on this cover is every woman, at every time, with every emotion hidden and yet the viewer knows they are there. HarperCollins has given me many superb covers, but these are two that I study, over and over, seeing more beauty and symbolism each time, as well as the hearts of the stories the covers enclose.

Thank you to Cristina Cappelluto for creating an extraordinary team; to Michelle Weisz and Yvonne Sewankambo for their magic, as each book finds its readership; and to all the others whose names and faces I don't know as I live and write in a valley far from the office, and in this second year of lockdowns we are all working from home, yet teamwork and friendship still blossom in the black print of emails.

Thank you to everyone.

Jackie French AM is an award-winning author, historian and ecologist. She was the 2014–2015 Australian Children's Laureate and the 2015 Senior Australian of the Year. In 2016 Jackie became a Member of the Order of Australia for her significant contribution to literature and youth literacy. She is regarded as one of Australia's most popular authors with her vast body of work crossing the threshold of genres and reading ages, and ranging from fiction, non-fiction, picture books, ecology, fantasy and sci-fi, to her much-beloved historical fiction.

jackiefrench.com
facebook.com/authorjackiefrench